A FLOOD OF EVIL

BOOK ONE: 1923-1933

By

Lewis M. Weinstein

Also by Lewis M. Weinstein

The Heretic (2000)

A Good Conviction (2007)

Case Closed (2009)

The Pope's Conspiracy (2012)

Hereje - The Heretic in Spanish (2012)

Author's Foreword

A FLOOD OF EVIL is a novel in two parts.

Book One, which is this volume, depicts the lives of Berthold Becker and Anna Gorska from 1923 to 1933, and follows their efforts to prevent Hitler's rise to power.

Book Two, currently being written, will cover the lives of Berthold and Anna from 1934 to 1946.

A Note on Historical Accuracy

Whenever historical events are presented, I have made every effort to be accurate, although it's important to recognize that quite often historians themselves don't agree as to what actually happened or why. Cause and effect are particularly elusive.

When the historians disagreed, I took the novelist's prerogative to choose the version that seemed to me the most likely.

Dedication

Edel Evantash

My grandfather Edel Evantash left the Polish *shtetl* of Ciechanow in 1908 and came to America. He brought his wife and oldest son to America a few years later. After a brief time in Philadelphia, they lived in Camden, NJ, where Edel became a successful home builder and a prominent member of the Jewish community while raising his five children, including my mother.

Edel returned to Poland several times to try to convince members of his family still living there to leave before it was too late. Some did leave, but others did not, and the Germans murdered all who stayed.

Some elements of this novel are loosely built on events in my grandfather's life. This does not include the famous train robbery carried out by Marshal Pilsudski in 1908. The train robbery did happen and my grandfather did leave Poland in that same year, but the two events were not linked except in my fictional version of events. My aunt, Edel's youngest child, told me, "Pop would never rob a train, but he wouldn't mind being portrayed that way in your book."

The photo of my grandfather and me was taken in 1941.

Appendices before the book ... things you might like to see before you read

SELECTED HISTORICAL CHRONOLOGY

FICTIONAL CHARACTERS

HISTORICAL CHARACTERS

Appendices at the end of the book ... for your reference during and after your read

GLOSSARY

BIBLIOGRAPHY

ACKNOWLEDGMENTS

SELECTED HISTORICAL CHRONOLOGY

1914 ... World War One begins

1918 ... World War One ends with Armistice

1919 ... Treaty of Versailles in Paris

1919 ... Poland re-established as an independent nation

1919 ... Weimar Republic established in Germany

***

1923 ... Hitler's Beer Hall Putsch fails in Munich

1928 ... *Amici Israel* initiative rejected by the Vatican

1932 ... Hindenburg wins German Presidential election

1932 ... Papen is appointed Chancellor, replacing Brüning

1932 ... Schleicher is appointed Chancellor, replacing Papen

1933 ... Hitler is appointed Chancellor

1933 ... Enabling Act makes Hitler an absolute dictator

1933 ... Dachau concentration camp opened

1933 ... Vatican signs Reich Concordat with Germany

***

1934 ... The Night of the Long Knives

1935 ... Nuremberg anti-Jewish laws

1938 ... Munich appeasement

1938 ... Kristallknacht

1939 ... Germany invades Poland

1944 ... D-Day invasion

1945 ... US forces liberate Dachau

1945 ... Nuremberg War Crimes Trials begin

MAJOR FICTIONAL CHARACTERS

in Germany
BERTHOLD BECKER

Elisabeth Becker ... Berthold's mother

Dietrich Becker ... Berthold's older brother, a war veteran

Richard Goldmann ... Elisabeth's employer, a Jewish businessman (Goldmann Department Store)

Judith Goldmann ... Richard's wife, Elisabeth's friend

Leonard Goldmann ... son of Richard and Judith, Berthold's friend

Monsignor Karl Johannes ... political aide to Cardinal Faulhaber in Munich

Albert Mueller ... a Nazi, Berthold's mentor at the Reichsbahn

Ernst Krueger ... Nazi Local District Leader in Northeim

in Poland
ANNA GORSKA

Evona Gorska ... Anna's mother

Jacob Gorska ... Anna's father, Orthodox Jew and businessman in Ciechanow

Danuta Gorska ... Anna's younger sister

Josef Gorska ... Anna's younger brother

in the United States
Edel Inwentarz ... Anna Gorska's great-uncle, living in America

Abraham Weintraub ... prosecutor of Berthold Becker at 1945 Nuremberg trial

Marissa Morgan ... Weintraub's daughter, a history professor at Brandeis University

HISTORICAL CHARACTERS

in Germany

Josef Goebbels ... propaganda chief of the Nazi Party

Hermann Göring ... World War One hero, Hitler's chief subordinate in the Nazi Party

Michael von Faulhaber ... Cardinal of Munich from 1917-1952

Ernst "Putzi" Hanfstaengl ... early associate of Hitler and foreign press secretary of the Nazi Party

Josef Hartinger ... Deputy Prosecutor of Munich

Reinhard Heydrich ... head of the Nazi political police (SD) and one of the main architects of the Holocaust

Paul von Hindenburg ... German Field Marshal in World War I, later President of Germany 1925-1934

Adolf Hitler ... Chancellor of Germany

Dorothy Thompson ... a well known American journalist

Hilmar Wäckerle ... Commandant of Dachau concentration camp

in Poland

Menachem Begin ... Zionist, later Prime Minister of Israel

Jozef Pilsudski ... Polish revolutionary hero, leader of Polish government from the mid-1920s until 1935

Irena Meltzer (real name Rosa) ... the first woman elected to the Polish parliament

Roza Robota ... portrayed fictionally as Anna Gorska's friend; actual leader of a 1944 Auschwitz uprising

in the Vatican

Eugenio Pacelli ... Cardinal Secretary of State 1930-1939, later Pope Pius XII 1939-1958

Achille Ratti ... Pope Pius XI 1922-1939

A Flood of Evil

Prologue

November 1945 - Nuremberg

Berthold Becker showed little emotion as his jailer unlocked his cell and escorted him along the dark corridor lined with soldiers. For several weeks he had sat quietly and watched as the trials of the other high-ranking Nazis had proceeded, and for the past two days he had paid somewhat greater attention as the evidence against him was presented, and what he regarded as a pathetic defense followed. It wasn't his attorney's fault. He was guilty. He had done horrible things. He couldn't change what he had done and now he would pay the price. He expected to be hanged.

In the courtroom, he walked past Hermann Göring, who still looked pompous and defiant, and Hjalmar Schacht, who smiled vaguely to himself, operating on a higher intellectual level than anyone else, or so he thought. Last night at dinner, Schacht had argued, as he often did, that he had committed none of the nonsensical crimes the War Crimes Tribunal had invented.

"What are crimes against humanity?" Schacht had ranted. "Or crimes against peace? There have always been wars. These charges are absurd."

Berthold understood the charges and did not object. He took his seat and watched the prosecutor, Abraham Weintraub, shuffle papers in preparation for his closing statement. The justices filed in - American, British, Russian and French - but before Weintraub could begin, Berthold's appointed defense attorney asked to speak. About what? He had finished his case the day before, and his closing statement would come after the prosecutor's.

"If it please the court, I have another witness."

The Chief Justice looked to Prosecutor Weintraub who made no objection, and all eyes turned to the now open door at the back of the courtroom and the woman standing there.

Berthold choked back the sounds that began to erupt in his throat but could not stop the tears that flooded from his eyes. The woman entering the courtroom had been his closest friend and lover for fifteen years. She was forever in his thoughts. He had not expected to ever see her again.

***

Anna Gorska looked at Berthold and smiled. He moaned and covered his eyes. When he looked up, she had already taken her seat in the witness chair, and he had heard her familiar voice state her name. She spoke clearly, but her hand quivered and she gripped the desk to steady it.

Q: Are you a Polish citizen?
A: Yes.

Q: Are you a Jew?
A: Yes.

Q: Were you and your family held in the ghetto established by the Nazis in Warsaw?
A: Yes.

Q: Were you later transferred to Auschwitz?
A: Yes.

Q: What happened to your family?
A: To the best of my knowledge, the Germans murdered every member of my family except me.

There was a sharp intake of breath in courtroom, then utter silence. Berthold imagined this was the first time most of those present had actually seen someone who had been a prisoner in a Nazi death camp.

Q: Did you know the defendant Berthold Becker before the war?
A: Yes.

Q: How did you manage to survive at Auschwitz when so many others perished?
A: I became a whore. I serviced prison guards, SS and German Army officers.

Anna looked across the courtroom and locked eyes with Berthold. He managed just the slightest curve of his lips and she nodded in return. He sobbed, feeling her love, even now, especially now, when their life together was over.

Q: Did there come a time when Herr Becker came to Auschwitz?
A: Yes.

Q: Did Herr Becker subsequently help you escape from Auschwitz?
A: Yes.

Q: How did he accomplish that?
A: He made up a story that whores were needed at another location and that it was an SS priority to move several of us to that location. He took us to Dachau.

Remembering their frantic trip from Auschwitz to Dachau, Berthold felt her touch, breathed her closeness, heard her sigh.

Q: What happened then?
A: The SS evacuated most of the Dachau prisoners to Buchenwald.

Q: But again you were saved?
A: Berthold kept me hidden.

Q: And then?

A: Dachau was liberated by the U.S. Army. I believe that you, Prosecutor Weintraub, were there that day.

Berthold's eyes spun to the prosecutor, who looked stunned. Weintraub had indeed been there, looking for high-ranking Nazis to arrest, but he had probably not noticed Anna.

Q: I understand you have a statement to make. Would you care to do that now?

A: Yes. Thank you.

Gorska slowly unfolded several sheets of paper, the soft rustling of which was heard throughout the courtroom. Her voice at first pulsed with emotion, but she quickly steadied herself.

"Berthold Becker was a member of the Nazi Party, and in that capacity, he participated in the commission of at least some of the crimes he has been charged with by this Tribunal. I am sure he expects to be punished." She paused. "But for reasons I will explain, he should not be put to death.

"Many Germans are guilty of acquiescing in the rise to power and subsequent crimes of Adolf Hitler and his Nazi associates. Most Germans offered no resistance to Hitler's program of unprovoked war and the murder of millions of innocent Jews."

Gorska paused again, looked at Berthold, and held his eyes with hers. Berthold's heart pounded as he felt a stifling mixture of joy and pain. Anna continued.

"This defendant is not now and never was an evil man. He was dragged into a maelstrom not of his choosing and from which he was unable to escape. It is easy to say he should have done more to stop the Nazis and in hindsight perhaps he would agree.

"However, Berthold Becker, unlike many others, did frequently take great risks to try to oppose the Nazis and

13

prevent their worst excesses. For the most part he failed in those efforts ... but at least he tried."

Gorska sipped from a glass of water, then addressed the French, American and British justices in turn, looking directly at each one as she mentioned their countries.

"Honored justices, may I ask what your nations did to save Jews from Hitler? Perhaps you know how inadequate those efforts were, but I think your record bears repeating.

"France participated quite willingly, some even say enthusiastically, in the roundup of French Jews - citizens of France - knowing they were destined for extermination.

"American and British forces had no direct contact with Jews headed for extermination, but your leaders knew of the death camps and your airplanes could have bombed the camps or the rail lines serving them. Your countries chose not to do that and thus allowed the extermination of Jews to continue, in some cases until the very day the camps were liberated."

Gorska slowly placed one page behind the others. She looked around the room, deliberately making eye contact, especially with those seated at the press tables. Almost everyone who met her stare looked away, made uncomfortable by her intensity.

"Berthold Becker, although a Nazi, did more than any of the great Allied nations to save Jewish lives. Many lives, not just mine. That is reason enough to spare his life now.

"But there is another reason, which I believe is even more important.

"Many Nazis who should be imprisoned or executed will perhaps never come to trial. Many Germans are already denying that mass murders of Jews ever took place or claiming that if such things did happen, they were not known to them.

"Such false denials must not be allowed. Those who supported Adolf Hitler or acquiesced in his evil must not be allowed to hide from the depravity in which they were complicit."

Anna looked directly at Berthold and he felt she was speaking to him, as if they were alone.

"Berthold Becker had a unique vantage point during the entire Nazi terror. He knows and will tell a truth that others deny."

Looking back to the justices, speaking slowly, she delivered each of her final words as if it were a dagger.

"You have the power to allow the terrible story of German evil and guilt to be known. Do not take the life of this defendant. Let Berthold Becker live to tell his story."

Her statement concluded, Gorska folded her hands in front of her and waited. Prosecutor Weintraub chose not to cross-examine and the witness was excused. She took a last look at Berthold in the defendant's chair, openly struggling to keep her emotions in check, then rose and walked to the rear of the courtroom. Several members of the press rose to follow her. Just inside the door, one of the reporters hugged her. Anna broke down in tears and left the room encircled by the reporter's arm.

Chapter 1

1990 - New York City

"I want to write a book about the people in your Nuremberg case," Marissa said between the first and second innings at Yankee Stadium.

A frown added to the lines in her father's face. "Why dredge that up again?," he said. "You know I've never considered it the shining moment of my legal career."

"Your case was presented brilliantly," Marissa said. "You convinced the judges that Berthold Becker was guilty of crimes against humanity."

"But the Nazi bastard didn't die," Abraham Weintraub said, his vehemence undiminished by the intervening forty-five years. "It was that Polish whore. Somehow she got herself to Nuremberg, and suddenly she turned up to testify in Becker's defense. But for her I'm certain he would've been sentenced to death."

"Exactly," Marissa said. "And what makes it even more remarkable is that many of Anna Gorska's family were murdered by the Nazis."

"We've both read her testimony," Abraham said. "What else is there to know?"

"There's got to be more. Did Gorska say anything else about Becker in subsequent interviews or statements?"

"I didn't have any more conversation with her," Abraham said. He looked ruefully self-critical. "I didn't even cross-examine her."

They watched the game for awhile and then Abraham asked, "Will this book further your career?"

Marissa chuckled. Her father, as usual, had gotten right to the crux of the matter. She waited while the crowd finished roaring for a play she hadn't seen. "It could," she said, flashing the smile she knew her father had adored since she was a child.

"My mentor at Brandeis will be retiring in three years. I need something special to give me a chance to succeed him."

"But there've been so many books," Abraham said.

"I know," Marissa said, "but most of the Holocaust literature has quite properly focused on the horrible things that were done to the Jews. I had a long conversation with my mentor about this and we agreed that the story of Berthold Becker and Anna Gorska might yield new insights into who allowed Hitler to come to power and then supported his horrible agenda."

She paused. "There's another reason. I want to work together with you. I'd like us to be co-authors."

Abraham closed his eyes and cupped his chin, a gesture Marissa had seen many times.

"Can you give me some time to think about it?"

"Sure, Dad. I understand."

They watched the rest of the game, had dinner in the city, and the next morning Marissa took the train back to Boston to await her father's decision.

***

"Becker's still alive," Abraham said when he called three days later. "He's in Munich in the same apartment where he lived as a child."

"Does this mean I have a co-author?" Marissa asked, her heart leaping.

"I couldn't turn you down. I've sent an overnight package: a copy of my file on Becker and a few notes about Gorska. It's all I have."

Over the next several weeks, Marissa contacted the International Tracing Service in Germany and the American Jewish Joint Distribution Committee in New York. Abraham called his contacts at the UN to arrange access to archived records. From these sources, Marissa learned that Anna Gorska had been among a group of Polish Jews smuggled into

Palestine in 1947 and that she was currently living in Jerusalem.

***

The next time Marissa called her father, he told her more about what he had seen at Dachau, his voice breaking as he talked about things he had never before related.

"There were piles of naked remains ... decomposing, some partially incinerated. There was a train of cattle cars filled with dead bodies."

Marissa knew her father still felt a visceral hatred of all Germans and all things German. He could not stand to hear German spoken, would not buy a German car, would not travel to Germany.

A quizzical tone came to Abraham's voice as he continued talking, as much to himself as to his daughter. "Becker was at Dachau, under arrest, and I had already questioned him briefly. When he was brought out for transfer to a detention center, he passed near me. I saw he was staring and followed his eyes to a woman who had clearly been a prisoner. Their eyes were locked until Becker boarded the transport vehicle. It must have been her."

Marissa debated, started to speak, stopped, then finally did. "Dad, the other day you called Anna Gorska a Polish whore."

"She called herself that," Abraham said.

"Do you think she chose to be that voluntarily?"

"I guess not, but she didn't explain or defend herself."

"No she didn't. I wonder why."

***

They had decided a letter to Berthold Becker was better than a phone call, which if it didn't go well, could end the project in a few minutes. A letter would give Becker time to consider his response.

18

Marissa wrote in German, going through many drafts, explaining who she was and the story she wanted to tell, emphasizing her objective of understanding why he and other Germans had come to support the Nazis. She said she would come to Munich and asked if she might meet with him as soon as possible. She held her breath as she addressed the envelope. While waiting for Becker's response, she commanded herself to think positively, organizing her materials and making tentative travel arrangements. Two weeks dragged by until the call came.

"Professor Morgan?"

"Yes," Marissa answered, her heart pounding.

"This is Berthold Becker calling from Munich."

Marissa slid comfortably into German, remembering the first time she took a German language course in college and her father had been so angry, until she explained she had decided to major in Holocaust studies and that German was thus an absolute necessity.

"I have taken the opportunity to research your record and your publications," Becker said. "If you come to Munich, I will meet with you. I make no promises, but I will meet."

***

Thirty-six hours later, Marissa's taxi turned east on Maximilianstrasse, inched forward in heavy traffic past the National Theatre, and turned right just before reaching the River Isar. She was in one of the few parts of Munich which had not been destroyed by Allied bombing during the war. The bright sun and the old buildings offered a pleasing prospect.

Becker lived on a tree-lined street of attractive nineteenth century apartment buildings, all of them four or five stories high. She passed a small grocery store and a restaurant with outdoor seating and reached his building. She pressed the button next to his name, was buzzed in without a word, and walked up the stairs to the third floor. Facing her in

19

an open doorway was a thin man standing stiffly erect. At eighty, he still projected iron discipline, his eyes focused and wary.

"Good day, please come in," Becker said without smiling.

He guided Marissa from the vestibule to his living room and pointed to an upholstered couch, while seating himself in a hard wooden chair opposite her. A large window covered by a thin curtain permitted just enough light to avoid the need for lamps. The furniture was in the style of a different era, but everything was clean and neat. She saw a piano in the next room. Two photos were displayed on the table next to Becker's chair.

"My parents," Becker said, following Marissa's gaze, "and my brother."

Marissa hoped Becker would control the crucial initial stages of their conversation. Once he began, if he began, her turn would come.

"How is your father?" Becker asked.

That question surprised her. She said her father was well.

"It was a big job your father had," Becker said. "Such a young man, prosecuting a Nazi war criminal in front of the whole world."

Becker's speech was clipped, his eyes impenetrable. "Your father was always well prepared and well organized. Of course he very much wanted me to hang, but even so, he treated me fairly."

And is that why you agreed to meet with me, Marissa thought, silently thanking her father. She offered the response she hoped Becker was seeking.

"If you're asking if I'll be like my father, the answer is yes. I will seek the truth, but I won't purposely trick you or seek to embarrass you."

Becker's face tensed, followed by an ironic smile.

"The truth will be embarrassment enough."

20

He reached for a thick folder and bent forward to give it to her. "I've made some notes." Another smile, this one for the first time seeming genuine. "As you know, I had quite a bit of time after the war."

Becker's eyes settled on the photos.

"I think we should begin in 1923 when I was living in this apartment with my mother and my brother Dietrich ..."

Chapter 2

March 1923 - Munich

Berthold Becker was working on a puzzle with his friend Leonard Goldmann. It was a glorious Bavarian scene, a railroad train passing below a turreted castle set on a heavily wooded hillside, snow-covered mountains in the far background. Berthold's mother Elisabeth came home, saw the boys occupied, and went to her piano, which she often did to relax. She worked her way through the opening phrases of Beethoven's *Moonlight Sonata*. She had often told Berthold how playing the piano brought memories of her deceased husband, sitting nearby and smiling lovingly no matter how many mistakes she made. Her gentle playing wafted through the apartment and relieved the tensions of her day.

Until her older son Dietrich arrived.

"Why is that Jew-boy in our house again?" Dietrich hollered when he saw Leonard.

Elisabeth froze, her fingers rigid above the keyboard. She shot up from the bench and rushed into the foyer to confront her older son.

"How dare you! Leonard is your brother's friend."

Dietrich's clothes were disheveled. His blond hair was sweaty and plastered to his head. There were smears of blood on his face and on his brown shirt; a wild angry look contorted his otherwise handsome features.

"You must not insult Berthold's friend," Elisabeth said. "Leonard's mother has been my best friend for years. His father gives me employment in his department store."

Dietrich snarled, "We should not take money from filthy Jews. Hitler says Jews are not true Germans. He says Germany can never be great again until all the Jews are gone."

Dietrich's face was now flaming red. Elisabeth started to cry and her tears seemed to take the sting out of Dietrich's fury. When he spoke again, there was a hint of gentleness in his voice that almost resembled the boy he had been before the war, but his words remained uncompromising and unyielding. He spoke pompously, as if he were a teacher and his mother a rather dull student.

"The facts are well known, Mother. The Jews started the war as part of their conspiracy to control the world. The German army was not beaten. No foreign soldier ever set foot on German soil. But the Jews stabbed our brave soldiers in the back by tricking us into an armistice, and then they dictated the Versailles peace treaty that still humiliates the German Fatherland."

Dietrich continued his monologue, but Elisabeth was no longer listening and eventually he stormed out of the house. Leonard followed a few minutes later. Elisabeth came to Berthold, still sitting mute in his chair, and placed her hand gently on his shoulder.

"Leonard is afraid of Dietrich," Berthold said softly. "I don't think he'll come here anymore." He tried to control himself, but there was a tremor in his voice. "He's my best friend."

"Leonard will come back," Elisabeth said with a confidence Berthold did not believe she felt. "I'll talk with his mother and I'll speak again with Dietrich. Your brother will not be permitted to act like that in this house."

***

Later that evening, Elisabeth told Berthold what had happened as she was leaving work.

"I was unable to leave the store," she said. "I stood just inside the main door. Brown-shirted men filled the street, shouting angry slogans; drums were pounding; it was terrifying. A second mob approached from a side street, howling and waving angry fists; these were the communists. Bottles were thrown and the melee began: fists, clubs, a flash of knives, a single gunshot. One of the communists was surrounded and beaten savagely by the brownshirts before his comrades dragged him to safety.

"Finally, whistles sounded and the municipal police arrived. As always, they drove the communists away but allowed the brownshirts to remain. With no one left to fight, the Nazis turned their attention to the store. They screamed: Jew store! Filthy Jews! Don't give your money to Jews! The police watched but did not interfere. Some customers hurried away but most defied the brownshirts and went inside. Eventually the thugs grew bored and dispersed. Once the streets were calm, I could leave."

"Was Dietrich one of those brownshirts?" Berthold asked.

"I didn't see him," Elisabeth said, "but I think he must have been there."

***

The next night Elisabeth told Berthold she had spoken with Leonard's mother.

"Frau Goldmann," Elisabeth said, "believes that Dietrich is like many other young men who are frightened and angry and confused, ready to believe Hitler's lies. She said Jews are used to being scapegoats whenever people have problems they don't understand and can't face. She said Leonard will come to visit us again, and that you, of course, are welcome at their home. She also asked if we would still come to Leonard's *bar mitzvah* next week, and I said we certainly would."

Chapter 3

April 1923 - Munich

Berthold and Elisabeth took the trolley across the city and walked up the imposing steps of Munich's Great Synagogue. From the outside, no Jewish star was visible. Four huge columns held up a classical portico and the building actually looked more like a church than a synagogue.

Berthold sat near the front with two other boys from the Wilhelmsgymnasium where he and Leonard attended school. Elisabeth sat alone at the back of the synagogue along a high wall graced with several stained glass windows. Over half of the more than one thousand seats were occupied. A resounding organ chord heralded the beginning of services. Berthold paid no attention until Leonard was called to the pulpit.

Standing next to his proud father, Leonard looked tiny. His voice broke several times as he chanted a prayer in Hebrew and then read from the scroll opened before him. He finished with a noticeable sigh of relief and was soon back in his seat, accepting the congratulations of family and friends.

The rabbi, smiling broadly, rose to present his sermon. Speaking in German, he congratulated Leonard and discussed the relevance of several passages from the portion of the Torah which Leonard had just read. Then his smiles ceased and his voice became somber.

"Since the time of Bismarck and the Emancipation, Germany has been a good place for Jews. We vote. We have legal rights. We pursue careers in business and law and medicine. We even participate in political life at the highest levels. For the past fifty years, life has been very good for the Jews of Munich."

The Rabbi's eyes scanned the synagogue; he nodded to his congregants, as if to confirm the prosperity reflected in their fine clothes and jewelry, but his look contained more sadness than joy.

"Since the war ended with such humiliation for Germany, angry voices are blaming Jews for our defeat and for everything else that's wrong in Germany. No matter that many Jews, including Richard Goldmann, the father of our *bar mitzvah* boy, fought bravely in the army and received decorations for their valor.

"As if that's not enough, vicious lies are being spread about a Jewish conspiracy to control the world and I have recently been informed that these lies are even put forward as historical truth by a supposedly learned professor in one of our finest gymnasiums."

Berthold had heard about this alleged Jewish plot in school and realized that Leonard, who was in his history class, must have told the rabbi.

"Some of you view this growing hatred of Jews as a temporary effect of the current economic and political crises, but I'm afraid you are seriously underestimating the problem. History has shown that once feelings against Jews begin to fester in a community, a momentum develops which is difficult to counteract ..."

A loud crash came from the rear of the synagogue. Several congregants pointed to a shattered stained glass window. Berthold heard his mother's voice and ran to her. A woman was applying a handkerchief to stop the bleeding from the back of Elisabeth's neck.

"Here it is," a man shouted, holding up a rock.

"I'm all right," Elisabeth said.

Then she began to cry. A doctor took her to a side room where he applied bandages, after which he pronounced the wounds to be superficial.

Several men who had run into the street returned, out of breath. "Whoever threw that rock is gone ... there are no others out there ... the police have been sent for ... the danger has passed."

On the pulpit, the rabbi shook his head.

"No," he said, concluding his sermon, "the danger has not passed. Our troubles have hardly begun."

***

Dietrich returned home several hours later, as Elisabeth was preparing the evening meal.

"I want to apologize to both of you for what I said about Leonard. He's Berthold's friend and I should not have been so harsh."

Elisabeth looked surprised, amazed really, and very pleased.

"That's very good of you, Dietrich," she said. "What Hitler says about Jews are lies. There's no truth to any of it."

"Perhaps," Dietrich admitted. "But still, you shouldn't have gone to the synagogue today. I told you not to go."

Berthold was horrified. Dietrich had indeed warned them not to go. Did he know the synagogue would be attacked?

"Someone threw a rock into the synagogue today," Berthold said. "Mother was cut by broken glass."

Dietrich looked shocked, but whether at the throwing of the rock or that his mother had been injured, Berthold was unable to tell.

"Are you hurt badly, Mama?" Dietrich asked.

"A little cut is all," Elisabeth said. "It will heal." She seemed to be weighing something, then made a decision and added, "Go on, Dietrich. Tell us more about Germany and Hitler."

Dietrich straightened to his full height, his powerful physique well displayed. He was obviously pleased to be taken seriously by his mother. He took a seat at the table and began.

"When we came home from the war, we were confused. We didn't know what had happened, why Germany had not

27

been victorious. But at least we thought the German people would welcome us back. They did not. There was no respect for us and our fight for the Fatherland. There were no jobs. There was no place for us in Germany. Everywhere we turned, we were made to feel unworthy. It was mainly the Communists and Jews who rejected us. Some of my friends joined the Nazi Party."

A look came onto Dietrich's face that Berthold had never seen before. He was literally shining with pride.

"Then Hermann Göring joined the Nazi Party. Hermann Göring, the commander of the Richthofen Fighter Squadron, successor to the Red Baron!"

It looked as if Dietrich was about to stand up and salute.

"One day I went to Göring's office. He greeted me with respect and we spoke for some time. He predicted the Nazi Party would become powerful and that the stormtroopers would be the battering ram of the Nazi movement, leaders in the coming struggle for German freedom. I told him I wanted to join and he welcomed me. He asked if I knew how to drive, and would I be interested in being one of Hitler's drivers."

***

Elisabeth had taken to buying food for an old Jewish lady whose husband had recently died. Their meager savings had been eaten up by the raging inflation, and she was slowly starving to death. Frau Keller and her husband had been Dr. Becker's patients before the war. Elisabeth asked Berthold to visit with the old woman on his way home from school, cautioning him not to injure her pride, and to understood how much it distressed her to need help.

Her tiny apartment was in a rundown building above several shops and a tavern. As Berthold climbed to the fifth floor, he wondered if Frau Keller even had the strength to manage the stairs. He was struck with the unsettling thought that she might be a prisoner in her own apartment.

Berthold quietly placed a small container on the dining table, hoping Frau Keller would be strong enough to eat the chicken soup and a precious hard-boiled egg he had been carrying with him all day. While the old woman sat motionless in her chair, her rheumy eyes unfocused, he tidied up, more as a diversion than because it was necessary, since there was hardly anything left in the house that needed tidying. Most of the furniture and other household things had been sold.

A prayer book, printed in German, lay open and Berthold read "Blessed are You, our God, who has commanded us to kindle the light of the Sabbath." There were candlesticks on the table but no candles; he made a mental note to bring some the next time he visited.

Frau Keller raised a frail finger to acknowledge his wave when he left.

***

Two days later, Berthold opened Frau Keller's door and immediately felt an ominous silence. There was also the smell of gas. He left the door open and walked quickly to the kitchen, where he found Frau Keller sprawled before the gas stove. He closed the valve and opened all the windows. The food he had brought was on the table, uneaten.

Also on the table was a pile of banknotes. Frau Keller had once referred to the "life savings" her husband had scraped together for their old age. Berthold counted seven thousand marks. It might have been enough, before the war, to purchase a small retirement house on a quiet street on the outskirts of Munich. Today it would buy a single discolored potato.

He lifted the old woman as gently as he could - she weighed almost nothing - and placed her in the bed, next to a photograph of her husband, so handsome and proud in his army uniform. He covered her with a blanket, closed the windows, and left carrying the now unneeded Sabbath candles.

Berthold and his mother were the only ones attending Frau Keller's funeral service, which Elisabeth had arranged and paid for.

Chapter 4

May 1923 - Munich

It took Berthold two weeks to get up the courage to approach his brother.

"I need to ask you something."

Dietrich crooked Berthold's head in his elbow and affectionately ruffled his hair. The brothers laughed together as they had not done in months.

"Let's go out," Dietrich said.

As they walked, Dietrich explained how Captain Göring was organizing the stormtroopers into sections - bicyclists, intelligence, a motorized squad, a cavalry, an artillery unit. Of course they didn't have cannons or even rifles, but they practiced as if they did.

"We've come a long way from the time we wore scraps of leftover Army outfits. Now we have uniforms and there's a real spirit of comradeship. We're a busy group, pasting slogans on walls, tearing down the Communists' banners, brawling whenever we get a chance."

A train whistled as it picked up speed, leaving Munich.

"Sometimes I go to the station to watch the trains," Berthold blurted out. "I love to imagine where they've come from and where they're going." He immediately felt foolish and juvenile compared to his older brother.

"I spent enough time on troop trains," Dietrich said. "I never want to see another train."

They approached the *Burgerbraukeller*, a huge beer hall on south bank of the Isar River. Outside were gardens and tables, some of which were occupied on one of the first warm days of spring. Inside were row after row of rough-hewn wooden tables.

"I think you're old enough to have a beer. What do you think?" Dietrich asked.

Berthold was afraid to answer but Dietrich decided for him. "Two beers, please."

When the buxom waitress brought the beers and leaned forward to place them on the table, displaying her considerable cleavage, Berthold gulped and blushed furiously while Dietrich laughed at his embarrassment.

"Time you grew up and got used to tits."

Dietrich waited until Berthold finally looked at him. "You said you had a question."

Berthold spoke rapidly, rushing to get the words out. "In school, my professor said Germany was not defeated in the war, that we actually gave up when victory was within our grasp. But my classmate said his brother, who was at the front, told him our soldiers were out of ammunition, that they were hungry and sick, and that they could no longer hold off the British and Americans. So who's right?" He felt unpatriotic even asking the question, but he had to know.

Dietrich nodded sadly. "Some of what your classmate said is true." His eyes glazed and his memories emerged in ragged chunks of words, as if the scenes of horror were playing in his mind. "Our trenches were wet ... smelly and disgusting ... stiff twisted bodies, lit by moonlight ... severed legs ... clouds of gas ... the smell of shit and piss ... oddly, in the morning, the sound of birds singing." Dietrich's voice was eerie, as if coming from some distant place. "I still have nightmares.

"But we were not losing!" Dietrich suddenly insisted. "We could have fought on; it was wrong to quit."

Dietrich's words were bold, but Berthold was not convinced. It did indeed sound like Germany was losing or at the least unable to win, much as his classmate had said. And it further seemed that this result arose from the realities of the battlefield, not from decisions made by Jews or Bolsheviks in Berlin. He wondered if Dietrich actually knew the German Army had failed but his embarrassment and patriotic pride made him unable to admit it, even to himself.

"Did our generals ask the Kaiser to call for an armistice?"

Berthold had surprised himself that he had the audacity to ask such a question and then was sorry when he realized he had added to Dietrich's discomfort. It took Dietrich several moments to answer, and when he did, it wasn't really an answer.

"Perhaps you would like to ask General Ludendorff that question. He was the Chief of Staff of the Army. He's the one, along with Hindenburg, who made those decisions."

"Sure," Berthold said. "I'll just phone him right now and see what he says."

"That won't be necessary," Dietrich said with a laugh. "General Ludendorff will be in Munich next week to meet with Hitler. I'll take you to see him."

Dietrich flexed his shoulders. A resolute look came into his eyes and he regained some of his enthusiasm. "The presence of men like Captain Göring and General Ludendorff within the Nazi Party is proof that Hitler is the one person who will lead Germany back to its proud and rightful place among the nations of Europe. Hitler is speaking here tomorrow night. Would you like to come with me?"

***

Berthold and Dietrich snuck out of the house after Elisabeth had gone to sleep. As they approached the *Burgerbraukeller*, loudspeakers on trucks blared and stormtroopers were giving out leaflets announcing Hitler's speech. Outside the beer hall, a brown-shirted group was savagely beating an elderly man.

"What did he do?" someone asked.

"The stupid communist called Hitler an idiot."

Berthold was frightened by the violence, but Dietrich said nothing and kept on walking. A large crowd had gathered and many were waiting in a long line to be admitted. Dietrich said Hitler always wanted the hall to be too small and thus filled to over-capacity. Berthold was impressed that his brother knew Hitler's thoughts, and even more impressed when Dietrich, wearing his swastika arm band, took them to the front of the line and then immediately inside.

The hall was already packed. Swastikas on bold red, white and black backgrounds were hung on every wall. A band played martial music. Many men and a surprising number of women were standing, jostling for position; the room was filled with smoke; everyone was drinking beer. Waitresses pushed their way through, carrying multiple mugs without a tray. Every conversation was a shouting match.

Dietrich maneuvered his way to a table near the front of the room where two men stood so he and Berthold could take their places. Soon after they arrived, a speaker took the podium; it was not Hitler.

"Is he coming?" Berthold asked.

"Don't worry," Dietrich said. "The *Führer* will be here. He's always late. Some people say he's purposely late, to increase the tension."

The speaker droned on, but no one could hear over the buzz of conversation, the band, and the intermittent outbreak of patriotic songs. Berthold listened to snatches of conversation between Dietrich and his friends.

"We collected twenty rifles on Tuesday."

"Collected? Or stole?"

"We followed Göring's orders."

"Do any of those rifles actually work?"

"Who would know? No ammunition."

Peering with difficulty through the smoke-filled room, Berthold saw that many of the men, perhaps half, were wearing the same brown stormtrooper uniform as his brother. A plump blond woman in her mid-twenties passed their table, purposely rubbing against one of the men. She turned and smiled as she walked away, swinging her hips. The others at the table exchanged knowing glances.

"Later," said the one who had been rubbed, "after she is, shall we say, excited by Hitler's speech, she'll want someone to share her excitement."

Suddenly there was a stirring at the door and the room tensed with anticipation. Several men entered, but again none was Hitler. Conversation resumed. This happened two more times, but nobody seemed discouraged or impatient. Each time, Dietrich said, "The *Führer* will be here."

And then he was, his white trench coat set off against a sea of dark uniforms.

Several men shouted "Heil Hitler!" and raised their right arms. Dietrich jumped up and did the same and soon "Heil Hitler!" blasted from one side of the hall to the other. Berthold felt conspicuous to remain silent, so he joined the shouting and even raised his arm. He saw the woman who had passed their table standing nearby, her own arm extended, a look of fierce passion in her eyes.

Hitler strode through the crowd, eyes straight ahead, his right arm bent at the elbow acknowledging the cheers. He grasped the podium with both hands and began in a normal conversational tone, almost professorial, calmly describing the revolutions which had convulsed Germany after the war. His voice was raspy but the words were clear. He spoke quietly that way for almost forty minutes.

Then he took a small sip of beer and as if a switch had been turned, he began to shout and wave his arms wildly. He broke into a sweat that quickly drenched his hair and face and clothes.

"We must call to account the Jewish Communist criminals of November 1918 who stabbed in the back our valiant and undefeated soldiers ... We do not pardon! ... We demand vengeance!"

Hitler screamed each denunciation louder than the one before. The crowd roared, and their adoration drove Hitler to new heights. Men stared at Hitler with wide-open mouths. Several women seemed to be in the grip of an ecstasy Berthold was powerless to understand.

"We will wage this struggle until the last Jew is removed from the German Reich!"

The words "last Jew" produced an even greater outburst of frenzied cheering, along with a cannonade of mugs pounding tables. Berthold felt sick to his stomach, worrying about his friend Leonard, remembering rocks thrown through synagogue windows.

A strand of hair plastered itself against Hitler's forehead. He propelled every sentence forward as if it were an artillery blast against the absent Jewish enemy, enveloping the audience in his frenzy. He spoke with no restraint, with furious gestures, a wild man. Dietrich hung on Hitler's every word. Berthold wanted to share his brother's enthusiasm, but he found Hitler's screaming and the audience's reaction equally repulsive.

"We will tear the Versailles peace treaty of the Jewish Communist criminals to shreds! ... We will create a mighty German Reich! I am showing you the only way! ... The people will rise up against the despoilers of Germany! ... Victory will not fail us!"

Hitler's head was thrown back, his right arm outstretched before him. He bounced up and down, his voice now hoarse and breaking with emotion. Berthold thought he looked silly.

"Deutschland! ... Deutschland!"

The entire hall reverberated, repeating *"Deutschland! ... Deutschland!"* Hitler's head fell forward onto his chest, soaked with sweat. The speech was over.

"Now he'll change his clothes and repeat the entire performance at another beer hall," Dietrich said, "but we, little man, will go home."

Several tables had been set up near the door where long lines of men and women were making contributions and completing membership applications for the Nazi Party. Dietrich's friend smiled as he left with the plump blond woman on his arm. Outside, men and women marched shoulder to shoulder, shouting "Heil Hitler! End the Jew Republic!"

Berthold was thankful Dietrich never asked what he thought about the speech, so he did not have to say it seemed to him like a well-choreographed circus act by a demented monster.

Chapter 5

November 1923 - Munich

Munich's summer of 1923 had been a nightmarish time. The hyperinflation continued and Germany's democratically elected government showed neither the ability nor the energy to make things better. Hitler spoke several times each week to increasingly hysterical crowds. A growing fleet of sound trucks prowled the streets and there was no escaping the Nazi message. Violence between Nazi and communist thugs exploded regularly, sometimes resulting in deaths.

One day, Berthold was visiting with Leonard at the same time Herr Goldmann was holding a meeting. Leonard explained that his father was worried about Hitler's growing popularity and had brought together important people, mostly but not all Jews, to try to develop means to counteract the Nazis' advances.

"Does Dietrich still drive for Hitler?" Leonard asked.

"Practically every day," Berthold said. "He takes him to meetings all over Bavaria. Mother tries to discourage him, but he doesn't listen."

Berthold hesitated. He had not previously repeated to Leonard any of the things Dietrich had told him about Hitler, but now, conscious of the people in the other room, he thought he should.

"Dietrich says there's tension within the Nazi movement. Some Nazis are even questioning Hitler's leadership. Dietrich says Hitler has fanned the flames and if he doesn't do something soon, he'll lose many of his followers. Dietrich thinks Hitler has begun to panic."

"Can I tell my father what you've just said?" Leonard asked.

"Yes. I think you should."

***

A few days later, Berthold came home from school to find Dietrich just leaving, wearing his best stormtrooper uniform, his old army pistol strapped around his waist.

"I have to go now," Dietrich said.

"What's happening?"

"I can't tell you. It's a huge secret. But in a few hours, everyone in Germany will know. It will happen at the *Burgerbraukeller* tonight."

***

As soon as Dietrich left, Berthold ran as fast as he could and fifteen minutes later he was banging on the Goldmanns' door.

""Tonight! It's going to happen tonight."

Leonard took Berthold to see his father.

"What's going to happen?" Herr Goldmann asked.

"I don't know exactly, but Dietrich said it'll be tonight at the *Burgerbraukeller*. He wore his best uniform and took his gun. He said all of Germany would know in a few hours."

"Thank you, Berthold," Goldmann said.

Berthold watched as Herr Goldmann shuffled papers on his desk until he found an invitation he had received but apparently ignored, to hear Gustav von Kahr, the recently appointed Commissioner of Bavaria, speak that night at the *Burgerbraukeller*. Goldmann called a friend, an attorney named Max Hirschberg, and then called the Munich police, speaking briefly with an inspector he knew. He put on his overcoat and went to say goodbye to his wife.

"Why are you going?" Judith Goldmann asked her husband. "It could be dangerous."

"There's no choice," Goldmann said. "We must know what's going on. Berthold should stay here tonight. Call the store and have Elisabeth come over as well. If there's trouble in

39

the streets, her apartment is too close to the *Burgerbraukeller*. I've asked the store to send two armed security guards here with Elisabeth. I'll be home as soon as I can."

***

Later, after it was all over, Herr Goldmann told Berthold what had happened. Hitler's red Mercedes had arrived at the *Burgerbraukeller*, with Dietrich driving. Hitler shouted orders to the municipal police to clear the streets, which, amazingly, they did.

The hall was jammed. Most of the important political and business leaders of Munich were inside. Richard found his friend Max Hirschberg and they sat together as Gustav Kahr took the podium and began to speak. About ten minutes into Kahr's speech, a commotion broke out near the main entrance.

"Out of the way! Clear the entrance!"

Hermann Göring bulled his way into the hall with a contingent of brownshirts. Everyone gasped when a machine gun on a tripod was set up facing the audience. Hitler, ludicrously dressed in a formal cutaway appropriate for a waiter in a third-class restaurant, stood behind the machine gun. He and the stormtroopers, waving pistols, elbowed people aside and forced their way toward the podium. Göring followed, brandishing a sword.

Commissioner Kahr had stopped speaking in mid-sentence, frozen in place. The din became overwhelming. Richard Goldmann watched in frightened disbelief as a number of men he knew to be police detectives stood and put on swastika armbands. More stormtroopers rushed in, but even with dozens of brownshirts struggling to clear a path, it took Hitler many minutes to reach the stage.

Hitler mounted the podium, raised his revolver and fired a single shot at the ceiling. The uproar instantly subsided. Then came Hitler's shrill voice, dialed to full volume.

"The national revolution has broken out. Six hundred armed men have this hall surrounded. No one is to leave."

Everyone looked around, fearful and confused. No one made a sound. No one tried to leave.

"I declare the Bavarian State government in Munich deposed," Hitler shrieked. "The Reich government in Berlin is also deposed. The police and army have joined under our swastika banner, which at this very moment is flying above the army barracks and police stations of this city."

Hitler turned and spoke politely to Kahr. "Excellency von Kahr, I must ask you to come with me. Everything will be settled in ten minutes. I shall guarantee your safety."

Herr Goldmann said he was surprised to see Kahr docilely follow Hitler out of the hall into a side room. Former Army Chief of Staff General Erich Ludendorff, in full uniform and wearing a metal helmet, appeared from somewhere and trailed after them. When the leaders had gone, the hall again erupted and some made as if to leave, but they were shoved back into their seats by the stormtroopers. Göring, medals sparkling, still flourishing his sword, leaped to the stage.

"This is not an assault on Commissioner Kahr," Göring bellowed in a parade-ground voice. "This action is directed solely against the Jewish Reich government in Berlin. Herr Hitler will return soon. Until he does, you must remain seated and follow the instructions of the guards."

Göring raised his sword, his voice even louder than before. "Long live the new Reich government. Hitler! Ludendorff!" Göring smiled and began to sing. Led by the stormtroopers, the entire hall joined in. "*Deutschland über Alles*" rang from a thousand voices.

Minutes passed and the crowd again became restless, but then Hitler returned, followed by Commissioner Kahr and General Ludendorff. The three men squeezed onto the podium and Hitler began to speak. Many in the audience climbed onto their chairs to get a better view.

41

"Now I want to explain what has been decided," Hitler said. "Commissioner Kahr will become Prime Minister of Bavaria. General Ludendorff will be the head of the Reichswehr."

A huge roar filled the hall. Hitler stood still and allowed it to roll to its conclusion, a joyous smile on his face. Then he reached over to Kahr and held their locked hands high, a visual portrayal of the new power arrangement in Bavaria. The crowd again roared. Letting go of Kahr's hand, Hitler spoke to the crowd.

"The government of the November criminals in Berlin is deposed and I hereby assume the political leadership of a provisional national government. We will rally the whole might of our country behind this new government. We will save the German people. We will march against the Jew-government in Berlin."

Led by the stormtroopers, cries rang out, repeated over and over again. "Heil Hitler! Heil Hitler!"

Ludendorff and Kahr each spoke briefly, making little impression after Hitler's histrionics. Hitler led those on the podium back to the side room and the crowd rose to leave, but their exit was very slow. At the door stormtroopers demanded that each person show an identification card or passport, which they checked against names on a list.

"Quick, follow me," Max Hirschberg yelled, pulling Richard Goldmann away from the door. "We can get out through the kitchen."

Hirschberg made it through, but Goldmann was stopped.

"Where do you think you're going," a stormtrooper said with a sneer. "Show me your identification." He compared Goldmann's card to his list. "Another Jew! Take him away."

Herr Goldmann was led to a crowded room on the second floor, crammed with Jewish men he knew. They were ordered to get down on their hands and knees. Two men who started to speak were hit in the head with clubs and lay bleeding on the floor.

***

Many hours had passed since Herr Goldmann had left and the tension in the Goldmann home had become unbearable. Finally there was a knock on the door. Max Hirschberg spoke to Judith in a frantic voice. "There's been a *putsch*. Hitler has taken control. Richard has been taken prisoner. They had a list and they kept all the Jews at the *Burgerbraukeller*."

Hirschberg rushed home to his wife and children. Judith Goldmann, who had always remained in control of herself, broke down sobbing, but when Elisabeth tried to hug her, she quickly pulled herself together, saying there was no time for tears. They decided it was safest to stay in the locked house with the two armed security guards. But how would they learn what was happening?

"We can use Papa's wireless," Leonard said.

"What's that?" Berthold asked.

"It's a special telegraph that works on radio waves and doesn't need wires. Papa has one of the few private sets in Munich. He taught me how it works. We can listen to police and army broadcasts."

"I'll telephone the *Münchener Post*," Judith added.

It took repeated tries, but Judith did get through to the newspaper, where she learned from a typesetter that the headline for the early morning edition proclaimed that Hitler and Ludendorff had taken over the Bavarian government.

"What will happen next?" Judith asked.

"Nobody knows," the typesetter said, "but the rumor is that Hitler will go to Berlin tomorrow and remove the Reich government."

"The Nazis have prisoners at the *Burgerbraukeller*," Judith said, trying to contain the hysteria she felt. "I've tried to

43

call the police, but I can't get through. Will you please try? My husband is there."

"We can't get through to the police either," the typesetter said. "And we can't leave. There's a mob of stormtroopers outside."

The telephone line went dead, which left the wireless set, glowing quietly on the dining room table, their only means of communication. Leonard thought he found the frequency on which the Munich police broadcast, but all they heard was static. Then there was a rapid repetition of short high-pitched signals.

"What do those beeps mean?" Berthold asked.

"It's called Morse Code," Leonard said, pushing a pad and a pencil toward Berthold. "You write."

Nothing made any sense to Berthold, just a series of sounds which Leonard said represented letters. Leonard listened and announced the letters. The first message, which told the weather in Munich, was repeated several times. Then came the words they were waiting for, although not what they wanted to hear.

HITLER DEPOSES
GOVERNMENT ... LUDENDORFF
AND KAHR PART OF PUTSCH ...
CITY HALL AND WAR MINISTRY
CONTROLLED BY NAZIS

"This is worse than anything we expected," Judith said. "Even Richard never predicted this. I can't believe that beast is going to run our country."

"He's only in Munich," Elisabeth said, "not all of Germany."

"But Ludendorff," Judith said, "was commander of the army. They'll follow him."

Hours later, long after their mothers had fallen asleep in their chairs, Berthold and Leonard were still glued to the wireless. Shortly after 3:00 am, a new message started. Leonard missed the beginning, but it was repeated twice. When the letters appeared on Berthold's pad, they stared in amazement, and then glee.

KAHR REPUDIATES
AGREEMENT WITH HITLER ...
REICHSWEHR AND POLICE
WILL PUT DOWN NAZI REVOLT

Leonard rushed to tell his mother. Berthold said he was leaving. Elisabeth protested, but he flew from the house, hollering, "I have to warn Dietrich."

***

Berthold had intended to run home, but since he passed the *Burgerbraukeller* on the way, he went there instead. He was amazed, first that he was allowed in, and second that virtually nothing was happening. A few people sat about, sleeping or drunk, but there were no preparations underway for any armed coup. He asked for Dietrich and was told his brother had arrived a few minutes earlier with Hitler. Just then Dietrich came down from the upper floor and saw Berthold.

"What are you doing here?" Dietrich asked.

"I came to warn you," Berthold said. "Commissioner Kahr has turned against Hitler. The Army and police are going to put down the *putsch*. I don't want them to shoot you."

"What? How do you know that?"

"Leonard and I heard it on his father's wireless."

"Where's mother?" Dietrich asked. "I was just going home to warn her to stay inside."

"She's at the Goldmann house."

"Damn!" Dietrich exclaimed. "They're out looking for Jews."

"But they won't go there," Berthold said. "Herr Goldmann is already held prisoner here at the *Burgerbraukeller*."

Dietrich hugged Berthold. "Thank you. I'll tell Hitler."

"Don't think I'm doing this to warn Hitler," Berthold said. "I don't care about him. I'm doing it for you."

***

Berthold went back to the Goldmann house and stayed there until daylight, when he and his mother went home. Dietrich had not been there. Berthold returned to the *Burgerbraukeller*, where he stood outside and watched, expecting the police to come arrest Hitler and let Herr Goldmann and the other Jews leave. If Dietrich was also arrested, he wanted to help him if he could. But no police came.

Just before noon, the doors of the beer hall flew open and a column quickly formed in the street outside. Swastika flags came first, then the leaders, Hitler in the middle, the collar of his trench coat turned up against the November chill, his holstered Browning pistol belted around his waist. Ludendorff and Göring were at his sides, Dietrich directly behind him. A small group of disciplined stormtroopers marched next in strict military order, followed by a larger unruly collection of poorly uniformed, ill-disciplined brownshirts, waving handguns and a few rifles.

Berthold did not know if Hitler had simply ignored the warning or if there had been some later development. He followed the group to the Ludwigsbrücke, where a small platoon of State Police moved forward to block the marchers from crossing the bridge. The two groups stared silently at each other while incongruous sounds of a carousel and children playing wafted up from a fair being held on the island in the middle of the river below them.

"Halt!" ordered the police.

Göring, his rubber coat belted tautly around his paunch, his *Pour le Merite* sparkling on his chest, counter-ordered, "Keep moving! Straight ahead!"

From the police side: "Load with live ammunition."

Göring responded, "Don't shoot your fellow war veterans!"

A trumpet sounded from the midst of the stormtroopers and Berthold heard someone yell "Charge the police!" A group of stormtroopers broke ranks and ran past the Nazi leaders. No shots were fired, but within seconds the thin police line had been shattered. Hitler had not uttered a word, either of command or encouragement, but he had won his first battle.

The march resumed, crossed the bridge and headed toward the center of the city. Many civilians now walked with them. The mood was festive. It seemed as if Ludendorff was now commanding the marchers while Hitler simply smiled and saluted the crowds. Many returned the stiff Nazi salute and shouted "Heil Hitler!" Hitler was conducting yet another performance and the crowd was loving it.

A flurry of wet snow began to fall as the marchers reached the Marienplatz, where swastika flags fluttered from the balconies of the City Hall, seemingly under the control of the Nazis. A photographer climbed high on the ancient Mariensäule column, holding on for dear life and struggling to point his camera. Thousands of people blocked traffic. Who had brought these crowds? Posters on poles announced that Hitler had taken over. Where had those posters come from? The crowd sang *Deutschland über Alles*. Some of the marchers joined in, others shouted "Heil Ludendorff!! Heil Hitler!"

A detachment of State Police arrived to block the way, supported by an armored car. The turret rotated to point directly at Hitler. Ludendorff commanded, "Follow me."

Totally serene, the old general seemed absolutely certain no German soldier or policeman would ever fire on the hero of the stunning German victories during the early days of the Great War. He was right. No shots were fired and the marchers obediently followed him into a narrow street.

**

Running ahead of the marchers, under the arches which lined the street, Berthold reached the *Feldherrnhalle*, the huge open loggia honoring Bavarian Field Marshalls of wars long past. Peeking from behind a column, he saw very substantial Army and State Police formations, much different from the small force on the bridge. The first marchers entered the square but the bulk of them were stuck in the narrow street. Hitler, Ludendorff and Göring stopped dead in their tracks, facing the police and Army just a few feet away. Berthold saw Dietrich standing behind Hitler. An eerie quiet came over the square; even the birds stopped singing.

A single shot rang out from somewhere and a police sergeant fell to the ground. Dietrich wrenched Hitler down and fell on top of him just as the police and Army opened an overwhelming barrage. The noise was deafening, but in thirty seconds it was over.

Hitler, covered with blood, crawled out from under Dietrich and ran to a car which seemed to be waiting for him in a side street. Göring limped off in a different direction. Ludendorff, who had remained standing at attention throughout the shooting, now marched alone, straight at the Army formation. The sun broke through grey clouds, reflecting off his pointed helmet and the Army lines opened to let him pass. The square was again silent.

**

Dietrich had not moved. Berthold ran to his side and dropped down on the bloody ground just as Dietrich opened his eyes.

"Did Hitler escape?" Dietrich whispered.

"What do I care about Hitler?" Berthold said. "He ran away and left you here. I tried to warn you and now ..."

"You take care of Mother now," Dietrich said, barely getting the words out. "Please do a better job than I've done. I've made a mess of everything."

Tears ran down Dietrich's cheeks. Berthold looked for help, but everyone was gone. He started to scream, but then he looked at his brother and realized there was no point. He had lost his father and now his brother was dying.

Dietrich coughed, his eyes closed, and his face suddenly held the pallor Berthold had often seen on bodies laying in the streets.

Chapter 6

1990 - Munich

Marissa was having coffee with Berthold Becker at an outdoor café near Berthold's apartment. She had spent several weeks in Munich, listening to Becker's account of the 1923 events, comparing it to her own knowledge of the history. She would soon go to Jerusalem to begin her meetings with Anna Gorska.

"Even though it happened sixty-seven years ago," Marissa said, "I still want to offer my condolences."

"Dietrich's death and his subsequent elevation to martyrdom by Josef Goebbels was the direct cause of my involvement with the Nazis seven years later. I became known as the *Putsch* martyr's brother, a title from which there was no escape."

"How long did it take until Richard Goldmann was released?"

"Later that same afternoon," Berthold said. "After the debacle at the Feldherrnhalle, the Nazi guards left the beer hall and the prisoners simply walked out. The police never did come to rescue them."

"Had they been injured?"

"A few, but all of them were terrified."

"What would Hitler have done with them if the *Putsch* had succeeded?"

"I guess we'll never know," Berthold said, "but Richard was well aware of Hitler's well-publicized intent to rid Germany of its Jews and expected the worst."

"Did you follow Hitler's trial?" Marissa asked.

"Not really," Becker answered. "We all thought Hitler was done. He was on trial for treason and would surely be executed or at least go to prison for many years. The violence in the streets had all but disappeared. The banker Hjalmar

Schacht had done something nobody understood which had magically ended the out-of-control inflation. Even the screaming against the Jews had quieted down. Things were almost normal again."

Marissa waited. She knew how unlikely it was that things were even close to normal for the Becker family, and she wondered if he would talk about it. Becker closed his eyes and took a deep breath.

"Mother told me she knew I had done everything I could but I still thought she blamed me for letting Dietrich stay with Hitler that morning. We were further shocked when Hitler was sentenced to what ended up being less than a year in jail.

"Thank goodness for Judith Goldmann. She came to our apartment many times in the next few months, more even than Leonard.

"Then one Sunday morning Mother opened the piano and began to play. It sounded so sweet to me. When she was done, she asked if I wanted to go out, and we walked for hours. She didn't say much, but I knew the time of mourning was over and now we could get on with whatever came next."

Marissa sensed Becker wasn't done; she waited.

"Of course I was devastated by Dietrich's death," Becker said softly, "but in a strange way I also thought I was very fortunate. I had been rather like a moth which had strayed too close to the flame, snared by Dietrich's involvement with the Nazis, but then the fire went out and I was saved."

Becker sipped his cold coffee, said quietly, "Later I got caught again. Years later, Hitler remembered my warning."

Marissa stood to leave and Becker asked, "You will see Anna now in Jerusalem?"

A sharp ripple of surprise went through Marissa. She had not mentioned her plan to meet Anna Gorska.

"Yes," Marissa said. "I'll be in Jerusalem for several weeks and then I'll come back to Munich as we've scheduled."

"Please tell Anna I'm comfortable talking with you."

***

On the way to the airport, Marissa thought about Becker's message for Anna. It was clear that Becker and Gorska had spoken to each other about her project, but if that was so, Berthold didn't need her to take a message to Anna. The message, she concluded, was for her; it was Berthold's way of saying he was pleased with their discussions so far.

From the airport, Marissa telephoned her father in New York. "I feel like I'm living in the history I once studied."

"Do you believe Becker's account?" Abraham asked.

"It's hard to be sure," Marissa said. "There's so much of his story where he's the only witness."

Abraham sensed his daughter's smile from four thousand miles away. "There is," Marissa said, "one piece of corroborating evidence."

"What's that?"

"Did you ever read *Mein Kampf*?"

"No. I hate everything about Hitler. Couldn't stand to read his book."

"Hitler wrote much of it in 1924 when he was in prison," Marissa said. "I looked at it this morning and saw something I'd never noticed before. The book is dedicated to the martyrs of the *Putsch*. Their names are listed. Dietrich Becker's name is among them."

***

1990 - Jerusalem

From the start, Anna Gorska had proven more difficult to reach than Becker. She had not responded to Marissa's letters or phone calls. It wasn't until Marissa left a message saying she'd begun meeting with Becker that Gorska called back and scheduled a meeting. Marissa taxied from the Tel

Aviv airport to Gorska's flat in Jerusalem, located on the sixth floor of a modern building not far from the King David Hotel.

Her father had remembered Gorska in Nuremberg as a beautiful woman, remarkably so given her years in the hands of the Nazis, and Marissa saw full evidence of that in the eighty-two year old woman in front of her. There was a spirit and a presence any woman of any age would have been pleased to project. She was saddened, however, by the thought of such elegance demeaned as a Nazi whore at Auschwitz. Gorska had prepared coffee and they made small talk for several minutes.

"Your English is excellent," Marissa said. "Much better than my Hebrew."

"I began as a child in Poland," Anna said. "Then of course I had lots of practice after the war when I helped the Americans as a translator. It's turned out to be useful here in Israel as well." Anna grew serious. "Is Berthold being cooperative?"

"He told me to tell you he was comfortable talking to me."

"Good," Anna said, nodding once, a small precise movement.

Marissa smiled tentatively and Anna returned the smile, a sign perhaps that she had passed some kind of test. So far. She decided to start her interview with a review of Gorska's career as a journalist.

"I've studied the archives of the *Haynt* and other newspapers which published your articles in Poland, Germany, London, New York and Philadelphia. You became a hugely important journalist in the 1930s, especially given that you started in a tiny *shtetl*. How did that happen?"

"I was very fortunate," Gorska said. "Marshal Pilsudski was a major help to my career, and then Berthold arranged for me to interview Hitler. In both cases, I was able to serve the interests of the people being interviewed; they helped me and I helped them." Gorska laughed. "At least Hitler and Goebbels *thought* I was helping them."

"When did you first meet Berthold?" Marissa realized as she said his name that she was getting comfortable referring to him as Berthold rather than Becker.

"It was in 1930 in Munich," Anna said.

"That long before the war?" Marissa sputtered. "I had no idea you and Berthold knew each other that early."

"How is he?" Anna asked.

"He's mentally quite sharp," Marissa said. "Wary."

"Is he able to tell his story? Emotionally, I mean."

"I don't know yet," Marissa said. "I think he's trying to tell me what he truthfully knows."

"But will he say what he felt?" Anna asked.

"I hope so," Marissa said.

Anna began talking about the time in Munich when she had first met Berthold, but Marissa didn't have enough context to make much sense of it and her confusion was obvious.

"Perhaps it would be helpful if I tell you how I got to Warsaw from my *shtetl* in Ciechanow and began the chain of events that led to meeting Berthold in Munich."

Marissa nodded and Anna continued, "The first inkling of my future was when a journalist from Warsaw came to our home for *Shabbos* dinner. That was in March of 1924 ..."

Chapter 7

March 1924 - Ciechanow

Anna's mother, due to deliver a child any day, was in bed under strict doctor's orders and thus unable to prepare the Shabbos meal. It was a big responsibility for a sixteen year old girl but Anna was determined that everything would be perfect.

Yesterday - Thursday - Anna had gone to the Jewish market to buy the fish, the chicken and the meat. She had also cleaned the house. Normally the cleaning was done on Friday morning, but Mama had warned she would not have time to do everything on Friday, since she had to do it all herself.

Up before dawn, Anna readied herself for what she knew would be a day-long, non-stop, high-tension race to have everything waiting when Papa and the others returned from synagogue that evening. She had done it before, but always together with her mother. Anna was not counting on much assistance from her younger sister Danuta, and of course her brother was completely useless.

Anna checked slowly and carefully for the third time to make sure every pot, pan, dish, cooking utensil and piece of silverware which had touched dairy foods was properly put away so nothing could possibly contaminate the meat implements she would soon be using. She kept going over the list, eyes darting, terrified she might overlook something. She tied a clean apron around her thin waist - it went twice around - and fixed a brightly colored kerchief on her head, just like Mama always wore.

She raised the cleaver and chopped off the fish's head, taking two swings to do what Mama always did in one. The next several hours were a blur of cooking - gefilte fish, challah bread, onions and potatoes, roasted chicken, beef, and finally, golden chicken soup.

Echoing repeatedly in her head was Mama's admonition, "Be careful with the fire. Only last month, Mrs. Zyserman was cooking and a fire started and their whole house burned down, although, thank you God, no one died." Anna knew that the Gorska home, also made of wood, was equally at risk.

"Danuta! Where are you?"

"I'm here." A reluctant reply.

"I want you to run to the market and get some garlic."

"But ..."

"Don't argue. Put on your coat. Here, take this money. Go. Hurry back."

Just in time, Anna remembered to remove the gefilte fish from the oven and place it outside in a metal box to cool. As soon as Danuta returned with the garlic, Anna crushed several cloves and rubbed them on the inside and outside of the chicken, before placing the bird on a roasting pan which she put next to the meat in the oven.

Anna was surprised when her Father appeared, home from his shop on his way to the bathhouse. Where had the time gone? He sniffed the cooking smells, smiled and gave her a big hug.

"It will be an excellent *Shabbos* meal." he said, patting her head lovingly. "How's your mother?"

"She's tired, but I don't think she's in much pain."

Jacob went into the bedroom and Anna could hear quiet voices. Soon he returned to the kitchen carrying a small leather bag which contained his silk caftan, velvet skullcap and clean underwear. He smiled wordlessly at Anna as he hurried off to the bathhouse, from which he would go directly to the synagogue.

Soon after Father left, the beggar who appeared every Friday afternoon knocked on the door. Anna took a coin from the jar set aside for that purpose and gave it to the thin poorly-dressed man, wishing him a *gut Shabbos*.

Anna's brother Josef burst into the house, ran to the children's curtained-off bedroom, changed from his after-school clothes into his *Shabbos* finery, and ran out of the house, having said not a single word nor even acknowledged his sister's presence.

Anna retrieved a portion of horseradish from the cool cellar under the house, taking a good whiff which brought tears to her eyes. While the chicken and meat continued to cook, she cleaned every utensil she had used, every kitchen surface, and any other corner of the house where even a speck of dirt revealed itself to her sharp eye. Finally, as the March sky began to darken, she took a deep breath. Everything was ready, and she had just enough time to wash herself with a cloth and cold water, after which she donned the heavy woolen dress she wore each *Shabbos*.

Anna went into her parents' bedroom and sat next to her mother, who was humming the *Lekhah Dodi*, the song of welcome to the *Shabbos* Queen. Evona pulled Anna to her and kissed her forehead.

"Everything is done, Mama," Anna said. "I even remembered to set aside the food for tomorrow. Will you join us for dinner?"

"I've not been to the ritual bath," Evona said, "so I don't think it's allowed for me to join Papa and the men at the table."

"But you couldn't go to the bath," Anna said. "You can barely walk."

"I'll discuss this with your father when he returns. But first let me tell you how proud I am of you. You will make a wonderful wife some day."

"Yes, of course," Anna said, but she was not enthusiastic and her mother noticed.

***

Anna peered excitedly through the window into the dark night, straining for the first glimpse of her arriving father.

57

What she saw instead was her brother Josef, dressed like a miniature Papa in his long black caftan and wide-brimmed hat, running boisterously, calling *gut Shabbos* at the top of his lungs. Behind Josef came her Father, her Grandfather Kamon (her mother's father), her Uncle Ezriel (her mother's brother), and a man she did not recognize. She rushed to set another place at the table.

Jacob frowned when he saw the unlit candles. *Shabbos* candles were supposed to be lit before sundown. What had happened to his wife since he had seen her just an hour before? He hurried to the bedroom and a minute later emerged with a big smile on his face. He gathered everyone at the sideboard where two candlesticks awaited, heirlooms of Evona's family, handed from mother to daughter for generations. But Jacob did not take up the hot coal to light the candles.

Everyone heard the quiet sounds from the bedroom and all eyes turned. Anna held her breath with pride as she watched her beautiful mother - in her best wig and wearing a recently altered dress of black silk, a single brilliant strand of pearls around her neck - walking with immeasurable dignity despite her condition. She faltered once, but Jacob took her elbow and gently guided her.

Jacob and Evona had been married for eighteen years. Jacob had the pale and ascetic look of the scholar he had wanted to be, his face thin, his nose sharp. At forty-two his beard and sidelocks were still dark but his hair was almost completely gray. Evona, two years younger and several inches shorter than her husband, was full-bodied in the hips and breasts, and now of course her belly was enormous. Three living children and two miscarriages had taken their toll, but everyone said her pleasantly rounded face and piercing dark eyes were still as beautiful as they had been on her wedding day.

Jacob took his wife's hand and helped her light the candles. With a shawl over her head and her hands covering her eyes, Evona chanted the prayer, her voice soft, pure and steady. The glow of the candles added to the soft light of the oil lamps. Jacob helped his wife to her seat. The stranger stood to be introduced.

"Evona," Jacob said, "this is Rachmiel Slowacki from Warsaw, where he is a writer for *Haynt*. We have been honored that our rabbi has selected us to invite Rachmiel to our *Shabbos* dinner."

"We are pleased to welcome you as our guest," Evona said.

Jacob then introduced Slowacki, very formally, to each of the children, explaining that *Haynt* (Today) was a very important Yiddish newspaper published in Warsaw. Anna, focused on the meal to come, hardly noticed.

Jacob washed his hands and poured the wine, including a weak honey wine for the children. He raised the family's silver *kiddish* cup and said the prayer, then broke off small pieces of Anna's *challah* which were passed from hand to hand until everyone had one, after which he said the prayer over bread.

Anna held her breath as everyone took a bite of the *challah*, exhaling with relief when nobody by face or gesture indicated anything amiss. She poked Danuta and the two girls left the table. Anna returned with the tray of gefilte fish and Danuta behind her carried the horseradish. Anna's anxiety rose again as her family began to eat.

Evona was the first to respond, smiling at her daughter. "This is delicious, Anna."

Evona took a few more bites, then rose awkwardly. Jacob started to go with her, but she waved him back and slowly returned to her bed. The rest of the dinner was eaten and everyone complimented Anna. The dishes were cleared, concluding prayers were sung, and the children sent off to bed.

Shabbos dinner, as always, had provided a foretaste of God's future world. Each participant was suffused with the sense they had shared a meal with the Almighty. Now the men's discussion of more worldly matters could begin.

***

Anna slid from her bed and crept surreptitiously to the curtain which separated the children's sleeping area from the dining area, as she had done many times before. She suspected Papa knew she was there and did not object. Rachmiel Slowacki, the guest from Warsaw, was reaching into his valise.

"Here," Slowacki said, "is one of the very first bottles of our great new Polish vodka *Wódka Wyborowa*." He added proudly, "This is Poland's first international trademark since we became - after one hundred twenty years - an independent state."

Jacob retrieved four narrow glasses from the cupboard and the men settled in for the traditional Friday night sharing of news, gossip and political opinions.

"What is Pilsudski going to do?" Jacob asked, and Grandfather Kamon quickly added, "Will the Marshal come out of retirement and overthrow the government?" Everyone in Ciechanow was asking those questions and they had a guest in their home who perhaps had some answers.

Jozef Pilsudski was, at the age of fifty-nine, a man of legend. He had been the major figure at every stage of Poland's recently acquired independence. Before the war he had fought the Russian occupiers. During the war, he led troops which he had recruited and trained, fighting first against the Russians on the side of the Germans, then abruptly switching sides to fight against the Germans. After the Great War, the Russians had again attacked Poland and Pilsudski's forces had defeated them in what every Pole knew as the miracle at the Vistula. He had been prominent at the peace conference at Versailles and subsequently in the creation of the new Polish nation, until one day he simply walked away from public life. Now, after several

60

years in retirement, there was speculation the Marshal would return.

"Marshal Pilsudski is disgusted with the political bickering and even more so with the corruption of government," Slowacki said. "He's been quietly organizing a team of potential officials, ready to take office should conditions require him to become the Prime Minister of the Polish Republic."

"Ach!" Jacob snorted. "Conditions! If Pilsudski wants it he'll create his own conditions. So the question is whether he wants it and if so, when he will act."

"The time may be getting closer," Slowacki said. "We've had fourteen governments in the past five years, and meanwhile our economy falls further behind the rest of Europe and the people suffer. Many believe a coup by Pilsudski is the only way to put Poland on the right track."

"I've seen your name in *Haynt*," Uncle Ezriel said to Slowacki. "You've written some excellent articles. Very keen analysis."

"Thank you," Slowacki said.

"Can you tell us why you're in Ciechanow?" Ezriel asked.

"I'm here to learn what Jews outside Warsaw think about the possibility of Pilsudski returning to the government. I'll go to five small towns and report what I hear."

As soon as there was a lull in the conversation, Jacob asked Grandfather Kamon to tell their guest about his experiences with Pilsudski during the revolution. Kamon was thrilled to relate what was his most precious memory.

"It was September 1908. There was a train carrying Russian tax receipts from Warsaw to Wilno. Marshal Pilsudski decided to attack at the Bezdany station. There were nineteen of us. My younger brother Edel and I were on the train posing as passengers. At Bezdany, we took out our pistols and shot the guards. Outside the train, other men cut the telegraph lines. A bomb blew open the mail car. We recovered enough rubles for

Pilsudski to equip many fighting squads and continue the insurrection against the Tsar."

"You were there!" Slowacki exclaimed. "Every Pole knows about this famous train robbery, but I never met anyone who was actually there. Were you arrested?"

"Several of our men were arrested and four received jail sentences. I was never identified, but my brother Edel had been recognized by one of the passengers and was being sought by the Russian police. That's when he decided it was time to leave for America, in a big hurry."

Anna had known, of course, that her Uncle Edel had gone to America, and that his wife and children had followed a year or two later, but she had never known that both Kamon and Edel had been involved in one of the most famous legends in Pilsudski's long history.

After Kamon finished, Ezriel began to tell of his involvement in Pilsudski's army during the Great War, but this story Anna had heard many times, and with her mind on other things, she left her hiding place and went to bed.

Chapter 8

Anna lay awake imagining her future. Warsaw was where she wanted to go, but how was she going to get there? She thought first of her Uncle Ezriel, who had moved to Warsaw and no doubt knew many people. Then her mind shifted to their *Shabbos* visitor, Rachmiel Slowacki, also living in Warsaw, who wrote important articles about the major political issues of the day. She began to wonder what it took to become a journalist like Slowacki.

Anna drifted off to sleep, but she rose early the next morning and wrote in the diary she had kept since she was eleven.

> *I used to be jealous that Josef*
> *could go to Hebrew school and I*
> *couldn't, but now I realize that just*
> *a Jewish education is not enough*
> *for me even if I was a boy.*
>
> *I must go to Warsaw, to*
> *university. I have two years to*
> *prepare. I need to read many*
> *books - history, science, novels.*
>
> *I must discuss these things with*
> *mother. There must be more to my*
> *life than making gefilte fish.*

It wasn't until she wrote the words *gefilte* fish that Anna remembered it was *Shabbos* and that she wasn't supposed to be writing. She hurriedly put away her diary and pen.

***

On *Shabbos* morning, the house was empty but for Anna and her mother. Evona Gorska had a well-worn Yiddish version of the Pentateuch, the five books of Moses which comprise the Holy Torah. Each year, all over the world, Jews read the entire Torah from Genesis through Deuteronomy, one section each week. In the current week's portion, Moses had led the Jews out of Egypt and received the Ten Commandments at Sinai, but they were still wandering in the wilderness, not yet deemed ready by God to enter the promised land of Israel. Sitting in bed and grimacing from time to time, Evona read aloud God's instructions for the preparation of a breast piece for the high priest.

> "You shall make a breastpiece and set in it
> mounted stones. The first row shall be of
> carnelian, chrysolite, and emerald. The second
> row: a turquoise, a sapphire, and an amethyst.
> The third row: a jacinth, an agate, and a
> crystal; and the fourth row: a beryl, a lapis
> lazuli, and a jasper. They shall be framed with
> gold in their mountings."

"Mama," Anna said, "These Jews had been slaves in Egypt. We are told they escaped with nothing but the clothes on their backs and a few pieces of unleavened bread. They were wandering in the wilderness for years. Where did they get gold and jewels and tools to make such things?"

"This is why, dear Anna," Evona said, "girls are not permitted to study Bible and Talmud with the boys. No boy would ask such a question."

"But what is the answer?" Anna insisted. "Does Papa know? Does the rabbi?"

Evona smiled through her pain. "I suspect any rabbi would have an answer, but I also suspect you would not be satisfied with what he would tell you ... if you asked him ... which you will not."

Evona closed her Pentateuch and lay back on her pillow. Anna knew she was not asleep. She was afraid to ask what was uppermost in her mind, but then she thought this might be the last time for a long while to be alone with her mother. Once the baby was born there would be few quiet moments in the Gorska home.

"Mama," Anna said.

Evona opened her eyes and Anna exhaled a single, hurried stream of words. "I want to go to university in Warsaw, I need to prepare for university exams, I need books to read, will you help me?"

Anna understood quite well the enormity of what she was asking. So far as she knew, no Jewish girl from Ciechanow had ever gone to university in Warsaw. Their Orthodox community would be shocked, Anna would be called brazen, and Papa would be harshly criticized for allowing his daughter to do such a thing.

Evona drew herself up, just slightly but enough to make her cringe. "You certainly have big ideas, Anna."

She motioned for Anna to sit closer and took her hand. "After hundreds of years without change, our Jewish world is suddenly being turned upside down. Jews argue endlessly about which way is right." Evona touched her daughter's cheek. "Women are changing too. We're now allowed to vote ..."

"More than that," Anna said. "A Jewish woman was elected to the Polish parliament. Her name is Irena Meltzer. She's coming to Ciechanow to give a speech. I saw a poster."

Evona smiled at her daughter, so full of energy and ambition, so excited at the prospects of her life, so unaware of the disappointments that inevitably lay ahead. She hugged her child and said, "I will speak with your father."

"Thank you, Mama. I do want to do more in my life than make *gefilte* fish."

Evona's eyes opened wide and Anna realized she had insulted her mother. "I'm sorry," she said.

"I don't disagree with you," Evona said. "It's a different world for you than it was for me when I was your age."

65

Anna breathed a sigh of relief; her body tingled at the possibilities which might soon be open to her. But mostly she understood she had an ally. Now she needed a plan.

***

When the men returned from the synagogue, there was another meal, featuring the food Anna had put aside the day before, after which the men prepared for several hours of study and quiet discussion. But Anna had a different idea. She approached Rachmiel Slowacki and asked if she could discuss something with him.

"Of course, Anna," he said. "And thank you again for a truly delicious meal. What is it you want to discuss?"

"Next week Madame Irena Meltzer will speak in Ciechanow," Anna said.

"Yes, I know," Slowacki said. "I'm sorry I'll have left by then. I would very much like to report on how she's received here."

"I could do it," Anna said. "I could go to the speech and interview her and prepare a report. I could mail it to you in Warsaw."

Slowacki looked at Anna in amazement. None of the Yiddish papers employed a female reporter, let alone a young girl who had never, so far as he knew, written anything. He started to shake his head when a voice startled both of them.

"You should give her a chance."

Anna spun to see her Uncle Ezriel standing behind her.

"She's the brightest girl I've ever known," Ezriel said. "If you give her good instructions, I think you'll be very pleased with what you receive." Ezriel came forward to face Slowacki. "What do you have to lose?"

Anna held her breath when Slowacki at first didn't respond. But then he said, "Anna, why don't you get your coat and come with me. I think best when I'm walking. Will you come with us, Ezriel?"

They walked for almost an hour, during which Slowacki outlined what he would want in an article and gave Anna more information about Madame Meltzer. He also told her to read everything she could find about the long-running dispute between Marshal Pilsudski and his political opponent Roman Dmowski, and why that dispute was important for the Jews of Poland.

***

Two days later, Anna wrote in her diary ...

> *My baby brother Yonah lived only three hours, not even long enough to be named at the synagogue or be circumcised, but the rabbi said any child born of a Jewish mother was a Jew, regardless of how long he lived.*
>
> *Even though we were sad for Yonah, Papa said we must thank God that Mother survived. She is pale and weak, and she suffered much pain, but she lives.*
>
> *It seems such a waste for a woman to carry a child for nine months and then he lives but three hours. What is God thinking?*

Chapter 9

1990 - Jerusalem ...

"When I prepared for what I hoped would be an interview with Madame Meltzer," Anna said, "it was the first time I did independent research."

Marissa thought about her first serious research paper, written when she was a junior in college. The more she learned about Anna Gorska, the more impressed she was.

Anna continued. "The library in Ciechanow had an archive of Polish and Yiddish newspapers. I read everything I could find about Roman Dmowski and the political party he headed. What I learned horrified me. Dmowski's hatred of Jews was just as strong as Hitler's."

"My mentor at Brandeis is one of the world's greatest scholars on Polish Jewry," Marissa said. "I'm familiar with Dmowski's history."

Anna smiled in a way Marissa thought was strange, but then she quickly returned to her research regarding Roman Dmowski. "So you know he opposed the rights for Polish Jews which had been mandated by the Versailles Treaty, and that he called Jews the enemy of true Poles, by which of course he meant Christian Poles. I read for days, and I couldn't wait to ask Madame Meltzer about these things."

Chapter 10

April 1924 - Ciechanow

Irena Meltzer, the first woman ever elected to the *Sejm*, the Polish national parliament in Warsaw, was scheduled to speak at one o'clock in the meeting room in the basement of the synagogue. The first to arrive, Anna and her friend Roza Robota settled on a bench just in front of the podium. They had each brought an apple and a piece of dark bread.

Anna had her research notes and a page filled with questions she wanted to ask, along with three sharpened pencils which she had stuffed into her coat pocket. She was so intent on reviewing her notes and questions that she failed to notice the heavy-set lady standing in front of her, until Roza poked her and jerked her head in the direction of the visitor.

"You seem quite absorbed in your papers," the lady said.

"Well," Anna said, "this is the first time I've been a reporter and I want to make sure I know the questions I want to ask ... if I get a chance to ask them."

"So you're a reporter," the lady said. "What newspaper are you working for?"

"The *Haynt* in Warsaw," Anna said proudly.

"Really," the lady said, not quite hiding the skepticism in her voice. "And may I ask how you came to get such a prestigious assignment?"

"Oh, yes, you may certainly ask. I was assigned this important job by Rachmiel Slowacki."

Madame Meltzer again looked skeptical; Anna explained. "Mr. Slowacki was our *Shabbos* dinner guest. That's when he asked me to cover this speech for him." Anna paused. "Well, actually, I asked him if I could, and he agreed."

"And what sort of questions are you planning to ask?"

"I've been reading about the views of Marshal Pilsudski and Mr. Roman Dmowski, especially regarding Polish Jews, and I would like to know what Madame Meltzer thinks about the differences between the two men."

"That's very interesting," the lady said as she turned to walk away. Looking back, she added, "I'll see what I can do to get you a chance to ask your questions."

Five minutes later, Anna's mouth dropped open as she stared at the woman who had mounted the podium and was being introduced by the head of the local Zionist Party. She blushed furiously when the lady looked down at her and winked.

"These are difficult times for Poland," Madame Meltzer began. "Our parliament is a mess. We don't seem able to compromise on anything and so we get nothing done. Unfortunately, our Jewish representatives are also divided. The assimilationists say we should become Polish in every way while the orthodox say it would be disastrous for Jews to cease being fully observant and the Zionists think we should leave Poland and go to Palestine."

"What do you believe, Madame Meltzer?" came a shout from a man somewhere behind Anna.

"You all know I'm a member of the Zionist Party. I think we should go to Palestine."

Another voice, this one a woman's: "Most of us cannot just pick up and leave our homes and families and businesses. What can we do if we have to stay in Poland?"

"I know it's difficult to leave, and there are also limits on how many Jews the British will allow into Palestine. For those who must remain in Poland, there are important decisions to be made. Roman Dmowski and his National Democrats have several times come close to a parliamentary majority, which if they ever achieve it, will be terrible news for Jews."

Everyone knew what was coming next. It was what they had come to hear. "It's an open secret the Marshal Pilsudski is considering a return to government. I think Jews will be much safer in Poland if the Marshal is in charge, so I would urge you to encourage him to return."

Several people clapped. Then more. Then shouts of "Pilsudski" filled the air. It was clear the Jews of Ciechanow would welcome Pilsudski, and it was also clear to Anna that this was the purpose of Madame Meltzer's visit. She was on a tour to drum up support for the return of Marshal Pilsudski.

Amidst the tumult, Anna tried but was not able to ask a question. She took notes and asked Roza to help her count the crowd and the proportion who were cheering for Pilsudski. Finally Madame Meltzer said she had another speech in another town that very night and she had to leave. Disappointed that she had been too shy to get involved in the discussion, Anna closed her notebook and started to walk away.

"Wait, she's waving to you," Roza said, grabbing Anna's shoulder.

Anna turned back and saw Madame Meltzer beckoning. She stood dumbfounded for a moment until Roza gave a push and they walked toward the podium. The most important female politician in Poland led the two girls to a corner of the room where they could talk privately.

Meltzer asked Anna about her family.

"Papa is Orthodox," Anna said. She hesitated, reluctant to be critical of her father's views. "But he's in business so he knows the world is changing and I think he understands we must adapt, even if he's unhappy with the changes."

"Are you familiar with the Zionist movement?" Meltzer asked.

"Not really," Anna said, hoping Meltzer would not be too disappointed in her.

"But," Roza interjected, "we're going to a Zionist meeting next week."

This was the first Anna had heard of any Zionist meeting, and she did not think Madame Meltzer was fooled.

"So, Anna Gorska, what would you like to ask me?"

Anna took out her list and asked a very patient member of parliament every question on it, taking copious notes. When she finally finished, Meltzer asked about Anna's plans.

"I hope to be the first Jewish girl from Ciechanow to go to University of Warsaw," Anna said. "And of course Roza will go too."

Meltzer seemed genuinely pleased. "We need bright young women like the two of you to become educated and convince Poles that Jews are a valuable asset to our country. Please let me know your progress and I'll do all I can to assist you."

***

Anna and Roza burst into the Gorska home, smiling and laughing, chattering non-stop.

"Shh, Mama may be sleeping."

"I'm not sleeping," came Evona's voice from the bedroom. "I've been waiting for you. Come tell me all about it."

When Anna had discussed her hopes for an interview with Madame Meltzer she had been apprehensive. Would she actually get to talk to the great lady? And even if she did, would there be anything to write that might please Rachmiel Slowacki in Warsaw? Now, as she and Roza related what had happened, it was clear she was on the verge of a major triumph, and a major change in her life.

"Madame Meltzer was very kind to you," Evona said, "and you've made a relationship with her that could prove quite helpful."

"Only if I get to Warsaw," Anna said.

"Which means you must carry out your plan to get yourself accepted to study at the University."

The mood turned somber as Evona and Anna remembered their talk on the *Shabbos* morning before Yonah's birth and death. "I'm so sorry for you, Mama," Anna said.

"I'm sad too," Evona said, "but life goes on." She smiled. "And your life ... aah, your life ... may turn out to be very exciting." Evona hugged Anna to her, then placed a hand on each of her shoulders. "Go. Write your story. Make your plans."

Anna and Roza sat at the table in the kitchen, several notebooks in front of them. Anna made a list: 1. write the article; 2. read, read, read; 3. find out requirements for admission to University of Warsaw; 4. ask for help: Uncle Ezriel, Rachmiel Slowacki, Madame Meltzer.

"You'll come, too," Anna said to Roza. "We'll do these things together."

"But I'm not as smart as you," Roza said.

"You will be," Anna said. "We'll read so many books we'll be the smartest girls in Ciechanow. No, in all of Poland."

While Anna drafted her article, Roza made a list of the books they should read.

"We must work on our Polish," Roza said suddenly.

"And also improve our German," Anna said.

Anna completed her draft of the article and gave it to Roza, receiving in exchange the list of books Roza had compiled. They made some revisions and then took the article and the list back into the bedroom. Tears came to Evona's eyes as she read.

"I'm so proud of you. Both of you. But you must add to your list books by our Hasidic masters. You may become a modern Jew, but you must not forget our traditions."

"And there's one other thing we must do, as soon as possible," Anna said when they were once more alone. Roza looked perplexed. They had not discussed any "other thing."

"Why are you surprised?" Anna asked. "You were the one who said it. We must join the Zionist Party."

"Yes, of course," said Roza. "They have the best parties and we can meet boys."

Chapter 11

Each Monday Anna went to her father's shop just off the market square, where she spent several hours organizing sales receipts, purchase orders, invoices and bank statements to produce reports of the previous week's revenues and expenditures for each of Jacob's businesses - the wholesale carpet business, the tobacco shop, the construction and agricultural equipment business, and the tailor shop - all run from the same small office with an adjacent warehouse, and all together barely producing enough income to support the Gorska family. Her bookkeeping tasks provided a very special time for her to be alone with her father, and many topics besides accounting were discussed.

"I see you got another bank wire transfer from Uncle Edel," Anna said, and in that moment the thought was born that perhaps her Grandfather Kamon's brother in America might help pay for her education at the University of Warsaw.

"It's almost twenty years since he left, but Edel continues to remember us." Jacob smiled and reached for a package on a shelf behind him. "He also sent this. It's a dress from a famous store in America which Edel hopes is your size."

Anna ripped open the package, held the dress in front of her and pirouetted. "It's beautiful!"

Jacob smiled at her enthusiasm, but Anna also saw sadness in his eyes. "My little girl is growing up," he said.

"I overheard Grandfather Kamon's story," Anna said, "about how he and Uncle Edel were train robbers with Marshal Pilsudski."

"I thought you were listening," Jacob said, his eyes twinkling even as he waggled his finger in disapproval.

"Did you ever think of going to America, Papa?"

"Many times I thought about it," Jacob said, sadness again passing over his face, "but always it seemed too complicated and now the opportunity has passed."

Although emigration to America had been slowed to a trickle by changes in U.S. laws, Anna knew that many Poles were still going to Palestine, legally or illegally. She didn't want to argue with her father, so she kept her thoughts to herself. Turning to her abacus, Anna slid the beads to make her calculations, enjoying the rapid clicking sounds. This week, Papa had made a profit, but Anna knew he never felt secure and never stopped worrying.

***

A week later, when Anna returned to do the bookkeeping, the latest edition of the Warsaw *Haynt* was spread out on Papa's desk. On the front page was a picture of Madame Meltzer and the headline "Zionist leader supports Pilsudski's return." And there, just below the headline, were the words "Reported by Anna Gorska."

It was hard to tell who was more excited, Anna or her father. Jacob hugged her, shaking his head and openly crying. They stayed like that for many minutes.

"I'm so proud of my daughter," Jacob said. "Here," he added, handing her an envelope, "they sent the payment for your article."

As she basked in her father's approval, Anna realized there would never be a better time to discuss her future. "Papa, I've decided to go to the University of Warsaw and I'm going to join the Zionist Party."

"You've decided?" Jacob said, frowning and pulling away from the hug. He kept his hands on Anna's shoulders, and then pulled her to him again, patting the back of her head. When they finally separated, the uneasy silence between them had grown oppressive.

Anna read her article; there had been some minor changes, but it was essentially what she had written. It was an incredible thrill to see her words and name in print. When she looked up, her father was staring at her with a sadness so profound it made her gasp.

"Poland is very different from what it was when I was your age," Jacob said. "We're split into a million pieces. We've always argued about Talmud, but now there's Zionism, communism, labor unions, politics ..."

Anna watched as a flood of emotions passed across her father's face; he made no effort to hide them. She saw anger, confusion, and doubt, and she felt sorry for her father, born into the world of the Polish *shtetl*, revering as he did the traditions of centuries, not knowing which way to turn as alternatives to those traditions appeared with frightening rapidity.

"I need to be part of this new world, Papa." She spoke softly, hoping they could talk, fearing his disappointment in her. He had been so proud a few minutes ago, but now her abrupt challenge to his way of life might be too much for him. A girl going to University! A Zionist in the family! She had been clumsy and tactless to express herself the way she had.

"I want you to know," Jacob said, "your mother has discussed your plans with me. She's excited by your ambitions. I am not ..."

He stopped speaking and Anna was afraid of what he would say next. *Not excited? Not certain? Not approving?* It would be a huge concession for him to admit being influenced by his wife. In Jewish households, at least as far as anyone was allowed to know, it was the man who made the decisions. Did he think the two women in his life were collaborating against him? Was he wrong if he felt that and found it painful?

Anna loved her father. She did not want to provoke his anger. Even more she did not want to humiliate him. And yet she had not asked his permission. Instead, she had told him what she had decided.

"I'm asking for your support, Papa. I need your support. I don't want to think that what I do makes you unhappy."

Jacob's face broke into a great smile, pleasing Anna even more because it was so unexpected.

"I understand," Jacob said, "you want more in life than to make *gefilte* fish." Anna's mouth dropped. Jacob chuckled. "Your mother told me."

Anna rushed to her father and threw her arms around him. She had a sudden understanding, not only of her father's support, but also of the courage and skill it had taken for her mother to prompt his reaction.

"I want to tell you something important," Jacob said. They still had their arms around each other but had pulled back a little, enough to see the tears in each other's eyes. "I hope that as you explore new ways as you are determined to do, you will never forget that love of God must always be fundamental to a Jewish life ..."

Anna heard the tremor in her father's voice as he struggled on. "... even the life of a bold young girl facing an uncertain new world. I want you to promise you will not ignore our traditions, that whatever else you study, you will also seek the word of God and the wisdom of our Hasidic masters. If you do that, even if I don't agree with other things you do, I'll be happy."

Anna had never loved her father more than at that moment. She knew he was uncomfortable with the life she was choosing. She knew, in his heart of hearts, he did not approve, and that he was also afraid for her. She knew he would continue to express his reservations, and in a way she welcomed them, as a check on her own enthusiasm. But with all that, her father was willing to let her make her own way, and that filled her with a strength and a confidence she had never imagined she would possess.

"I promise, Papa," she said. "Whatever else I become, I will always be a Jew."

***

77

Several days later, the newspapers reported that Marshal Josef Pilsudski had emerged from retirement to once again take charge of the Polish national government. Evona received a letter from her brother Ezriel who had been among those marching into Warsaw and was with Pilsudski when the Marshal commandeered the presidential palace.

In a postscript for Anna, Ezriel wrote, "I think, when it is time for you to apply to the University of Warsaw, I will be in a position to ask Marshal Pilsudski to put in a good word for you."

Chapter 12

June 1924 - Ciechanow

Every priest in Poland offered the centuries-old Easter prayer *perfidis Judæi*, and some took care to explain, lest anyone miss the point, that all Jews alive today are as guilty of killing the Son of God as those who were actually in Jerusalem nineteen hundred years ago.

The pogrom arrived in Ciechanow three days later.

***

Anna turned a corner and confronted a mob. She froze, but the mob's attention was focused on an old man standing alone, obviously Jewish in his black caftan and long beard. They began with taunts.

"Poland is for Poles," they screamed. "Christ-killing Jews must leave!"

Someone threw a rock. It missed, but the next one struck, and the one after that. The old man writhed on the ground while thugs poked him with sticks and kicked him. A young man raised a large cobblestone and smashed it down on the man's head. When the mob went looking for more victims, Anna approached the still form lying in the street and understood immediately he would never move again.

"Anna Gorska, come over here. You must get out of the street."

Anna did not recognize the woman calling to her, but with more rioters approaching, she followed the woman into a nearby building and down narrow cellar steps, leaving behind the sounds of screaming and crashing.

"Thank you," Anna said as soon as she caught her breath.

"You don't recognize me, do you," the woman said. "I've been a customer in your father's shop; I've seen you working there."

At the mention of Papa's business, Anna jumped up. Where are the hoodlums going? Will they attack Papa? Will they throw rocks at our home? She started towards the steps.

"You mustn't go out there."

Anna broke free and ran up the steps. Moving quickly, staying close to buildings, she ran to her father's shop. There was broken glass on the street and stores had been looted, but the rioters had moved on. Anna approached Papa's door. He must have been peering through the curtain since the door opened and Papa grabbed her arm and pulled her inside.

"You put yourself at risk coming here," Jacob said. "They just left; now we must get home."

They went outside, looking around cautiously. Then they ran together, ducking into side streets whenever they heard the pogrom ahead of them. They passed several policemen who were standing quietly, doing nothing, and then reached a street where a group of rioters had stopped and seemed confused. Facing them was a group of Jewish men, most of them holding clubs. A large blacksmith waved a sledgehammer and walked slowly toward the rioters. Two men, war veterans, walked behind him with raised rifles. The rioters turned and fled.

"Jacob," the blacksmith said. "Come with us, we'll take you home."

Evona and the other children were in the house when Jacob and Anna arrived. The blacksmith and his group moved on, looking for more rioters to confront, and soon returned with Anna's Grandfather Kamon, who had been bloodied but was walking proudly.

"He was trying to fight two thugs all by himself," the blacksmith said. "We took care of them."

When Josef and Danuta saw their grandfather, they began to cry.

"Hush," Evona said. "He's fine. Just a little blood."

Evona and Anna bandaged Kamon. Jacob took a large club and stood outside the door, ready to bash heads if anyone came. When darkness fell, they could still hear sounds of rioting, and from time to time, Jews who had organized the defense ran down their street. Gradually the night became quiet.

Jacob went out at dawn. Aside from groups of Jews who were still patrolling the streets, things seemed normal. Later in the day, a battalion of the Polish Army arrived and took up stations in the town.

"Three Jews were killed," Jacob reported, "and many more were injured seriously enough to be hospitalized. Almost every Jewish business, including mine, has been damaged."

There was no more violence, but neither were charges brought against any person responsible for any of the mayhem, including the three murders.

Chapter 13

1990 - Jerusalem

"I still haven't told you how I got to Warsaw," Anna said. "The first time was soon after the pogrom. Papa had business in Warsaw and took me with him. When I was there, Uncle Ezriel took me to meet Marshal Pilsudski. I wore the dress Uncle Edel had sent and we talked about the train robbery. The Marshal had fond memories, and also appreciated that Edel sent money every year to help support his political activities. He promised to help me when it was time to apply to the University."

Marissa pictured the sixteen year girl old from the *shtetl* sitting across a desk from the most powerful man in Poland. Anna's face had lit up when she mentioned the dress, and Marissa imagined how pretty and enthusiastic she must have been.

"What was Pilsudski like?"

"He looked older than the photographs I had seen, but he was still a vibrant man. To me that day he was friendly and gentle, but of course I knew he was also a fierce fighter, both in war and in politics. I could see the fire in his eyes."

"You were still in what we call high school?"

"Yes. One good result of the Minorities Treaty after the war was the opening of public schools to more Jews. I got an excellent education, especially the last two years when I studied even harder than before. Roza and I read constantly - history, philosophy, economics, literature. When it came time, Marshal Pilsudski did put in a good word for me, and for Roza as well, even though he didn't know her."

"Did you enjoy your experience at university?"

"Yes. Roza and I kept together, studying all the time, reading everything. We didn't go out with boys a lot. Well, I didn't. Roza did. I wrote more articles for *Haynt*, and that put me in contact with some important people. It also required a lot of specialized study outside my course work. Madame Meltzer became both a source and a friend."

"And how did you get from Warsaw to Munich?"

"My publisher decided he wanted a story about the problems Jewish students were having in Germany. I mentioned that I had a relative in Munich, and off I went."

They left Anna's apartment and went to a nearby café for lunch. Watching Anna, entranced by her story, coming to like her as a person, Marissa was increasingly haunted by the image of this awesome woman at Auschwitz.

"Can I ask you something about your testimony at Nuremberg?"

Anna nodded.

"You said you saved yourself at Auschwitz by ..." Marissa couldn't say the words.

"I said I became a whore."

"But you didn't explain ..."

"I was at Nuremberg for one reason - to save Berthold's life - and I could not allow anything to confuse my focus. I had forbidden my attorney to ask any more about it."

Anna met Marissa's gaze.

"Very few people survived at Auschwitz. I knew if I could stay alive long enough, Berthold would come get me. So I did what I had to do. Of course it was disgusting and demeaning, but gradually I came to understand that those words applied to the Nazis who were fucking us, not to us. So I had peace with it, and I also managed to get some food to take to other women, to give them an extra day of life."

***

1990 - New York

Abraham quietly pulled at his chin, a puzzled look on his face. Marissa had just told him what Anna had said about her time at Auschwitz.

"I've been thinking about Gorska," he said. "For one thing, I surely underestimated the impact of her testimony. Think about it. She didn't deny any of the crimes Becker was accused of. She openly presented herself as a whore and made no effort to justify it. She didn't care what the Justices thought of her, but she got them to do what she wanted."

After a long pause and a sip of coffee, Abraham continued, "What you just told me fits with what I've been thinking. Gorska had to mention Auschwitz but what happened to her there was not the important part. Her objective was to establish her credibility to focus the Justices on her accusation of Allied complicity in the murder of the Jews. She had been there. She knew. Her point was that their countries - France, England, America - had done nothing to help Jews while Berthold Becker had."

Marissa put her hand on her father's shoulder.

"And it worked," Abraham said. "The Justices, perhaps for only that moment, felt guilty. To assuage that guilt, they allowed Berthold Becker to live. Gorska's strategy was brilliant."

Chapter 14

1930 - Munich

Berthold Becker, twenty years old and a second-year student at the Ludwig Maximilian University of Munich, was attracted by a poster advertising an informal talk by a recent graduate of Munich's Technical University who was now employed by the Reichsbahn, the German National Railway. Berthold had originally intended to become a research scientist but now he was thinking he might prefer a more hands-on engineering career. This possibility, and his life-long fascination with railroads, brought him to the small meeting where he folded his muscular six-foot frame into the small lecture seat and waited.

Albert Mueller looked just like the engineer he was, about five feet nine, somewhat plump, three-piece tweed suit, pencils and pens clipped in his jacket pocket, wire framed glasses. Rather fussily, he arranged his papers on the lectern, smiled at everyone, and began.

"Following the end of the war, the Reichsbahn was created by consolidating the railways of the individual German states. In just over one decade, we've become the most advanced railroad company in the world and the largest employer in Germany.

"I work out of the Munich division headquarters in close coordination with senior engineering staff in Berlin. My general area of responsibility is the assignment of our 690,000 freight cars over a 54,000 kilometer network of track. I'm here to recruit bright young men to join our company."

The meeting lasted almost ninety minutes, during which Berthold learned about Mueller's current project involving improvements to the railroad's communication system. Berthold was impressed that Mueller always cited exact numbers, which showed the precise way his mind worked. His own mind began to spin with plans to study electrical engineering and work for the Reichsbahn. Mueller wasn't that much older than he was and yet he already had a very responsible position.

After the meeting, Mueller asked Berthold to stay and they had further discussion on the questions Berthold had raised. Then Mueller asked, "Did you have a brother?"

It had been seven years since Dietrich Becker had died, but Berthold was still uncomfortable discussing his brother's Nazi history, especially with a stranger.

"Dietrich ..."

"... died in the *Putsch*," Mueller finished gently. "I know. I was part of it, but not where the shooting took place. I was with Rohm at the War Ministry."

Mueller kept talking but Berthold could barely listen, his head swarming with images and sounds of the horrible day when Dietrich had died in his arms.

"I never met your brother," Mueller was saying, "but of course I knew who he was. I saw him several times when he was driving Hitler. Everybody knows Dietrich Becker saved the *Führer's* life."

Berthold wanted to learn more about the Reichsbahn, but he was worried that an association with Mueller might lead to an affiliation with the Nazis he did not want to make. Best to clear things up right away.

"Dietrich acted bravely," Berthold said, "but I think the beer hall *Putsch* was ill-conceived and poorly carried out. Many men died for no good reason."

"I agree," Mueller said.

"Are you a member of the Nazi Party?" Berthold asked.

"Not now and never was."

Yet you called him Führer.

"Hitler's attempt to take over the government by force was a big mistake," Mueller said, "but he's changed his approach since he got out of prison. Much of what Hitler is

86

now proposing would be far better for Germany than the ineffective policies of the Weimar Republic."

Perhaps Mueller saw the uncomfortable look in Berthold's eye because he added, "I care much more about the railroad than I do about politics."

Berthold followed Mueller's lead away from the Nazis and back to the Reichsbahn. "I'm considering switching to an engineering program."

"What are you studying now?"

"I'm a physics major."

"Perhaps you could take some courses at the Technical University." Mueller smiled. "Would you like me to speak to the admissions officer? You might be able to start right way."

Berthold agreed but his uneasiness remained.

**

Berthold left the meeting and walked to the fountain in front of the University where he had arranged to meet his friend Leonard Goldmann. Leonard was not there and as he waited, Berthold's attention was attracted by a disturbance on the opposite side of the Ludwigstrasse. A group of students had surrounded someone and were hurling taunts at their victim. Berthold crossed the street.

"Jew!" was the first word he heard. "Rich filthy Jew. Taking a space that should go to a German."

Pushing into the group, he saw it was Leonard who was being harassed. One of the students smacked Leonard across the face, sending his glasses flying. Leonard did not attempt to hit back. He looked puny next to his large attacker.

"What seems to be the problem here?" Berthold asked.

"You stay out of it."

"Don't you want a fair fight?" Berthold said, moving between Leonard and his attacker. Not waiting for an answer, he threw two punches in rapid succession, a short left jab to the stomach and a right cross to the jaw. His opponent crumpled to the ground.

"Anybody else want a turn?" The others shuffled around but none stepped forward. "If you do this again, I'll come looking for you."

Berthold picked up Leonard's glasses and said, "Let's go."

"Where did you learn to punch like that?" Leonard asked. "You hit like Max Schmeling."

"Hardly like Schmeling, but thank you," Berthold said. "I joined the university boxing club several months ago and I've also been lifting weights regularly. Never dreamed it would come in so handy."

"Do you still want to grab a beer?" Leonard asked.

"Absolutely."

They walked to the nearby Schwabing district, enjoying the "Bohemian" feeling created by the artists, writers, expatriates, and those native Bavarians considered completely mad by the respectable people of Munich. They chose one of the many cafés, found a table, sipped their beer.

"Has this happened before?"

"Not this bad, but it's been getting worse," Leonard said. "These boys hear anti-Jewish propaganda all the time. Many of their parents are unemployed and can barely keep food on the table. They're afraid of the future and jealous of me. They find it easy to blame a Jew for their problems."

"You're being far too understanding," Berthold said. "Those thugs meant to do you serious harm. Things are tough for many Germans. So what! They should learn to deal with their problems instead of blaming someone else."

"Hitler plays on their anger," Leonard said. "The Nazi message is all over - posters, meetings, newspapers, speeches. They've completely taken over the German Student Union."

"Who pays for all that stuff?" Berthold asked.

"I don't know, but there seems to be plenty of money. I keep hearing about wealthy older women who are enamored with Hitler. Can you imagine him a charmer?"

"After the *Putsch*, we all thought Hitler was done," Berthold said. "Now he's back, stronger than before."

Leonard took a deep breath and Berthold sensed something important was about to be said.

"My father has decided I should go to America and attend New York University, beginning with the fall semester. He says the University of Munich is no longer a suitable place for a Jew."

Leonard had discussed this possibility before although the timing was sooner than Berthold had expected.

"Is he going to move the whole family to America?"

"Not yet," Leonard said, "but I think he wants to have a backup plan in case things get unbearable for Jews here in Germany. There's a family from Munich whose relatives own a department store in New York called Bloomingdales. I'm to work there and learn about American business."

"Do you think it will ... get that bad?"

"Yes ... Yes I do."

A painful silence hung in the air before Berthold said, "I'll miss you."

"Me too," said Leonard. "I don't want to go to America. My English is terrible. I never thought I would leave Munich, and I'm afraid it's not temporary."

Leonard paused and shook his head sadly. "Tell me about your meeting. How did it go?"

Berthold reported on his discussion with Albert Mueller and the possibility of taking extra courses at the Technical University.

"I know somebody who's doing that," Leonard said. "It's a heavy load, but you could handle it." He laughed. "You've always liked trains. Did you ever finish that puzzle?"

"I put it back in the box," Berthold said. "Never looked at it again. It was a reminder of a very ugly time."

"What did you think of Mueller?" Leonard asked.

"He's smart," Berthold said, "and ambitious, already advanced in his career. He said he's not a Nazi, but that may not be the truth. I'm not sure I can trust him."

***

Berthold hurried home, anxious to discuss the day's events with his mother. The sounds of Beethoven's *Moonlight Sonata* greeted him, even before he opened the door. His mother often played that piece just after work. Berthold knew she used the piano as a means to feel close to his father, long dead in the war, who had listened so lovingly to her stumbling efforts when she was learning to play. Now, her passionate play made it clear she was no longer a novice.

When Elisabeth finished, Berthold joined her in the music room. The piano was one of the few good pieces of furniture which had survived the sell-off during the runaway inflation of the early 1920s. The Becker family, due to Elisabeth's employment at the Goldmann Department Store, had done well enough since those days. They were not wealthy but they were comfortable, and most of the furniture had been replaced.

"How was your day?" Berthold asked, bending over to kiss his mother on the cheek.

"Not bad," Elisabeth said. "Most of the dresses I've ordered for the spring season have arrived, and I've begun working on the fall line."

"People are still buying, despite the market crash in America?"

"There's some fall off at the low end, but high-end merchandise is flying off the racks."

"I have something I'd like to discuss with you," Berthold said. "May I have the honor of your company this evening at the Cafe Luitpold?"

"Well! Aren't we getting sophisticated. Quite the young college man."

As they walked, they discussed books, their favorite topic of conversation. Both were voracious readers.

"I'm enjoying *Buddenbrooks*," Elisabeth said. "It tells the story of a German family which thought it would continue to prosper forever, but now has to struggle to retain its position and dignity."

"Just like so many in Germany today," Berthold said.

They strolled past the Opera House where the audience for a performance of Wagner's *Siegfried* was making its way through slow-moving streetcars and horse-drawn taxis. Suddenly, Adolf Hitler emerged from a limousine and hurried into the Opera House, barely acknowledging the stiffly raised arms and "Heil Hitlers."

A chill passed through Berthold, but as Elisabeth gave no indication she had seen Hitler, he recovered his poise and they continued walking. Berthold saw their reflections in the large picture windows of brightly lit stores. He was proud of his own appearance, tall, lean, strong, but it was his mother whose startling looks he admired. At fifty, Elisabeth Becker had once again become a beautiful woman, no longer the haggard person who had struggled to keep herself and her sons afloat during Germany's terrible times.

They reached the Café Luitpold, the most elegant restaurant in Munich. Berthold had made a reservation and they were seated at one of the few remaining tables, near a window with a view of well-dressed couples passing by outside. Waiters moved smoothly and a string quartet played softly. The first course arrived and they chatted quietly as they ate. Eventually, Elisabeth asked Berthold what he had wanted to discuss.

"I'm thinking of taking some courses at the Technical University."

Elisabeth smiled. "What prompted that?"

"It's all about trains. I think I might want to work for the railroad."

Berthold summarized his conversation with Albert Mueller, then paused before adding, "Herr Mueller was part of the *Putsch*."

"Is he a Nazi?"

Berthold took his time answering. "He says not. He said his interest is trains, not politics."

"I noticed how you stiffened when we saw Hitler outside the Opera."

So she had seen him.

"I hope," Elisabeth said, "our government can survive the new crisis. There are many who think it won't, that it can't, that democracy just doesn't work, at least here in Germany."

They discussed the Goldmann's plan for Leonard to go to America and then ate silently for a while, before Elisabeth said, "I'm going to Paris next week."

"Wonderful," Berthold said. "Is it a buying trip?"

"Yes ... but also part pleasure. I'll be meeting a gentleman there for dinner."

***

Several days later, Berthold and his mother sat together at breakfast. The conversation was strained, as it had been since Elisabeth had told Berthold about her upcoming trip to Paris.

"Out with it, Berthold," Elisabeth finally said. "What's bothering you?"

"That's a silly question, mother. You know very well what's bothering me. Who are you having dinner with in Paris?"

"His name is Henri Bousquet," Elisabeth said gently.

"Henri? He's French?"

Elisabeth smiled. "Yes, he's French. He's fifty-five years old, a widower, and actually a very charming and educated man. I think you'd like him."

"It's just ..."

Elisabeth didn't help him.

"It just ... doesn't seem right."

"Do you think I'm being unfaithful to your father?" Elisabeth said, a gentle smile taking the edge off her words. "It's been thirteen years since he died. I love him still - I really do - but I've had no choice but to build my life without him. My life at work ..." Elisabeth took a long pause before adding, very softly, "... and my life as a woman."

Berthold took a deep breath and exhaled slowly. Elisabeth took his hand and they sat together silently for several minutes. A tear came to Berthold's eye.

"I'm sorry for being selfish, Mama. Of course you should have a full life. It's just a little hard for me to get used to. I promise I'll try."

They smiled at each other.

"How did you meet him?" Berthold asked.

"He owns a small Paris design firm. I buy dresses from his firm."

"So you've known him for some time?"

"Almost a year. But this is the first time we have an actual date."

***

On the day his mother left for Paris, Berthold went to the university gym and worked out for over an hour, lifting weights, shadow boxing, jumping rope, basically exhausting himself. Finally, he sprawled across a bench and put a towel over his head.

"I think maybe you're tired enough now," said a voice.

"For what?"

"For me to dare to get in the ring with you."

Berthold removed the towel and saw a tall, fit-looking, blond-headed man standing next to him.

"My name is Reinhard," the man said. "I'm looking for some exercise. Will you accommodate me?"

Berthold pulled himself off the bench. Reinhard was about his height and weight; his arms and legs looked strong.

"Sure," Berthold said, and the two men walked to an empty ring and climbed in. Berthold pointed to the protective head gear laying on the lip of the ring, but Reinhard shook his head. For several minutes, they warmed up with lightly thrown punches. Reinhard was quick.

"Ready?" Berthold asked.

"I am," Reinhard said.

Berthold set the three-minute timer. The men came together and after a few feints, Berthold threw a hard left hand. And missed. While still registering surprise, he was hit with a stunning blow just below his heart. He saw the follow-up punch readied and not thrown.

"That's your one present," Reinhard said. "You've been fairly warned."

They went at it for another two minutes until the timer rang, both landing hard body shots but neither, by unspoken agreement, aiming at the other's head.

"One more round?" Reinhard asked.

When they finished what turned out to be a fairly even match, they finally got around to finishing their introductions.

"Berthold. Berthold Becker."

"Reinhard. Reinhard Heydrich.

Chapter 15

January 1930 - Paris

Henri Bousquet was handsome and suave and devastatingly French. When they had first met, it was all very businesslike, with Elisabeth inquiring about materials and styles in the upcoming line. They shared a cup of coffee and Elisabeth convinced herself it was nothing special.

She knew she was wrong the next time she went to Paris and Henri sought her out. That time they had a glass of wine at Les Deux Magots and talked for almost two hours as the sun set on a gorgeous summer day, their talk made easier by the effort Elisabeth had made to improve her French. Then, two weeks ago, Henri had called and asked if she would be available for dinner when next in Paris. Not even her considerable powers of denial could convince her that nothing was going on.

She was staying at a small hotel in the Sixth Arrondissement. Henri arrived to pick her up at seven thirty. He kissed both her cheeks in the lobby and led the way to his chauffeur-driven car. They chatted nervously as they were driven across the Seine and into a section of Paris Elisabeth had never seen before, a place where elegant stone buildings faced wide tree-lined boulevards. They turned onto a side street and stopped in front of a small restaurant which exuded a quiet ambiance and the promise of marvelous cuisine.

Henri made menu suggestions and Elisabeth agreed. They ate and chatted until finally dessert had come and gone much too quickly. Henri suggested a nightcap at his apartment. Elisabeth nodded her approval.

The car was waiting and the ride took less than five minutes. They stopped before a large stone building on Boulevard de Courcelles. Henri unlocked a wrought iron gate and they entered an elegant courtyard. He led her to a small elevator for which another key was needed. They rose to the fourth floor where the elevator opened directly into the anteroom of an apartment that took Elisabeth's breath away: high ceilings, thick carpets, lustrous paneling, comfortable furniture, large windows looking down on the lights of the boulevard below.

Henri poured drinks and offered a tour. There was a spacious study, a well-equipped kitchen, two small bedrooms, and finally, the master bedroom, where Henri lit several waiting candles.

Supremely confident as, Elisabeth thought, he had every reason to be, Henri took her in his arms. His kiss was gentle, but the heat that coursed through her body made her feel she was melting. It had been thirteen years.

Henri took off his jacket and reached carefully to unfasten her dress. The next thing she remembered clearly was lying exhausted on luxurious silk sheets under a warm cover, naked except for the pearls around her throat. There were vaguer memories of his mouth in places no mouth had ever been before, and her mouth - incredibly, unbelievably - exploring his body in a manner that seemed so natural when it should have been utterly beyond the wildest imagination of a respectable unmarried woman in her fifties.

"I cannot understand," Henri had said before they fell asleep, "why our countries have such difficulty getting along, when it is so obvious we are enormously compatible."

In the morning, Elisabeth woke to sounds of breakfast being prepared. Henri came into the bedroom carrying a silk robe. She slid out of bed and rose to be clothed. Henri draped the robe over her shoulders and reached to cup her breasts, pressing gently against her from behind. Her quick breath provided an instant answer. The robe fluttered to the floor.

"Breakfast can wait," Henri said.

"Won't anything burn?"

"Just us, my dear. I turned off the flames in the kitchen."

Chapter 16

March 1930 - Berlin

Not long after Albert Mueller had helped Berthold arrange to take several engineering courses at the Technical University, he also invited him to visit the railroad's headquarters in Berlin.

"I have an ulterior purpose," Mueller said. "I want to recruit you into my section."

They went a few weeks later during a short break in the academic calendar. Mueller procured first-class tickets on the special fast corridor train which left Munich just after noon, made one stop at Nuremberg, and arrived in Berlin that evening, precisely on schedule. During the ride, they carried on a non-stop discussion about rail lines, train composition and signal technology. Their first two days in the Reichsbahn's Berlin headquarters were devoted to more of the same.

At night, Mueller took Berthold out to see the sights of Berlin. They walked by the Reichstag and other government buildings, were revolted by the slums and seedy pubs, and passed a cinema that was showing the first German sound film, *Blue Angel* featuring Marlene Dietrich and Emil Jannings. Mueller said Hitler had condemned the movie as pornographic trash.

How did Mueller know Hitler's opinion?

On their second night in Berlin, they attended boxing matches in an overcrowded smoke-filled beer hall where a ring had been installed for the night. Berthold paid close attention to the boxers' techniques and learned more than he ever had in the classes he had taken at the university. Max Schmeling, who had recently won the heavyweight championship of the world, came into the ring and shook hands with the boxers who were that night's featured attraction. As he left the ring, smiling and waving, he passed by Berthold's aisle seat and reached over to shake Berthold's hand.

The next day all hell broke loose and Berthold's life was irrevocably changed.

A week or so before they had arrived in Berlin, a young Nazi stormtrooper named Horst Wessel had been shot and critically wounded in the squalid slum district where he lived. Wessel was well known to the Nazi leadership for writing lyrics to a new fight song which had been published in Josef Goebbels' propaganda newspaper.

Goebbels, the Nazi Party boss in Berlin as well as Propaganda Chief, saw a golden opportunity and moved quickly to take advantage of it. He went several times to Wessel's bedside and reported each visit with breathless solemnity. When Wessel died, Goebbels organized a massive public funeral for the new "martyr" to the Nazi cause. Stormtrooper units as far as fifty miles from Berlin were mobilized. Goebbels himself would deliver the eulogy.

Mueller convinced Berthold that since they were in Berlin it was a spectacle not to be missed. Berthold was nervous about attending a Nazi event but, under Mueller's prodding, agreed he would be well hidden in the crowd which police were estimating would exceed thirty thousand.

It didn't turn out that way. They hadn't been there more than ten minutes when a uniformed stormtrooper appeared before Berthold, standing sharply at attention.

"Goebbels wants to see you."

"Why does anyone want to see me?"

"Are you not the brother of *Putsch* martyr Dietrich Becker?"

"How do you know that?" Berthold asked, glaring at Mueller, knowing instantly it was he who had arranged this, despite his feigned look of surprise.

Displaying a level of anxiety that bordered on panic, the stormtrooper insisted, "You must come with me. I have been ordered to bring you. Goebbels is waiting. There is little time."

Berthold was furious but felt he had little choice but to follow as the stormtrooper brusquely pushed people aside, announcing repeatedly, "Make way for the *Putsch* martyr's brother."

Berthold kept his head down, ignoring the exclamations and outstretched hands of the crowd as he passed. They reached the podium and Goebbels motioned for Berthold to climb up and stand next to him.

"We're deeply honored you're here today," Goebbels said without smiling. "Please stand near me. I'll introduce you during my remarks."

Goebbels began to speak, his face a portrait of concern and consolation. The crowd roared repeatedly and even Berthold was caught up in the eloquence and power of Goebbels' words.

> We think of the two million in the
> graves of Flanders and Poland who
> gave their lives upon the altar of
> the future so that Germany might
> be established again ...
>
> We greet you, dead ones, as
> Germany is beginning to glow
> anew in the dawn of your blood ...
>
> Let us sound the march-beat of the
> brown battalions for Germany and
> freedom.

Thirty minutes into his eulogy, Goebbels put an arm around Berthold's shoulder. The crowd grew silent in anticipation.

"Horst Wessel is not the first martyr of our movement," Goebbels said. "Seven years ago in Munich, a young man sacrificed his own life by placing himself between our *Führer* and the line of fire, saving Hitler's life for Germany. That man was Dietrich Becker, and his is the blood that stains our sacred Blood Banner."

Goebbels paused for several dramatic seconds, his solemn face scanning the silent crowd. "Standing here is Berthold Becker, Dietrich Becker's brother, who was also at the Feldhernnhalle that fateful day."

Goebbels raised Berthold's hand in his own. The applause was deafening and sustained. Flashbulbs popped. They stood there for several minutes until Goebbels thanked Berthold again and indicated he should leave the podium.

Berthold angrily confronted Mueller. "Why did you make me a part of this?"

"I did no such thing," Mueller said. Berthold was certain he was lying.

The funeral of Horst Wessel was the most important story in the Nazi world. *Der Angriff* featured Goebbels' speech on its front page. Further back in the paper were two photographs, Goebbels holding Berthold Becker's hand high and Dietrich Becker resplendent in his stormtrooper uniform. The caption proclaimed both brothers as heroes of the Nazi movement. Berthold was now part of Goebbels' carefully constructed web of Teutonic myth and heroic doom.

***

When Berthold returned to Munich, he started to tell his mother what had happened but she already knew.

"Richard Goldmann showed me the photograph."

"I'm so sorry," Berthold said.

"Dietrich did such foolish things," Elisabeth said, "and now his mistakes have reached out to ensnare you."

"It's not Dietrich's fault," Berthold said. "I should have known better."

"Probably it will pass and nothing will come of it," Elisabeth said, failing in her effort to be reassuring. "Do you think it was Herr Mueller who planned it?"

"Not all of it," Berthold said. "Horst Wessel had not yet died when we left for Berlin. But when the funeral was scheduled, and we were still there, I think Mueller went to Goebbels."

"How would he know Goebbels?" Elisabeth asked. "How would he get to him?"

"I think the answer is obvious ... and frightening," Berthold said. "Do you think the Nazis will keep coming after me?"

"Of course they will," Elisabeth said. "Now that they've found you, they'll never let go. They are nothing if not relentless."

Chapter 17

August 1930 - Munich

Five months had passed and nobody in Munich had mentioned the photo. Towards the end of the summer, the Goldmanns organized a party for Leonard before his departure to New York. The ballroom at the Hotel Bayerischer Hof was filled with elegantly dressed guests. A band played American jazz-style music.

Leonard was standing near his parents, saying goodbye to his friends and family. Berthold wandered along the large buffet table, adding to his plate and nibbling as he went. A girl just ahead of him in line smiled at him and he smiled back. When she had filled her plate and left the line, he waited until she found a table, then followed her.

Berthold never forgot that moment, which was unique in all his life. Why had he been so instantly and profoundly attracted to that particular girl? She was pretty, and he soon learned she was smart, but he decided it was the smile. He had been entranced by her smile before he knew her name or she ever said a word to him.

"Would you mind if I join you?"

"Please do."

"My name is Becker. Berthold Becker." He made a small bow.

"I'm pleased to meet you, Herr Becker. I am Anna. Anna Gorska."

Anna smiled again. Berthold sat down and caught his breath and tried to think of something to say. Something not too stupid. She rescued him.

"I'm related to Leonard," Anna said. "One of my cousins is the brother of Richard Goldmann's aunt. Something like that." She laughed and Berthold thought it was the most beautiful sound he had ever heard.

She was speaking German but he detected an accent he didn't recognize. Should he ask? No, that would be rude and suddenly he was terrified to do anything that might offend Anna Gorska. He knew other girls and had been on dates but he had never felt anything like this.

"I know who you are," Anna said. "Leonard talks about you all the time. I think he'll miss you more than his own family when he goes to America."

"I'll miss him too," Berthold said. "We've been close friends for a long time."

There was an awkward silence. Berthold was desperate to say something. "Did you come to Munich just for this party?"

"Actually, I'm here on an assignment from my newspaper in Warsaw. I'm to write a story about the treatment of Jews in German universities. I told my editor I had a cousin in Munich and he couldn't wait to send me here."

"I can help you," Berthold said, expelling the words in a rush, as if he was afraid someone else might volunteer before he had the chance. "I know many students at the University of Munich." He paused. "It's not good, you know, how Jews are treated. That's why Leonard is going to America."

"I know," Anna said. "It's not good in Poland either. I was hoping Leonard could help me, but he's been so busy, and now he's leaving tomorrow."

"Did I hear my name? I was going to introduce you, but I see you've already met."

Leonard nodded to Berthold ever so slightly, the twinkle in his eye communicating in the manner of long-time friends that he understood and very much approved. Leonard moved on and Berthold asked Anna about her life in Poland. He delighted in the sound of her voice as she described growing up in a village she called a *shtetl* and said she now lived in Warsaw, where she was both a student at the university and a reporter at a Yiddish daily newspaper. All of this was so different from anything he had experienced or even remotely imagined, an exotic tale from another world.

***

The next morning, Berthold joined the crush of family and friends seeing Leonard off at the main Munich train station. Anna had waved to Berthold as he approached and his heart leaped. He wanted to go to her but first he had to say goodbye to Leonard. They hugged and promised to write to each other, and both wondered if they would ever meet again.

After the train left, Berthold nervously approached Anna. He had thought of her constantly since their conversation the night before. He was thrilled that he could help with her story, if only he could speak without stumbling over the words.

"Would you like a cup of coffee?" he managed to say.

"Yes. That would be nice."

They walked to a small café, where each ordered a pastry as well as coffee.

"What are you studying at the University of Warsaw?"

"Mostly literature, history, and languages."

"Your German is excellent. What else do you speak?"

"If you live in the part of Poland where I come from," Anna said, "you grow up speaking Russian and German as well as Polish, and of course also Yiddish and a little Hebrew. I've also started to study English and French. And you, what do you study?"

Berthold explained that he was a physics major at the University of Munich but was also taking engineering courses at the Technical University.

"I'm fascinated by science, although I know very little," Anna said. "The closest I come is when I pass the statue of Nicolaus Copernicus, Poland's most famous scientist."

Now here was something Berthold knew about! They became delightfully engaged in a conversation about the wonders of modern astronomy and how the laws of physics in space seemed to be the same as those on earth.

A sound truck blaring Nazi slogans interrupted them and Berthold heard Nazi marchers singing the words Horst Wessel had written.

"What's that all about?" Anna asked.

Berthold panicked. Of course the song reminded him of the photo of him with Goebbels at Wessel's funeral.

If Anna ever sees that photo, she'll hate me.

"The Nazi thugs have started to sing it all over the place," Berthold said. "I don't really know what it's about."

Could she hear the lie in his voice, see it in his eyes?

Anna cringed. "They sing with such hatred. Is it the same at the universities?"

"Unfortunately it is," Berthold said, pleased to change focus. "Maybe it would not be good for you to conduct your interviews on university grounds. Suppose I invite several students to meet us at a beer hall. How long will you be in Munich?"

"Another week," Anna said.

Plenty of time and yet not nearly enough.

***

Berthold arranged several meetings at a small beer hall near Munich University. The first of these were with Christian students, most of them about to enter their last year at university. Each faithfully echoed the standard anti-Jewish message, expressed approval for quotas on Jewish students and professors, and claimed that Jews took too many places which were needed for Germans.

"But aren't the Jewish students also German?" Anna asked, always smiling sweetly.

Taken aback, the boys stumbled with their answers while Anna took notes: "... not real Germans ... the law says they are but they want to be different ... different holidays ... different foods ... they think they're special ... look down on Christians ... it's our country, not theirs ... if they wanted to be Germans, they would convert to Christianity."

"But Hitler says conversion isn't enough," Anna insisted. "According to Hitler, anyone with Jewish ancestry is still a Jew, even after they convert."

None of the boys had an answer to that, but Anna always stopped pushing before tempers flared. When they had a break, Anna asked Berthold what he thought of the students' attitudes toward Jews.

"What you heard," Berthold said, "is typical of the feelings of most students, although some are more aggressive and violent."

"What do you think about German Jews?" she asked.

"I don't see Jews as that different. They pray differently and they don't believe in Jesus." He paused and thought for a moment. "Actually, I don't really know any Jews except for Leonard and his family."

"What do you think of the explanations the boys gave for why Jews are not true Germans?"

"I think Jews do want to be different," Berthold said. "They stay apart, with different customs." He paused and thought. "But I've heard Leonard's father say that since Emancipation there's been significant movement toward blurring all the differences except religion."

"In Poland," Anna said, "sometimes it seems Jews are more hated when they try to assimilate than when they choose to live apart from Christians."

This discussion brought to the surface the huge differences between himself and Anna which until that moment he had managed to ignore. Not only was she Jewish while he was Catholic, but she was two years older and immeasurably more mature. She had experienced and thought about things he had never considered.

Why is she wasting her time with me?

"How did your friendship with Leonard come about?"

"As far back as I can remember, my mother was always friendly with Leonard's mother. After Father died in the war, Herr Goldmann hired my mother to work in his department store. Our families have always been close."

Berthold thought for a moment. "Our relationship is unusual. Most Christians don't know any Jews except if they deal with them in business. I think Mother and I were the only Christians at Leonard's bar mitzvah."

"It's the same in Poland," Anna said. "My father deals with Christians all the time, as customers or suppliers, but they never come to our home and we don't go to theirs. Of course their food is not kosher, so we couldn't eat it. I think it's fair to say that we Polish Jews have not gone out of our way to create opportunities for friendship with Christians."

"I'm very happy we have the opportunity for this friendship," Berthold said, blushing that he had dared to speak out.

"So am I," Anna said softly.

***

Next Berthold sought out Jewish students to meet with Anna. It wasn't easy, since he didn't really know any except for having seen them in class, but the fact that he was Leonard's friend helped, and soon Anna was being told about harassment and beatings, and the many Jews who had dropped out, giving up the dream of a university education.

Suddenly one of the Jewish students said to Anna, "You're not like most of the Eastern Jews in Munich. You're educated, well dressed, and if I may say so, very attractive. And you speak German."

Anna asked the student to expand on his thought. He was reluctant at first, but when Anna assured him that was exactly what her newspaper wanted to learn, he opened up in a way that made it clear he had discussed this topic before.

"Jews in Munich are divided into four groups. At the top are the very wealthy families, many of whose children are being baptized and married to non-Jews. Next come well-to-do businessmen, doctors, lawyers and other professionals. The third group are German Jews who have moved to Munich from small German towns. At the bottom are the Eastern Jews from Poland and elsewhere. They dress in strange-looking black clothes and speak a language no one understands. Forgive me, but many German Jews think these Eastern Jews are unclean and slovenly. There have been attempts to expel them, but they keep coming and they have a very high birth rate. Many have become smalltime racketeers and thieves."

Anna took notes furiously. When she looked up, the student added, "I'm sorry to say these things to you, but you insisted."

"Please don't apologize. It's important for Jews in Poland to understand."

Between the meetings with students, Berthold and Anna spoke about books. "Have you read the stories of Sholem Aleichem?" Anna asked "You could learn a lot about Polish Jews from those stories."

"Have they been translated into German?"

"I believe so," Anna said, and then added softly, as if to herself, "We're so different."

This is it, Berthold thought. She's had her interviews and that's the end of me. He waited for Anna to explain what she meant by different, and while he did, he studied her appearance as if he might never see her again. Her face was round, her hair dark and adorned with curls, her eyes perfectly placed and penetrating, her lips pink and luscious. She was much shorter than he was and although he couldn't see now because she was sitting, her hips swayed enticingly when she walked. Her breasts were ...

"Can we be friends anyway?" Anna asked.

Berthold almost blurted out his amazement that she would even think of wanting to be his friend.

"We can try," he said, and he knew from her smile it was the absolutely perfect thing for him to have said.

***

For the second time in a week, Berthold stood at the train station saying goodbye to someone he cared about. He knew he was in love with her, but as pleasant as Anna had been, and despite her suggestion that they could be friends, and as interested as she seemed to be in what they had talked about, she had not uttered a single word from which he could draw hope that her feelings in any way matched the intensity of his.

The conductor called "all aboard" and Berthold looked at Anna in a way that even his mother later described as pathetic. He moved closer and Anna amazed him with a quick kiss on his cheek. With the train whistle screaming and puffs of smoke encircling their legs, he put his arms around her. She did not pull back. Their eyes locked and they shared a real kiss.

One kiss, and a moment later she was gone.

***

Berthold was brimming with emotions he did not know how to express, was in fact afraid to express or even think. He struggled to compose a letter, puzzled over it for two days, then finally said to his mother, "I've been trying to write a letter to Anna, but I can't seem to figure out what to say."

"I think your look at the train station said everything. Tell her how you feel."

"I don't think I dare. Suppose she doesn't feel the same way."

"I think your chances are good, but you'll never know if you don't try."

Berthold absorbed that advice for several minutes, then his look turned pensive. "There's a problem," he said.

"Yes, a big problem," Elisabeth said. "She's Jewish."

"More than that," Berthold said. "It's that damn picture of me and Goebbels. I didn't tell her about it and I'm afraid if I do tell her she won't want to see me again. Not that I would blame her."

"She's a reporter," Elisabeth said. "She'll find out. It would be better if you tell her first."

Several more days went by and still Berthold had not written.

Chapter 18

September 1930 - Warsaw

"What are you going to tell your parents?" Roza screamed after Anna had told her about Berthold.

"I don't have to tell them anything," Anna said. "I'll probably never see him again."

"You better hope that's true. He's Catholic and he's two years younger than you. What were you thinking?"

"If I was thinking it would never have happened. He is so good-looking, and intelligent, and considerate. He even reads books. He's perfect. Well, maybe not perfect."

"So what are you going to do now?"

"We'll write some letters. Nice, polite letters. Then we'll forget about each other."

They had been walking, as they did most mornings, from the apartment they shared in the Jewish section of Warsaw to the Royal Way, and then to the University. Anna stopped abruptly when the statue of Nicolaus Copernicus came into view ahead of her.

"What are you staring at?" Roza asked.

"Nothing," Anna lied.

Roza made a face and shook her head in exaggerated disbelief, until Anna broke up and started to laugh. They had been friends since they were little girls in Ciechanow and there were no secrets between them, not for long anyway.

"Berthold knows all about Copernicus." Anna said

Roza howled. "Anna Gorska," she declared, "you're in love."

Anna did not deny it.

***

Dear diary, I cannot lie to you. I only
told Roza part of the story. As close as

we are, I was embarrassed to tell her the rest.

I knew from Leonard that Berthold would help with the students. Leonard said it was just the kind of thing Berthold would do because he was so nice. I saw Berthold (I'm really being silly; I just love to write his name) heading to the buffet table and I got there ahead of him. I smiled at him and sought out a table with two empty seats, hoping he would follow.

But I didn't expect to fall in love with him - I choked when I just wrote that. I have never been in love and this was not the one I would have picked. So wrong.

To make conversation, I asked him how he came to know Leonard, as if I didn't know the whole story already. What a phony I was.

Now, do I feel better? I don't think so. It's good nothing will come of this because I could never tell my parents.

***

Anna wrote two articles about the plight of Jewish students in German schools and her stories attracted the attention of her fellow students in Warsaw. She had come to expect angry looks from Christian students, along with occasional not-so-veiled statements that Jews like her were taking spots in the University that belonged to real Poles, but now it escalated. A note was inserted into one of her books.

Anna Gorska, We don't like your stories. You don't belong here. Why don't you and your Jewish friends just get out of Poland.

The next day, as she was leaving class, Anna was surrounded by several male students, pushing against her. An elbow was driven into her ribs. A hand reached between her legs. She slammed her knee into the groin of the boy who was grabbing her and looked for someone else to hit, but the others backed off. She studied each of their faces, one by one, saw the hatred flashing from their eyes, then turned and walked away with all the dignity she could muster. Later, she found Roza and told her what had happened.

"How do they even know what I write?" Anna asked. "None of them reads Yiddish."

"They force one of the neighborhood Jewish boys to translate," Roza said. "Whenever your name appears in *Haynt*, they go right to him. He's afraid not to do what they demand."

"What am I going to do?"

"I have an idea," Roza said.

Roza took Anna to meet one of the largest and strongest of the Jewish students at the University, well known by his nickname "Samson." The next day, Samson went with Anna to the class where she had been attacked and Anna discretely pointed out the student who had groped her. That night, the student was severely beaten and the note that had been left in Anna's book was stuffed down his pants.

"Did it work?" Roza asked a week later.

"So far," Anna said.

***

Not everyone was pleased with Anna's approach. After *Shabbos* services a few days later, Anna was approached by several of the synagogue's most prominent women.

"We've discussed what you had done to that student, and we think it's a mistake."

"Who is *we*," Anna asked, "and why is it wrong for a woman to defend herself against hooligans?".

"Your violence will only make things worse."

"Who put you up to this?" Anna demanded. "Men who won't talk directly to a woman? Men who cower in their caftans while Jews are beaten? Tell them I won't cower and I won't submit. Tell them they must wake up and see the world as it is, not like it was in some idyllic past - which, by the way, was never as idyllic as they imagine."

The women were too shocked to answer.

"You'll never tell them, will you," Anna said. "At least tell your husbands to talk to me themselves instead of hiding behind their wives' skirts."

But they never did. Anna found another synagogue. She wondered how her father would react when he learned she had left the Orthodox synagogue he had chosen for her and joined one dominated by Zionists.

***

Anna finally wrote to Berthold. She thanked him for his help with the student interviews. She told him about her mauling at school and how "Samson" had beaten up the one who had grabbed her. She wrote about her disappointment with the response of the Jewish ladies at synagogue.

She formulated the next sentence in her mind ... *I think often of the way we said goodbye and hope we can meet again some day ...* when she realized that was the last thing she should ever write.

Think straight, Anna, she said to herself. Here you are on Nalewki Street in the middle of the most Jewish section of the most Jewish city in Europe. He's a Catholic! You should forget you ever met him. She hastily signed the letter and mailed it, enclosing copies of her articles about the German universities which she had translated from Yiddish to German. Then she moaned aloud. *Why is this so impossible?*

Chapter 19

December 1930 - Warsaw

Warsaw was not all tension and trouble. In fact, it was the center of an amazing eruption of Jewish political and literary activity. Anna and Roza made every effort to enjoy their lively and modern city which believed it could compete with Berlin and even Paris as a cultural capital. Plays, movies, readings, lectures, cabarets, concerts and operas made almost every evening a potential celebration. In the past month alone, Anna and Roza had seen several politically cynical cabaret shows, an American movie, and performances by two of Warsaw's thriving Yiddish theater groups. They had just left the theater after seeing a revival of *The Morality of Mrs. Dulska* by Gabriela Zapolska.

"Zapolska's writing is such an inspiration," Roza said. "She is always brutally honest, never shirking from the immorality and squalor she sees in the lives of poor people, prostitutes, and Jews."

Anna thought about her own writing and more broadly the potential of journalism to influence events. She had published dozens of articles, but did anything she wrote actually make a difference?

Roza kept talking but Anna did not hear. Roza raised her voice to get Anna's attention. "Listen to me. My friend Chaim asked me to go with him to the New Year's Eve party at the Hotel Bristol. He also asked if I knew someone who might want to accompany his friend."

Roza winked. "So do I know such a person?"

Anna thought about Berthold, but they had made no promises to each other, and she had not been on a date since her return from Munich.

"Does this friend of your friend have a name?"

***

Two weeks passed quickly. Purchasing new gowns was out of the question, but Anna and Roza scraped together enough money to have their best dresses refurbished and also for the ultimate splurge on hair and nails.

It had been snowing for several days. When the open-top horse-drawn *droshky* arrived at Nalewki Street, the wheels had been replaced and it was a sleigh. Anna and Roza were waiting in the tiny foyer of their building. Chaim and his friend Morris, dressed in the most fashionable tuxedos and topcoats, escorted them to their carriage. Covered with blankets, the two couples sat facing each other and began the slow drive through the crowded streets of the Jewish district. Small bells attached to the horses' harnesses announced their approach.

"So, the famous Anna Gorska," Morris said. "I've read your articles in *Haynt*. I think you really did us all a service with your article about the Arab riots in Palestine. It's best we have no false illusions."

"Enough," Roza said. "No politics tonight."

"But Roza, my dear," Chaim said, "politics is what tonight is all about. The most famous and powerful people in Warsaw will all be at the Bristol, and most of the conversations will be about politics."

The snow transformed Warsaw into an enchanted city with flickering lights piercing the darkness. They left the Jewish district and entered the Royal Way where the intellectual and cultural life of the city was concentrated. In the open *droshky* they looked up at the tall thin column of King Sigismund in Castle Square.

"Everyone wave to the ancient Polish King," Roza commanded, and they all did, feeling boisterous and happy and patriotic and very much in the holiday mood as the brilliantly lit Bristol Hotel came into view. They joined the line of carriages waiting to disembark, in no hurry as they gawked at the beautiful people entering ahead of them. When it was their turn, Morris paid the driver and made arrangements for him to return at three o'clock in the morning. Anna, still thinking about Berthold, was nevertheless excited to be on a date.

***

They found their table and stared at the glittering elite of Warsaw society, a *mélange* of Polish, Russian, German, French and English accents drifting over them. Prominent politicians, businessmen, the Cardinal Archbishop of Warsaw, the Chief of Police, many army officers, and a few famous writers passed by. The twinkle and flash of crystal goblets and candles were complemented with lush red poppies and sunflowers, so unexpected in December.

A sudden stir in the crowd and a fanfare from the orchestra brought all eyes to the main entrance. Marshal Jozef Pilsudski had arrived. Accompanying him in the place of his ill wife was parliament member Irena Meltzer.

Anna told Morris and Chaim about how she and Roza had met Madame Meltzer in Ciechanow many years before, and that the article she wrote describing Meltzer's visit to her *shtetl* was her first published work.

As Pilsudski and Meltzer crossed the open space which would later be the dance floor, Madame Meltzer saw Anna. She whispered something to Pilsudski and started walking toward Anna, motioning for the Marshal to follow, which, to the surprise of many, he did. With the entire ballroom watching, they reached Anna's table. She rose and stepped out to meet them.

"Anna, so good to see you," Madame Meltzer said, and to Marshal Pilsudski she added, "You met Anna Gorska several years ago. You know her uncle Ezriel and also her grandfather Kamon Inwentarz and his brother Edel, now in America."

"Kamon and Edel," Pilsudski said to the speechless Anna, a warm smile creasing his face. "You know we robbed a train together." Pilsudski laughed loudly. "They're both still well?"

"Yes, Marshal, they are," Anna managed to say.

"Well, tell them I think of them and always hold both of them in warm regard."

Pilsudski started to walk away, but Madame Meltzer again whispered in his ear and he turned back. "I understand you write for *Haynt*," Pilsudski said to Anna. "Perhaps if you come to my office, we can find something of interest for your readers."

Pilsudski and Meltzer continued their walk, stopping at several other tables along the way. Anna floated back to her table.

"Oh, I'm so sorry," she said. "I didn't introduce you."

"Don't trouble yourself about that," Morris said. "I can't believe I was so close to the Marshal. And he knows you!"

Dinner was served by an army of waiters and the evening passed in a blur of food, drink and dancing. Anna danced with her date Morris and also with Chaim. She was on the dance floor when her publisher at the *Haynt*, Yitzhak Gruenbaum, tapped on Morris' shoulder.

"May I have a short dance with my famous employee?"

Gruenbaum said to Anna. "You're the talk of the room, my dear. We must meet before you interview the Marshal." He danced a few more awkward steps and released her back to Morris.

The New Year was welcomed with traditional midnight festivities, after which the orchestra launched into a song familiar to every Warsaw resident as the theme song of Hanka Ordonowna, Warsaw's leading cabaret performer. Her voice came floating from off-stage, and then there she was - blond, vivacious, sexy, singing as she walked.

"Love will forgive you everything,
it will change sorrow to laughter.
Love will forgive you everything,
because Love, my dear, is me."

Hanka bowed, her low cut gown displaying a great deal of her more than ample cleavage. She entertained for the next thirty minutes, a dazzling combination of song and chatter, then finished with an announcement. "Perhaps you've heard I have a new show opening next week. It's a one woman show." She smiled. "Of course, when the woman is Hanka ... there's no need for another."

The audience laughed and cheered as Hanka walked off, every slow swing of her hips a seductive invitation. Anna watched, unable to tear her eyes away.

"You know she's Jewish," Roza said.

"Not like any other Jewish woman I've ever seen," Anna said. "We'll have to practice walking like that."

Chapter 20

January 1931 - Warsaw

Several days later, Anna arrived at the offices of *Haynt* to find her publisher Yitzhak Gruenbaum deep in discussion with Irena Meltzer.

"Marshal Pilsudski has never before granted a private interview to *Haynt*," Gruenbaum said. "We must get it right, which is why I invited Irena to join us. Have you thought about topics for your interview?"

"Actually," Anna said, "I thought since Marshal Pilsudski invited me, he probably already has a topic or two in mind."

Meltzer bust out laughing while Gruenbaum almost choked. "Ach ... why do I hire the smart ones?"

Anna bit her tongue and Meltzer jumped in, still barely repressing a smile. "Of course the Marshal will tell you what he wishes to discuss, but you should be prepared if you have the opportunity to ask questions."

Thirty minutes of discussion, mostly regarding the continuing worldwide depression and the stunning Nazi election successes in Germany the previous September, produced several questions which Anna duly noted.

***

Anna met alone with Marshal Pilsudski in the Belvedere Palace, where he lived as well as worked. The Marshal directed her to a comfortable chair and sat next to her. He wasted no time.

"I was told that in your article about the riots in Palestine, even though you write for a Jewish newspaper, you reported aspects of the Arab position. Irena Meltzer was impressed with your objectivity."

Pilsudski didn't expect Anna to respond. He immediately went on to state his fundamental belief that Poland was best served if all of its minorities, including Jews, were vibrant participants in all aspects of Polish life. Then he raised the issue which Anna had no doubt was the reason he had granted her this interview.

"My concern is that I'm not totally convinced of Jewish loyalty to the Polish state."

Does he mean the Polish state, Anna thought, or does he mean loyalty to him? The problem was that there was not a single Jewish viewpoint on anything. Many Jews were supportive of Pilsudski, but others less so. Be aggressive, Gruenbaum and Meltzer had stressed. He reacts well when he's pushed.

"How much evidence do you need to be convinced?" Anna asked, recognizing the challenge in her question. "The Jewish members of parliament always vote for whatever you want. My Uncle Ezriel was but one of many Jews who came to Warsaw to fight with you when you needed help to return to government. My Grandfather Kamon and his brother Edel robbed trains with you."

"That was long ago and it was just one train," Pilsudski said, but he could not keep from smiling.

Anna returned Pilsudski's smile and said sweetly, "Apparently one was enough." Then she plunged in.

"Perhaps it's not you, Marshal, who needs convincing about Jewish loyalties."

She met Pilsudski's surprised glance and raised her own questioning eyebrow. *I can't believe I said that.*

"Let me explain," she said. "The Christian population of Poland, beset with unemployment and inflation, is looking for someone to blame. Both the Catholic press and Roman Dmowski's Endek Party say that Jews have a conspiracy to take over the world, that Jews are stealing jobs from Poles, that

Jews are corrupting Christian morals. None of this is true but when it's repeated often enough, people believe it."

Anna wondered if she had gone too far, but forward was now the only possible direction, so she continued before Pilsudski could respond. "In this harsh anti-Jewish environment, the only rational political choice for Polish Jews is you. You are the only one standing strong for Jews. Jews would be foolish if they fail to support you with every ounce of energy they possess. This applies to all Jews - Zionists, Orthodox, assimilationists, traditional."

"You will write this in *Haynt*?" Pilsudski asked.

"Of course. It's the truth. I'll get statements from every Jewish faction. May I quote your belief that Poland is best served if Jews are - she consulted her notes - 'vibrant participants in all aspects of Polish life?'"

Pilsudski agreed, then started to rise, indicating the end of the interview.

"May I ask a few questions?"

"You continue to surprise me," Pilsudski said, resuming his seat. "Where did you learn to be so audacious?"

"Perhaps it runs in my family," Anna said. "Train robbers, you know."

He smiled and looked at his watch. "One question."

"Should Jews in Poland fear Hitler?" Anna asked.

"All Poles should fear Hitler," Pilsudski said. "Jews, Christians, everyone. I believe Hitler's rhetoric about Jews is not political posturing. He truly does hate the Jews. He also sees Poland as rightfully belonging to Germany, and if he gains power, he'll want to get it back."

"What can we do?"

"You mean what can I do?" Pilsudski said, holding up two fingers to let Anna know this was her second question. "I will tell you, but you cannot write it, not yet. I'll let you know when you can. Do you give me your word?"

"Yes," she said. "I'm honored by your trust."

"At the moment," Pilsudski said, "Poland has more troops and weapons than Germany, but this will not last much longer if the Allies fail to enforce the Versailles provisions limiting German rearmament."

The Marshal was silent for several moments, perhaps deciding how much to reveal. Finally he said, "Poland must act. Perhaps we should initiate military action against Germany while we still have the advantage."

"Why are you telling me this if I can't write it?"

"You can't quote me," Pilsudski said, "but perhaps what I said will inform your questions when you meet with other sources. I have every reason to hope you *will* write about these issues."

"And what I write in Yiddish in *Haynt* will have broad influence, when no one but Jews reads that paper?"

Pilsudski smiled. "Don't worry, my dear. You'll soon find other newspapers interested in your thoughts."

"How ...?"

Pilsudski chuckled.

Chapter 21

1990 - Jerusalem

Marissa was with Anna in her Jerusalem apartment, concluding what had been a full week of intense daily discussions.

"You were very bold in your approach to Marshal Pilsudski. Were you concerned you might antagonize him and lose your great opportunity?"

"Of course it was a possibility," Anna said, "but I knew Madame Meltzer had said good things about me, and that the Marshal had a warm spot for my Grandfather Kamon and Uncle Edel, so I took a chance. In hindsight, I think that may have been one of the best decisions I ever made. The stories I wrote based on that interview changed my career and ultimately my life."

"Did you think Pilsudski was serious that Poland might actually invade Germany?"

"Oh yes, he was serious," Anna said. "I think he would have done it if he had ever been able to get the French to help."

"Did Pilsudski follow through on his hint about non-Jewish papers?"

"Within a week," Anna said, "Gruenbaum began getting requests from the major Warsaw dailies to reprint my columns."

Anna went to the kitchen to refill their coffee cups.

"Marshal Pilsudski and I understood," she continued as she walked back into the living room, "that our relationship benefitted both of us, and we were both willing participants in that partnership. We also came to like each other on a personal level. I know I cared about him and I believe he cared about me."

Anna grew pensive before adding, "Everything changed when he died in 1935. Polish Jewry never had a chance from that point on."

Chapter 22

April 1931 - Warsaw

Anna and Roza stood in a crowd near a large bonfire in one of the few empty lots in the Nalewki section of Warsaw. *"Lag b'Omer* is the strangest of the Jewish holidays," Roza said.

"There are so many strange things about us. Is it any wonder Christians are puzzled?" Anna asked. "Why the bonfire?"

"Some say the fire symbolizes the immense light introduced into the world by Rabbi Shimon bar Yochai."

"Who?" Anna asked.

"What? You skipped that class?" Roza broke into uncontrolled laughter. Then, in her best imitation of a stern Talmudic scholar, she lectured, "Shimon bar Yochai was a rabbinic sage active in Jerusalem in the first century just after the destruction of the Temple. He was a disciple of Rabbi Akiva, and is said to be the author of the *Zohar*, the central work of the *Kabbalah*, about which more undecipherable words have been written than any other topic in Judaism."

Unable to stay serious, Roza broke out in a huge laugh.

"There's no end to this story, is there," Anna asked.

"That's why men spend their lives studying and arguing."

"And for this," Anna said, "they give thanks to God they were not born women?"

***

The next morning, because of, or perhaps despite, Roza's explanation, Anna went to *Lag b'Omer* services in the small Zionist synagogue she had been attending irregularly for six months. She was a passive participant, vaguely trying to remember what Roza had said about the biblical commandment to count forty-nine days, while on another level pondering on the fact that the Zionists, so different in many ways of daily life from Orthodox Jews like her family, still said the same prayers. What a strange and unfathomable tribe we are, she thought. Despite all our diversity we are yet one people. A familiar melody caught her attention and she pictured her father chanting the same prayer in Ciechanow at the exact same moment in time.

Gradually, without having sought it, there grew within her a sense that God not only existed but that He was calling to her, to Anna Gorska, right here on Nalewki Street in Warsaw, right now. It didn't matter what God might be saying to others; for Anna, His message was suddenly and brilliantly clear.

God is depending on me.

Polish Jews are confused and disheartened. From this chaos must somehow emerge the eternal truth. I, Anna Gorska, a journalist, have become a truth-seeker. God needs me to search for truth and reveal it to the Jewish people. She was immediately frightened by the scale of the challenge. How can one little *shtetl* girl aspire to such a monumental task? Her answer was quick and surprisingly simple. God does not ask us to do that which we cannot.

She heard her father's voice as if he was next to her. Even as you explore new ways, Jacob had said, you must remain close to God. Traditions can change, but love of God must be fundamental to every Jewish life, now and forever. Papa was so right. Start with that truth. Build from there.

As she left the synagogue she was given a small blue and white can with slot in the top. This is a *pushke*, she was told. Fill it with coins and bring it back. The money will help restore our Jewish homeland in Palestine.

A thin young man wearing a disheveled tan suit approached Anna outside the synagogue. "You're Anna Gorska," he said, so serious as to be almost comical. "I've read every one of your articles in *Haynt*. You're a very good writer, and you always concern yourself with important matters."

He held out his hand timidly. This was yet another consequence of Anna's change from an Orthodox to a Zionist synagogue. Zionists were much more relaxed about interactions between men and women, an attitude which Anna rather liked.

"My name is Menachem Begin," he said, his hand still extended. "I'm a student at the University. I've seen you there many times, but until now I was too nervous to speak with you."

Anna took his hand and smiled. "And your closeness to God today has helped you overcome your shyness?"

"One of the many blessings God has given me this morning," Menachem said.

There was between them an immediate comfortable feeling that Anna had rarely experienced with other young men she knew. Menachem wasn't handsome, but there was an undeniably compelling presence about him. They spoke for several minutes before he excused himself and started to walk away.

"I'll see you at the University," Anna said.

Menachem turned. "I look forward to that."

***

Roza, who had been talking nearby with a middle aged couple, brought them over to meet Anna, saying they had asked to be introduced to the famous Polish journalist.

"My name is Ascher Lowenfield," the man said. "This is my wife Rayzel."

Anna knew that Ascher Lowenfield was the head of a huge department store and one of the wealthiest Jews in Warsaw. It turned out the Lowenfields were hosting a guest from America who was a reporter for TIME Magazine.

"We'll be having dinner tonight at the Bristol Hotel," Rayzel Lowenfield said to Anna. "Will you and your friend be so kind as to join us?"

Glancing at Roza, who seemed enthusiastic, Anna accepted the invitation. Walking home, Anna laughed to herself. Oh Papa, she thought, I have come to synagogue, and I have felt truly Jewish and close to God and to you, but now I will spoil the day by eating in a non-kosher restaurant. She imagined her father saying 'I'll take what I can get' but immediately doubted there was any chance Papa might actually react that way. It seemed far more likely, however, that God would accept her compromise.

**

During dinner, the American reporter asked many questions about Poland, Zionism and Hitler, and seemed impressed with Anna's answers, saying several times, "You know more about that topic than any of our Polish correspondents." Later he added, "TIME Magazine's readers could benefit from your perspective. Would you mind if I discussed with our editors the possibility of having you write for us?"

Anna said she would not mind.

Chapter 23

May 1931 - Northeim

Berthold had, with Albert Mueller's assistance, entered into the Reichsbahn's work-study program and had been working two days each week in a small town called Northeim, located roughly midway between Munich and Berlin. His job was to study procedures being developed to manage the installation of new signaling technology. He was to attend meetings where these procedures would be discussed and try to anticipate problems that might arise during implementation.

"You'll be an independent observer," Mueller had said. "It'll be quite an opportunity to impress the bosses in Munich and Berlin."

Berthold traveled to Northeim each week by train. The trip took three hours and the rhythmic click of the wheels on the rails prompted a relaxed state of mind and plenty of time for his thoughts to wander.

Mostly he thought about Anna. They had exchanged letters periodically so he knew about articles she had written and that she would soon graduate from the University of Warsaw. But, he reflected with sorrow, he knew nothing about what she was feeling, especially what she was feeling about him. Closing his eyes, he brought to mind the one kiss they had shared on the train platform in Munich, and Anna's warm touch and taste seemed as real to him as it had been then.

He arrived at the Northeim rail station after dark and went directly to the hotel where the Reichsbahn had reserved a room for his use for the duration of his project.

"Welcome back, Herr Becker. Your room is clean and ready, and your laundered clothes are in your dresser."

In the morning, he enjoyed a hearty breakfast in the hotel dining room and walked to the railroad facility just as dawn was breaking. He noticed a significant increase in the number of Nazi propaganda posters, including announcements of two major Nazi Party meetings to be held in the next three days.

Berthold's first order of business each Thursday morning was to attend a regular meeting of the engineering staff. His assignment was to listen and learn but he had also begun to ask questions ... *How many labor hours are saved by the new switches? How much increased business might result from faster switches and signals?*

Berthold was always polite when he asked his questions and he never challenged any of the answers given, but he always asked for the supporting data and the assumptions on which they were based. As the weeks passed, he felt his contribution was more anticipated and more welcome.

But not by everyone.

"Have you always been a smart-ass?"

The question came from a mid-level engineering manager named Ulrich Walther who had been employed by the railroad in Northeim for over twenty years. They were walking together from the meeting to the work site where the new signals were being tested. Berthold considered his options. If he was aggressive in defending his questions, or if he cited his authority from upper management to ask them, he would probably get into an argument. But if he backed off, he would seem weak and could expect a serious crack in whatever credibility he had so far established.

When he spoke, he hoped it was with no trace of arrogance. "I have a feeling you're going to teach me something I want to learn." He saw the surprise on Walther's face while he kept his own expressionless. After several seconds he added, "Where do you think I'm missing the boat?" And then, "Would you like to have a cup of coffee and tell me?"

***

Sitting alone in his hotel room, Berthold repeatedly re-read the letters Anna had written to him, which he carried back and forth with him each week. There was warmth in her letters but not any passion comparable to that he felt for her. He knew - just knew - she felt the same but neither of them ever expressed it. Still, all these letters had to mean something.

He wrote "Dear Anna," threw the paper away and started again with "Dearest Anna," enjoying the tingle the words provoked. He wrote about his exchange with Herr Walther which he said had resulted in some very good ideas and the prospect of future collaboration. He wrote about the book he was reading and commented on the book she had said she was reading. He explained that, as he was taking more classes at the Technical University, it made sense to actually transfer to that university while continuing to take a reduced number of courses at the University of Munich.

This was all very nice, but he remained frustrated at his inability to find a more romantic way to express what he was feeling.

**

Late one afternoon when Berthold was at his desk at the Reichsbahn offices in Northeim, a young man appeared requesting that he come to the Local District Office of the Nazi Party.

"Goebbels has asked Herr Krueger to meet with you."

How did Goebbels know he was in Northeim, or for that matter, even remember his name? They had met just the one time, at the funeral of Horst Wessel. Berthold shuddered as he always did when he thought of the photo of himself with Goebbels. He was sure it was Albert Mueller's doing then, and his mentor was no doubt responsible for this new summons as well.

Ernst Krueger was a feared man. He was the Nazi boss in Northeim, said to be ruthless. Berthold found him at a messy desk in a small, stuffy office that smelled of sweat and beer. On the desk was a framed copy of the photo of Berthold with Goebbels.

"Goebbels says your brother was a *Putsch* martyr in Munich," Krueger said. "I wish I had been there."

So you could be dead too, Berthold thought. He hated to be reminded of Dietrich's useless death, but knew that so long as he had any contact with the Nazis, he would be known as the brother of a Nazi martyr.

"Goebbels also says you're an excellent organizer."

How would Goebbels know anything about his organizing ability unless Mueller had told him?

"We need people like you in Northeim," Krueger continued. "There is constant pressure to do more, always more. If we have three meetings in a week, they want to know why we didn't have four. All this takes arranging - choosing speakers, scheduling bands, arranging food and drink, following up. Something always goes wrong. Then there's the stormtroopers, always unhappy, looking for a fight. If there's no one to fight, they fight amongst themselves. Some days I wish the communists were more active, just to keep the stormtroopers busy."

Suddenly Krueger didn't sound so ruthless. Instead, he sounded overworked, frustrated and more than a little afraid.

"I'm very busy myself," Berthold interjected. "I'm still at university, and my job with the railroad is very demanding. I really don't have time to help you."

Krueger's face stiffened; he looked shocked. "Germany," he said, "cannot wait until you have more time. We must march now - for Hitler! for freedom! Shall I tell Goebbels you refuse to help?"

Berthold had not expected to be confronted in such a direct and threatening manner and he didn't know how to respond. "I don't want to join the Nazi Party," he said softly, barely squeezing the words out, his voice croaking. It occurred to him that the Nazi leader in Northeim was not a man who was used to being turned down, and now Krueger would have to report his failure to Josef Goebbels. Berthold was sure this was not the end of the discussion.

Chapter 24

May 1931 - Warsaw

Anna had written to her Uncle Edel in America. She told him how happy she was in Warsaw, but that it was getting worse all the time for Jews in Poland. She asked him to encourage her parents to leave. She also mentioned how fondly Marshal Pilsudski had spoken of him and enclosed several of her articles from *Haynt*. She told him her graduation was coming soon and thanked him again for his assistance. Finally she remembered to ask about his wife and children, and the growing number of grandchildren.

Edel wrote back, saying how proud he was of Anna, and asking her to please continue to send her articles, since only some of them were published in his local Yiddish paper. He added that he had tried to convince Anna's family to come to America, that he could guarantee work in America for her father which meant he could get a visa, and that he would gladly send the money for the trip.

Anna put Edel's letter back in the envelope. She sat quietly, crying silently, knowing her father would never go, knowing she would never go without her family. Poland is no place for Jews but there are three million of us and there is no other place for us to go. Uncle Edel has offered our family a rare opportunity but we will not take it.

Another letter had arrived from America, from the TIME Magazine reporter Anna had met at dinner with the Lowenfields, saying he had obtained English translations of several of her articles and discussed them with his editor. As a result, Anna was invited to write an article describing the impact in Poland of the Nazi successes in Germany, maximum five hundred words. "I know you have much more to say than five hundred words," the reporter had written, "but it will be a start."

Writing a short article was always much more difficult than a long one. Anna took out her notebook and began an outline, which was itself more than five hundred words.

***

The weather was perfect. White chairs had been set out for the graduates and their families in the large garden behind the library. Anna's parents had arrived in Warsaw the day before, along with Grandfather Kamon. Two hundred graduates, including Anna and Roza, prepared to receive their diplomas. Marshal Pilsudski was on the stage to deliver the commencement address.

At the reception after the ceremony, Anna introduced her proud family to her Warsaw friends and to Marshal Pilsudski, who was delighted to see Kamon Inwentarz after so many years. Pilsudski whispered something in Jacob's ear that brought as big a smile as Anna had ever seen on her father's face.

That night Anna read the diary entry she had written seven years before: *I must go to Warsaw, to the university ... there must be more to my life than making gefilte fish.*

So many people had helped her - Madame Meltzer, Yitzhak Gruenbaum at *Haynt*, Marshal Pilsudski, Uncle Edel, her parents - and now she was a proud graduate of the University of Warsaw. She was also a respected journalist with a sparkling future ahead of her. And to her surprise, she had learned that making *gefilte* fish was not such a bad thing after all.

***

Anna received a note asking her to come to Irena Meltzer's office; she left immediately.

"Do you have a story for me?" Anna asked.

"No," Meltzer said.

"What's the matter?" Anna asked, alarmed by the look on Meltzer's face.

"This is very upsetting," Meltzer said. "When you wrote those stories about students in Munich, you mentioned you had been helped by a German boy named Berthold Becker. You said he became your friend."

Meltzer handed Anna a copy of the Nazi newspaper *Der Angriff* from March 1930. "Gruenbaum gave this to me last week. He thought it would be better if I gave it to you. I waited until your family had left Warsaw."

Anna stared at the photograph of Berthold Becker standing next to Josef Goebbels. She gagged and almost fainted, then she cried, huge sobbing tears. Meltzer came to her and held her gently. The quiet satisfaction Anna had been feeling about her graduation, her loving relationship with her parents, and her thriving career prospects shattered like a broken mirror.

***

Anna stumbled from Meltzer's office to the synagogue where she sat alone, holding her bowed head in her hands. Time passed; she didn't know how much; she didn't care. Without seeing or hearing anyone approach, she became conscious of someone sitting behind her.

"Is there anything I can do for you?"

The voice was familiar but she did not immediately recognize it. "You could leave me alone," she said.

"Of course. I will leave."

Anna heard feet shuffling behind her and finally looked to see who it was. "I'm sorry, Menachem," she said. "That was rude. Please stay."

"I don't mean to intrude," Menachem said. "I just want you to know a friend is here if you have need of one."

Anna stood and slowly walked to Menachem. She hugged him, quietly said "Thank you," and left the synagogue.

***

It was dusk when Anna returned to her apartment. She mounted the stairs and was sitting quietly in the dark when Roza arrived.

"What are you doing?" Roza asked, visibly startled.

"I don't know."

Roza knew enough from the friendship of a lifetime to wait until Anna was ready to talk. She poured two glasses of wine and sat down next to her. Anna gave the photo to Roza.

"Is this Berthold?" Roza asked.

Anna nodded.

"Where was it taken?"

"Berlin."

"When?"

"Over a year ago."

"So it was before you met?"

"Yes."

Roza came closer to Anna and hugged her; Anna shook in her friend's embrace, her tears flowing.

When they separated, Roza said, "He is quite good-looking."

Anna smacked Roza lightly and managed a weak smile.

"Do you think that helps?"

Chapter 25

June 1931 - Munich

Elisabeth had been distraught ever since Berthold told her he had been asked to work with the Nazis in Northeim, even though he had said no, perhaps especially because he had said no. She knew Berthold would be back in Northeim in connection with his work for the Reichsbahn, and this would provide opportunities for Herr Krueger to ask again. Goebbels would make him ask. The Nazis would never let go of Dietrich Becker's brother.

Whatever Berthold's response, whether he joined the Nazis or rejected them, he was carrying a time bomb of which he was unaware. For days, Elisabeth tortured herself trying to decide how best to tell Berthold things he simply had to know. She discussed her thoughts with Judith Goldmann and finally made up her mind.

***

Elisabeth chose the quiet time after dinner. She played her piano to calm her nerves, then went to her son who was in the living room reading a book.

"I have something I need to discuss with you."

Berthold looked up, frightened. Despite her decision to proceed, Elisabeth felt faint and unequal to the task, but she knew she could not delay any longer.

"Over fifty years ago," she said, "a young woman from a small village in the north of Germany took the path from Judaism to Christianity. Perhaps she was revolting against her family, or maybe she simply found her religious peace in Jesus. I don't know. In any case she abandoned her Jewish past, moved far away to Munich, adopted a new name, sought out a priest for instruction, and became a Catholic. Some years later she married a Catholic man."

"Why are you telling me this?" Berthold asked.

"That woman was my mother ... your grandmother."

Elisabeth stopped speaking to give Berthold time to absorb what she had said. When his eyes met hers, she continued.

"I was born and raised a Catholic. So were you. But according to Jewish law, the child of a Jewish mother is a Jew. Under that tradition, I'm a Jew and so are you."

Berthold shook his head, confused, stunned, afraid.

"My mother told me this just before she died," Elisabeth said. "As far as I know, my father never knew he had married a woman who had been born a Jew. Certainly your father never knew."

"Why are you telling me now?"

"You must know, to protect yourself." Elisabeth steeled herself. She had to be completely honest, even if she felt selfish. "And to protect me."

"Protect against what?"

"The Nazis have their eyes on you. I'm afraid of what will happen to us if they find out we're Jews."

"How would they find out?"

"I'm sure the trail is not completely hidden. My mother said her family was furious when she left to become a Catholic. They destroyed all mention of her name in family records and to the extent they could in the town records as well, but I have no doubt something is still out there, if someone looks hard enough."

Berthold closed his eyes. He felt sick. "Who will look?" he asked. "Who would care?"

"The Nazis want to revere you as a hero," Elisabeth said. "Goebbels took a thug like Horst Wessel and made him into a martyr. Think what he could do with the brother of a real Nazi martyr. This man in Northeim will ask again."

"I told him I wasn't interested."

"Do you think they'll give up? Nazis don't quit."

"I'll keep saying no."

"And eventually," Elisabeth said, "Goebbels will want to know why you, who should be a Nazi hero, are rejecting them. He'll find whatever records still exist, and then he'll come after you ... and me. We'll be attacked in *Der Angriff*. Stormtroopers will harass us on the streets, and you'll be harassed at school like Leonard was. The Goldmann store will become a Nazi target, even more than it already is. We'll always be looking over our shoulder, waiting for the next rock to be thrown. You'll lose any hope of a career with the Reichsbahn. And if that monster ever gets to be Chancellor, we'll be ..."

Elisabeth couldn't finish. She couldn't predict what Hitler would do; she only knew it would be horrible.

"I can't work with the Nazis," Berthold said. "For many reasons, not least of which is that Anna will hate me."

"Perhaps not if she knows the whole truth," Elisabeth said. "I've spoken to Judith Goldmann and she discussed it with Richard. He has an idea. It's complicated. It might involve Anna."

"What is it?"

"I think we should all discuss it together, but first, there's something else you need to know."

Elisabeth was trying to dole out the surprises one by one, knowing how overwhelming this must be to her son. He sat down and waited, a welter of emotions, all bad, moving across his face.

"My grandmother and Judith Goldmann's grandmother were sisters."

Berthold shook his head, stunned again. "What are you telling me? We're related to the Goldmanns?" After a brief pause, "Is there more? Was my grandfather Hitler's uncle?"

Elisabeth had to smile. "Not so far as I know," she said.

"Does Leonard know we're related?"

141

"No. Judith and Richard know, but not Leonard."

She could see Berthold's brain working, struggling to put the pieces together.

"Anna," he whispered. "Anna is also related to the Goldmanns. That's why she was here last August." Then Berthold's face went completely white. "Oh my God, are Anna and I some sort of cousins?"

"No," Elisabeth said. "You're connected to Judith's family and Anna is related to Richard. Two separate families."

***

Berthold, Elisabeth, Judith and Richard were seated around the Goldmann's dining table. There was food on the table but no one ate. They talked about Jewish cousins, Catholic cousins, family feuds, and who knew what when.

Richard Goldmann sat quietly through the discussion of family history - it wasn't his side of the family - then brought them back to the present.

"Hitler boasts that once he's in power, he'll deal with those responsible for the misfortunes of our nation. He says heads will roll, and there's no question whose heads he means. In *Mein Kampf,* Hitler said Jews should be treated like germs, eliminated by extermination."

He looked at Berthold. "But we have a more immediate problem. Berthold, who we now know is Jewish, at least by Nazi standards, is being recruited by the Nazis. What is he to do?"

None of the others spoke. Richard continued. "I see four choices. One, Berthold can become a Nazi. Two, he can completely reject them. Three, he and Elisabeth can leave Germany. Or, four, he can provide some assistance in Northeim but not become a member of the Nazi Party."

"It is repulsive for me to think of being a Nazi," Berthold said.

"But if you reject them outright," Richard said, "they'll be infuriated because of Dietrich. They'll try to find out why, and they'll probably learn about your Jewish ancestry."

"But even if they found out, why would they make it known?" Berthold asked. "Whatever they learn about me also applies to Dietrich. Wouldn't it be embarrassing for them to admit that one of their supposed martyrs was a Jew?"

"Maybe," Richard admitted, "but do you want to take that chance? Goebbels would make up lies to minimize the damage to them even as he destroyed your life and your mother's. That's why I recommend the fourth alternative. You could pretend to work with the Nazis while actually working against them."

"How could I do that without joining the Party?" Berthold asked.

"There are people who help the Nazis but are not Party members," Richard said. "The banker Hjalmar Schacht is one."

"I'm not so important as he is," Berthold said.

"I think you are," Richard said, "but for different reasons. However they portray it, it would be disastrous to the Nazis if Dietrich Becker's brother rejected them."

Berthold started to say something, then stopped, waiting for the rest of Richard's plan. Elisabeth took his hand but her hand was shaking and he was not comforted.

"Too many people," Richard said, "even Jews, don't take Hitler seriously. I think it's very important to convince Jews in Germany and elsewhere, especially England and America, that Hitler would do terrible things to Jews if he ever has the power. We must not allow anyone to be fooled by the interviews Hitler has recently given to the foreign press claiming he's not really so anti-Jewish."

Richard paused, but everyone else waited for him to continue. "My thought," he said, "is for you to appear to work with the Nazis but actually work against them. If you help the Nazis in Northeim, and get to know other Nazis here in

143

Munich, you'll learn things that will expose the truth about them. Perhaps that knowledge would spur others to work more effectively against them."

"How will anybody find out what I learn?" Berthold asked.

"Perhaps Anna could write about those things," Richard said. "We could ask her."

At the mention of Anna, Berthold's stomach tightened. It had been over a month since he had heard from her. He had no idea why her letters had stopped, but the last thing he wanted was for Anna to know anything about his Nazi connections.

The room was ominously still as everyone tried to digest what Richard was proposing.

Richard waited patiently, then said, "We shouldn't make any decisions today. We all need to think. In the end, Berthold, it's your decision and you need to be comfortable with whatever's decided."

"Comfortable!" Berthold said, making no effort to hide his anger. "How could I possibly be comfortable? My whole life is being turned upside down. Until yesterday, I thought I was going to get an engineering degree and work for the Reichsbahn. Now I find out I'm Jewish and you're asking me to spy against the Nazis."

Berthold stood and walked around the room. How could he possibly be clever enough to do what Richard suggested? He would be found out in a second.

"Could we really go to America?" he asked.

"It might be possible," Richard said. "It would take several months to find out, and in the end the answer might be no. But you may need to do something before that if the Nazis continue to pursue you."

Elisabeth went to her son and hugged him. She looked completely exhausted as she wiped tears from her eyes and pulled back so she could see Berthold's face.

"I'm so sorry about all this," she said, suppressing a sob. "I didn't imagine I'd ever tell you about your grandmother. If the Nazis weren't trying to bring you into their web, I would never have said anything. We were both born Catholic. Being Jewish has never had anything to do with us."

Judith Goldmann spoke for the first time. "I think we've said enough for now. We all need to think further, especially Berthold. Since time may be important, let's meet again tomorrow evening."

***

"We spent hours talking about this," Berthold said when they re-convened. He took his mother's hand; they both looked on the verge of tears.

"Mother and I have agreed we will to go to America, if that is possible. But we understand it will take time and if the Nazis pressure me again, I have to be prepared to respond. I think the best of the bad choices is to try what Herr Goldmann has suggested, even though I'm terrified to think I can put anything over on the Nazis. I'm also not sure that whatever I do, even if I don't get caught, will actually make much difference."

"It might," Richard said, "and meanwhile I'll try to find a way to get you and your mother to America."

Chapter 26

July 1931 - Munich

Three weeks had passed since Berthold had learned of his Jewish ancestry. He had been to Northeim twice, but the Nazi leader Ernst Krueger had not approached him, raising the hope that Richard's insanely dangerous plan would never have to be put into action. His letters to Anna continued to go unanswered.

Learning that he was Jewish had started Berthold thinking about why Jews were so hated. His thoughts went to the harsh views about Jews expressed by his church and he asked his mother to explain why the Catholic Church hated Jews.

Elisabeth sighed. "The church hates Jews because Jews deny that Jesus Christ is God."

"But so do Muslims and Buddhists and Hindus and who knows how many other religions. Why is the Jews' refusal so troubling?"

"Jews matter more," Elisabeth said, 'because Christians believe Jesus was a Jew. The Christian Bible says Jesus lived as an observant Jew, preached to Jews and died a Jew. Christianity is based largely on Jesus' Jewish roots and Christian doctrine claims that numerous sections of the Jewish Bible foretell the coming of Jesus.

"But Jews, who presumably know their own Bible best, reject the idea that the Old Testament has anything to say about the coming of Jesus. The implications of that rejection are potentially devastating for the whole concept of Christianity. If the Jewish view is correct and Jesus is not foretold in the Jewish Bible, what happens to the foundations of Christianity?"

"You didn't just come up with all that, did you? You've been thinking about it for some time."

"Judith Goldmann and I have had many conversations on this topic."

Berthold thought about that, then asked, "Have you ever spoken to someone in the Church about their hatred of Jews?"

"No," Elisabeth answered, "but if you want to learn more, perhaps you could speak with that priest you know from your school, who by the way has also been my confessor for several years."

***

Berthold spent many hours in the university library before he sought out Monsignor Karl Johannes. The two men sat in a pew in the cool darkness of Munich's cavernous and otherwise empty Cathedral.

"Thank you for meeting with me, Monsignor," Berthold said. "My mother suggested I speak to you. I want to understand why the Catholic Church seems so adamant in its hatred of Jews."

A noticeable wince appeared on Monsignor Johannes' face as Berthold continued.

"I've been reading the Catholic press. According to several articles in *La Civiltà Cattolica*, all of Christian civilization is gravely threatened by the Jews' plan to dominate the world. Other articles say the Jews killed Christ, use the blood of Christians in *matzoh*, poison wells, perform sexual abominations, and are in league with the devil. All of these accusations were printed within the past year."

Monsignor Johannes looked away, avoiding eye contact. His hands were joined, fingers interlocked tightly together. He rocked slowly, took a deep breath, visibly gathering resolve. He rose and began to walk, motioning for Berthold to follow. The sound of their heels echoed in the otherwise silent space. They stopped near a large dark painting.

"This depiction of the denunciation of Christ by the Jews before Pontius Pilate marks the beginning of the terrible history of the Catholic Church and the Jewish people."

Berthold expected the Monsignor to say more about the painting but he didn't and they continued walking silently until they were back where they had started, again seated side by side.

"Cardinal Faulhaber," Johannes said, "is pained by the hostility of the Church toward the Jews that you saw accurately reflected in the Catholic press. Several years ago, he launched an effort to remove the words 'perfidious Jews' from the Easter liturgy. Perhaps surprisingly, the Cardinal's initiative, which was called *Amici Israel*, gained the support of almost two thousand priests and several bishops and seemed headed for success. But then it was derailed in Rome by the Vatican."

Berthold had been unaware of *Amici Israel*, which had not been mentioned in any of the sources he had read.

"I'm pleased that you came to me," Monsignor Johannes said. "There's more to say about this topic, but not today. I'll speak with Cardinal Faulhaber and then we'll meet again."

***

It might have been coincidence, or perhaps Monsignor Johannes had spoken with Cardinal Faulhaber and that conversation had evoked the same passion that had previously led to his *Amici Israel* initiative, but Faulhaber's sermon two weeks later was stunning.

"You are all aware," Cardinal Faulhaber had said, "of the prayer in the Easter liturgy that calls on Catholics to pray for the perfidious Jews, that they may know Jesus Christ our Lord and be delivered from their darkness. This prayer has been a central part of our Easter liturgy for many centuries and it has often aroused Catholic hearts against the Jews, sometimes leading to violent actions.

"There are two things wrong with that prayer ... the Jews are not a perfidious people ... and they do not live in any darkness from which they need to be delivered."

Faulhaber's steely gaze circulated slowly among his congregants, who looked at each other in confusion which in some turned to anger.

"There are some in our city," the Cardinal said, "whose malicious campaign against the Jews has gone beyond all decent bounds of what Christians know to be proper and true. Among other indecencies, there has been publication in these last few weeks of a scurrilous, fraudulent document known as the *Protocols of the Elders of Zion*. This document purports to be minutes of meetings in which the leaders of the Jewish people are making plans to take over the world."

A pin dropping at that moment would have sounded like a rifle shot.

"There were no such meetings. There is no Jewish conspiracy to take over the world. The so-called *Protocols* is a fraud invented many years ago by agents of the Russian Tsar."

Faulhaber, showing his emotions in a manner none of his flock had ever seen before, took a deep breath.

"Christians must remember that Jesus our Lord was himself a Jew who never preached harm against his own people and certainly never called them perfidious."

Faulhaber turned and walked slowly to his seat.

Still astonished when they left the Cathedral, Elisabeth told Berthold that nothing like it had ever before been heard in Munich.

Chapter 27

Thomas Mann, a recent recipient of the Nobel Prize for Literature, had lived in Munich for much of his life. It was thus a major event when he spoke, and both Elisabeth and Berthold were in attendance. Mann talked first about his novels, then pointedly put aside his notes.

"These are difficult times," Mann said. "Families all over Germany and Europe are confused and frightened, much as my fictional family in *Buddenbrooks*. I urge all Germans to remember that we are very new at democratic government, barely ten years. It is a difficult form of government, far from perfect even at its best, but if we persevere, I believe it will be worth the effort. The Weimar government *is* making progress."

Mann drew himself up, nodded to his audience, then added, "We Germans are an intelligent people, cultured and capable of great things. A democratic government and free speech are the best ways to achieve that greatness."

His voice was soft but it captured his sadness and anger. "The violent ways of the Nazis are not a proper path for a cultured people."

Angry shouts exploded from the rear of the hall. "Jew lover! ... Communist!"

Berthold stiffened, expecting violence as police started to move, but Mann intervened.

"Let them stay. Perhaps they can learn something here."

He tried to resume his talk, but a second chorus of loud catcalls interrupted him. A group of tough-looking men, incongruously dressed in ill-fitting tuxedos, rose from their seats, pulled on Nazi armbands, and ran down the aisle toward the podium. Police immediately jumped into their path, forced several of them to the ground, and pushed the rest toward the back of the hall and out the door.

Mann waited until the hall was quiet. "These people are a terrible burden for Germany," he said. "Their attacks on Jews are hideous. I will continue to speak out."

Berthold and Elisabeth walked with the crowd to the back of the hall, where Josef Goebbels stood near the door, a smirk on his face. He seemed pleased with what he had undoubtedly orchestrated. Berthold imagined his article full of lies for the next edition of *Der Angriff* was already written. They tried to slip by unnoticed, but Goebbels saw Berthold and tipped his hat. Berthold nodded and hurried his mother out the door.

***

The next day an embossed envelope was delivered to the Becker home. In it was a hand-written note, signed Dr. J. Goebbels, politely asking Berthold to come see him at the Brown House at his earliest convenience.

***

Berthold stared at the giant swastika festooning the front of the Brown House, the Nazi Party headquarters in Munich. He noticed the bronze tablets mounted on either side of the entrance and walked closer to see his brother's name listed with the other *Putsch* martyrs. As always, he was angry. The ill-conceived and abysmally executed coup had failed and Hitler should have been washed away in its aftermath, deported if not executed. But here he still was, a plague on Germany, and Goebbels' propaganda had managed to transform a colossal failure into an heroic moment in Nazi history. Dietrich had died for nothing, except to ensnare him, eight years later, in the Nazi web. Berthold made himself known and waited in a large room where typewriters clattered and messengers scurried about.

"Thank you for coming," Goebbels said when he appeared a few minutes later. "Seeing you the other night reminded me of your conversation with Local Group Leader

Krueger in Northeim. The poor man was devastated by your rejection."

He motioned for Berthold to follow him and lurched off, his right leg noticeably shorter than the left. Berthold followed, thinking with every step that the plan he had so quickly agreed to was truly insane. They climbed a grand stairwell to the second floor.

"The *Führer* is in Berlin today," Goebbels said, "as are most of the others, but I can show you his office."

Berthold was startled to see a life-sized portrait of Henry Ford, the U.S. automobile manufacturer, displayed prominently in Hitler's office. Why was it there? He would ask Anna. Then he remembered Anna was no longer answering his questions. There were also large paintings of Frederick the Great and Bismarck.

Goebbels pointed to the paintings and said, "I've commissioned a composite portrait - Frederick, Bismarck and Hitler together - to show the continuity of German greatness."

As if Hitler deserves a place with the greatest men of German history, Berthold thought, glancing up to see if Goebbels had read his mind.

Hitler's office was elegantly furnished and thickly carpeted, with a huge desk plus a round table surrounded by leather armchairs for small conferences. Surprisingly, Hitler's bookcases were packed with Karl May's stories of the American West. May had been one of Berthold's childhood favorites, and it was unsettling that he and Hitler liked the same author.

"My office is much more modest." Goebbels said as they walked down the hall. He took his seat behind his desk, over-sized but not nearly so much as Hitler's, and motioned for Berthold to sit opposite him.

"We've come a long way in the last several years," Goebbels said. "Soon, we'll control Germany."

Berthold could not contain the look that jumped to his face and Goebbels saw it. "This prospect does not please you?"

he said sharply. "Well, Herr Becker, it doesn't really matter whether you are pleased or not. It will happen, and all Germans, including you, will accept it and adjust. There will be no other alternative."

In that moment, face-to-face with Goebbels' overwhelming confidence, Berthold found it easy to believe the Nazis might indeed come to rule Germany. Judging from Goebbels' smug smile, the fright he felt must have shown.

"The other night," Goebbels said with a smirk, "should be a good lesson for you. When your Thomas Mann provides a thoughtful analysis of the dangers which he fears will follow the Nazi assumption of power, and expresses dismay at the collapse of the humanist and idealistic values of the nineteenth century, and further decries the emergence of the wild, crude and primitive emotions of mass society ... he speaks a truth ... to which no one will listen."

Goebbels picked up a book from his desk and put it back down.

"Whereas Hitler, with uncanny intuition, senses the ills his audience is suffering, tells them what they want most desperately to hear, and convinces them he is the only one who can lead Germany to a glorious future. He reaches people in a way Thomas Mann can never do."

It was hard to admit Hitler was the better of Thomas Mann in anything, but Berthold agreed with Goebbels and understood more deeply the true danger Hitler posed. It wasn't what Hitler knew or did; in most cases he was ignorant of history and economics, and a failure in everything he had tried. But in selling himself, with Goebbels' assistance, he was a genius.

"Some," Goebbels was saying, "have called our propaganda a synthesis of unconnected and oversimplified ideas. You may be surprised to learn I do not disagree. We Nazis offer an easy-to-absorb clarification for those who are confused and frightened. We take the incomprehensible hodgepodge of political rhetoric and create a coherent myth for the masses which they can understand and want to support."

Goebbels smiled and Berthold saw the piercing, ice cold calculation in his eyes. He shivered with the thought that such calculations were at this moment directed at him.

Goebbels opened the leather-bound book which was lying on his desk. There was Hitler's signature, personally inscribing a copy of *Mein Kampf* to Berthold Becker in recognition of his services to the *Führer*. Berthold's eyes became unfocused and a queasy feeling rose in his gut.

"Hitler remembers your brother Dietrich coming to him the night of the *Putsch*, bringing a message from you that the army and police had turned against him. He very much appreciated that warning, as a result of which he had a car waiting for him at the Feldherrnhalle and was able to escape when the shooting broke out. Hitler does not forget those who help him."

I warned Dietrich, not Hitler.

Goebbels rose from his chair indicating that the meeting was coming to an end.

"The future will be here soon enough," he said. "But for today, our movement requires a significant contribution from the little town of Northeim. Can Local Group Leader Krueger count on your help to accomplish the goals I set for him?"

A meaningful pause, his eyes focused on Berthold.

"Keep in mind," Goebbels said, "we also have great plans for you. Your recent career-enhancing opportunity at the Reichsbahn was not an accident. Herr Thyssen, who builds locomotives and has associates on the Reichsbahn board, is a very good friend of the *Führer*.

Another pause. Goebbels' eyes bored into Berthold like a dagger.

"So what will it be?"

Berthold followed the plan he had accepted and managed to say "I will help Herr Krueger" in the most enthusiastic voice he could muster. He did not think Goebbels was fooled. Goebbels nodded and Berthold turned to leave.

"Did you forget?"

Berthold, who was already walking away, turned back, confused.

"Heil Hitler!" Goebbels snapped, raising his right arm.

Berthold hesitated just a split second, long enough for the corners of Goebbels' mouth to turn, then raised his arm and returned the salute. Again he started to walk away, but again Goebbels called him back, pointing to the autographed copy of *Mein Kampf* lying on his desk.

***

Berthold still felt immersed in Goebbels' filth as he stepped into the ring a few hours later. He had entered the university boxing tournament weeks before, but the timing could not have been more perfect. He wanted to hit and be hit.

He fought like a crazy person and reached the finals, where his opponent was the leader of the Hitler Youth group at the Technical University. Perfect. It was supposed to be a three round match, but Berthold charged from his corner, throwing one punch after another until his surprised opponent was completely overwhelmed. A powerful right cross dropped him to the canvas.

The referee raised Berthold's hand to signify the victory and that's when he saw Reinhard Heydrich at the back of the crowd, smiling and offering a wry salute.

Had Goebbels sent Heydrich to follow him?

Chapter 28

1990 - New York

Marissa was back in New York, comparing notes with her father and organizing the next phase of her interviews with Anna and Berthold.

"You can literally see the trap closing around him," Abraham said.

His voice trailed off and Marissa sensed a loosening of his hatred, a willingness to at least consider why Berthold had acted as he did.

"And yet," Abraham continued, "had Anna argued mitigating circumstances at Nuremberg, the judges would not have been moved, nor would I."

"We've all learned a lot in the past forty-five years," Marissa said.

"I was surprised to learn about Henry Ford's portrait in Hitler's office," Abraham said.

"Hitler often said Ford was his inspiration," Marissa said, taking on her professorial manner. "For ninety-one successive weeks, Henry Ford's company newspaper featured articles on the corrupting influence of Jewry. Those newspapers were distributed in every Ford dealership. Ford also published a truly scurrilous book called *The International Jew* and re-published the infamous *Protocols of the Elders of Zion*, which was of course a staple of Nazi Jew-hatred. Only when he was about to lose a libel suit did Ford recant and apologize, but nobody ever believed he had changed his views. There's no question that Ford's repeated attacks on Jews set a tone which contributed to the antisemitic attitudes of many Americans, and maybe Germans as well."

"Hitler's hero," Abraham said. "I'm sorry I ever owned a Ford."

Chapter 29

August 1931 - Munich

Each time Berthold returned from Northeim, he rushed through the accumulated mail, searching ever more desperately for a letter from Anna. It had been almost three months. Again he wrote to her, feeling pathetic and without hope: *I miss you so much. Why have you stopped writing?*

***

Berthold reported to Richard Goldmann as he did after every visit to Northeim

"Local District Leader Krueger started me out with easy tasks, detail work, no real challenge. He also put up that photo of me and Goebbels and I became a hero. Everyone seemed to know I had met personally with Goebbels and had actually been in Hitler's office.

"I now spend many evenings in beer halls talking with men who've joined the Nazi Party. They remind me of Dietrich and his friends when they came home from the front, with no jobs and feeling abandoned by their government. It's been almost fifteen years and nothing is better. In their minds, the Weimar government is incompetent and only Hitler can lead them to a better life."

"You're learning a lot," Richard said.

"I'm also learning just how little the Socialist and Catholic parties are doing to counter Hitler's message."

"But there are articles every week in both Socialist and Catholic newspapers attacking Hitler and his ideas," Richard said.

"Do you think the men who are attracted to Hitler read those articles? The Nazis have meetings all the time. They repeat a powerful message, simplified by Goebbels. Their audience is frustrated and afraid, and they believe what they hear. The Socialists and Catholics have no idea how to reach that audience. The Nazis have invented a new way of doing politics, and they have the whole field to themselves."

***

Several days later, Elisabeth told Berthold that Richard and Judith Goldmann had invited hem to dinner.

"They want to talk about Anna."

Berthold began as soon as they walked in the Goldmann's door.

"Anna has stopped answering my letters and I'm afraid something has happened to her. What do you know?"

Richard and Judith exchanged a look. "She saw the photograph of you with Goebbels," Judith said. "She's angry and upset."

"Why didn't you tell me?"

"We just received her letter two days ago."

Dinner was served and nobody said anything more about Anna. Berthold sulked and said nothing about anything.

***

The fall semester began and Berthold attended classes, but he barely listened and often failed to do the readings. He went back and forth to Northeim, although his once intense interest in the railroad had waned. When he was in Northeim, he could not avoid Local District Leader Krueger.

As Berthold watched and participated in the relentless Nazi campaign to secure influence in Northeim, he realized that what he was learning needed to be known and he became ever more desperate that he had no way to communicate outside of telling Richard, which he felt was worthless. Then he remembered Richard's original idea, so long ago, that Anna could write about what he was learning.

***

"I have an idea," Berthold said to Richard the next time they met.

"Have you considered the risks?" Richard asked, aghast at the boldness of what Berthold was proposing.

"I have," Berthold said, "and I've also considered the possible gains. Right now our plan to spy on the Nazis is useless and I've lost all contact with Anna. How could things get worse?"

They both knew and left unsaid that things could indeed get much worse, but they talked it through for over an hour and finally agreed on a plan.

As the first step, Richard agreed to call Anna at the *Haynt* offices in Warsaw and ask if she would be agreeable to Berthold's suggestion. He also agreed to tell her there was an explanation for the Berlin photo and urge that she should withhold judgment until she heard all the facts from Berthold himself.

When Richard reported back that Anna had agreed, Berthold steeled himself and went to the Brown House, mumbling over and over to himself "the *Fuhrer*, the *Fuhrer*, the *Fuhrer*."

***

Ernst Hanfstaengl was born in Munich and educated at Harvard. He had been a supporter of Hitler for years and had recently begun serving as Hitler's liaison to the foreign press. His job was to place favorable articles about Hitler in American and British newspapers. He was just the man for what Berthold had in mind.

Hanfstaengl had an office in the Brown House and Berthold made an appointment. Upon arrival, he was taken to a tiny room on the third floor which could barely contain the man who worked there, let alone a guest. Hanfstaengl was well over six feet tall, with a very large head covered with thick, unruly hair. He seemed to be in his mid-forties, vigorous and fit.

"Berthold Becker," Hanfstaengl said cheerfully. "Are you the little boy I used to see sometimes with Dietrich?"

Berthold nodded.

"Your brother was a good man. The *Führer* misses him still. Goebbels says you're doing good work in Northeim. What can I do for you?"

"Thank you for seeing me, Herr Hanfstaengl ..."

"... Putzi, please call me Putzi. Everyone else does."

Hanfstaengl had a reputation for being garrulous, so Berthold let him talk. With no prelude and no obvious relevance, Putzi went into a long story about his undergraduate days in America and his family's art business in New York, finishing with what to him was the hilarious manner in which he had obtained his nickname.

"Putzi of course means 'little fellow.' My family started calling me that when I was a baby. The name stuck, and when I started to grow so large, it became a real joke."

Putzi stopped talking and Berthold sensed it was finally time to explain why he was there. To say he was nervous would be a gross understatement.

"The *Führer*," Berthold said, pleased he didn't gag on the word, "has been granting interviews to members of the foreign press. I believe you are the one who arranges these occasions."

Putzi nodded.

"A friend of mine is a journalist for a Polish newspaper. There's much interest, and I may add concern, regarding the *Führer* in Poland, and I wonder if it might be possible for my friend to interview Hitler."

"Which Polish newspaper?"

"The *Haynt*."

"So your friend is Jewish."

"Yes, she is."

"And a woman. How old?"

"Twenty-three."

Putzi's face for the first time registered surprise. "So young. Does she speak German?"

"Fluently."

"Is she attractive?"

"Yes."

Berthold remembered something Anna had written in the last letter she had sent. "She also writes for TIME Magazine in America."

"Well, that strengthens the case."

Putzi wrapped his head in his huge hands and thought for a moment.

"It may be possible. Hitler likes being with pretty young women. How did your friend get to be so prominent at such a young age?"

"She knows Marshal Pilsudski."

"You should have said that first," Putzi said with real enthusiasm. "They'll all want to meet with her, Goebbels for sure. They'll want to question her regarding Pilsudski's plans. I'll talk to Adolf and get back to you. Thank you for bringing this to us."

Berthold was stunned. He had never heard anyone refer to Hitler as Adolf.

Chapter 30

August 1931 - Warsaw

Berthold's telegram hit like a lightning bolt: YOUR INTERVIEW WITH HITLER APPROVED. COME TO MUNICH AS SOON AS POSSIBLE.

Anna had been prepared by Richard Goldmann's telephone call and had alerted her publisher Yitzhak Gruenbaum. When the confirming telegram arrived, Gruenbaum contacted Irena Meltzer and arranged a meeting.

"My, my," Meltzer said. "How far we have come since the Marshal trusted you with that first story. So many articles. So many papers in so many countries. But still, why would Hitler grant an interview to a young Jewish girl from Poland?"

Gruenbaum answered. "He's been interviewed several times recently by members of the foreign press - British and American mainly. Since the big advances made by the Nazis in the last elections, he wants to appear more reasonable, even regarding Jews, in order to broaden his support among right-wing businessmen.

"Of course Anna must talk with Marshal Pilsudski before going to Munich. He might not want her to go, and he certainly would have some thoughts about what she might say."

***

"Have you told Berthold you saw the photograph?" Meltzer asked as they walked away from the *Haynt* offices..

"No, but I told Richard Goldmann and he told Berthold."

"So Berthold's had no chance to explain?"

"What explanation can there be! This photo had already happened when we first met in Munich, and he didn't tell me."

"Do you still love him?"

Anna took a deep breath and exhaled noisily. "It's quite possible."

"Then you need to know the truth. You must give him the opportunity to explain."

"He's written many letters that I haven't answered."

"So he sent a telegram he knew you couldn't ignore." Meltzer smiled. "He's a bright boy."

"Yes," Anna said.

"You should tell Marshall Pilsudski about Berthold," Meltzer said. "And you should show him the photograph."

***

Anna, Irena Meltzer and Marshal Pilsudski strolled in the park that surrounded Belvedere Palace, enjoying the warmth of a sunny September day, armed security discreetly at a distance. Pilsudski had greeted them outside, looking far better than recent press reports of his health might suggest. Perhaps he had good days and bad days. Anna explained that she had an invitation to interview Hitler.

"So the *Führer* wants to meet with our Anna. That's good."

"The fact that I know you was a major incentive in granting the interview. I gather you don't object."

"Quite the opposite. We should take advantage of this unexpected opportunity. But please tell me more about how it came about. Who is this Becker fellow? How do you know him?"

"I met Berthold Becker at the home of relatives of mine in Munich when I was there doing a story on the persecution of Jews in German universities. He was very helpful."

Anna looked at Meltzer who said, "You must tell him."

"Since then," Anna said, "it appears that Berthold has made connections with prominent Nazis."

Anna gave Pilsudski the photograph of Berthold with Goebbels. Pilsudski looked at it and then at Anna. He reached out to take her hand, something he had never done before.

Anna was startled; she had expected anger and instead she saw concern.

"Is Becker a Nazi?" Pilsudski asked.

"This photograph seems to say so."

"How does he explain it?"

Anna hesitated, then said. "We haven't discussed it."

"I can see the pain in your face," Pilsudski said. "You like this boy and you don't understand. Perhaps you should hear young Becker's explanation before you condemn him, and meanwhile, you can also talk with Hitler and find out what's on the monster's mind."

Anna blinked away the tears that had started to form, and Pilsudski place a gentle hand on her shoulder. They walked several steps in silence until they came to a grouping of iron chairs and Pilsudski indicated they should sit.

"It's my view," Pilsudski said, "that Hitler has a very good chance to take over the government of Germany. If he obtains power, he will cast his eyes on Poland and on Jews. He's a patient man. He'll build Germany's army even as he tries to convince the world he means no harm."

The Marshal took several deep breaths.

"I'd like to know more of Hitler's temperament when he's not carrying on like a raving maniac. I'd like your opinion as to whether his speeches are an act; I think they are. But mostly I'd like to know anything he says or implies about Germany's Army and about Poland, especially Danzig. He likes to brag, so he may let something slip."

Pilsudski motioned for Anna and Meltzer to come closer and bent toward them in a conspiratorial style. He spoke in a whisper.

"Here's what I would like Anna to tell Hitler about *my* views and intentions."

Chapter 31

September 1931 - Munich

Richard Goldmann met Anna at the train station and brought her by taxi to the Goldmann house where Berthold and Elisabeth were waiting. When Anna appeared, Berthold felt faint, his stomach queasy. He had taken a huge chance by arranging the Hitler interview and here she was, so that was good, but the look on her face was not encouraging.

"Did you have a pleasant trip?" Elisabeth asked.

"Yes. Quite pleasant."

Anna looked back and forth between Berthold and Elisabeth without smiling, and her voice was flat, with no emotion. Judith Goldmann took Anna to her room to freshen up.

The others went to the living room. Berthold placed the newspaper with the photograph on a small table around which chairs had been arranged. Elisabeth gave him a hopeful smile; Richard said it would be all right.

Anna came back into the room and Richard directed her to the chair next to Berthold, facing the table and the photograph. Berthold stared at her, terrified but knowing what he had to do.

"I should have told you," he said. "I didn't know how."

"Tell me now."

Berthold explained how he had been in Berlin with Albert Mueller on Reichsbahn business and how Mueller had insisted they go the Horst Wessel funeral.

"I shouldn't have gone," he said. "That was my first mistake. We hadn't been there for ten minutes when Goebbels sent for me to come to the platform. Mueller must have gotten word to him that Dietrich Becker's brother was in the crowd."

"So you just paraded on up there," Anna said. "Why didn't you just walk away?"

"I didn't think I had that choice," Berthold said weakly, his head hanging down. "There was an ugly mood in the crowd. Thousands of drunken Nazi thugs were looking for any excuse to pounce on someone. They had already beaten several people they claimed were communist spies."

It sounded lame to Berthold even as he said it. Anna will think I'm weak and a coward as well as stupid, he thought. He winced, expecting a blizzard of questions and accusations, but Anna said nothing. Berthold looked to his mother to continue, as they had agreed.

"There's more," Elisabeth said.

Anna turned to Elisabeth and waited, her face still expressionless.

"My grandmother," Elisabeth said haltingly, "was Judith's grandmother's sister."

Anna looked back and forth between Elisabeth and Judith. She seemed shocked. Elisabeth continued.

"My mother changed her name and her religion many years ago, before she met my father. She told me this shortly before she died. Her husband, my father, never knew; my own husband never knew. I told Berthold after he was approached by the Nazis in Northeim."

Anna understood how complicated decisions could become in the face of violence. She had seen fear in the faces of young people in Warsaw and in Munich. She had seen it in her parents, and she had felt it herself. She understood it now in Elisabeth and Berthold.

"What happened in Northeim?" Anna asked Berthold, the edge beginning to disappear from her voice

"I was in Northeim working for the Reichsbahn. I was asked to help the Nazi Local Group organize their efforts. I said no."

Elisabeth again picked up the story.

"After Berthold was approached in Northeim, I told him about his Jewish ancestry and we met with Richard and

166

Judith, at my request. We agreed that if Berthold rejected the Nazis out of hand, it would raise red flags. The Nazis would want to know why the brother of one of their heroes hates them so much. They would dig into Berthold's background, and mine. They would learn our secret and our lives would be ruined."

Anna sat stone still, waiting for the rest. "So you became a Nazi?"

"No," Berthold answered, his face white as chalk. "Herr Goldmann had said if I worked for the Nazis, I might learn things that would be valuable for those who oppose Hitler. So when Goebbels insisted that I work with the Nazis in Northeim, I said I would. Since then, I've been gathering information, but I haven't joined the Nazi Party."

Anna's mind was spinning. The idea of Berthold being a Jewish spy within the Nazi ranks was far beyond anything she could have imagined, even more stunning than his Jewish ancestry. Her first reaction was to wonder if Berthold was strong enough to carry out a dangerous secret mission under the eyes of the Nazis. He had needed his mother to share the burden of this disclosure to her. He had gone to the stage in Berlin when he could have walked away.

On the other hand, he had arranged an interview for her with Adolf Hitler, something no newspaper in Poland had ever had. Her final realization, of which she was immediately ashamed, was that it would be an enormous boost to her journalistic career to have an ongoing source within the Nazi establishment.

"Our conclusion," Elisabeth was saying, "was that Berthold must continue to deceive the Nazis until arrangements can be made for us to go to America."

"America?" Anna gasped. "You're going to America?"

Richard answered. "We're exploring that possibility."

Elisabeth suppressed a sob, then said, "It's the best plan we could think of."

Anna closed her eyes. Elisabeth looked at Berthold, who seemed about to say something. She motioned for him to wait, but Anna slowly shook her head and an uneasy silence engulfed all of them. Finally Anna spoke.

"I have to think about all this and right now I'm too tired to think clearly. I've been traveling since last night."

"Certainly," Judith said. "Perhaps you'd like to lie down and rest."

"Yes, that would be good. When is my meeting with Hitler?"

"First there's a meeting with Hanfstaengl," Berthold said. He consulted his watch. "In three hours."

***

Anna cringed at the sight of the swastika outside the Brown House, and even more when they passed near the fortunately unoccupied offices of Hitler and Goebbels on their way to Hanfstaengl's tiny space on the third floor. Anna and Berthold squeezed together on two armless chairs facing the big German who sat behind his desk.

"So here is the famous Anna Gorska, friend of Marshal Pilsudski, come to meet our *Führer*."

"Thank you for arranging this, Herr Hanfstaengl," Anna said.

"Please. Nobody calls me that. Call me Putzi."

Anna grinned and said, "Perhaps you should know I speak Yiddish."

Hanfstaengl looked surprised, then he blushed, and finally he roared with laughter and turned bright red.

"I'll explain later," Anna said to a confused Berthold.

"You can call me Putzi, but Hitler will expect you to call him *Führer*," Putzi managed to say through his laughter.

"Then he'll be disappointed," Anna said. "He is not my leader."

Putzi again laughed uproariously and Berthold was now sure this whole scheme had been a horrible idea, from so many perspectives. Anna was being far too aggressive.

"He will also expect an honorarium." Putzi managed to say between guffaws.

"I'm prepared for that," Anna said, "but of course *Haynt* does not have the resources of the Hearst newspapers."

Anna knew Hearst had paid one thousand marks for each of their interviews with Hitler, and also that Hanfstaengl took a thirty percent share.

"We can pay one hundred marks."

After a short pause, Putzi said, "That will be fine."

"Shall we now talk about the questions?" Anna asked.

"You want questions?" Putzi blurted. "Hitler doesn't answer questions. He talks. You're supposed to listen and take down what he says."

Anna phrased her next remark as diplomatically as she could, which she realized was not very diplomatic at all.

"I have come to Munich to ask questions which are important to my readers and to Marshal Pilsudski. I have other business in Paris, so if there are to be no questions, this meeting is over and I will be off to Paris in the morning."

Putzi looked shocked that anyone would make such demands and threaten to walk away from an interview with the *Führer*. He stared at Anna for a two full minutes. Berthold was stunned by the audacity of Anna's demand, but Anna just waited, seemingly unconcerned. Then Putzi smiled.

"You will have three questions. I will review them in advance."

"Five questions," Anna said, "and that is the end of this negotiation. Shall we discuss the questions?"

Chapter 32

Anna met Putzi at the Brown House the next morning, where she learned that the venue for her interview had been changed to Hitler's house. Putzi offered to take her by taxi and on the way, she asked why the change.

"I have no idea," Putzi responded. "Hitler often changes schedules at the last minute. Sometimes he doesn't show up at all."

"Will you be there when I meet with him?"

"No. He doesn't like any other people present when he's meeting with the press."

"Why is that?"

In what to Anna was an unexpected flash of honesty, Putzi said Hitler wanted to be free to claim he had been misquoted, with no witnesses to disagree. This also has advantages, Putzi explained, for the potential witness, who cannot be shot for contradicting the *Führer*. At the time, Anna thought Putzi was making a joke.

Hitler had recently moved into a handsome nine-room apartment on Prinzregentenplatz, one of the most expensive neighborhoods in Munich. Hanfstaengl walked with Anna up the elegant stairs to the entry, where they were met by a pretty young woman. Putzi, who obviously knew the woman, did not seem pleased to see her, but he said nothing and left abruptly. Anna was led to a small sitting room.

"Uncle Adolf is not ready yet, so he has asked me to entertain you. My name is Geli Raubal."

Over the next fifteen minutes, sipping coffee and saying almost nothing, Anna learned from Geli, who talked non-stop, that she was a student at Munich University, her course of study as yet undetermined. She also took singing lessons. "Uncle Adolf thinks I can become a Wagnerian heroine, but I have my doubts." In a whisper, Geli confided she was having an affair with one of Hitler's drivers. She giggled and added, "Won't Uncle Adolf be angry if he finds out?"

Anna was not forced to speculate, since a butler appeared and escorted her to a large, beautifully furnished room.

"The *Führer* will be here shortly."

Shortly turned out to be almost thirty minutes, but then the door opened and it was indeed Adolf Hitler who entered. Anna rose politely and smiled. Hitler took her hand and kissed it, quite the gentleman. Anna fought down the terror and revulsion she felt at feeling his touch.

"You're a very attractive young lady."

Anna thought Hitler's attempt at a compliment came off awkward and stiff, as well as being inappropriate. Hitler motioned for her to be seated and took himself to a facing couch. From his jacket pocket he withdrew a single paper.

"Your first question has to do with my plans for Germany. I will answer."

For twenty minutes, Hitler spoke in the manner of a university post-graduate student presenting a paper. He described Germany's humiliation after the Great War, the failures of the Weimar Republic, the arrogance of the French, and finished with a condemnation of what he claimed were excessive reparations payments. He never paused and Anna did not interrupt. She took very few notes; there was nothing new in his remarks.

"Your next question is whether I am planning another *Putsch*. The answer is absolutely not. We will take power legally, through the electoral process, in full accordance with the Constitution." He could not resist a small smile. "Then, of course, we may make some changes."

Again Anna resisted her inclination to ask more. So it went for questions three and four, as Hitler said he did not intend to make war on anyone and that he particularly looked forward to good relations with Poland. He did not mention Danzig.

"Question five has to do with the Jews," Hitler said. "As I have told other newspapers, I renounce antisemitism. In a recent interview with the *London Times*, I gave my assurance that I have no wish to be associated with pogroms. I also stated that the Nazi Party had no objections to decent Jews."

Now, finally, was Anna's time to be confrontational.

"But you also said in that interview, Herr Hitler, that should Jews link up with Bolshevism, they would then be regarded as enemies. Since you always claim that Jews and Bolsheviks are actually one and the same thing, are you not still as opposed to Jews as you have always been?"

Hitler started to speak but Anna interrupted him. Perhaps because he was so unused to being interrupted, or that he had been lulled by the tranquility of the past hour, or that he was beguiled by his clear vision of Anna's knee as she chose that moment to cross her legs, he let her go on. She spoke in the sweetest voice she could muster.

"In Munich two years ago, in a tent jammed with thirty thousand people, you stated that the Jews are Germany's mortal enemy, parasites and scoundrels, swarthy, greasy, hook-nosed, and stinking. In *Mein Kampf*, you wrote that Jews should be exterminated like germs."

Hitler scowled, but Anna hurried on before he could speak.

"So my final question, Herr Hitler, is whether the Jews of Poland can take comfort from what was reported recently in the *London Times* or whether they should believe what you have just said?"

Hitler looked at his watch. "I have another meeting," he said. "Goebbels will continue this discussion."

Without appearing in the least ruffled or angry, Hitler rose, bowed a formal little goodbye, and left. Anna was not upset. Hitler's non-answer would be fine for her article.

A few minutes later, Josef Goebbels arrived. He, unlike Hitler, appeared to be seriously rattled. Anna could only imagine what Hitler had said to him. Yet, in what Anna took to be a supreme effort at self-control, he smiled. It was a sickening smile but a smile nonetheless.

"The *Führer* offers his apologies. He asked me to continue the interview. Can I order some coffee for you?"

"No thank you," Anna said. "Are you prepared to answer the question Herr Hitler refused to answer?"

"The *Führer* did not refuse to answer your question," Goebbels said. "Your appointment ran longer than expected and he has other business. But I will answer: Hitler has no objection to decent Jews."

"How do you reconcile that with what Hitler has said and written before?"

"As I said, Hitler has no objection to decent Jews."

"Did you write that for Hitler to say?"

"Yes, of course." Goebbels seemed pleased that Anna recognized his role. "We discuss things regularly. Now, since we have answered all of your questions, I have a few questions for you."

"Go on," Anna said.

"Is Marshal Pilsudski conspiring with the French against Germany?"

Anna was amazed at how clumsily Goebbels had phrased his question, but she answered exactly as she and Pilsudski had discussed. "The Marshal has talked with the French and he expects those talks to continue. He does not regard such discussions as a conspiracy against Germany."

Goebbels did not react but went directly to his next question. He has his own list, Anna thought.

"Would Marshal Pilsudski be willing to talk with Germany about different arrangements for Danzig? You know the arrangement dictated by Versailles is not viewed favorably by us."

"You understand that I'm a reporter, not a diplomat," Anna said.

"But perhaps you've heard something in the course of your reporting," Goebbels said, his lips curling slightly.

Anna smiled.

"Yes, Herr Goebbels, I have. It is well known in Warsaw that the Marshal would like to expand Polish influence in Danzig." This was word for word what Pilsudski had asked her to say.

"And of course you know that would be contrary to our wishes," Goebbels said.

"Marshal Pilsudski would be willing to talk about that," Anna said sweetly. "Perhaps a compromise might be found."

Anna responded to several more questions, faithfully repeating everything Pilsudski had asked her to say about Danzig and the corridor to the sea, Poland's interactions with the French, rumors of an imminent treaty with the Russians, and the Marshal's health. Each time, she made herself seem reluctant to answer, citing lack of knowledge or confidentiality, but then she provided the agreed upon information in response to Goebbels' persistent and increasingly frantic questioning.

Does Goebbels guess what I'm doing?

Eventually, Goebbels rose and said how pleasant their meeting had been.

"Hanfstaengl will come to take you home," he said.

Then, after he had started to walk away, he turned back, as if something had just occurred to him.

"Perhaps you could enlighten me about something. How is it that you know our colleague Berthold Becker?"

A chill went through Anna. *What has Berthold told Putzi?* She should have prepared for this but had not.

"I met him at the University of Munich when I was here last year working on a story about harassment of Jewish students," she said, praying there would not be any follow-up questions, frantically trying to formulate answers if there were.

"Yes of course. I read your story."

Goebbels nodded and this time he did walk away. He didn't need me to answer that question, Anna thought. He already knew the answer. He just wanted to match my answer to Berthold's. Anna's heart was still pounding when Putzi arrived and asked where she would like to be taken.

"I need to go to the library at the University of Munich," she said.

Chapter 33

Anna rummaged through card files, scribbled meaningless notes, and looked furtively to see if she had been followed. An hour later, she took a cab to the Goldmann home.

"Thank God you're back," Judith said. "We were worried."

Anna forced a smile. "After I finished with Hitler and Goebbels, I went to the library and pretended to do research."

"Why did you do that?" Richard asked.

"Goebbels frightened me," Anna said.

She turned to Berthold. "Goebbels asked me how I knew you. I had no idea what you had told Putzi, so I wasn't sure how to answer."

All of the color drained from Elisabeth's face.

"I said I met you at the University when I was doing research for my story. I never mentioned the Goldmann family. I didn't come directly here when I left Hitler's house because I didn't want to be followed here."

Anna paused, then asked, "Berthold, what did you tell Putzi about us?"

"I told him you were a friend of mine and a journalist. Also that you knew Marshal Pilsudski. I never mentioned the Goldmanns. I should have told you that. I put you at risk."

"I should have asked," Anna said. "There's a lesson here that we'd better both learn."

Berthold's heart jumped. Learning lessons implied future interactions.

"I'm sure Goebbels will follow up," Anna said. "He'll learn about connections between the Becker and Goldmann families."

"Let's not over-react," Richard said. "So what if Goebbels learns that Elisabeth works at the store, or that Berthold and Leonard are friends, or even that Anna is distantly related to me? The only way those connections will raise suspicions is if we lie about them and they find out the truth, so we should tell the truth if asked."

"I agree," Anna said. "That's what I was thinking through at the library."

"But if they learn that Judith and I are related ..." Elisabeth said, her voice quivering.

"That is a different matter," Richard said. "But that connection is also much more deeply hidden."

"Not deeply enough," Elisabeth said softly. "I'm sure there are records somewhere."

Silent and wary looks passed between all of them. Then Berthold asked Anna what she thought of Goebbels.

"I think his mind absorbs everything but his questions were clumsy. Maybe he's not as smart as he thinks he is."

"He's smarter than Putzi," Berthold said. "Deceiving Josef Goebbels is not the same as fooling Putzi Hanfstaengl."

He paused, straining to express the emotions he was feeling, then added, "I'm very relieved you're back safely."

Berthold felt his words had been awkward, but when Anna looked at him, it seemed her eyes had softened. Or was that just his hopeful imagination?

**

Dinner conversation was polite but not in any way intimate, or even warm. It seemed to Berthold that everyone was nervous and uncertain, deep in their own thoughts, unable to speak freely about anything important. After dinner, Anna drew Berthold aside.

"I really do have business in Paris and I'll be leaving in the morning."

Berthold looked down hoping Anna would not see the sadness he felt. She had completed her interview with Hitler, and now she would leave. He might send her more information, they might even exchange letters, but the chances were good he would never see her smile again.

Anna came close to him and put her hands on his shoulders. He saw something in her eyes that made his whole body tingle.

"Would you like to come with me? To Paris? We have much to talk about."

She waited patiently for his response.

"Yes," he said. "I would love to go to Paris with you."

Later still, Elisabeth gave Henri Bousquet's telephone number to Berthold. "Call him if you need anything in Paris."

Chapter 34

Early the next morning, when Anna and Berthold arrived at the train station, they saw the headline in the *Münchener Post* and froze. They bought the paper and read the article.

GELI RAUBAL SHOT DEAD IN HITLER'S APARTMENT

Geli Raubal, a 23-year-old music student who is Adolf Hitler's niece, has killed herself ... there are reports of a quarrel between Herr Hitler and Fraulein Raubal ... the weapon which killed Raubal was Hitler's pistol

On the train many kilometers outside of Munich, Anna was still shaking.

"I was with her yesterday. She came to entertain me while I was waiting for Hitler. Oh my God, she was a flighty little thing. She said she was having an affair with Hitler's driver and wouldn't Uncle Adolf be furious if he found out. Maybe he did find out. Maybe he shot her in a jealous rage. Should I tell the police?"

With no hesitation, Berthold said, "There's no benefit and much risk in talking to the police. They've already concluded it was suicide, so what Geli said to you has no bearing."

"How terrible for a life to end so young," Anna said. "Geli was the same age as Dietrich when he died." Tears formed in Anna's eyes. "Tell me about him," she said softly, her head tilted to listen.

Berthold took several moments to gather himself before he managed to speak. He started by saying that Dietrich was a good brother and that he loved him and missed him. He explained how Dietrich was scarred by the war and enamored with Hitler.

"Did Dietrich know what Hitler said about Jews?"

"Of course. How could anyone not know? Dietrich repeated those things. I remember one terrible time when he came home and found Leonard in our home. He screamed and ranted, but later he apologized." Berthold fought back the sob in his throat. "I tried to warn him the night of the *Putsch*, but he followed Hitler and so he died."

Berthold was aching to hold Anna's hand but did not dare to do so. It was as if his hand was glued in place and no power on earth could make it move. But then Anna placed her hand over his and allowed it to rest there. He turned his hand and their fingers engaged.

The train rumbled on, and for much of the next hour, both of them, emotionally drained, stared at the high mountains, farmers working in fields, a river winding in the distance. All the while, Berthold didn't let go of Anna's hand until they reached Stuttgart, where they changed trains. Later, on the train to Paris, they once again found each other's hands.

"Marshal Pilsudski has defended Jews in Poland," Anna said suddenly.

She had been silent so long that Berthold jumped at the sound of her voice.

"Everyone else in Poland hates the Jews. We will have a horrible life in Poland when Pilsudski is gone."

"What sort of life will we have?" Berthold asked.

"Are you asking about a life for Jews in Europe, or for the two Jews sitting here on this train?"

"Do we have a life ahead of us?" Berthold asked.

"Sometimes you're an idiot," Anna answered, smiling openly for the first time in two days.

Somehow being called an idiot made Berthold feel terrific. He returned Anna's smile.

"Would I ask you to come to Paris with me," Anna said, "if I didn't think we might have some kind of life together?"

***

They arrived at Gare de l'Est in Paris in the late afternoon. Anna took a paper from her pocket and gave it to a taxi driver. Only when they were underway did she explain.

"My newspaper in Warsaw has a counterpart in Paris and my editor wants me to establish a connection."

To describe the tiny space on the fifth floor of a decrepit building just off Boulevard Saint Germain as an office was exceedingly generous. A man named Nachum Wolman introduced himself as the editor of the *Parizer Haynt*. He said he'd been expecting her. Out of deference to Berthold, they spoke in German.

"Where's your press?" Anna asked, slightly out of breath from the climb.

"We have no press," Wolman replied. "We rent time to print our few pages every week."

"You publish weekly?" Anna asked. "*Haynt* means today."

"Well, it's always today when we print."

Anna laughed out loud, then said, "I have a story for you, an exclusive interview with Hitler, but you can't print it until I get back to Warsaw and we print it first."

"That's reasonable."

"I want to send a short summary now. Can you arrange a telegram?"

"Can you pay for it?"

Anna gave him a page she had written on the train including a postscript saying she would be back in Warsaw with the balance of the story in two days.

"We'll need rooms," Anna said to Wolman.

Rooms? Berthold's hopes crashed.

Wolman made a telephone call. "You have reservations at a hotel just a few blocks from here."

***

The hotel was a narrow eighteenth century townhouse located just one block from the Seine. It was clean and quiet, not extraordinary in any way, but to a wide-eyed Berthold, his pulse racing, it was a forbidden paradise. They left their suitcases in their rooms, met back in the foyer, and walked to a restaurant near the hotel. The delay was, for Berthold, a heightening of his already flaming erotic tension.

"What is *coq au vin*?" he asked.

"Chicken, braised and cooked with wine," Anna said without hesitation.

"How do you know?"

"I've eaten at several fine French restaurants in Warsaw." Sensing Berthold's surprise, Anna added, "Since the war, Warsaw has become a very cosmopolitan city."

Baked onion soup arrived, then the *coq au vin* for Berthold, roasted duck for Anna, followed by a cheese course, accompanied by a wonderful red wine. Berthold offered to pay, but Anna said she would be reimbursed by her newspaper.

After dinner, they walked. Paris after dark was beyond enchanting. Street lights flickered as did occasional lights peeking through curtained windows. On the wide boulevard were horse-drawn carriages, a few taxis, and many couples, just like them, walking hand in hand. They headed toward the river, passing under broad trees. Crossing the bridge they saw to their right the great towers of Notre Dame. A few minutes later, standing in awe at the edge of the wide plaza fronting the Cathedral, they saw another couple stop, embrace and kiss.

The moment was irresistible. Berthold turned to Anna and, after a brief hesitation, she came into his arms. Their bodies pressed together in eager embrace and their lips met,

182

warm in the cool evening air. Neither was willing to break away, neither was sure what to do next.

"We're involved in a dangerous business," Anna said when they finally came up for air.

"Kissing?"

"That too," Anna laughed, "but I was thinking of spying on the Nazis. It seems so presumptuous to imagine that you and I can help keep the Nazis from gaining power. But others," she added, "could take the information you provide and use it effectively."

Berthold, still trembling from the kiss, struggled to organize his thoughts and speak coherently, distressed that Anna was once again talking about Nazis.

"Marshal Pilsudski?"

"Exactly."

They walked along the side of the Cathedral to the far end of the island, where they stood on a small bridge and watched the reflection of a full moon in the river, rippling as boats slowly passed. On the other side of the bridge was a small restaurant and in its window, a sign said *crème glacée*.

"Is it too cold for ice cream?" Anna asked.

Berthold was irritated by yet another delay, but he took Anna's hand and they walked across the short bridge. They were the only patrons. A man who introduced himself as Monsieur Berthillon led them to a small round marble table.

"*Nous voudrions crème glacée*," Anna said, impressing Berthold with her French, and apparently communicating adequately, since they were soon presented with a small bowl of ice cream and several cookies. They ate with two spoons from the same bowl.

Back outside, Berthold walked closer to Anna, put his arm around her, and was excited by the occasional feel of her hip against his.

"The *Parizer Haynt* has a matchmaking section," Anna said. She saw his crestfallen look. "I'm not looking for a match. I'm thinking we could transmit messages in advertisements."

Berthold said it was a good plan. By this time, after the dinner, the walk, the kiss, the ice cream, he was literally about to explode and would have agreed with any plan Anna suggested as long as they kept walking in the direction of their hotel.

***

When they paused in the lobby, Anna gave Berthold what he chose to interpret as a questioning look.

"I'll give you five minutes," he said, "and then I'll come to your room?"

She touched his cheek. Her finger was trembling and he wondered which of them was more nervous.

Berthold counted the three hundred seconds, each one an agony. He knocked lightly and the door opened. She stood in a thin black nightgown that took his breath away, then came into his arms; he felt for the first time the softness and heat of her body. Even in the midst of his passion, he knew this moment could never be repeated and that they would remember this embrace for as long as they lived. He wanted it to be perfect, but was suddenly terrified he would do something wrong.

Anna backed away.

"I've never done this before."

"Neither have I," Berthold said, but realizing she was as frightened as he was gave him confidence.

Anna watched as he undressed, then stood absolutely still as he raised her nightgown and dropped it to the floor. They stared at each other, savoring the sight.

"I have a condom," Anna said.

Shortly after dawn, Berthold felt the warmth of her bare leg against his. Opening his eyes, he saw her face. Even in his dreams, he had never dared to imagine her sleeping naked next to him. The feelings that swelled in him could never be reduced to words, but from somewhere came the belief that he and Anna fit together in some mysterious way in their special part of a vast and unknowable universe.

Then his heart went cold. The universe he shared so lovingly with Anna Gorska also included Adolf Hitler and Josef Goebbels.

***

Berthold eased his way out of bed, dressed quietly and left the room, returning with coffee and several croissants. Anna was still sleeping and he thought her face against the pillow was the most beautiful sight he had ever seen. When she opened her eyes and smiled, he walked over and kissed her tenderly on her cheek.

They ate ravenously, after which they heated water over a gas burner and bathed each other, soaping and caressing until the excitement became unbearable and they ran dripping to the bed to make love again. Hours later, they reluctantly dressed for Anna's appointment at the *Parizer Haynt*.

Wolman had many questions about the status of the Zionist movement in Poland, and Anna reported that the inability to get to Palestine was devastating to many Polish Jews, but there was hope the situation might change.

"Don't fool yourself," Wolman said. "The British have taken their position and will not change. If Jews want to get to Palestine, they'll have to do it illegally."

There was more discussion between Anna and Wolman about deteriorating conditions for Jews in Poland, the Polish and French attitudes toward Hitler, and the future prospects of the Communist Party inside and outside of Russia.

"Can I purchase an ad in your matchmaking column?" Anna asked when there was a lull in the conversation.

Wolman looked pointedly at Berthold, then said, "Of course."

"Could I send you a telegram from Warsaw and have you print a message? And Berthold from Munich could do the same?"

Wolman nodded and they worked out the logistics. Berthold would be known as "Rolland" and Anna would be "Threepenny." Wolman never asked why they wanted to do this, nor did he ask for payment.

**

On the way back to their hotel, they stopped for provisions: two baguettes, several packages of cheese, a bottle of wine, and after a discussion they could not have without giggling, several more condoms.

They rushed into Anna's room, made love with energy and haste, shared a piece of baguette slathered with soft creamy cheese, and made love again.

"Do you think we have enough condoms?" Berthold asked.

"We'll see," Anna said. "I've always thought Roza was more "adventurous" than me, but not any more."

Berthold was reluctant to comment on their lovemaking, nervous that any discussion would reveal how little he knew, and perhaps also reflect negatively on his performance. But Anna had no such reservations.

"This is everything I could have hoped for," she said.

Berthold took a chance. "Not bad for a first time?"

"Not bad at all," Anna said. "Besides, doesn't last night count?"

Anna took a bite of bread. "You know, we have a very small house in Ciechanow. Certain things you hear." She blushed and stopped.

"My mother has a boy friend," Berthold said. "Actually he's here, in Paris." Berthold snuggled behind Anna and caressed her shoulders, her back, her bottom, several times each. "Mother gave me Henri's phone number, in case we needed anything while we were here." He kissed the back of her neck. "But I think we have everything we need."

"It's so strange," Anna said, "to think of our parents naked with each other."

Neither of them chose to say anything more about the idea. For them at that moment, it was as if they had just invented something entirely new, just for them, never done by any other human being, especially their parents.

"How," Berthold asked, "did you come to have such a close relationship with Marshal Pilsudski?

"Back to the real world?"

"Just for a while."

"I'll take that as a promise," Anna said. She took a minute to frame her thoughts. "It starts in 1908. Pilsudski was organizing a revolution against the Russians and needed money to equip and train his fighters; he decided to rob a train carrying Russian tax money to Vilnius. My Grandfather Kamon and his brother Edel were part of Pilsudski's gang. They stopped the train and stole the money; quite a bit of money."

"Was anyone killed in the robbery?"

"I think there was, but Grandfather never really says. Edel was recognized and had to flee the country; he went to London and then America. Anyway, Marshal Pilsudski is very fond of both Kamon and Edel, so when Madame Meltzer introduced me to him, he sort of took me under his wing."

"Madame Meltzer?"

"She was the first woman elected to the Polish parliament. She came to Ciechanow when I was still in high school, part of a political tour to drum up support for Marshal Pilsudski to return to the government. I interviewed her and wrote an article which was published"

Anna prepared more bread and cheese, poured two full glasses of wine, and served Berthold, who had remained in bed, wearing a huge smile and nothing else, watching every turn of Anna's naked body as if it was the first woman's body in the entire history of the world.

"Your turn," Anna said between sips of wine. "How did you manage to get this strange man Putzi to arrange my interview with Hitler?"

"I had been to see Goebbels, so I knew that Putzi also had an office in the Brown House. You had stopped answering my letters and then I learned you had seen the photo. I was desperate to see you again, so I came up with a crazy idea. I figured I had nothing to lose."

Anna started to giggle.

"What are you laughing about?

"Putzi's name."

"What about it?"

"Do you know what *putz* means in Yiddish?"

Anna was staring at Berthold's erect penis.

"How would I know that?"

Anna pointed.

"No," Berthold said.

"Yes."

***

Later, still wrapped in each other's arms, Anna said, "I also lost a brother, but he died the day he was born, so it wasn't the same. You had the opportunity to love your brother for many years."

"More than that. He was my hero, bigger, stronger, a veteran of the war, involved in important events. What was your brother's name?"

"Yonah, but of course I never got to call him that."

Berthold put on his shirt, found a spare blanket in the closet, and wrapped it around Anna.

"You lost your brother, and then your best friend went to America," Anna said. "You must be so lonely."

188

"And then you went away from me."

"I was shocked by that photo. I didn't understand. But now I'm back, thanks to you and Putzi."

"I don't want to ever be apart again," Berthold said. "I don't mean just physically."

"I know what you mean. I want the same thing."

"I don't know if I can continue to fool the Nazis."

"I think they'll help you," Anna said. "They want to be fooled. They need you to be their hero."

"What will we become?" Berthold asked.

"Whatever it is," Anna said, "I think it will be very different from whatever our dreams have been until now. But we will share our futures, whatever they will be.

Chapter 35

Berthold's train ride back to Munich was bittersweet. He kept imagining Anna in the seat next to him and once he almost reached for the hand of the elderly woman who was actually sitting there.

He finally fell asleep and then awoke with a start, drenched with sweat, his breath coming in gulps, his pulse racing. The nightmare of Hitler's speech, when Dietrich had taken him to the Burgerbraukeller, had never been so real.

***

Berthold barely had time to say hello to his mother before they were startled by heavy pounding on the apartment door; whoever it was must have been lurking outside.

"Herr Hanfstaengl needs to see you immediately."

At the Brown House, Putzi was indeed frantic.

"The newspapers are going crazy. Hitler is having a nervous breakdown. What did Geli tell Anna? Will Anna write about her? Where have you been? I've been trying to find you for days."

"I was in Paris," Berthold said, "and you can relax. Anna is not going to write anything about Geli Raubal."

This didn't stop Putzi. "There have been stories every day in the socialist newspapers. Some blockheads are even suggesting Hitler killed her or had her killed."

Did he? Berthold almost asked before he caught himself.

Putzi flew from one issue to another, all related to Geli. "There's resentment about party money Hitler spent on expensive clothes for Geli ... my view is she was just an empty-headed little slut with no brains or character ... she did have nice tits ... he was infatuated with her ... paid for her singing lessons, thought she could become a Wagnerian heroine."

Putzi came up for air and took a deep breath before archly passing judgment on that idea.

"She was not an apt pupil."

***

Putzi went on relating the latest Nazi gossip, in the course of which he mentioned the name Reinhard Heydrich. Berthold remembered the name and the right cross to the chest Heydrich had landed.

"I've met him," Berthold said. "Who is he?"

"He's Himmler's new chief of the party's intelligence service. Been working here in this building for several weeks now, supposedly building a network of spies and informers to root out anyone who says something bad about Adolf. How did you meet him?"

Berthold explained.

"Be glad if he's your friend," Putzi said. "I think he'd be a dangerous man to have as an enemy."

Chapter 36

"Did you use the condoms I gave you?" Roza asked.

"Yes." Anna blushed. "And we bought more."

"Oh my God! Tell me everything!"

Anna first felt embarrassed. Then she felt disloyal. Then she told Roza every single intimate detail she could remember and perhaps even added a few embellishments. She also told Roza about her meetings with Putzi, Hitler and Goebbels, but said nothing about Berthold's Jewish ancestry or their plans to spy on the Nazis.

Roza asked about the Berlin photograph and Anna repeated Berthold's story. Roza looked skeptical but Anna said she thought it was the truth.

Later, when she was alone, Anna allowed herself to consider whether the way her body tingled when she thought about Berthold did not make her less questioning about that photo than she might otherwise have been.

She was also honest with herself that she was using Berthold in furtherance of her own career. That didn't make her proud, and it created a confusing tension that affected all her thoughts and feelings. In the end, she justified her actions and the risks by considering the horrible flood of evil that would come to the world if Adolf Hitler ever achieved power. She wrote none of these thoughts in her diary.

***

Later that day, Anna and Irena Meltzer met with Marshal Pilsudski.

"Did you tell Hitler what I told you?" Pilsudski asked

"Hitler left. I told Goebbels."

"That will do. Goebbels tells Hitler everything."

Anna started to say more but Pilsudski interrupted. "Did your friend explain that photograph and were you satisfied with his explanation?"

"Yes."

"He's not a Nazi?"

"It's complicated but no, he's not, although he does have connections with Nazi leaders and insiders that ... might be helpful."

Anna described in great detail her interviews with Hitler and Goebbels, about which she was writing several long articles for *Haynt* and a shorter article for TIME Magazine in America.

"Of course I will not include anything you think should remain confidential."

They discussed what could and could not be written and then Pilsudski cupped his chin in his hand and sat deeply in thought for several minutes. A smile gradually filled his wrinkled face. Anna could not remember seeing him so pleased.

"Thank you, Anna," he said. "You've provided a very valuable service for Poland. Hitler will be confused. Perhaps he'll send someone to talk to me, which will give me the chance to learn more about his intentions and decide what I must do."

Pilsudski rose and took several unsteady steps, looking weaker than Anna had ever seen him. He coughed violently, but then his eyes took on a sparkle.

"I want Hitler to think Poland is afraid of him ... right up to the moment the Polish army marches into Germany."

Anna was stunned and Meltzer looked to be in shock.

"We will have one chance to defeat Germany and maintain our independence," Pilsudski said. "Only one."

Chapter 37

1990 - Munich

Marissa had invited her father to come to Munich to meet Berthold Becker face-to-face, and he had said he would, but she did not fully believe him until he had actually boarded the plane, and by that time she was sorry she had asked him. She knew he still hated all Germans and had not forgiven those who had lived during the Nazi years for what they had done or failed to do. He found it despicable that forty-five years later many Germans still refused to express what he considered sufficiently sincere repentance, and he could find no words harsh enough to describe those who still thought Hitler had been a great leader.

Marissa feared Abraham's feelings might be so clear to Berthold, who missed nothing, that he would clam up, destroying the project and her chances of academic advancement. She had taken the risk because she wanted his face-to-face perspective on Berthold Becker, and also because she wanted to work with him, to enjoy his company and his mind.

Now they were in Munich and the time had come. Abraham was outwardly nervous when Berthold joined them for coffee at the Hotel Bayerischer Hof, but he stiffly extended his hand and Berthold took it. Marissa watched, tense and not overly hopeful. Abraham spoke first, in English, "My daughter says her sessions with you are going very well."

"You can be very proud of her," Berthold said, also in English. "Her mind works like yours in many ways."

All of Marissa's discussions with Berthold had been in German, and she had expected to be called on to translate. She was thrilled by Berthold's decision to speak English, which she felt was a confirmation of the respect Berthold had previously expressed for her father. Berthold suggested they meet for dinner that evening at the Café Luitpold. Abraham stiffened and Marissa imagined how difficult it would be for him to have dinner in public with the Nazi he had prosecuted and still had not forgiven. But he did not object and they made the arrangements.

**

At the Café Luitpold, Berthold spoke to the headwaiter and they were led to the particular table he had reserved.

"Sixty years ago, when I was still at university," Berthold said, "I came here with my mother. We sat at this very table just after we had seen Hitler going to the Opera."

Marissa remembered what Berthold had said about that conversation with his mother, how he had felt repulsed by Hitler. She believed he was telling the truth about his feelings then, but then why had he later done the things that brought him to the dock at Nuremberg?

They placed their orders and exchanged small talk through dinner, skirting around sensitive issues, until Abraham said, "There were things about you I had no idea of in Nuremberg."

"Some of which you now know," Berthold said, the edge of a smile in his eyes.

Some, Marissa thought, as she watched her father begin to react angrily to Berthold's smile, then rein himself in. She cautioned herself not to push faster than either man felt comfortable going.

"Would it have made a difference at my trial if you had known about my Jewish ancestry?" Berthold continued, apparently determined to provoke a reaction.

"Yes, of course," Abraham answered without hesitation or undue emotion. "It would have been stunning information for all of us."

"Would it have made it better or worse for me?"

Abraham and Marissa had discussed that very question many times; now Abraham answered Berthold as he had answered his daughter, saying, "I really don't know. By itself, it might well have made things worse for you, but it would not have been by itself. It would have led to other disclosures."

"It wouldn't have changed what I had done," Berthold said, his eyes now sad, focused directly at the prosecutor who had tried so hard to see him hang.

***

Marissa and Abraham met with Berthold several more times over the next two days and also went with him to visit some of the sites in Munich that were part of his story, including the now empty lot where the Great Synagogue had once been, destroyed during Kristallknacht.

"I can still hear that rock crashing through the window at Leonard's bar mitzvah," Berthold said, grimacing.

On their last day in Munich, father and daughter had a hurried breakfast before heading to the airport, from which Marissa would go to Jerusalem, Abraham to New York.

"I re-read Anna's Nuremberg testimony last night," Marissa said. "Why do you think she didn't mention Berthold's Jewish background?"

"Perhaps she wasn't sure if it would help or hurt."

"What do you think of Berthold now that you've met him?"

"I don't like him any more now than I did then," Abraham said, flashing the anger he had worked hard to hide for the past several days. "He admits he did terrible things."

Marissa thought for a moment. "Yes, but it's the other things he did that we need to know about, the things that brought Anna Gorska to Nuremberg." She smiled at her father. "You were good with Berthold."

"I didn't want to create problems for your book - our book. I know how important it is to you. And now that I don't have a case to win I can be more patient."

They laughed together and then Abraham asked, "Do you think he's sorry?"

"Yes I do. My sense is that Berthold is consumed with regret." Marissa paused. "And the fact that Anna came to Nuremberg for him says a lot."

"She was in love with him," Abraham said.

"I don't think that's the whole story."

"Berthold is still trying to work things out," Abraham said. "After all these years, it seems he's still wondering if there were other options he might have chosen."

Marissa noted that Abraham had said 'Berthold' instead of 'Becker.' It was the first time he had done so. She had been considering a bold move with her father and now decided to propose it. She took a deep breath. "Why don't you stay in Munich and work with Berthold for a few days while I go to Jerusalem?"

"Good idea," Abraham answered even before Marissa had completed the question.

Then he added something he must have been mulling over. "You know, it wasn't just the Nazis who were pulling at him. His mother, Richard Goldman, and of course Anna, were all trying to direct his actions. In 1931, he was just twenty-one years old. It must have been confusing and overwhelming for him."

They finished breakfast and Marissa went to the airport while Abraham went to the hotel desk to let them know he was not checking out after all.

***

In Jerusalem, the conversation returned to Paris.

"Those two days," Anna said, "were the most wonderful time of my entire life. Those memories sustained me through many dark times."

Anna's eyes sparkled with the look that must have captivated Berthold sixty years before. Marissa wondered how many more times they had been together, if they had ever again made love, and what their relationship was now.

"At Nuremberg," Marissa said, "you never mentioned Berthold's Jewish ancestry."

"My only goal at Nuremberg was to keep Berthold alive, so I said what I thought would achieve that goal, and nothing more."

Anna grew reflective and Marissa waited.

"When we were in Paris," Anna said, "we truly thought we could make a difference. We believed that if those who understood Hitler's demented thinking - and many did - could summon the courage and will to act against him, then Weimar democracy would have a chance to succeed, and if it did, Germany would have no need for a *Führer*. We thought we could help that happen. We were so young."

***

Abraham was uncomfortable, full of second thoughts about his decision to stay in Munich. Instead of moving forward with Berthold's story, his focus kept returning to Nuremberg.

"If Anna Gorska had argued mitigating circumstances at Nuremberg," Abraham said to Berthold, "the judges would not have been moved, nor would I."

"How do you know?" Berthold asked. "You have no idea what those circumstances might have been."

Abraham was startled by Berthold's challenge. Berthold saw his reaction and acknowledged it with a nod.

"The Allies' sole purpose at Nuremberg," Berthold said, "was to punish some prominent Nazis, not to explore why any of us might have acted as we did."

"Were there facts in your case that might have made a difference to a more open-minded tribunal?"

"That's really two questions," Berthold said. "Of course there were reasons why I did what I did, but would any of that have made a difference at Nuremberg, even if the judges were open to hear it?" His eyebrows rose. "I think not," he said, then added, "Will it make a difference to you now?" He sighed. "I know you hate Germans, and you hate me."

Their eyes locked. Abraham looked truly surprised.

"Any German with a conscience understands he is hated wherever he goes," Berthold said. "I don't expect to change that, but I do want you to understand why so many Germans clearly saw Hitler's evil and still allowed him to come to power. Not only Germans. The French, the British, the Americans, and the Vatican were all culpable, and they've all been trying to hide their failures ever since."

***

This was the moment, Abraham later told Marissa, when he realized the full potential of what they were involved in. Berthold Becker had experienced the Nazi horror from a unique perspective, and he was willing to share what he had seen and knew. Anna Gorska had pursued this goal for forty-five years, beginning at Nuremberg or maybe even before. Now Marissa and he were privileged to be picking up that cudgel.

"Gorska's testimony was brilliant," Abraham said, expressing his understanding even as it suddenly came to him. "She worked out the only possible way to save Berthold's life and presented it flawlessly. Now here we are, all these years later, seeking to understand how Hitler came to power and who could have prevented it, just as Anna so eloquently argued at Nuremberg."

Chapter 38

November 1931 - Northeim

Berthold had been in Northeim for several days, working intently on the new Reichsbahn signaling systems. When he had time, he went to Nazi headquarters and performed whatever tasks Local Group Leader Ernst Krueger assigned.

"The big day is coming," Krueger said, referring to the November 9 anniversary of the *Putsch* march. Ghastly memories, Berthold thought, his stomach tightening.

"We want you to join us on the stage."

This was something Berthold wanted very much *not* to do, but knew he could not refuse. The Nazi chains were tightening, and there was nothing he could do about it.

When the day came, a large crowd assembled at Northeim's circus grounds. Berthold felt their angry, anxious mood. Conditions in Germany had not improved. Extended unemployment had driven many to confusion and depression. The suicide rate had risen. And the Weimar government seemed pathetically impotent.

Berthold stood on the small stage, shivering in the cold. Ernst Krueger read (from *Mein Kampf)* Hitler's description of the *Putsch* and the names of the martyrs. He adjusted the order so that Dietrich Becker's name came last. Krueger raised Berthold's hand in his.

"Here," he shouted, "is the brother of the revered *Putsch* martyr Dietrich Becker who gave his life to save the *Führer*."

Signs suddenly appeared, boldly printed in red and black, emblazoned with the Nazi swastika and containing two names: Dietrich Becker; Berthold Becker. A prolonged ecstatic cheer rose from the crowd. "Heil! Heil! Heil!" Berthold had become a real-life hero, an antidote for troubled minds. He raised his right arm like everyone else. He felt numb and sick.

After the ceremony, Berthold was invited to join a group of stormtroopers at a nearby beer hall, but he declined, saying truthfully he had a pounding headache. He walked slowly back to his hotel, huddled in his coat, his breath fogging the air, his mind trying to make sense of what he was getting ever deeper into.

His grandmother was a Jew. He felt an irrational anger at his mother for telling him about his ancestry, and was ever more fearful of becoming the object of Hitler-provoked Jew-hatred. Leonard had often felt that hatred.

He missed Leonard, far away in America, and Anna, far away in Warsaw. Instead of them, his days were filled with loathsome Nazis, and he could not imagine how that was ever going to change.

***

"You were quite the man last night."

Berthold looked up to see the smiling face of Albert Mueller.

"You were there?"

"Oh yes, far back in the crowd. It seems you're taking your commitment to Goebbels seriously."

"I do what I'm asked," Berthold answered flatly.

"Such enthusiasm," Mueller said. "You still have reservations?"

"I understand why the Nazi message is so appealing. Germany is in trouble, Hitler says he'll make things better, and many Germans are desperate to believe him."

Berthold paused and Mueller said, "But ..."

"It's the violence, Albert. And the hatred of Jews. Do you know that Jews are harassed now on trains. Stormtroopers get on the trains and beat up Jews. On our trains!"

"Why do you care about Jews?" Mueller asked.

A stab of fear grabbed at Berthold's gut and he felt faint. He looked down at the papers on his desk, hoping Mueller had not seen his face. *Did he know?* No, of course he didn't know; nobody knew. But Berthold understood he had made a serious mistake, one which Mueller would surely report to Goebbels. Frantic, no words came to him, until finally he sputtered, "It's just not right to treat any people like that, and on our trains it's a disgrace."

"Jews are our enemies!" Mueller said, raising his voice as he quoted Hitler. "Jews are the cause of all of Germany's problems. Germany cannot be great until the Jews are put down."

An ugly smile crossed Mueller's face. "Do you have a problem with our *Führer's* policies about Jews?"

Berthold was too frightened to answer, but Mueller saved him, at least for the moment.

"This is not an argument we should be having," Mueller said. "I came here to tell you the Reichsbahn is very pleased with your work. When you graduate, you'll be offered an important management job in the Munich regional headquarters."

***

The next day Krueger sent a message asking Berthold to come see him when he was finished his work.

"You have a new assignment," Krueger said, "direct from Goebbels. He wants you to meet with men and women who have recently joined the Nazi Party to find out what it was that attracted them. He doesn't say why - he never does - but I suspect he wants to fine-tune his propaganda message based on what seems to have worked before."

Berthold held back a sigh and responded with as much enthusiasm as he could muster. "Will you send someone to their homes and invite them to a meeting? No stormtroopers. I want a quiet, uninterrupted meeting."

"Yes, of course," Krueger said. "Everyone will be thrilled to meet the brother of our *Putsch* martyr."

Krueger's words expressed confidence, but he looked uncomfortable. "You know," he said, "this is very important for me. What we do in Northeim is reported in Munich and evaluations are made about our leadership here. Failure is not tolerated. I need you to do a good job with this."

Chapter 39

1990 - Munich

"Those few days in Northeim," Berthold said to Abraham the next time they met, "changed everything. From that point on, all of my work, whether for the Reichsbahn or the Nazi Party, was haunted by the twisted face of Josef Goebbels."

"Tell me about the meeting with the new Nazis," Abraham said.

"There were several hundred people there. Krueger provided three secretaries so every word could be taken down and sent to Goebbels. The first man to speak was a respected physician who read from prepared notes. He recounted Germany's problems and argued persuasively about the ineffectiveness of Germany's parliamentary government. Then his conclusion: We need a strong leader to take charge. I believe Adolf Hitler is that leader."

"Was that the general feeling?" Abraham asked.

"Yes. Many others said essentially the same thing. One young man put it particularly well: Our lives are an unending humiliation and we have nothing more to lose. We're willing to take a chance on Hitler and the Nazis."

"Did anyone mention Jews?" Abraham asked.

"Not until I asked if anyone shared the views of the Nazis regarding Jews. Then several spoke up and others nodded their agreement. The consensus was that Germans should listen to Hitler when he says the Jews are not good for Germany."

"But that had not been at the top of their minds?" Abraham asked.

"I think it was just beneath the surface, and deeply held, a quiet feeling that was actually more frightening to me than Hitler's rants and taunts. Germans saw no need to defend Jews, verbally or physically, and of course as time went on, most of them never did."

***

When Abraham repeated this conversation to Marissa upon her return from Jerusalem, she offered her analysis. "It seems to me that most Germans never matched Hitler's level of Jew-hatred. But, and it's a big but, they had been conditioned to dislike Jews and to blame them for whatever was bad in their lives. They accepted the premise of Hitler's arguments, if not the vehemence."

"Conditioned?"

"There were many causes. Some Germans resented the freedoms Jews had obtained in the nineteenth century and the success they had made of their lives since the fetters had come off. Others accepted the scapegoating of the Jews for losing the war. Some were frightened by the association of international Jewish financiers with both inflation and depression and by the often repeated insanity that this was part of the Jews plot to take over the world. Almost everyone accepted the constant linkage of Jews with communists. And underlying all that, they accepted as gospel truth the Catholic and Lutheran demonizing of Jews which had gone on for centuries and had become increasingly virulent during the 1920s."

"So whatever the problem," Abraham said, "Germans believed Jews were the cause, which was certainly easier than actually taking responsibility themselves."

Chapter 40

January 1932 - Warsaw

One of the letters Berthold sent from Munich had not reached Anna in Warsaw. Following the system they had worked out, Berthold had placed five short messages to "Threepenny" in the *Parizer Haynt* and subsequently mailed five letters to Anna in Warsaw, each one dealing with a separate topic. Anna had received four of the letters and confirmed each with a short message to "Rolland." To make sure he understood, Anna wrote an otherwise innocuous letter to Berthold, mentioning as an aside how much she appreciated the four letters she had received from him.

Resting her pen, she closed her eyes and saw Paris - the old buildings and narrow streets, the moon shimmering on the river, croissant crumbs on the sheets. Longing to express her feelings but unable to conjure the right words, she finished her letter with a quote from a poem she had recently read ...

I see your eyes everywhere.
Your eyes kiss me.
From afar your eyes love me.
From afar your eyes kiss me.

***

Marshal Pilsudski was away from Warsaw on an inspection tour of Polish military units; upon his return Anna asked for a meeting. First on her agenda was Berthold's report on Hitler's recent interactions with Hindenburg, which had not gone well for the *Führer*. Pilsudski laughed out loud at the image of the old Field Marshal berating the corporal and refusing to appoint him Chancellor, but he quickly turned serious.

"I knew Hindenburg before and after the war," Pilsudski said. "He was never very bright, nor imaginative, and I expect his discernment has not improved with age. He may despise Hitler as beneath him, but I think there's a good chance the corporal will eventually out-maneuver the Field Marshal. Hitler is forty-three, Hindenburg is eighty-five. Hitler's game is to be there when Hindenburg falters, as indeed he must."

Pilsudski paused, a pensive look on his face, and Anna wondered if he was reflecting on the state of his own health. Or maybe he was thinking about his own *coup*, knowing just how easy it had been to take over a government. But when he spoke, it was about Berthold.

"You've developed a remarkable source of information. How does your friend learn these things?"

"Much of it comes from that strange man Ernst Hanfstaengl, and Berthold also sees Goebbels from time to time."

"This is a dangerous business for a young man. How is he managing?"

Anna was often tormented by just this question; she wasn't really sure how Berthold was holding up under the pressure and said so to Pilsudski.

"One of the most important aspects of your job is to help him be strong," the Marshal said. "Whatever happens."

***

As Anna was wondering how she could help Berthold stay strong when they never saw each other or even spoke, Roza came into their apartment with a bouncing step and a huge grin.

"What are you so excited about?" Anna asked.

"I have a job! Yesterday I went to see Ascher Lowenfield. Remember we met him and his wife after *Lag b'Omer* services. I don't know if he remembered me but he surely knows who you are." She drew herself up proudly. "You are now speaking to the newest junior administrative assistant at the Lowenfield department store."

"How wonderful," Anna said. "I'm thrilled for you."

Roza looked at the papers spread all over the apartment. "Is this your big article, the one Gruenbaum wants you to write about Jew-hatred in Poland?"

"I'll tell you about the article, but first there's something I should have shared with you long ago. It's about Berthold."

"There's more to that beautiful boy than a quick jump into bed in Paris?" Roza said with a laugh. "But let me guess. You know what I think? I think he sends reports to you which you pass on to Marshal Pilsudski."

"You figured that out?"

"I've been putting pieces together," Roza said, her mood darkening. "Berthold is really taking some serious chances."

Anna started to tear up and Roza put her arm around her.

"We may already be compromised," Anna said. "One of the letters Berthold sent has not been received. Probably it just got lost, but it's terrifying to think the Nazis might have caught on. Since I failed to confirm one of his messages, he hasn't sent any more. We need a different system."

Roza's frown changed to a smile. "I have a suggestion." She paused to elevate the suspense; Anna waived her hands to prod her on. "One of my new duties at the Lowenfield store will involve correspondence with other department stores all over Europe, including a certain Goldmann Department Store in Munich."

"Roza, you're a genius."

"So I've been trying to tell you."

"I'll talk to Ascher Lowenfield," Anna said, "and see if he'll go along with your idea." Then she added, "Do you think any of this can actually do any good?"

"It's certainly better than doing nothing," Roza said. "Your columns may have more impact than you realize. Besides, nobody has a better plan."

Chapter 41

February 1932 - Munich

Berthold learned from one of Putzi's offhand remarks that the Nazis were having serious discussions with the Vatican. He went as soon as he could to discuss this development with Monsignor Johannes.

"I should have gotten back to you long before this," the Monsignor said when Berthold arrived. He collected some papers on his desk and put them in a folder, then said, "Now, where did we leave off?"

"Actually," Berthold said, "I'm not here to continue our previous discussion. As important as the sad history of Jews and the Church may be, I think my topic today may be even more consequential, at least in the short run."

Monsignor Johannes looked surprised. "You have my attention."

Berthold had carefully rehearsed how he would open the conversation, and as a result he spoke a little stiffly. "It has come to my attention that there are talks underway between high-ranking Nazis and the Vatican, and that Hitler regards an alliance with the Vatican as critical to his efforts to become Chancellor. It is my belief that these discussions, if they are known to you, would not be seen favorably by yourself and His Eminence Cardinal Faulhaber. If my assumption is correct, I would like to work with you to hinder any deal Hitler wants to make."

Monsignor Johannes sat like a statue, his eyes focused on the wall behind Berthold. There was no evidence he was breathing and it seemed he had even stopped blinking.

"Your mother told me you were a very special person," Johannes finally said, "but this is beyond anything I might have imagined. How on earth have you learned what you just told me?"

"Are you aware of these discussions in Rome?"

Monsignor Johannes lips showed the briefest flicker of a smile, and Berthold thought he was perhaps not used to having his questions answered with a question. But there was no anger in his response.

"We are aware of the discussions in Rome," Johannes said, "and you are correct that we do not view them favorably."

Berthold now answered Johannes' question. "I learned about these meetings from a Nazi named Ernst Hanfstaengl. Do you understand the danger to me in having this conversation with you?"

"Yes," the Monsignor said. "There is danger on our side as well. I want to talk more, but first I must receive authorization. You can be assured that, this time, it will not take six months to get back to you."

***

Two days later, Berthold was back in the Cathedral.

"From this point forward," Johannes said, "we're in this together and I promise to be fully honest with you. There will be no secrets. Will you agree to the same?"

Berthold nodded his agreement. Monsignor Johannes took a few seconds to compose himself and then said, "We are going to discuss matters which involve German Chancellor Brüning, Cardinal Secretary of State Pacelli, and Pope Pius XI."

Berthold began to say something but Johannes held his hands in a manner to suggest patience.

"I'm going to trust you," the Monsignor said, "with confidential information that could be very damaging to Cardinal Faulhaber if it reached the wrong ears."

Berthold felt tension but not fear. He was excited by what he recognized as a potentially powerful liaison, perhaps comparable to Anna's relationship with Marshal Pilsudski, and was comforted to think he might now have a collaborator with whom he could share the growing complexity of his life.

"Chancellor Heinrich Brüning," Johannes said, "is a good Catholic and has long been a major figure in the Catholic Center Party. Last summer he met with Cardinal Secretary of State Eugenio Pacelli in Rome and tried to convince him of the dangers Adolf Hitler poses to Germany and to the Catholic Church. Cardinal Pacelli was not receptive to Brüning's warnings, and also failed to pass on to the Holy Father, as Brüning had requested, a collection of documents supporting the case against Hitler."

Johannes looked at Berthold for a long moment and then said, "You're probably wondering why I told you this story."

Monsignor Johannes smiled and Berthold could literally feel their conspiracy taking shape.

"It so happens," Johannes said, "that Marshal Josef Pilsudski has a special relationship with Pope Pius and often exchanges correspondences with the Holy Father which do not pass through Cardinal Pacelli."

"What does Marshal Pilsudski have to do with me?" Berthold asked, probing to learn what Johannes knew.

"It has come to our attention that you have a friend who is quite close to Marshal Pilsudski. She is also a respected reporter with international connections."

"How do you know that?"

"There is virtually nothing we cannot find out if it is important to us," Johannes said.

Again Berthold started to speak and again the Monsignor stopped him.

"Perhaps," Johannes said, "it is not beyond the realm of possibility that such an industrious person as your friend Anna Gorska might obtain a copy of Chancellor Brüning's documents from some unknown source and in turn present these to Marshal Pilsudski in such a way that he would be inclined to pass them on to the Holy Father, unbeknownst to Cardinal Pacelli."

Johannes placed a thick envelope on the table.

"Cardinal Faulhaber and many other German bishops have repeatedly issued condemnations and warnings regarding the threat posed by Adolf Hitler and the Nazis. Cardinal Pacelli cannot be allowed to keep these warnings from the Holy Father."

"Why," Berthold asked, "doesn't Cardinal Faulhaber simply take the documents to Rome and give them to the Pope?"

Taking a deep breath, Johannes said, "The Cardinal would be subject to the same rules as any other bishop wishing to see the Pope about matters of international consequence. In order to get an audience with the Holy Father, he would first have to present himself to the Cardinal Secretary of State. Cardinal Faulhaber would not be treated any differently or with any greater respect than was Chancellor Brüning."

Berthold was stunned by the substance of Johannes' request and also by his frankness regarding the limitations under which Cardinal Faulhaber was constrained. It was hard to accept that a man who had so much power in Munich could be so powerless in Rome.

"I know how difficult this will be," Johannes said, "and how dangerous. I would never ask such a thing if the Cardinal and I did not believe that Hitler, if he ever becomes Chancellor, would be an utter catastrophe for Germany."

Berthold reached for the envelope and Johannes placed his hand over Berthold's so that both were holding it.

"Thank you," the Monsignor said.

***

Berthold had walked home from the Cathedral with the envelope concealed inside his coat, checking repeatedly to make sure it was still there. Now it commanded the center of the Becker's dining table like an unexploded bomb. Richard, Judith, Elisabeth and he all stared at the envelope as if it was a live thing mutely daring them to act.

"It's not sealed," Berthold said. "Nothing with Monsignor Johannes is unintended, so I conclude he wants us to read the documents before sending them to Anna."

They each read Chancellor Brüning's carefully reasoned arguments regarding the Nazi threat and looked at copies of Hitler's speeches and other Nazi propaganda that proved the threat was real. All the while Berthold's anger was rising.

"It's infuriating that Cardinal Pacelli would keep this from the Pope," he said. "Do we agree to send this to Anna?"

They all nodded.

"If you will write a cover note," Richard said to Berthold, "I'll post it to the Lowenfield store first thing in the morning."

***

"I'm pleased that you are working with Monsignor Johannes," Elisabeth said after the Goldmanns had left, "but there are things I must now tell you."

Berthold heard the tension in his mother's voice and feared what was to come.

"When Anna was here to interview Hitler," Elisabeth said, "and it became clear that this business was even more dangerous than we might have imagined, I decided to see if I could get the Church to destroy its records of my mother's conversion. I went to Monsignor Johannes, who is my confessor and who I trust completely, and asked him to find and destroy the records, which he did. Those records are now gone."

"Why did you not consult with me before you went to Monsignor Johannes?"

"Perhaps I should have, but at the time you had taken on such a huge burden and I thought it would just add more pressure on top of everything else. Did I make a mistake? Are you angry with me?"

"I think you did make a mistake," Berthold said. He saw his mother's face sag. "But I'm not angry. I know you would only do what you thought was best."

Elisabeth collapsed into Berthold's arms; it was the first time their roles had been so reversed.

Chapter 42

Anna delivered the package to Marshal Pilsudski and sat quietly while he read Chancellor Brüning's documents.

"These papers were given to Cardinal Pacelli to be forwarded to the Pope and Pacelli failed to do so?"

"So it appears," Anna said. "Brüning says the papers were not passed on and Cardinal Faulhaber's sources in Rome indicate that is true."

"Faulhaber's sources are impressive," Pilsudski said. "He learns about Berthold's connection to you, and your association with me. And of course he is right in wanting to share Brüning's fear of what Hitler would do if he ever achieved power."

"You will help?" Anna asked.

"My military aide is going to Paris next week," Pilsudski said. "I'll direct him to stop in Rome on the way. My friend Pius will see him."

Chapter 43

February 1932 - Munich

Berthold was meeting with Putzi, this time in the Brown House. In the midst of a flow of innocuous conversation, Putzi asked, "Do you think it odd that Hitler never mentioned Jews in his big speech to industrialists at Dusseldorf?"

Berthold didn't answer. Putzi cocked an eyebrow. "But you seem to mention them all the time. Apparently you expressed concerns about Jews being beaten on trains. Goebbels wonders why you have such interest in Jews."

Mueller had reported his comment to Goebbels. While Berthold's insides quivered and sweat broke out on his forehead, Putzi kept right on talking, giving no indication he had noticed Berthold's reaction.

"Actually, I agree with you," Putzi said, "and so does the *Führer.*"

Still Berthold waited, confused and frightened.

"I told Goebbels," Putzi added, "you were concerned that an emphasis on Jews at this time is not helpful to the Nazi movement. That's exactly why Hitler didn't mention Jews in his Dusseldorf speech, why he directed Goebbels to tone down Jew-hatred in all Nazi publications, and why he ordered the stormtroopers not to attack Jews. Hitler is hoping the world will forget his 'excessive attitude' toward Jews, at least until after he becomes Chancellor."

Putzi made a tiny nod and held his hands open just so before him, his wordless gestures communicating that he expected Berthold to recognize what he had done for him by twisting the words Berthold had actually spoken to Mueller into something quite different.

Why is Putzi protecting me?

"Goebbels, by the way," Putzi said, moving on, "was quite impressed with your feedback from Northeim. He said he's

217

already planning some changes in his propaganda as a result of your work." Putzi again switched topics. "What did you think of Marta Huber? Her mother is one of my wife's best friends."

Marta Huber had been present at a recent gathering in Putzi's apartment, Putzi's wife had introduced them, and Berthold had spent some time talking with her. "She's very nice," Berthold said, "but I'm really too busy to think about girls."

"I see. Well, not to worry, there'll be more young ladies set out for your inspection. Just stop bringing up Jews all the time and you'll have a slew of juicy young things to choose from." Putzi smiled. "Or maybe you prefer Jewish girls," he added, clearly amused. "How was Anna Gorska in Paris?"

Berthold's heart rate sputtered and he felt faint, but Putzi didn't expect an answer.

"Goebbels, by the way" Putzi said, "was thrilled with the reaction of the industrialists at Dusseldorf to the *Führer's* speech. He wonders if your Anna wrote an article. If she did, could you please get me a copy as soon as possible? Depending on what she wrote, maybe I can get her another interview with Hitler."

***

It was already dark when Berthold left Putzi's apartment to go to his previously arranged meeting with Richard Goldmann. Since he was walking very fast, he could not help but notice a short man in a non-descript overcoat, a hat drawn down over his eyes, scurrying to keep up with him. He slowed down; the man did likewise.

What am I going to do now?

Berthold heard sounds of yelling and headed toward them. As he had hoped, it was a group of communists, hollering slogans and looking for a fight. Predictably, Nazi stormtroopers appeared and obliged them. Berthold negotiated his way through the brawl, putting the chaos of fifty fighting men between himself and the man in the hat. He checked behind him several more times but his tail, if that's what it was, was no longer there.

Richard greeted him and led the way to his home office. Berthold had been in this room only once, nine years before on the night of the *Putsch*. The old wireless set had been pushed into a corner of one of the bookcases.

"How is Leonard?" Berthold asked. It had been well over a year since Leonard had left Munich. "My last letter from him is already several weeks old."

"We spoke on the transatlantic telephone yesterday."

While Richard reported on Leonard's recent progress both at New York University and at Bloomingdales, Berthold marveled at the idea of sitting in Munich and talking to someone in New York.

"There's something you should know," Berthold said. "A man followed me when I left Putzi's apartment, but I think I lost him before I came here."

"It has to be Goebbels," Richard said. Berthold, who had not yet told Richard about his blunder with Mueller, now did so, adding that Goebbels had learned of his remark and that Putzi, surprisingly, had covered for him.

When Berthold left the Goldmann house, the man he thought he had lost was standing across the street, not even trying to keep hidden.

***

At breakfast the next morning, Elisabeth asked about Berthold's meetings with Putzi and Richard, and in the course of answering, Berthold mentioned Marta Huber.

"I know her," Elisabeth said. "She's Henriette's daughter. Both she and her mother are my customers." She laughed scornfully. "The Nazis hate Jews but they have no problem buying Henri's designer clothes at the Jewish-owned department store."

It had been over two years since Berthold had first learned about Henri Bousquet. They had met several times when Henri had come to Munich and Berthold was well over his initial negative reaction to his mother having a lover. He was actually pleased she had found a partner with whom to share her life.

"I was followed from Putzi's flat to Richard's home. I'm pretty sure the man was sent by Goebbels."

Tears welled in Elisabeth's eyes. Berthold reached across the table and put his hand on his mother's shoulder.

"I'm so sorry to have gotten you into all this," Elisabeth said. "Are you sure you're not angry with me?"

"No, of course not," Berthold said, thinking maybe that was not quite true and that his mother knew it. "But it keeps getting worse. I'm being pulled in deeper and deeper. Whenever the Heil Hitlers begin, I feel sick to my stomach. I almost threw up the other night in Northeim."

"You should be at such a happy point in your life, about to graduate from college and begin your career."

Mother and son looked at each other, not happy with anything except the way their own relationship had grown and strengthened.

"I made a bad mistake the other day in Northeim. I told Albert Mueller it was awful that stormtroopers were attacking Jews on our trains. He passed on my remark and Putzi told me Goebbels mentioned it to him.

"Mueller is Goebbels' spy?"

"I had suspected so and this proves it. It's crazy, isn't it? Goebbels spies on me while I spy on him. The problem is he's likely much better at it than I am."

"Tell me more about this Albert Mueller."

Berthold recounted his recent interactions with Mueller. Then a thought came to him and he practically jumped out of his seat.

"I can call her! I can say I went to Richard's house last night to make arrangements to use Richard's telephone to call Anna to tell her about the possibility of a second interview with Hitler. If I tell that to Putzi, he'll tell Goebbels. Oh that's very good."

***

"Anna! Anna! It's so good to hear your voice."

Berthold was in Richard's office at the Goldmann store, talking to Anna at the *Haynt* offices in Warsaw.

"It's so nice to hear from you," Anna said, but her voice sounded restrained and puzzled, and Berthold understood why. This was a significant break from the protocol of contacting each other they had agreed upon, and she wasn't sure how to react. They were still nervous about the missing letter and were in fact still posting messages in the *Parizer Haynt*, although these were now decoys and were not followed by letters.

"Putzi asked me to find out if you heard Hitler's Dusseldorf speech and if you wrote an article about it."

"I did hear the speech, in Pilsudski's office," Anna said, her voice beginning to relax.

"Did you write an article?"

"Yes, it's already been published in *Haynt* and several other papers. Gruenbaum told me it's going to be in the *Muenster Post* tomorrow."

"Putzi won't read that socialist paper but I'll make sure he gets a copy. What did Pilsudski think?"

"It's all in the article."

"Putzi said if Hitler likes what you wrote, he'll try to get you another interview. Were you very critical?"

"Actually no. I summarized what Hitler said and suggested that his industrialist audience was likely to be favorably impressed. Some of those who attended were quoted later saying that if Hitler was willing to bend his message to court them, then he would also moderate his behavior if he became Chancellor and thus they could work with him."

"Hitler will like that," Berthold said.

There was a long silence until Anna said, "I hope you know what I'm thinking."

"Yes, I believe I do."

"I think of Paris every day," Anna said. "Roza says I walk around with a goofy smile, but I don't care."

There was another long silence and then at the same moment, they each whispered, "I love you."

After a long pause, Anna said, "You can tell Putzi I will have discussed the prospect of a second interview with the Marshal."

"They'll be drooling to talk with you," Berthold said. "Pilsudski is the hook."

* * *

Berthold appeared without an appointment in Albert Mueller's Reichsbahn office in Munich. "So you told Goebbels," he demanded.

"Of course," Mueller said. "What did you expect?"

"Did you tell Goebbels directly or did you tell Krueger and have him move it up the line?"

"I speak to Goebbels; I have no relationship with Krueger."

Berthold was pleased to have extracted that little piece of information from Mueller but he wasn't done.

"Is that why Goebbels now has me followed?"

"I don't know anything about that," Mueller said. "Goebbels doesn't tell me what he does. He did ask me to find out about your relationship with the Jew Richard Goldmann, and he's curious to know why you prefer 'Jewish pussy' to our fine German girls like Marta Huber."

"That is none of Josef Goebbels' fucking business," Berthold roared.

"So you think."

Mueller very pointedly looked around his office, which was spacious and well furnished, the lair of a successful junior executive.

"I like working for the Reichsbahn," he said. "It was my hope that you would also enjoy the benefits of such a career, but it seems you're on the verge of throwing that away. I would urge you to think deeply about these matters and consider adjusting your attitude. It's only the *Führer's* gratitude toward your brother that has kept your prospects alive even this long."

Berthold didn't think Hitler's gratitude had anything to do with it. For Hitler, gratitude was a short-lived emotion. Besides, Goebbels was his patron, not the *Führer*. Goebbels had made him a Nazi hero and he would be embarrassed if he had to admit he was wrong. Mueller's onslaught, however, suggested that Goebbels might be nearing the end of his rope.

Chapter 44

1990 - Munich

Marissa interrupted Berthold's narrative to pursue what she was beginning to suspect was a far more interesting relationship between himself and Putzi than Berthold had as yet revealed.

"Were there any other indications," she asked, "that Putzi may have known your true feelings toward Hitler and the Nazis?"

Berthold didn't answer, which raised Marissa's curiosity even more.

"A colleague of mine," she said, "met Putzi in the 1970s. He was back in Germany by then, still playing piano at cocktail parties. I'm sure you know he had left in 1936."

"1937," Berthold said.

"Did you see Putzi in Munich after you were released from prison?"

"Yes." Berthold's look suggested he understood what Marissa was reaching for but he was still unwilling to accommodate her. "I saw him several times. He was very helpful in getting me re-acclimated to civilian life."

"Why did he protect you?"

"I think," Berthold said, finally relenting, "that Putzi was as afraid of Hitler as I was, and that we were caught in the same Nazi trap."

Chapter 45

March 1932 - Munich

The headline in every German newspaper was the same.

HINDENBURG WILL RUN!

With his seven year term as President nearing its end, Field Marshal Paul von Hindenburg had decided to run for re-election. A few days later, Josef Goebbels, at a Nazi rally at the *Sportpalast* in Berlin, announced that Adolf Hitler would be the Nazi Party's candidate for President of the German Republic. There was also a Communist running but neither the Social Democrats nor the Catholic Center Party fielded a candidate.

In Munich, Putzi said, "It's not even clear that Hitler knew Goebbels was going to make that announcement, but we're in it now." As usual, Putzi went on with news Berthold would want to communicate to Anna. "Now that he's running for president," Putzi said, "I suppose it would be nice if the *Führer* was actually a citizen of Germany."

"He's not a citizen?"

"Adolf Schicklgruber was born in Austria and never bothered to become a German citizen, although he did change his name. I think he's going to get some university to give him a minor position that somehow also includes citizenship."

Putzi roared with laughter. "Can you imagine thirty thousand voices yelling 'Heil Schicklgruber!'"

Berthold didn't understand how a university could grant citizenship but decided not to ask. Eventually Putzi stopped laughing.

"By the way," he said, "Goebbels agreed to invite your friend to interview Hitler while he's campaigning. I think we'll be able to schedule it in Northeim, although the dates aren't set yet."

When Berthold called Anna with the news, she asked where Northeim was. "It's north of Munich and west of Berlin. Hitler's campaign schedule hasn't been set and will probably change once it is. Can you be flexible?"

"Yes of course."

Then Anna's voice changed, tenderness replacing businesslike. "Will I get to see you? I mean, when I'm not with Hitler."

"If it's humanly possible to arrange," Berthold said. "Can you stay for more than one day? Perhaps we could plan a trip."

"That would be wonderful," Anna said softly, then added, "You and I, what a surprise, like a sudden burst of sun in the midst of a winter storm."

Berthold could see the smile on Anna's face. "I can never say it as well as you do," he said, "but please know I feel the same. Thank you so much for giving me the opportunity to love you."

Chapter 46

March 1932 - Northeim

Ernst Krueger had never been more nervous. So much could go wrong for which he would be blamed. Berthold worked ceaselessly to help Krueger make plans for Hitler's appearance, and just as quickly change them. Fifteen thousand tickets had been sold within hours. A minute-by-minute agenda was developed and reviewed in both Munich and Berlin, where everyone suggested changes which were mutually inconsistent and had to be reconciled. They also had to be flexible. It was highly unlikely that Hitler would arrive on schedule. If he was late, the crowds had to be kept in place, perhaps for hours, which meant innumerable mundane but indispensable aspects of food service, entertainment and toilets had to be arranged.

A contingent of Hitler's SS bodyguards arrived and threw everything into chaos: change this; this is not acceptable; what dunce made these arrangements? But finally everything was in place and everyone seemed to be satisfied. That's when Anna called Krueger's office from Berlin, fortunately when Berthold was there.

"I'm fine," she said, "but I'm not coming on the train tonight. Hanfstaengl was waiting for me in Berlin and there's been a change in plans. I'm to fly to Northeim in Hitler's plane, but I don't think Northeim is the first stop."

***

Of course Hitler was late. The crowd stood in a cold driving rain and waited for the *Führer* to descend from the dark clouds in the first airplane ever to land in Northeim. A Nazi fife-and-drum corps played to entertain them. Berthold was terrified the plane would crash and Anna would be killed.

He checked with Krueger every ten minutes but there was no word.

Finally at five o'clock, three hours behind schedule, a small plane dropped to a low altitude and buzzed over the hysterically cheering crowd. Then it soared upward and headed off. Was the *Führer* leaving? Had he decided to skip Northeim? Krueger calmed everyone by announcing that the plane would land in a field outside of town.

Twenty minutes later, a black limousine slid to a halt and black-uniformed SS men ran to stand at attention. The door opened and Hitler emerged, followed by Goebbels and then Putzi, who could barely fit through. Finally, as Berthold watched in amazement, Anna Gorska, his Anna, looking flustered and bewildered, stepped out of Hitler's limousine. Berthold's feelings of pride were quickly buried by concern and fear. Anna had gone from a *shtetl* in Poland to flying with Hitler. It was not an easy path to fathom, but the dangers were obvious.

Hitler strode quickly to the platform where he saluted the crowd. He seemed to be in an excellent mood, notwithstanding what must have been a grueling day. The rain had slackened and Hitler directed that his umbrella be removed so he could stand like the audience with his bare head exposed to the drizzle; the crowd applauded wildly at this gesture.

Berthold rushed to Anna's side, but there was time for only the very briefest of hugs before Goebbels began to introduce Hitler. Anna's notebook flashed open, pen at hand.

Putzi came up behind Berthold, leaned down and whispered, "Quite a girl you've got there. She's captivated the *Führer* all day."

Goebbels introduced Hitler who spoke calmly for fifteen minutes, finishing with his standard promises to defeat the communists, abolish the Versailles Treaty, and resurrect a powerful and defiant Germany. He never uttered the word Jew nor did he attack his opponent Hindenburg. Berthold, who had seen the manic intensity Hitler brought to other speeches, had the impression Hitler did not expect to win the Presidency and did not really care.

After the speech, Anna started to explain to Berthold that she could not stay overnight in Northeim since she had to continue on with Hitler, but just then an apologetic Putzi came over to tell her she had been bumped from the plane in favor of a reporter from the London Times.

Goebbels grabbed Putzi's arm to hurry him along, and as he did, he noticed Berthold standing next to Anna. Goebbels sneered and mouthed the words "Jewish pussy." In the background, Putzi shook his head.

***

Anna and Berthold sat despondently in a corner of the bar at Berthold's hotel, speaking quietly, or not at all whenever anyone came close. The joy of seeing each other had evaporated into dismay induced by the relentless progress of Hitler's Nazi bedlam. This was surely not the reunion they had so eagerly anticipated.

"I hate them both," Anna said, referring to Hitler and Goebbels, "but give them their due. They've transformed Adolf Hitler from an insignificant little corporal who failed at everything he ever tried into the most compelling politician in Europe. Even people who find Hitler repugnant are fascinated by him."

"Will anybody stop him?"

"The Marshal thinks that's still possible ... but not likely."

Anna thought about what she had said, tense and fidgeting and increasingly miserable. "In any case," she added almost as an afterthought, "it won't be the Pope who interferes with Hitler's march to power. Pilsudski's man did get a private interview with His Holiness, but Pius took one look inside the envelope and gave it right back to him."

"He never read it?"

"Colonel Beck said he read one page, just enough to see it was from Chancellor Brüning."

After a short pause, Berthold asked, "Why are we doing this?"

That loaded question sat in the air for several minutes, like a bad smell, until Berthold finally said, "Are you going to answer?"

Anna's eyes flashed a hard look Berthold had never seen before. "I feel soiled," she said. "I've been immersed in dirt for six hours. We flew to four other locations before Northeim, each time taking off and landing on bumpy fields. All day I had to sit next to him, just behind the pilot, constantly answering questions from him and from Goebbels about Pilsudski's plans and intentions. Whenever the plane veered and my body rubbed against Hitler's I thought I would be sick."

Still she hadn't answered his question.

"It's all an act in the grand play Richard Goldmann invented," Berthold said, pushing again. "But you know that. After all, I'm just an actor. You, on the other hand, are one of the directors."

"I do understand," Anna whispered, looking down, not daring to make contact with his eyes. "I know we've put you in a horrible place and I feel guilty all the time. Here I am advancing my career while you're the one who's in danger. I know it's not fair." She looked up. "Do you want to stop?"

"Maybe my mother and I should just go to America with Richard Goldmann and forget about all this."

"Would you really go?"

The tension between them had grown to the bursting point. No smiles. No loving looks. No tender touches.

"I would not," Berthold said softly. His voice caught and he blinked back a tear. "I couldn't bear the thought of never seeing you again."

That broke the tension, although both knew the issues they had raised remained unresolved. Anna took Berthold's sad face in her hands.

"Does your room have a tub?"

Chapter 47

Putzi had suggested a lakeside lodge in Lower Saxony, a four hour drive from Northeim, and Ernst Krueger had agreed that Berthold could borrow his automobile. The next day brought a glorious morning, warm for March. Berthold put the top down, Anna wrapped her head in a scarf, and off they went.

"Two days alone," Anna said. "No Nazis, no stories to write. Whatever will we do?"

Berthold reached over and gently rubbed Anna's thigh.

"I think we'll figure something out."

But it turned out their conversation in the car was all about Nazis. They jumped from topic to topic, but always it came back to Hitler.

"Do you think Hitler is stable?" Berthold asked.

"I've thought a lot about that," Anna said. "He's a very private person so it's hard to know for sure, but I think he's ferociously focused on every opportunity and every risk relevant to his political success. Of course, he has nothing else. If he's not the *Führer*, he's nothing at all."

She thought for a few seconds, then added, "In his speeches, he gives the crowd the emotional performance he thinks they want, but off the stage, he's a very serious person who thinks rationally, except about Jews. He's nervous all the time, sometimes despondent and even desolate, but then he snaps out of it and keeps on going."

"That's exactly what Putzi says about Hitler," Berthold said, after which they drove in silence for several miles before he resumed the conversation.

"Does Hitler expect to beat Hindenburg for the Presidency?" Berthold asked.

"No," Anna said, "but that's not his goal. He wants to be Chancellor, not President. However, the Presidential campaign is raising him to a new level of prestige in Germany, and in the world. He is now seen as one of the two major politicians in

Germany, and the other one is very old and generally thought to be senile. Hitler is moving ever closer to his goal of being Germany's only obvious leadership choice. It's frightening."

Their enthusiasm dampened by all these negative thoughts, they had driven quietly for several miles and had reached the outskirts of Hanover, when Anna said, "Enough about Hitler; let's talk about us. In two months, you'll graduate from college and start your new job. Are you excited?"

"Yes. I think it'll be challenging. The Reichsbahn is a great company, looking to get even better, and my project with the signals systems has gone very well."

"Do you know what your assignment will be?"

"Not yet."

Anna took a long look at Berthold and he felt something significant coming.

"I want to tell my mother about us."

"She won't be happy to learn that you like a Catholic," Berthold said.

"There are two things wrong with that sentence," Anna said. "We are well beyond the stage of 'liking' each other, and you are not a Catholic." She thought for a minute. "I guess you are a Catholic, but you're also a Jew. Which do you think you are?"

"I know next to nothing about being a Jew," Berthold said, "but when I go to church I sometimes find great comfort in the message of Jesus."

"If I tell my mother we're in love, I must also tell her about your Jewish ancestry." Berthold didn't respond. "If you'd rather I not," Anna said, "I won't."

"But you want to?"

"Very much so. I want to share what I feel about you. I need someone to talk to. It's too wonderful to keep all to myself. My mother is getting older. I want her to know how happy I am."

Berthold chose each word with great care. "I'm sure you understand the dangers my Jewish ancestry poses for me and my mother." He glanced at Anna sitting erect and tense next to him. "I'm also sure you trust your mother to keep what you say confidential."

Anna's face relaxed as Berthold continued, "Our lives are in each other's hands; I trust you to make the right decisions and I do very much appreciate that you asked my permission."

"If I were not already sure how much I love you," Anna said, "I would be now."

Berthold pulled over to the side of the road and they exchanged a crushing hug and kisses made wet with tears.

Driving further north from Hanover, they were entranced by the beauty of Lower Saxony. The lodge Putzi had recommended was small but luxurious, located directly on a lake whose name they could never remember. Putzi had called ahead and they were treated like royalty - Nazi royalty. The lodge's brochure offered a wide choice of activities which, except for a few minutes strolling along the lakeside, they completely ignored.

Anna had brought the black nightgown which had taken Berthold's breath away in Paris; it was the first time she had worn it since. Midway through the second day of lovemaking, a naughty look passed over Anna's face.

"What?" Berthold asked.

"I heard Herr Goebbels ask if you prefer ..."

She couldn't say the words, nor could Berthold, but neither could they stop laughing. Finally Berthold managed to say, "Very much so," and they fell into even more uncontrolled and raucous laughter. "Let me continue to demonstrate," he added, to which Anna answered in the most demure and prim voice she could summon, "By all means do."

Chapter 48

March 1932 - Munich

Hitler was not mentioning Jews in his campaign speeches, but when Berthold returned to Northeim, he had found a few pamphlets leftover from the thousands which had been distributed to every home in Northeim in his absence. He felt sick as he showed his mother the Nazis' plan for Jews ...

1. A Jew cannot be a citizen;

2. No Jew may hold public office;

3. All Jews who have come into Germany after 1914 will be expelled forthwith;

4. No Jew may edit or contribute to any newspaper or periodical;

5. All land and houses belonging to Jews will be taken away from them;

***

Monsignor Johannes was not surprised when Berthold told him Pope Pius had refused to look at the Brüning materials. He left to tell Cardinal Faulhaber and returned almost immediately, saying the Cardinal wanted to talk with Berthold directly.

Without the magisterial attire he wore in the Cathedral, Cardinal Faulhaber looked very much like any other priest, trim and erect in a plain black suit and clerical collar, but Berthold, awed by his presence, felt his pulse racing and his breath coming in gulps.

"We appreciate your efforts," the Cardinal said, coming around his desk and leading the way to a comfortable seating area in a corner of the large office.

"Would you tell me about this young woman who has Marshal Pilsudski's ear."

Berthold explained who Anna was, where she was from, and how her uncle's connection had led to her close relationship with Marshal Pilsudski.

"I understand you first met Frau Gorska at Richard Goldmann's home," Faulhaber said. "I'm impressed with Herr Goldmann's business acumen and also his political inclinations. I understand he is increasingly well respected among the Social Democrats."

Faulhaber looked at Johannes and then at Berthold.

"If," he said, "the Catholic Center Party and the Social Democrats are ever to work together, it will be due to men like Richard Goldmann. Unfortunately, the Vatican incorrectly equates socialism with communism and opposes any cooperation between the Catholic Center and the Social Democrats."

Berthold was surprised at Faulhaber's forthright assessment and a quick glance at Monsignor Johannes revealed that he too had not expected the Cardinal to speak so frankly. Johannes asked Berthold to tell the Cardinal exactly what had happened in Rome.

Berthold repeated what Anna had told him. "Marshal Pilsudski sent Chancellor Brüning's materials to Rome with a very high level emissary, a Colonel Jozef Beck who I understand will soon be appointed Foreign Minister of Poland. The Pope received him cordially but as soon as he understood the nature of the materials Beck wanted to give him, he terminated the interview."

"Was Cardinal Pacelli involved?" Faulhaber asked.

"Colonel Beck did not meet with Cardinal Pacelli," Berthold said, "but he believes the Pope knew he was bringing the Brüning materials before he actually presented them, and further believes that knowledge came from Cardinal Pacelli."

Cardinal Faulhaber closed his eyes and brought his clenched hands together at his chin. He nodded rather forlornly, and Monsignor Johannes indicated to Berthold they should leave.

***

On March 13, 1932, President Hindenburg received almost nineteen million votes, a fraction short of the 50% needed for an outright victory; Hitler was second with eleven million. In the runoff election several weeks later, Hindenburg won handily. Berthold breathed a little easier. Hitler still had no power and no clear path to obtain that power.

Chapter 49

1990 - Munich

Marissa asked Berthold if he knew why the Pope had refused to read the Brüning papers.

"When I asked," Berthold said, "Monsignor Johannes cited the Vatican's fear of atheistic communism."

"The Vatican has always linked their support of Hitler to their fear of communism," Marissa said.

"But Johannes said there were other reasons."

Marissa held her breath. This was a point on which historians still strongly disagreed, and about which the Church had not released any documents, if indeed there were any.

"Johannes said Cardinal Pacelli desperately wanted a Concordat between the Vatican and the German Reich but felt it could never be achieved as long as there was a parliamentary government in Germany. He also knew that Hitler, if he ever achieved the Chancellorship, was determined to make a radical change in the German constitution by passing what he called an Enabling Act which would make the Reichstag a rubber stamp for his policies and directives. Johannes said Hitler's willingness to negotiate a Reich Concordat in return for the Catholic Center Party's support for an Enabling Act was the essence of the deal being negotiated in Rome. At the time I didn't know what either of those was."

"And of course," Marissa said, "within a year, the Enabling Act was passed, with Catholic support, and the Reich Concordat was signed. Pacelli had his agreement and Hitler was an absolute dictator. The Vatican has always denied any *quid pro quo*, but the evidence seems to point otherwise."

Chapter 50

May 1932 - Warsaw

Anna was working quietly at her desk at the *Haynt* when a messenger handed her a note, hand-written in Yiddish: *Dear Anna. I am at the Bristol Hotel. Can you come to see me? Edel Inwentarz.*

Anna ran to the Bristol and burst through the revolving door into the lobby. A man who looked to be about sixty years old rose to greet her. He was of medium height and thickly set, a strong man, a man who looked like he could indeed have robbed a train with Marshal Pilsudski. Anna came into Edel's arms and they hugged each other.

"You're just as beautiful as your photographs," Edel said, a broad kindly smile capturing his face.

Anna blushed as questions spilled out, "Does Kamon know you're here? Does the Marshal know?"

"No one knows. It was a last minute trip. I'm here for the Joint, replacing a man who had a heart attack the day before he was to leave. I was on the boat and at sea before I had a chance to write."

Anna knew that the American Jewish Joint Distribution Committee, referred to by everyone as "the Joint," was the major source of charitable funding for Jews in Poland and elsewhere in eastern Europe. She had not known her Uncle Edel was as prominent in it as he apparently was.

"How's my brother?" Edel asked, "and your parents?"

"Grandfather Kamon is well, although he and my parents are under great strain and none of them is fully healthy. Will you come to Ciechanow?"

"Of course. Just as soon as my business here for the Joint is finished and I get to see my old friend Pilsudski."

"The Marshal will be thrilled to see you," Anna said. "I'll call his office. It's not far; we can walk there."

But it turned out Pilsudski was away and would not be back for several days, so Anna had the pleasure of showing her great-uncle Edel around the center of Warsaw as he marveled at the modern buildings, the electric tram, and the other changes that had occurred in the quarter century since he had left Poland.

They came to the University of Warsaw, passed through the black iron gates and stopped on the tree-lined path which led to the library. Anna took Edel's hand.

"It's just over a year since I graduated," she said. "You helped make this possible for me and I am so very grateful."

"And I am so very proud of the result," Edel said, looking at her with a gentleness that brought a tear to her eyes.

**

The next morning, Anna and Edel walked from the Bristol Hotel to the *Haynt* offices where Yitzhak Gruenbaum was waiting for them.

"It takes a while for the *Haynt* to get from Warsaw to America," Edel said, "but I read every paper as soon as it arrives."

"Thank you," Gruenbaum said. "Your niece has brought a new dimension to our reporting. Her relationship with Marshal Pilsudski is invaluable."

"And with Hitler," Edel said.

"Yes, of course," Gruenbaum agreed. He hesitated, looked to Anna and received her unspoken permission, then added, "But perhaps her most important connection is the young man she met in Munich, which is how she got her interview with Hitler."

Edel turned to Anna, clearly surprised.

"My uncle is not yet aware of my German friend," Anna said. "I am planning to tell him about Berthold at lunch today."

Edel nodded, smiled, and asked an unrelated question, "Anna's recent article about anti-Jewish feeling in Poland had quite an impact on us in America," Edel said. "How was it received here?"

"It brought much Jew-hatred to the surface, and also doubled our circulation."

"Is my niece in danger?" Edel's immediate reaction warmed Anna's heart.

"No," Gruenbaum said. "Her well-known connection to Marshal Pilsudski protects her."

They talked for another few minutes, after which Anna showed Edel the small cubicle where she worked. He insisted she sit on her chair while he stared at her for several long moments, storing a memory.

***

Anna had wanted to share everything about Berthold for months. Edel's combination of kindness and distance made him the perfect confidant for her and at lunch she held back nothing, including Berthold's Jewish ancestry and Nazi connections, the plan to spy on the Nazis, and their times together in Paris and Lower Saxony. She talked for over an hour. At some point, Edel took her hand in his and she kept talking. When she was done, he smiled but said nothing for what seemed like forever. It occurred to Anna that her uncle was carefully going back through her story, putting pieces together, and perhaps identifying problems and issues she had not yet anticipated. She felt more comfortable than she had in a long time.

Finally Edel chuckled. "I thought I had an active life as a young man, but I was thirty-four years old when I left Ciechanow. You are only twenty-four and already your history reads like a story-book." He paused. "This German boy is very important to you. Do you love him?"

"Yes, Uncle, I do. But I'm afraid for him. He's brave and very intelligent, but he's in great and growing danger, in large part because of me and my desire for information for my articles."

"Does he understand that?"

"Yes, we've discussed it."

"Then you're not deceiving him."

"I don't know if he's tough enough to do what he'll have to do."

"Nobody can measure their toughness until the time comes to act," Edel said. "Besides, your friend took on his role as a spy to protect his mother. He did that before you were involved. You're as much an accomplice in his plan as he is in yours."

Anna nodded as she absorbed Edel's perspective, so obvious now that he had said it.

"I want to tell my mother everything," Anna said. "She'll be shocked that I've taken a Christian boy as my lover."

"He's Jewish."

"Technically, but in every real way he's Catholic. Mother will be disappointed that I've taken a lover of any kind. She'll blame loose living in Warsaw, and my parents will blame each other for letting me go there in the first place."

"Then they will blame me as well," Edel said, "for encouraging you and paying some of the bills."

A devilish look came into Edel's eyes.

"You were born the year I left Ciechanow," he said. "I was already married and had a child. Your mother found it easier to talk with me than with her own father, much as you are finding it easier to do the same thing now." Edel paused. "I will not reveal any secrets, but I can assure you Evona will not be shocked that you and Berthold became lovers without the benefit of marriage."

"My mother was pregnant before she was married?"

Edel smiled. "I never said that. But I will say you are not the first in our family to have the urges you felt and acted upon."

242

Anna shook her head and laughed. "No child can imagine her parents as young." She jumped up to put her arms around her uncle and hug him tightly. "Thank you."

***

Anna and Edel came to Marshal Pilsudski's office at the Belvedere Palace, where they were greeted by an aide and taken to the private family quarters. Pilsudski rose from the table where he was playing solitaire. He and Edel hugged and then Anna sat silently for almost an hour as the two old friends reminisced. It was a history of early twentieth century Polish revolutions only Pilsudski could have related and Anna was utterly enthralled, writing in her notebook many ideas for potential articles. While they were talking, the Marshal's wife arrived, a young girl in tow.

"Aleksandra," Edel said, jumping up to hug her. To Anna, Edel said, "This one was the spark of our group. She was beautiful and daring, and we all fell in love with her."

"Good thing you never mentioned that then," Pilsudski said. He introduced his wife and daughter to Anna and then they withdrew while the two men continued their conversation. Anna sat quietly, listening, taking notes.

"Edel," Pilsudski said, "what do Americans think about what's happening in Poland and Germany?"

"Of course there's concern about the increasing anti-Jewish feeling," Edel said, "and the Joint has increased its relief efforts. But so far there's not much being done by our government. Many Americans believe their efforts in the Great War were sufficient and now Europe should take care of its own problems."

"That's too bad," Pilsudski said, "Please try to convince American Jews that ignoring Europe is a bad mistake. Germany is falling apart. Too many Germans seriously under-estimate Hitler. Hindenburg is an old man who is increasingly unable to focus. There are still ways to stop Hitler, but time is running short."

Pilsudski paused and his face assumed a wry expression. "You've been polite not to mention my own obvious physical deterioration, but that doesn't make it go away. I'm very fearful about what will happen to Poland's Jews when I die."

The Marshal rose and walked awkwardly to Edel, and the two old comrades hugged. Seeing them together, Anna understood just how much Josef Pilsudski had come to be like another great-uncle for her. She was sure this was the last time her uncle and the Marshal would meet and was very much aware she was watching a piece of Polish history slip away.

Chapter 51

May 1932 - Ciechanow

Anna's entire family and many friends were waiting for the bus from Warsaw. Someone had made a sign - WELCOME HOME EDEL! WELCOME HOME ANNA! Anna was surprised that she was mentioned until she realized with an embarrassed start that it had been over a year since she had last visited Ciechanow.

Kamon was the first to greet Edel. The brothers looked at each other carefully, no doubt taking note of the changes almost a quarter of a century had made; then they hugged and cried together. Whatever they said was lost in the sound of the bus moving on to its next stop. Anna hugged her parents, and then her brother Josef and sister Danuta. Her parents looked older than they should have. Jacob was only fifty, Evona two years younger, but the strain of being a Jew in Poland was taking its toll.

The group walked to the synagogue where long tables had been set up outside and lunch was served. As word of Edel's presence spread, hundreds more of Ciechanow's Jews arrived. Women kept bringing more food and the meal went on for hours, ending only with the call to evening prayers.

After the service, everyone stayed at the synagogue and Edel answered questions about his work and family in America: they kept kosher; most Jews went to synagogue; his five children spoke English and were all doing well; he had become a home-builder; he was not confronted with any significant anti-Jewish behavior where he lived.

Then the Gorska family went home where Evona served yet another huge meal featuring a stew that had been cooking overnight.

***

Anna was awakened very early the next morning when Edel whispered through her curtain.

"We're going to take a walk," Edel said. "Will you join us?"

The brothers never stopped reminiscing as they wandered along the narrow streets in the Jewish section. At the cemetery they stood before their parents' graves and talked about their childhood. At the edge of the town, they stared at fields of potatoes and sugar beets while a small herd of cattle grazed in the distance. Back in the town center, they stood near the City Hall from which they could see the sixteenth century castle of King Sigismund. Edel lingered at the market where his wife had long ago purchased fruits and vegetables. Along the main street of shops, he stopped by a place where shoes were repaired.

"Do you remember this shop, Kamon. I worked here for several years. Repairing shoes was also how I earned my living in London, and then again for several years in America."

As they completed their long walk and neared the Gorska home, Edel said, "In Warsaw, everything is different, but here, everything is the same. I wonder for how long."

For Anna, this morning walk provided an unforgettable emotional connection to the place where she had been born.

***

The moment Anna dreaded had finally arrived. For two days, she had spoken with her parents about her work in Warsaw and what was happening in Ciechanow, but they had avoided the crucial issue Edel wanted to raise. Now they were gathered around the table, sharing another cup of after-breakfast coffee.

"Sometimes," Edel said, "you have to admit you're fighting a battle you cannot win. The Jewish people have achieved much in Poland, and this should be remembered and revered forever." He paused. "But now that time is over."

Kamon and Anna's parents listened respectfully, but it was clear Edel was delivering a message they would not accept.

"Marshal Pilsudski will certainly do his best to protect Jews as long as he lives, but he's old and ill, and when he dies there'll be no voice in Poland to stand against the hateful attacks of the Catholics and Endeks about which Anna has so accurately reported. The Minorities Act will be repealed and all the gains Jews have made will be gone: Jews who have money and businesses will lose their wealth; Jews who have jobs will be let go; Jews who have homes and farms will find they cannot keep them."

Edel continued to pour out his heart to people he loved.

"I can't save all of Poland's Jews, but I can save you. I can bring all of our family to America, where I can help you start new lives. Danuta, Josef, and of course Anna can all have good lives in America, just as my children and grandchildren are already enjoying."

"I'm too old to travel to America," Kamon said. "And I'm not well. I wouldn't survive the trip."

"I will not leave my father," Evona said.

"I will not leave my wife," Jacob added.

Edel did not turn to Anna. Perhaps he didn't ask because his heart told him he did not want to hear what she would say. Instead, he continued to plead with the others.

"You would not be abandoning Polish Jewry," he said. "No. You would be offering this great civilization a chance to continue living. You could be a voice to convince American Jews to fight harder for their fellow Jews in Poland and Germany."

Edel composed himself, then started a new tack.

"Perhaps you're saying to yourselves that you're not capable of influencing Americans. You're probably right."

Her grandfather and parents looked surprised, but Anna knew where Edel was going.

"Kamon, Jacob, Evona," Edel said. "You've produced a remarkable young woman. Surely you must recognize that Anna is capable of doing things which you cannot. Her voice, which is already great, would be even more influential if she were to speak from America, and if she could meet American leaders face to face."

Anna was crying, but Edel would not stop.

"I believe Anna wants to come to America," he said, "but I'm afraid she won't leave if you decide to stay. I implore you. Please leave Poland before it's too late."

Facing the painful stares of people whose minds were long ago resolved, Edel reached the end of his plea, knowing he was defeated and that Anna was condemned to stay in Poland, come what may. He looked away, unwilling to meet Anna's eyes.

***

Edel spent much of the next two days with his brother Kamon as both men recognized it was probably the last time they would see each other.

Anna took the opportunity to get re-acquainted with Josef and Danuta. When she had first left for Warsaw and the University, Josef had been thirteen and Danuta ten. Although she had visited Ciechanow since then, she had not spent much time with them, and now that they were eighteen and fifteen, it was like meeting new people. They spoke as they walked, wandering without destination, finally pausing at the crumbling old castle.

"Sometimes the Zionists meet here," Josef said. "Once we lit a bonfire in the courtyard and stayed until dawn."

"Do you want to go to Palestine?" Anna asked her brother.

"Yes," Josef answered. "But it's almost impossible to get a visa from the British."

"Perhaps I could help," Anna said. "Have you heard the name Menachem Begin?"

"Of course," Josef said. "He's one of the most famous people in the Zionist movement in Poland."

"Menachem is my friend," Anna said. "I could ask him to help you get a visa." Anna paused, then added, "Better yet, you can come to Warsaw and meet him yourself. But before you do, you must prepare. You need to be fluent in Hebrew and familiar with the history of Zionism and with current conditions in Palestine."

"What do you think we do in our meetings?" Josef said, laughing. "Do you think you're the only one with brains in this family?"

"Please forgive me," Anna said, returning Josef's smile and feeling closer to him than she had ever been. "I should come to Ciechanow more often. That will change now, especially with the new bus line. Do Mother and Father approve of you going to Palestine?"

Josef answered, 'They understand how difficult it is to get work here, even for Poles but of course much worse for Jews. I think they would not object. What about you? Will you go to Palestine?"

"Maybe some day," Anna said, "but not now. There are things I must do here in Poland, stories that must be written."

Out of the corner of her eye, Anna saw Danuta, left out of the conversation, about to burst. "You too, Danuta," she said. "Will you come to Warsaw for a visit?"

"I would love to," Danuta said. Then her eyes widened and, taking her opportunity, she whispered, "Do you still see that German boy?"

"What do you know about any German boy?"

"I heard you say his name the last time you were here and after you left, I asked Mother about him. She didn't say much, but I could tell he was important to you. Do you still see him?"

Josef had walked ahead, giving the sisters privacy, but now Anna asked him to join them.

"His name is Berthold Becker," she said. "I met him in Munich at an event hosted by our distant cousins Richard and Judith Goldmann. We became friends."

Then, Anna thought, I saw his photo with Josef Goebbels and met his Nazi friend Putzi Hanfstaengl and he arranged for me to interview Adolf Hitler. And still I love him. How can I possibly explain any of that to my little sister? She's fifteen years old, bursting with energy, and she wants to know everything, but thankfully she's too timid to ask.

"Berthold and I are still friends," Anna said, thinking to put the matter to rest.

"I have a boy friend," Danuta whispered so Josef couldn't hear, and Anna realized she had again under-estimated her not-so-little sister.

"When you come to Warsaw," Anna said, "we'll have a long sisters conversation, just the two of us."

***

"It's been a long time since we had a serious talk," Evona Gorska said to her daughter. "Too long."

Anna began by talking about Yitzhak Gruenbaum and her experiences at the *Haynt*. "Do you remember my first interview with Madame Meltzer? We've become close friends and colleagues."

"You always knew what you wanted to do," Evona said. "Being a journalist, going to University. Now you meet with Marshal Pilsudski and interview Adolf Hitler. What was it like to be with Hitler?"

"After I flew with him I needed to take a bath," Anna said, remembering who she took that bath with. Her smile and poignant pause alerted Evona, who rarely missed an unspoken signal.

"I think it's time for me to tell you about Berthold," Anna said.

"The boy you met in Munich at the Goldmann's house? The one who helped you with the story about Jews in German universities?"

"Yes. That one."

Evona smiled. "There's more?"

"Much more." Anna took a deep breath. "We've become far more than casual friends."

"You've slept together?" Evona asked, and even though Anna had hinted at their relationship, she was startled by her mother's directness. "We don't have many opportunities to talk," Evona said, "so I think we should get right to the point."

"I agree," Anna said. "I love him and he loves me ... and we have slept together."

"So you've fallen in love with a German Catholic," Evona said, her voice taking on an edge, "and all of our worst fears in sending you to Warsaw have been realized. You know you can never marry him."

Evona was not pleased, but as Edel had predicted, her anger was tempered, no doubt by her own experience.

"We're not talking about marriage," Anna said, "but I need to tell you something. Berthold is Catholic, but he's also Jewish."

Anna smiled, then laughed. "If I'm honest, I must admit I fell in love with him before I knew he was Jewish, but I suppose God knew and was just waiting for me to find out."

It took over an hour to tell the story: Berthold's Jewish grandmother; his brother Dietrich's death in the *Putsch;* how Berthold had been dragged into the Nazi fold; the decision to use his access to high-level Nazis to try to prevent Hitler's ascent; his connection with Cardinal Faulhaber and Monsignor Johannes; the way Marshal Pilsudski was making use of information provided by Berthold; the danger to Berthold and his mother if their secret was revealed.

Evona listened intently and asked many questions. When Anna finished, she said how proud she was to have such a daughter.

"I was excited every time I saw an article of yours, but this is so far beyond anything I imagined. I'm not speaking of your associations with famous people, stunning as they are. I'm speaking of you, your abilities, your mind, and most of all of your Jewish heart. What more can a mother want?"

A cloud passed over Evona's face and she asked, "Can we tell these things to your father? He would be so proud."

"I told you first because if you did not find my life acceptable, I could never tell Papa. But if you'll help me, I want Papa to know everything I've just told you."

***

The conversation with Jacob went well, but it led inevitably to criticism of Anna's decision, almost two years before, to switch from an Orthodox to a Zionist synagogue. She had written to her parents at the time, but they had never fully discussed the matter.

Anna heard Edel coming into the house and asked him to join the conversation, hoping he would be a voice in her support, but Kamon, who was with Edel, also joined, and he set an immediate confrontational tone.

"You've become a *goy*," Kamon said, using the Yiddish word for gentile.

Anna's face fell. She could think of no way to explain why she had changed synagogues without causing enormous pain. Edel came to her rescue.

"I've been with Anna in Warsaw for several days," Edel said. "I have seen her at work, with the Marshal, and in her synagogue." He paused and took Anna's hand. "This beautiful Jewish girl is certainly not a *goy*. She is a different kind of Jew than you are, brother Kamon, but she is surely a Jew. More than that, she is exactly the kind of Jew our people desperately need. I think you should listen to what she has to say."

Encouraged, Anna took up the argument, speaking softly but firmly. "Why is it not Jewish to speak Hebrew instead of Yiddish? Why is it not Jewish to wear modern clothes instead of those worn hundreds of years ago? Why is it not Jewish to want to go to Palestine when we are so obviously not wanted here?"

"It is not Jewish to fail to keep the *Shabbos* and the other commandments," Kamon insisted.

"No Jew keeps all six hundred thirteen commandments all the time," Anna said. "God has set a target and given us the freedom to approach that target as best we can. What is important is that we understand that every Jew - and also every gentile - is part of the same infinite world God has created."

Anna found herself saying things she had never said aloud before, but which came naturally, as if they had somehow been completely formed in her mind.

"The small part of the universe that encompasses Poland has changed, and more changes are coming. To remain faithful to our Jewish God, we must survive in this new world, and I believe survival requires that we change on the outside even as we remain as Jewish as we can on the inside."

"You must understand," Jacob said gently, "how frightening these changes are to many Jews, including your family. We see our world crumbling around us. We're frightened when our Torah is challenged by secular studies we don't understand."

"This is not new, Papa," Anna said. "Jews have been interpreting the word of God since it was first received at Sinai. It is over a hundred and fifty years since Moses Mendelsohn translated the Five Books of Moses into German and thus introduced new interpretations required by a different language."

"That translation was immediately banned by Orthodox Jews," Jacob said.

"That didn't stop Jews from reading it," Anna said, "and the Jewish Enlightenment movement which Mendelssohn initiated ended Jewish isolation and brought us into the world. It also led to the creation of Jewish culture, the study of Jewish history, and more penetrating analysis of what a Jew really is. It led to previously unimaginable political freedoms, including the right to vote and run for office."

Kamon started to speak, but Jacob beat him to it.

"But in their haste to live in the non-Jewish world," Jacob said, "many Jews have cast away the very things which make us Jews. I'm afraid we're losing God, and then what will we be? How can we bring God's message to the world if we fail to study and observe His words? There is not enough room in a Jewish life to include the secular along with the Jewish."

Anna was impressed with her father's analysis; he had gone beyond the anger many Orthodox Jews felt and expressed. Their minds were engaged and she was thrilled.

"Your Mendelssohn," Jacob continued, "thought Yiddish was a ridiculous language, ungrammatical and unable to express man's higher thoughts. But we love that language. The Yiddish stories of Sholem Aleichem and Peretz reveal the very essence of who we are. If we're too intent on becoming like everyone else, we'll lose what makes us unique."

"We must do both," Anna said. "We must carry with us into the modern world all the values of Jewish learning and Jewish living that have sustained us for so many centuries, but the lessons of Torah and Talmud are not defined by the clothes we wear or the language we speak. God hears us in whatever language we speak, as long as we speak to Him."

"Do you think," Jacob asked, "that Jews can love God and remain true to His commandments while surrounded by the pulls and chaos of the modern world? Can you do that?"

"I can try, Papa. I think God is not unaware of the changes taking place in our world. This is the challenge He has given us."

Jacob smiled and looked at Evona, who in turn looked at Kamon.

"We should not fight Anna's way," Kamon said. "Nor should she fight ours. If Jewish life is to survive, we need to draw strength from old and new alike."

"Amen," Edel said, placing his hand on his older brother's shoulder.

***

The following morning, Anna and Edel took the bus back to Warsaw. The day after that, Edel left for his long journey to America.

Anna, of course, did not go with him. She understood that any hope she may have had to go to America was now gone. She and Berthold were committed to live with whatever future derived from that decision. In part she was proud, but she could not deny the feeling of terror she expected would be her constant companion until the day she died.

Chapter 52

May 1932 - Munich

"Good morning," Henri said as Berthold came into the dining room. Henri Bousquet had arrived in Munich several days earlier. This was the first time he had stayed at the Becker home. Berthold had taken his suitcase to what had been Dietrich's room but was fairly certain that was not where Henri was sleeping.

"Are you excited to be graduating?" Henri asked as Elisabeth brought Berthold's breakfast.

"Yes," Berthold said, smiling. "I think I've had enough school and I'm looking forward to working fulltime with the Reichsbahn."

In response to Henri's questions, Berthold explained his new job and Henri seemed suitably impressed.

"We met your friend Herr Hanfstaengl yesterday," Elisabeth said.

Berthold was stunned to hear his mother refer to Putzi as his friend in front of Henri, which meant they had discussed Berthold's association with the Nazis. He tried to keep the anger off his face, but his mother saw it.

"Henri knows."

"Knows what?" Berthold asked, his voice harsher than he wanted it to be.

"Everything," Elisabeth said softly. "Henri is Jewish. He understands what that means in Germany."

"And Putzi?" Berthold said. "Does Putzi know Henri is Jewish? You should have discussed this with me first."

"You're right. Henri said the same thing. I'm sorry, but there can be no secrets between us."

Elisabeth took a deep breath and smiled.

"Henri and I are engaged to be married. I was planning to tell you this morning."

Then her voice stiffened and she added sharply, "And we did not discuss the matter of Henri's religion with Herr Hanfstaengl."

"You have no right to be angry with me," Berthold said. "It's the other way around. Do you have any idea how complicated and frightening my life has become? Now I have this to worry about."

Berthold forced himself to take a bite of toast and a sip of coffee before continuing. "Do you know how easy it would be for Putzi put the pieces together, or mention something inadvertently to someone else who would put it together? Nobody trusts anyone in the inner group around Hitler; everybody's always looking to get something on somebody else."

They sat silently for some minutes before Berthold asked, "How did you come to meet Putzi? Does he know you're my mother?"

"Herr Hanfstaengl's wife and mother often shop in our store. Yesterday they came particularly to meet Henri. We've been advertising he would be there, and the Hanfstaengl women have each purchased several items from his line in the past year. This time, for the first time, Helene's husband came with her."

She paused; Berthold waited for more bad news.

"Helene introduced me to her husband. When he heard my name, Herr Hanfstaengl asked if I was related to you and Dietrich. He said the *Führer* thinks highly of you and remembers with deep appreciation Dietrich's actions during the *Putsch*. Henri heard all that and that's why, later, I had no choice but to tell him the rest."

Berthold again did not - in fact could not - respond; his thoughts were simply not coherent. He rose and left the house, but he after taking a few steps outside he stopped and returned.

"Mother, I am so upset about many things, but I came back to tell you I'm pleased at your decision to marry. I'm truly happy for you. You've been alone for too long."

"I have not been alone," Elisabeth said. "I've been with you, and I will continue to be with you."

Berthold put his arms around his mother and they hugged deeply.

"Henri," Berthold said rather stiffly, "I'm happy for you and mother. I hope you can make a life together." He paused. "I know what it's like to care for someone who's living in a different country and with so many secrets."

He offered his hand and Henri took it, silently, solemnly, awkwardly.

"We will talk more," Henri said.

**

The Technical University of Munich was founded in 1868 by Bavarian King Ludwig II and soon became one of the leading European institutes of technology, with high-ranking academic departments in mathematics, the natural sciences, engineering and economics. The graduation ceremony was held on the lawn which fronted the library. The weather had cooperated and it was a glorious spring day. Seventy-five graduating students sat before a raised platform; behind them were parents and friends, including Elisabeth and Henri, and Richard and Judith Goldmann. Off to one side Berthold saw Albert Mueller, who waved.

The university president introduced those sitting on the platform, including a faculty member who had recently received the Nobel Prize in chemistry. Then of course the president made a speech, far too long by Berthold's standards. Several awards were announced; Berthold joined in the polite applause.

"The award for overall excellence in mathematics and engineering, the top academic award, goes to Berthold Becker."

Berthold, stunned, climbed onto the platform as the president went on, "Herr Becker has pursued a specially designed curriculum combining electrical engineering with business economics and management, a new program developed by the university and officials of the Reichsbahn, intended to produce young men who will become the leaders of Germany's industrial rebirth."

Berthold shook hands with the president, then turned to face the audience and smile at his mother, who was clapping excitedly. His gaze moved to a large man at the back of the crowd who was standing and also clapping with great enthusiasm: Putzi.

When the ceremony was over, both Albert Mueller and Putzi Hanfstaengl approached and there was no alternative but to make introductions all around. Putzi's twinkling eyes took in the Goldmanns and Henri, as well as Berthold and Elisabeth, all of his charm on full display.

"It's a great pleasure to meet you, Herr Goldmann," Putzi said, a wide and engaging smile on his large face. "Of course I've often been in your store. My wife and mother are both good customers of Frau Becker. It's so good to see you all together and happy, honoring my good friend and associate who seems to be much smarter than even I had suspected."

Albert Mueller, standing behind Putzi, stepped forward to offer his congratulations, to which he quietly added, "Herr Thyssen was very pleased with your recognition."

Berthold's joy collapsed. Thyssen, who was a major industrialist with ties to the Reichsbahn and also an important supporter of both Hitler and the Technical University, had apparently known about the award before it was announced. Had he earned it or had Thyssen had arranged it? He felt as if he was being squeezed into an ever-contracting, ever more strangling Nazi encirclement, a cold and lonely space which blocked out the glorious sunshine and what should have been the joy of this special day.

***

Elisabeth had planned a small dinner party; the Goldmanns, Beckers and Henri squeezed into Richard's car for the short drive to the Becker apartment. The dinner was pleasant although Berthold was tense, worrying about Mueller's comment. Richard and Henri talked about new trends in retail business and fashion. Elisabeth and Judith chatted about Paris. Berthold heard without really hearing.

Mostly Berthold watched his mother. She looked happy. She also looked beautiful. She was fifty-two years old and her appearance seemed more elegant than Berthold could remember. She had become a capable businesswoman and an important cog in the management of the Goldmann store, taking on responsibilities beyond her own department. And she was very obviously in love. Berthold vowed to do everything in his power to keep her safe and let her enjoy this new phase of her life.

When they had finished eating, Richard called Berthold aside and then announced that the two of them had an errand to run and would be back in about an hour. Richard drove to the Goldmann store, turned his car over to the doorman, and escorted Berthold to his office.

"Leonard first," he said, looking at his telephone. Richard's secretary, forewarned, was already placing the call.

Berthold and Leonard talked for almost fifteen minutes, a significant graduation present given the rates for transatlantic calls. Most of their conversation was about school and work. Because he had lost a year transferring schools, Leonard had another year to go at New York University. His part-time job at Bloomingdale's was going very well and he was excited about the American business methods he was learning.

"Have you thought more about coming to America?" Leonard asked.

"I think I would love it," Berthold said, "but it's not going to happen."

"Anna?"

"That's one reason," Berthold said. "There are others we should not talk about on the telephone."

Berthold and Leonard finished their conversation and Berthold gave the phone to Richard for a few last words.

"While we get Anna at the *Haynt* offices in Warsaw," Richard said, "you should know that I have this phone line checked every day to assure no one is listening in." When the connection was made, Richard briefly said hello to Anna and then left the room.

***

"Hello, Anna."

"Oh, I love to hear your voice saying my name."

"I whisper it to myself day and night. Are you well?"

"I'm fine."

There was a long pause and both understood the unspoken emotions they were feeling.

"There's good news," Berthold finally said. "Mother and Henri are engaged." Berthold told Anna about the events of the past few days, including his graduation award. He also expressed his concerns about Mueller, and Putzi's unexpected appearance at the graduation ceremony. "There's no escaping the Nazis in my life."

"Do you think Hitler will ever gain power?" Anna asked.

"Putzi says Hitler will find a way, even if no one else sees it now."

"Pilsudski agrees with that," Anna said, then added, "Is Putzi suspicious of your connection with Richard Goldmann?"

"When Mother first told me about Putzi being in the store, I thought it was a very dangerous development, but now I think it may not be. Putzi's wife has known Mother for years, so the connection between the Goldmann and Becker families doesn't seem unusual."

Berthold paused, then said, "But I do have a problem with Albert Mueller. Have I told you about him?"

"You mentioned him once or twice."

"He is much too involved in my life. He's suspicious about my commitment to the Nazi cause, and also about what he sees as my sympathy for persecuted Jews. I think he reports to Goebbels regularly."

Berthold heard a sharp intake of breath. He waited for Anna to compose herself.

"It's so precious for us to be able to talk," she said. "I hate to waste this time discussing Nazis."

"There are no conversations any more that don't include Nazis," Berthold said. "We made our choices and now we must play them out, wherever they lead."

He hesitated, then added, "Will you think less of me if I tell you I'm afraid? Sometimes my head seems to explode with all the intrigues bouncing around in there. It would be so easy to make a fatal mistake."

"I do understand," Anna said, "and it's only going to get worse. I know you have to do things you don't want to do. I wish I could share those things with you." She paused. "I wish - so much - that we could just have normal lives."

"You mean marriage and children?" Berthold said, amazing himself with his bold leap. "I want that too."

"Was that a proposal?"

"Yes, but I think you proposed first."

They were both stunned by what had just happened and neither said anything for several moments.

"This must be the strangest engagement ever," Anna said, "and we can't tell anyone."

"But I can tell myself," Berthold said. "In my nightmares, when I hear Hitler screaming in my head, I'll think of being engaged to you and his voice will disappear and it will be blissful. Thank you for that."

Richard knocked gently on the door.

"I think that's Richard telling me it's time to hang up," Berthold said. "I love you."

"And I love you too, my dear ... fiancé."

Chapter 53

June 1932 - Northeim

After his long part-time apprenticeship with the Reichsbahn, Berthold now began his first real assignment. He was responsible for implementing his Northeim project across the Reichsbahn's entire Hanover operating region, of which Northeim was a part. It was exactly what he had hoped for.

He started by bringing selected technical people from the other sections of the Hanover division to a three-day working meeting in Northeim where they could get familiar with the new equipment and systems. Berthold asked Ulrich Walther, who had worked with many of those attending, to conduct the sessions, some in a classroom and others out in the yard.

At the end of the seminar, they set a goal to implement the new switch and signal technology in all Hanover Division locations within six months, during which time Berthold would work with headquarters cost accounting and financial personnel to monitor what they hoped would be demonstrably improved operating results.

***

Shortly after noon the next day, a young Nazi arrived demanding Berthold's immediate presence in the office of Local Group Leader Ernst Krueger. Berthold told the messenger he was busy and it was not possible to come immediately but he would see Herr Krueger at the conclusion of his working day. When he arrived at Nazi headquarters that night, he encountered a swarm of chaotic activity, even more confused than usual.

"What's happening?" Berthold asked the first person he saw.

"The Reichstag has been dissolved; an election is scheduled for July 31."

Berthold, who had been forewarned by Putzi, was not surprised. Elections were not required for two more years, but Franz Papen, the new Chancellor who had recently replaced Brüning, had dissolved the Reichstag and called for new elections.

When Krueger saw Berthold, he screamed across the room, "Who do you think you are? Seven hours later you finally show up!"

It occurred to Berthold that in the relative and always ambiguous power structure of the Nazi organization, he needed to be in a stronger position than the man who was yelling at him, and that it was time to make that clear. He had considered this likely confrontation throughout the afternoon and a solution had come to him; he was prepared to bluff his way forward. He motioned for Krueger to go into his office, followed him, and closed the door.

Berthold spoke slowly and without raising his voice, "Do you know, Herr Krueger, the nature of the work I'm doing at the Reichsbahn and who was instrumental in placing me there to do such work?"

Krueger looked perplexed. That was not the response he had expected and he did not have an answer at hand.

"Who ...?" Krueger started to ask, but Berthold interrupted him.

"It is not for me to tell you," Berthold said, "and until someone in higher authority decides to inform you of my mission here in Northeim, I would advise you to speak very carefully to me. As a first step, when we leave this office, you will make clear to everyone out there the high regard you hold for me and I will then do you the favor of very openly returning that regard."

Krueger, who had been standing, sat down heavily in his chair. He would never, Berthold was sure, ask any questions. Bullies, once confronted, almost always backed off. Berthold smiled and took the chair facing Krueger across his desk.

"Apparently you've just learned what I have known for a week," Berthold said. "I'm here to help you all that I can. What is your plan?"

Krueger, his demeanor now as if he was reporting to a superior, explained that he had been surprised by the sudden call for elections and, as yet, there was no plan. Over the next thirty minutes, Berthold made several suggestions which Krueger readily accepted, and the beginnings of a plan took shape.

The brief sense of satisfaction Berthold felt from his successful skirmish with Ernst Krueger lasted only until he left the headquarters and heard a group of stormtroopers singing what had become their favorite refrain.

"When Jewish blood spurts from the knife, good times are once more here."

***

The next morning, Albert Mueller charged into Berthold's office and challenged Berthold with the same words Krueger had used.

"Who do you think you are?"

"When did you get here?" Berthold asked softly. "Did Goebbels send you?"

A split second hesitation was enough for Berthold to conclude that Mueller had not talked with Goebbels, but he nevertheless asked, "What exact message did Herr Goebbels ask you to deliver?"

The frown on Mueller's face told the whole story. He knew that Berthold could and would check anything he now said. Mueller's bluff had been called, and he had no way to know if Berthold was also bluffing. But Mueller did not give up.

"There's something not quite right with you, Becker."

This was a statement Berthold had not expected, and it terrified him. He felt his pulse start to race.

"Maybe you think you're protected by your friend Hanfstaengl," Mueller said.

Berthold had learned from his interactions with Putzi that much could be gained by waiting and listening, and that's what he now did. After another long moment of silence, Mueller said, his eyes narrowed and his mouth twisted, "Richard Goldmann."

As much as Berthold tried to conceal his reaction, he knew he failed. Mueller smiled, sensing Berthold's weakness.

"You and your mother have far too many connections with Jews," Mueller said.

Berthold could no longer hold his tongue or his temper.

"Before my father died during the same battle in which our *Führer* was injured, he was physician to the Goldmann family. When he didn't return from France, and our family was on the verge of becoming destitute, Richard Goldmann invited my mother to work at his store."

Berthold realized even as he spoke that offering an angry defense was a mistake which would only heighten Mueller's curiosity. He stopped but it was too late. Mueller would now dig deeper into the relationship between the Becker and Goldmann families, spreading suspicion as he went, and eventually finding the proof he was looking for.

Chapter 54

It took just seconds.

Did he actually think it through in advance or were his actions in response to an unexpected opportunity that presented itself? He had no recollection of making a plan and yet was forever haunted by the thought it had transpired too perfectly to have just happened.

Berthold stepped out of the shadows and onto the train to Munich just as it was pulling out. As was his habit, Albert Mueller had boarded the last passenger car and was walking forward, heading to the dining car. Berthold stood quietly and waited.

Mueller didn't see Berthold move out behind him as he stepped onto the narrow platform between the third and fourth cars. He may or may not have understood the significance of Berthold's grip on his shoulders. Perhaps he saw Berthold's face above him as he lost his footing.

Berthold pulled the emergency cord to stop the train.

Mueller's body, when fully recovered several hours later, was in three pieces.

Chapter 55

June 1932 - Warsaw

Josef and Danuta stepped off the bus, their eyes wide. Anna walked with them for hours, allowing her adopted city to penetrate their *shtetl* senses: Warsaw University, the Presidential palace, the Great Synagogue, the offices where she worked at *Haynt*. A poster advertised a boxing match featuring a Jewish boxer and Anna promised to take them. She finished their tour at Marszalkowska Boulevard, where they were overwhelmed by the bustling crowds, clubs, cafés, horse-drawn cabs, automobiles and electric street cars, all jostling together in a huge swirling caldron of old and new Warsaw.

At dusk, they met Menachem Begin at a coffee shop near the university where they talked about the excitement and difficulties of life in Palestine. Anna and Menachem argued over who was responsible for the conflicts with the Arabs that flared regularly.

"There's plenty of land," Menachem said, "enough for Jews and Arabs to share."

"Are you willing to recognize that some Arabs may not agree with that assessment?" Anna asked. "Do you accept that some times it is the Jewish settlers who provoke the violence?"

"You have never been to Palestine," Menachem said. "You don't know what goes on there."

"I have talked to many Jews who have been there," Anna said.

These issues were not resolved, but both Anna and Menachem worked hard to restrain their combativeness, to keep the discussion civil, and to avoid damaging a friendship that was clearly important to both of them. Eventually, Menachem reviewed with Josef the latest procedures for obtaining a British visa to Palestine. He tested Josef's proficiency in Hebrew and his knowledge of Zionism, and deemed him a fit applicant.

"Tomorrow," Menachem said, "we'll go to the British consulate and see what we can do to get your application started."

"How old do you have to be to get a visa?" Danuta asked.

"We prefer at least sixteen," Menachem said.

"I'll be back," Danuta said.

Menachem patted her shoulder and said, "I know." Then he added, "There's a meeting tonight. Would you like to come?"

***

The Zionist meeting and the boxing match occupied the next two evenings, and the days were spent further exploring the wonders of Warsaw. Anna encouraged Josef and Danuta to go off by themselves, sensing a growing closeness between them.

On their last morning, Anna got Danuta aside. "I haven't forgotten. Tell me about your friend."

"He's very nice. And cute. His father works for Papa."

"Does he listen to you when you talk?"

"Yes, of course."

"No, I mean does he pay attention to your ideas?"

Danuta hesitated, then said, "Sometimes."

"That's the second most important thing," Anna said.

"What's the first?"

"Don't get pregnant," Anna said as Danuta blushed wildly.

"I'm serious," Anna added. "If you get pregnant you won't be able to go to Palestine."

"How old were you when you, you know, did it?"

Anna smiled at how cleverly her sister had asked the question.

"Who says I have?"

Danuta waited, using a reporter's technique Anna had perfected and taught her.

"I was twenty-two. You have seven years."

"I don't think so."

Anna shook her head, smiled, and handed Danuta a package of three condoms.

"You're too young to have sex, but if you do, use these."

Danuta smiled, surprised, no longer blushing, thrilled to be accepted into the sisterhood of the sexually aware.

An hour later, as Anna watched her brother and sister board the bus and followed its progress until it was out of sight, she knew both of them far better than she ever had before. She also felt the frustration she usually suppressed but which the discussion of condoms had unleashed with a vengeance. It had been three months.

***

That night, alone in her apartment, tears ran down Anna's cheeks as she read Chaim Bialik's poem.

> *Distant islands, lofty worlds*
> *   of our dreams,*
> *they made us strangers*
> *   wherever we went.*
> *They made our lives hell.*
>
> *And on these islands we remain*
> *   friendless, like two flowers*
> *in a desert, two lost souls searching*
> *   for an eternal loss*
> *in a foreign land.*

Anna could accept that she and Berthold would stay in the desert that Europe was becoming, but if it took all the energy she would ever possess, she was determined that Josef and Danuta would see the flowers of a different land in Palestine.

Chapter 56

June 1932 - Munich

"I killed him. I made it look like an accident, but it wasn't. It was murder."

Berthold sobbed as he told his mother what had happened on the train.

"I had to do it," he said. "Albert would have raised suspicions. Goebbels would have investigated."

Elisabeth tried to comfort her son, but they both knew a crucial line had been crossed. Berthold had taken an innocent man's life to protect their secret. She was horrified. "This is all my fault," she said. "I should have let the truth be known."

"It is not your fault," Berthold said. "You made the right decision. The Nazis are suspicious of everyone, including their own Party members."

That night, unable to sleep, Berthold lay in bed re-reading the anti-Jewish propaganda brochure the Nazis had distributed in Northeim. It came to him just before dawn that now was the time to take the next step.

***

Berthold found Goebbels at the Brown House.

"I understand you were on the train," Goebbels said. "It must have been awful."

"Yes," Berthold answered, his heart pounding, "and I might even have caused the accident. I was coming one way, Albert the other. He seemed startled to see me and began to slip. I tried to grab him, but ..."

After extolling Mueller's virtues for several more minutes, but raising no questions which challenged Berthold's account of how he had died, Goebbels provided an opening when he said, "We've lost a good man."

"To honor Albert," Berthold said quickly, "I would like to join the Party."

"Wonderful," Goebbels said. "Of course I'll sponsor you, and I'm sure the *Führer* will want to be part of the ceremony. He's asked me several times if you had joined yet."

Hitler was in Munich, and the ceremony took place in his office that very afternoon. Putzi was there, along with several other leading Nazis, including Reinhard Heydrich, and there was much talk about Dietrich. Berthold received a membership card which duplicated Dietrich's low number, indicating the prestigious status of Nazi Party membership since the early days. The truth didn't matter; as always, the truth was what Hitler said it was.

As soon as he could get away, Berthold found a small alley and retched until he thought he would die.

**

Wandering aimlessly for hours, Berthold found himself alone in the huge Cathedral, images of Albert Mueller alive and dead filling his mind. He had killed a man who had befriended him. Was anything he might yet accomplish worth taking the life of another human being? Was he as bad as the Nazi monsters?

Sitting alone in the cool vastness of the empty Cathedral, signs of faith all around him, he had an eerie thought that Jesus might be speaking to him, though he heard no words and felt unworthy of such attention. Slowly he began to formulate a view that his guilt and his secret were but trivial pieces in a far more complex puzzle. There is a flood of evil coming, he thought, and each of us who perceives its approach has an obligation to do what he can to prevent it. Thus he recast the killing of Albert Mueller as his first major initiative in the service of something far more significant than simply protecting himself and his mother. Perhaps it could even be seen as an act of war, where killing was not a sin.

He walked out into the warm summer night where millions of stars testified to the unknowable chasm which stretched from the insignificance of his individual earthly presence to the grandeur of a unified creation. And so, on the day he officially became a Nazi, Berthold also experienced his Christian faith more intensively than ever before, although he was also nagged by the thought that this carefully structured religious exoneration was in truth a shallow justification for his heinous act.

Chapter 57

1990 - Munich

"It was a huge victory all over Germany," Marissa explained to her father. "The Nazis doubled their vote, from 6.4 million to 13 million, and won 230 seats in the Reichstag. But despite the largest election victory of any party in any of the Weimar years, they still did not control enough seats to form a government with Hitler as Chancellor."

Berthold, Marissa and Abraham were in Munich discussing the situation in Germany as it existed in the aftermath of the July 1932 elections.

"This," Marissa continued, "was the moment when Hitler's future and that of Germany were poised on a razor's edge. Some thought it was possible Hitler had put himself into a corner from which he could not emerge."

"The Nazis understood that clearly," Berthold said. "I heard Goebbels say several times the Nazi vote total had peaked, and also that they were broke, which made it likely, if there was another election in the near future, they could not even maintain what they had.

"Hitler was clearly depressed and desperate. He had struggled for a decade and his party had more votes and Reichstag seats than anyone had ever imagined it might achieve, but it was not enough, and he had no prospects for more. His dream, his movement, the only focus his life had ever had - all of it seemed to be over."

"Out of that desperation," Marissa interjected, "he took another huge gamble. He went to Hindenburg to demand the Chancellorship when there was no reasonable hope the old man would give it to him."

"And Hindenburg turned him down?" Abraham asked.

"In twenty minutes," Berthold said. "The meeting was a set-up. Newspaper headlines appeared even before Hitler returned to the Kaiserhof, screaming that Hitler had been reprimanded and humiliated by the Reich President, calling his demands a 'shocking pretension.' It was an embarrassing defeat and there was at that moment a real possibility the Nazi Party could split apart."

Chapter 58

September 1932 - Munich

The Hanfstaengl apartment sparkled with light, champagne and a collection of Munich's Nazi notables. Lest he have any illusions about his own importance, it was swiftly made clear by Putzi's wife Helene that Berthold was there as a 'party favor' for the daughters of her friends.

Surrounded by several young ladies, Berthold did not at first notice who came into the room after him, but later he saw a man whose photo appeared regularly in the newspapers. Vaguely listening to one of Helene's young ladies, Berthold searched his memory for what he knew about Dr. Hjalmar Schacht.

Schacht had of course been lionized for miraculously ending the out-of-control inflation which had plagued Germany in the early 1920s, although nobody seemed to know precisely what he had done. Based on that accomplishment, he had been named President of the Reichsbank for life, a position from which he had recently resigned for reasons not clear. Berthold moved closer to where Dr. Schacht was happily answering questions from a circle of admirers.

"Do you think Hitler would be a good Chancellor?"

"Yes," Schacht answered. "In fact, I'm going to write to President Hindenburg to ask him to appoint Hitler at the next opportunity."

Berthold gasped. Hitler's career was so close to over and Schacht was about to resuscitate it. Schacht looked up and saw that the industrialist Friedrich Thyssen had joined the group of listeners.

"Fritz," Schacht said, "will you join me in petitioning President Hindenburg to appoint Hitler?"

"Of course," Thyssen said.

Putzi joined the group and after a boisterous exchange of the latest Nazi gossip, the three men - Schacht, Thyssen and Putzi - moved off to a corner of the room. Berthold didn't dare follow and was soon joined by another of Helene's young ladies. The woman, pretty but flighty, did not require much of Berthold's attention and he found himself wondering why such intelligent and worldly men like Thyssen and Schacht would support Hitler for the Chancellorship. He concluded that these men had simply run out of patience with the Weimar experiment. Democracy had not worked in Germany and Hitler had positioned himself as the only leader who could energize Germany to regain its rightful place in the world. His carefully constructed speech at Dusseldorf had set their minds at ease.

"Can I steal him away for a few minutes?" Putzi asked the girl standing next to Berthold. "I promise to return him none the worse for wear."

Putzi led Berthold over to Schacht and Thyssen.

"Here's the young man we were talking about," Putzi said, "the one who won the award. Berthold Becker, may I introduce Herr Fritz Thyssen and Dr. Hjalmar Schacht."

They all shook hands and then Thyssen said, "We have both lost a good friend. I understand you were with Albert Mueller when he fell onto the tracks."

Berthold closed his eyes in what he hoped would be seen as an expression of sorrow rather than the sinking feeling he had whenever Mueller's name was mentioned.

"Albert was slipping," he said, "and I tried to grab him. I have nightmares about it all the time."

"We both miss him," Thyssen said, quickly followed by, "I spoke to one of my friends in the Reichsbahn the other day and your name came up. My friend says you're a future star."

Thyssen, Schacht and Putzi resumed the conversation they had been having. Berthold smiled, never said another word, and listened intently, picking up isolated words: Dusseldorf, Danzig, Guderian.

Soon after, Schacht and Thyssen left, and Berthold went to say goodbye to Helene Hanfstaengl, who of course noted that he was leaving alone. She allowed a naughty smile to capture her face and he knew what was coming.

"I'll keep trying," Helene said, "until you take one of these beautiful young women with you when you leave. They're all willing, you know."

Berthold glanced at the luscious bottom of the last girl he had spoken to as she slowly walked away, trying to remember her name and wondering what she would be like. His body stirred; it had been six months. Helene followed his glance and smiled.

***

"I recognize Dusseldorf and Danzig," Berthold told Richard when they next met, "but who is Guderian? Thyssen seemed very excited about some military analysis this fellow had prepared."

Several days later, Richard reported to Berthold that Heinz Guderian had been one of the bright young officers selected to remain in the reduced-size German army after the war. In the early 1920s, he had been active in the defense of Germany's eastern frontier, after which he had been placed in command of the Army's motorized units in Berlin. He was the author of numerous papers on what he termed new concepts in mechanized warfare.

"How did you learn these things?" Berthold asked.

"The Socialist Party has a comprehensive file on the progress of German rearmament, which we strongly oppose as a violation of the Versailles Treaty."

"Why don't you say these things in political campaigns?"

"Unfortunately," Richard said, "socialists are much better at research than we are at politics." He gave Berthold a thin folder. "Here's Guderian's latest paper, making the case that tank warfare is the wave of the future. I would imagine this is what Thyssen was so excited about. He probably expects to manufacture the tanks."

Chapter 59

October 1932 - Ciechanow

Anna and Menachem disembarked in Ciechanow after a comfortable trip on the bus that took, still amazing to Anna, under two hours. Menachem had come to recruit for *Beitar*, the youth component of the Zionist movement.

Begin's visit had been announced in advance, and an excited crowd, including Anna's brother Josef and sister Danuta, was there to greet him. Menachem and the young Zionists went off to the old castle to prepare for the meeting to be held there that night. Anna went home with her parents and grandfather.

"You've become very famous here," Evona said to her daughter. "*Haynt* is now delivered by the bus on the same day it's published and copies are always available at the library. If there's an article by you, I post it on the bulletin board."

"I don't suppose everyone always agrees with what I write," Anna said.

"That's certainly true," Grandfather Kamon said in a low voice.

Evona gave her father a quick look. "This is no way to welcome Anna home," she said. "We've had this discussion; no more.

***

The young Zionists assembled at the Ciechanow Town Hall; carrying torches, they marched across the bridge to the castle. The huge round towers and high exterior walls stood out starkly in the moonlight. The great gate was permanently wedged open on rusted hinges and inside, whatever walls had once enclosed medieval living spaces were long gone and the ground was bare.

The bonfire prepared earlier was lit and once it was burning fiercely, the head of the Ciechanow Zionist Party introduced Menachem. "This young man, only nineteen years old, is already recognized all over Poland as one of Zionism's most important leaders."

Anna, standing next to Danuta, asked, "Have you made application yet?"

"I have the forms," Danuta said.

"Have you told Mama and Papa?"

"No." Danuta grabbed her older sister's arm. "I was hoping you would help me."

"There are now over 50,000 *Beitar* members, more than half of them in Poland," Menachem was saying. "How many here are members?" About half of the crowd raised their arms and cheered. "How many will now join the Ciechanow chapter of *Beitar*?" Every remaining hand shot up, except Anna, who was busy taking notes.

"We have uniforms here for all who want them," Menachem said.

Many young people came forward, boys and girls alike. Each was given a uniform and each removed his or her outer clothes without the slightest embarrassment and put on a *Beitar* uniform. As Danuta change her clothes, Anna saw the lithe body of a stunning young woman. She was certain that several of the boys had also noticed.

It occurred to Anna that the Zionist movement was making girls the equals of boys in many ways, and that this was one more reason the *shtetls* of Poland would have to change. These girls would never submit to the arranged marriages and domestic lives their parents might want for them.

***

"I'm sad and I'm also afraid," Danuta said as she and Anna walked home from the Zionist bonfire.

"How could you be otherwise," Anna said. "Your whole life is changing in ways no one can predict. You're very brave, and I'm proud of you."

"I have so much to learn before I can go to Palestine, even if I get a visa. Hebrew. English. How to be a farmer."

"How to be a farmer?" Anna asked, laughing. "I don't think so. I have a different idea for you. Why don't you see if you have a talent for journalism? Menachem said there's a great need to tell the story of the Zionist settlements in Palestine. You could start with an account of his visit to Ciechanow."

"I thought you were going to write that story," Danuta said. "I saw you taking notes."

"I have plenty of stories to write," Anna said. "I'll give you my notes."

***

Early the next morning Menachem took the bus to another stop on his seemingly endless recruiting mission. Later in the day, the Gorska family, including Josef and Danuta, gathered around the dining table to talk.

"This is so rare," Evona said. "We should cherish this moment together; there may not be many more like it. Josef will soon go to Palestine. Maybe Danuta wants to go as well."

Danuta's head spun to her mother; she had never mentioned her intention to emigrate to Palestine.

"It wasn't hard to figure out," Evona said. "Your new uniform was a clue."

Jacob and Evona shared a look which mixed pride and profound pain. Anna imagined how lonely they would be in a home empty of their children, with grandchildren, if any, born elsewhere.

Jacob spoke to his children. "Your mother and I, and Grandfather Kamon, have talked about this many times. We've decided that we will stay in Ciechanow, despite Uncle Edel's repeated offers to bring us to America. We've also decided we will not oppose Josef or Danuta if either of you make plans to go to Palestine. Of course we'll miss you terribly but we understand and we'll help you any way we can."

Danuta looked like she was about to cry. Evona opened her arms and rushed to hug her.

When everyone had returned to their seats, Evona turned to Anna. "You are the puzzlement for us," she said. "Maybe you could explain why you're not planning to go to Palestine. With all of your connections, you could surely get a visa. I think it's important for us to know why you're choosing to stay in Poland."

"Several of my friends have gone to Palestine," Anna said, "and although it's a hard life, they seem to be happy there. I encourage every Jew who can go to do so, including Josef and Danuta.

"But the fact is that most Polish Jews will never be able to go to Palestine, so those who remain must find a way to live here, no matter how difficult it becomes. At least for now, I've decided my place is with those who stay, where I'll use the platform *Haynt* has given me to tell of the struggle of Polish Jewry in Poland."

Chapter 60

November 1932 - Warsaw

Anna had received several long communications from Berthold, including a description of Major Heinz Guderian's plans for a mechanized army. She arranged a meeting with the Marshal and sat quietly while he read.

"Napoleon would attack," Pilsudski said when he put down the last page.

What attack, she thought? Was the Marshal actually considering an armed attack on Germany?

"Come walk," Pilsudski said suddenly, leading Anna through rooms of the Belvedere Palace she had never seen. They passed several servants who looked attentively to see if they were needed but made sure to keep their distance. Large windows gave glimpses of bright sunlight bouncing off bare trees in the park outside.

"I told Aleksandra you were coming and asked her to meet with us," Pilsudski said as they entered the private living area.

"So, here is Anna Gorska," Madame Pilsudski said, "the woman who spends more time with my husband than any other woman but myself."

They took seats on comfortable chairs near a blazing fireplace. Pilsudski repeated the essence of Berthold's reports to his wife, then asked her, "What do you think we should do?"

"My husband has a better grasp of European politics than any other leader on the continent, yet he asks for my advice. Why, Anna, do you think he does that?"

Anna understood she was being tested, that her answer must neither patronize Madame Pilsudski nor insult the Marshal.

"My guess, Madame Pilsudski," Anna said, "is that you make your husband think harder. You don't accept his conclusions easily, and thus his decisions become better than they might otherwise be."

Pilsudski laughed with genuine joy. "Well said, Anna! Most of my colleagues don't dare to question my judgments, at least to my face, but Aleksandra has no such qualms."

He paused to let this praise of his wife sit in the air for a moment, then continued, "So let's begin by clarifying our objectives. What are we trying to accomplish?"

Pilsudski turned to Anna. Another test.

"It seems to me," Anna said, "that your overriding goal has always been to safeguard Polish independence." Another pause, then Anna continued. "In the short-term, this means keeping Hitler from power. Poland cannot do this alone so the challenge is to find allies to assist with that objective."

"Brilliant," Madame Pilsudski said.

"Do I dare," the Marshal said with a smile, "disagree with a political analysis supported by two such intelligent and charming women?"

"Only at your peril," Madame Pilsudski said. "Shall we go through the list?"

Anna imagined they had been through this 'list' many times, sitting before the very fireplace that was warming them now, as changing circumstances altered the perspectives and interests of potential allies and enemies.

"Russian negotiators," Pilsudski said, "have recently signed a non-aggression treaty with us and I expect it will be ratified by both governments in the next several weeks. This has raised concerns in Germany."

Pilsudski sat back and beamed with a look of satisfaction and mystery Anna had never seen before.

"Of course," he said, "these concerns are soundly based. If I could convince Russia to stand aside, I could then induce France to attack Germany from the west while we simultaneously attacked from the east. We could each take a little territory, but more importantly, we would put teeth into

286

the League of Nations' monitoring of German rearmament by claiming it was fear of that illegal rearmament which prompted us to attack in the first place, which is at least partly true."

"Is there any chance France would join such an *audacious* initiative?" Madame Pilsudski asked, dragging out the French pronunciation of audacious.

"Ah the French," Pilsudski said. "They won't act without British support, which would be meaningless even if His Majesty's government offered the most solemn of promises. Furthermore, the Brits are not interested in Poland and don't trust me."

"Which distrust, my dear," Madame Pilsudski said, "you have well earned."

"Still it would be good to talk again with the French," Pilsudski said. "They have as much reason as we do - perhaps more - to want to contain Germany while it's still feasible to do so. I'll schedule a meeting with the French military attaché."

There was a lull in the conversation until Madame Pilsudski said with a knowing grin. "Whatever have we forgotten?"

"Well, there is the Catholic Church," Anna said.

"So indeed there is," the Marshal said. "Please repeat what you told me before."

"Göring has once again been in Rome," Anna said, "reportedly offering Hitler's commitment for a Reich Concordat in exchange for the support of Catholic Center delegates for an Enabling Act."

"Hitler is negotiating deals as if he was already Chancellor," Pilsudski said. "Remarkable."

Madame Pilsudski raised her eyebrows. "Yes, amazing," she said. "Who else do we know who did things like that before he had official power? But tell me, dear, what's so important about this Concordat?"

The Marshal smiled and rested his hand on his wife's knee before he answered, "A Reich Concordat is basically a contract between the Vatican and the German government specifying the rights and rules of operation of the Catholic Church in Germany. It's been one of Cardinal Pacelli's major goals for years. There are several valid reasons to have one - we have one in Poland - but my guess is that what the Cardinal Secretary of State Pacelli really wants is to be able to exercise greater control over what he perceives as the much too independent politics of the German bishops, especially Cardinal Faulhaber in Munich. Former Chancellor Brüning told Pacelli several years ago that the Reichstag would never pass a Reich Concordat, so Pacelli needs Hitler in power to get it."

Pilsudski glanced at Anna and added, "This is all connected with the rejection of the Brüning documents. Pacelli does not want the Pope to focus on how horrible Hitler would be. He just wants Hitler in office so he can get his Concordat."

"My sources say Pacelli is well aware that Hitler cannot be trusted to honor a Concordat," Anna said.

"That supports my argument," Pilsudski said. "The provisions between Germany and the Vatican might become meaningless, but the restrictions on the German bishops would remain firmly in place."

"And what is this Enabling Act which is being traded for the Concordat?" Madame Pilsudski asked.

"As Hitler has quite openly stated," Pilsudski explained, "one of his first acts as Chancellor will be to amend the German Constitution to allow the passage of laws and decrees without the concurrence of either the Reichstag or President Hindenburg, which would of course make the Chancellor an absolute dictator. It takes two thirds of the Reichstag to amend the Constitution, which means Hitler needs the votes of the Catholic Center delegates to get an Enabling Act passed."

***

Marshal Pilsudski did indeed arrange a meeting with Colonel Alain Bélanger, the military attaché assigned to

France's Warsaw embassy, to which he invited Anna and Colonel Josef Beck, the recently appointed Polish Foreign Minister.

"So, Marshal," Bélanger said, "have I been summoned to learn that your troops are massed at the border, ready to invade Germany?"

Beck choked on his drink, Anna looked down and bit her tongue, and Pilsudski was completely unflustered.

"Poland's invasion plans," Pilsudski said with a roguishly icy overtone, "should such plans exist, are a military secret that would only be revealed to allies who chose to become participants." He allowed a smile to appear on his face and continued, "Can Poland count France in that select group?"

"As the Marshal well knows, France has been Poland's ally by treaty since 1921," Bélanger said. "Has Poland been the victim of an unprovoked attack which, under the terms of that treaty, is the pre-condition that would compel France to provide diplomatic and military assistance?"

"The pace of German rearmament suggests that such an attack may well be forthcoming," Pilsudski said. "Your government's unwillingness to constrain German rearmament is a shortsighted policy that will inevitably lead to war, perhaps sooner than later."

"My government," Bélanger said, "is not aware of any German rearmament."

Turning to Beck, Pilsudski said, "You see how much we can learn from French diplomats. Colonel Bélanger is able to lie with a perfectly straight face."

Facing Bélanger again, Pilsudski continued, "I have of course anticipated your duplicitous response. Anna will soon summarize for you what she has already published about German rearmament, and Colonel Beck will reveal additional details which have not been published. When they have completed their presentations the French government will no longer be able to claim ignorance as a basis for its spineless national policy."

"That is most undiplomatic language, Marshal," Colonel Bélanger said.

"We have tried diplomatic language and it hasn't had much effect," Pilsudski said. "You have two choices. You may stay and listen, or if you would rather maintain the facade of French ignorance, you may leave. If you stay, be assured we will make no notes of your participation and will not refer to this conversation without your concurrence. Anna, of course, will not mention you directly or by implication in any articles she writes."

Colonel Bélanger stayed fixed in his seat and Pilsudski motioned for Anna to begin.

"Germany began re-arming immediately after the Great War, but substantive rearmament," Anna said, referring to her notes, "didn't commence until after the Inter-Allied Control Commission left Germany in early 1927. Krupp's artillery design group immediately reactivated their main works in Essen and its engineers were tasked with designing a new generation of self-propelled guns, torpedo launching tubes, periscopes, armor plate, remote control devices, and rockets. The prototype of an 88 mm antiaircraft-antitank gun and blueprints for cannons, howitzers and light field guns were also soon completed. Tanks went into production in 1928. Artillery firing ranges were operational in 1929."

"Lest you continue to delude yourself that these activities are for defensive purposes," Pilsudski interjected, "Colonel Beck has learned something which will startle you."

The information had actually come from Berthold but they had of course agreed not to mention him.

Beck spoke without notes. "Major Heinz Guderian, the chief of the Wehrmacht's new motor transport command, has argued that tanks should be concentrated in armored divisions, and even more radically, that all other forces should be made subordinate to the tanks. He conducted a demonstration in 1929 with little automobiles draped with canvas to resemble tanks. The other officers laughed at him then, but they're not laughing now. Earlier this year, Germany produced a prototype five-ton, two-man tank armed with two machine guns."

Colonel Bélanger fidgeted as Beck continued.

"Guderian has developed plans for what he calls a *panzer* thrust, a sharp surgical strike at the enemy's central nervous system, designed to paralyze the ability to respond."

Beck paused, looked ominously at Bélanger, and added, "There is nothing defensive about such a plan."

Pilsudski also stared at Colonel Bélanger. "So far," he said, "France has been unwilling to heed any evidence that might have led to sanctions against Germany."

Pilsudski drew a deep breath and his voice took a sharper edge. "France has engaged in purposeful self-deception, choosing to believe the preposterous cover stories put forward by German military and political leaders. Perhaps your businessmen, like industrialists in Germany, see opportunities for profit in the rearmament of the Reich and have convinced French political leaders not to object."

Pilsudski paused but Bélanger offered no response. Pilsudski asked Anna to summarize the current political situation in Germany.

"Leading German generals," she said, "are aligning with major industrialists with the goal of bringing about a right-wing government dedicated to Germany's resurgence as a military power. Recently, there have been credible approaches, from prominent men like Hjalmar Schacht and Franz Thyssen, asking President Hindenburg to appoint Adolf Hitler to be Chancellor of such a government."

"There is however," Pilsudski interjected, as he and Anna had scrupulously scripted, "a viable alternative. There is a revolt ongoing within the Nazi Party, focused around a man by the name of Gregor Strasser. Discussions have been initiated, the goal of which is to bring Strasser and a sizable number of Nazi delegates into a coalition government which would *exclude* Herr Hitler."

Colonel Bélanger's attention was now riveted. This appeared to be something he had not heard before.

"How do you know these things?" he asked, his head rotating between Anna and Pilsudski.

"My sources cannot be revealed," Pilsudski said. He and Anna had agreed that the Marshal would claim all sources as his, thus hoping to divert Bélanger from speculation about any possible sources unique to Anna. They understood that Bélanger was no fool and that such a strategy was not guaranteed to work.

"But," Pilsudski continued, "accepting for the moment that what you've just heard is true, would you not agree that it should be the common goal of France and Poland to oppose Adolf Hitler's dangerous lunacy, and that this will be much easier to accomplish before he gains power than after, and that we have before us at this very moment a marvelous opportunity while Hitler is being weakened by a revolt within his own party."

"What do you propose?" Bélanger asked, breathing out all of his tension with the words.

Anna was euphoric. The French attaché was engaged. She was so proud that the information provided by Berthold had helped produce this result.

Pilsudski rose and paced as he spoke.

"I do not believe we need to actually invade. The German generals know full well they cannot adequately defend their borders. My proposal is that France and Poland open secret discussions with President Hindenburg, being careful not to upset the old man's Prussian pride. We would allude to the possibility of invasion, but our only actual demand would be that Hitler must not become part of any German government, let alone its head."

Bélanger was thinking intensely, and Pilsudski waited until he looked up.

"In return," the Marshal continued, "I propose that France and Poland will agree to take a joint initiative at the League of Nations to relieve Germany of the most onerous of the Versailles restrictions, including what even I consider the unfair and unrealistic limits placed on the German military. This would be purely symbolic, since they are already violating these provisions, but symbolism is important. I believe Field Marshal Hindenburg would find both aspects of that proposal quite attractive."

The room went silent. There was no more to be said by anyone except Colonel Bélanger, who downed his cognac and rose, delaying the moment as long as he could.

"I will take what you have said to my superiors."

Resolution grew visibly on Bélanger's face and he even seemed to grow taller.

"You have put forward a very sophisticated proposal that touches on every aspect of the problem we're facing. I will recommend that this proposal be considered with the same seriousness in which it has been offered."

Chapter 61

December 1932 - Berlin

"Goebbels wants you to come to Germany," Berthold exclaimed as soon as Anna came onto the phone. "He says you should see for yourself that Hitler's accession to the Chancellorship is being widely discussed and supported by a broad spectrum of German politicians, businessmen and military leaders."

"Does he want me to report the truth?" Anna asked.

"Apparently Goebbels is interested in stories about Hitler in the foreign press, and doesn't care if they're positive or negative. For his purposes, as he has said many times, rumors are as good as facts, lies as good as the truth, and any attention, even outright condemnation, has its value."

"I'll be on the next train."

***

The day Anna arrived in Berlin, General Kurt von Schleicher was appointed Chancellor by President Hindenburg, replacing Franz Papen who had held the office for less than six months. The next morning, while all the other reporters chased after Chancellor Schleicher, Anna went to Papen's not-yet-vacated office at the Chancellery, where she found she was not alone.

The woman sitting in the outer office looked up and said, "It seems that two of us at least have the nose for the less obvious but perhaps bigger story. My name is Dorothy Thompson."

"I know who you are," Anna said. "Your fame has reached as far as Warsaw."

Thompson waited.

"Oh, I'm sorry. My name is Anna Gorska."

"The young woman from Poland who writes such well-researched and analytical stories in English," Thompson said.

"You've heard of me?"

"Don't underestimate your fame. Everyone has seen the photo of you in Hitler's plane. What are you doing in Berlin?"

"Goebbels invited me."

"I guess he didn't mind that you pointed out the hypocrisy of Hitler's recent avoidance of derogatory remarks about Jews. By the way, I agree with you. He's not fooling anyone who doesn't want to be fooled."

"Actually, Putzi said Goebbels was quite satisfied with my article."

"Putzi? Your range of acquaintances is impressive."

The door to Papen's office opened and they were invited to enter. A secretary brought coffee and then disappeared.

"Why are you here?" Papen asked amiably. "I would think my former champion who has now become my enemy would be the story today."

"General Schleicher's remarks are quite predictable," Thompson said. "Yours are not."

Thompson paused while opening her notebook. Anna did likewise, more than a little overwhelmed at working side-by-side with the most famous female correspondent in the world.

"Are you planning to retreat quietly into retirement?" Thompson asked.

Papen laughed, revealing the answer before he said a word.

"As you are no doubt aware," he said, "I have been unable to form a parliamentary government, either with Herr Hitler or without him. This situation is very uncomfortable for President Hindenburg. I resigned to give someone else an opportunity."

Thompson smiled, revealing her skepticism, but Papen, understanding the absurdity of what he had just said, showed no displeasure.

295

Anna, her heart pounding, asked her first question, "Goebbels thinks General Schleicher's Chancellorship will last two months at the most. Do you agree with him?"

Now Papen looked surprised, as did Thompson.

"Did Goebbels publish that this morning?" Papen asked. "I didn't see it in *Der Angriff*."

"No," Anna said. "He mentioned it last night at the Kaiserhof. He predicted that Schleicher would be a disaster and if Hindenburg did not put a new cabinet in place before the reconvening of the Reichstag at the end of January, the entire government would collapse in chaos."

Papen laughed. "For once," he said, "Herr Goebbels and I agree."

"Will you be doing anything to help Goebbels' prediction come true?" Thompson asked, nodding to Anna in recognition of what now seemed to be an investigative partnership.

"Perhaps," Papen said, "you could report I'm not pleased with the way General Schleicher has manipulated events over the past days. Also, that we do not agree on the best way to structure and manage Germany's government. Nor do we agree on the best way to involve the Nazis in the government, without which nothing productive can be accomplished."

"So the game is not over," Anna said.

"Perhaps not," Papen said, standing.

Their interview concluded, Anna and Dorothy Thompson left Papen's office and walked into the huge Reichstag chamber, eerily empty and quiet.

"Well, Miss Gorska," Thompson said. "I think you and I just made quite a combination. We must definitely talk more. Perhaps we can even share sources. Would lunch tomorrow fit into your schedule?"

***

Berthold had planned to work on his Reichsbahn assignment at the railroad's corporate headquarters in Berlin, but Goebbels grabbed him first.

"There's new information every hour," Goebbels said, "and I'm overwhelmed with constant demands and questions. Everyone's confused and tempers are flaring. I want you to deal with the Gauleiters and Local District Leaders in my place. You'll communicate information I provide, answer their questions, and let me know what's on their minds. I've made arrangements for an office and secretarial assistance here at the Kaiserhof."

Berthold put in a token appearance at his Reichsbahn office, explained what he had been asked to do for Goebbels, and received permission to take whatever time was needed. Someone, probably Herr Thyssen, had spread the word that Berthold's Nazi-related business was always to be a priority.

***

At the end of the day, Berthold caught up with Anna, who was staying at the nearby Hotel Excelsior. Over a glass of wine, they discussed their day's activities.

"This is the first time we've ever done this," Anna said.

Berthold look puzzled.

"We're like a married couple who've gone off to work and come home at dinner time to share their day's experience."

"I like that," Berthold said.

"You may not like this. Dorothy Thompson wants us to share sources."

"Not me!" Berthold exclaimed.

"Well, why not? It's no secret to the Nazis we have a relationship, and there've even been times when you've been asked by Goebbels or Putzi to give me certain information."

"But," Berthold said, "there have been other times when the information provided was definitely not what the Nazis wanted you to know." He paused. "Plus there's the other thing."

"If we try to hide our relationship from Thompson," Anna said, "she will sense our deception and that will only serve to raise her curiosity."

"Can you trust her?" Berthold asked.

"It's too soon to know. We'll have to test her."

They spent the next hour carefully identifying every piece of information Berthold had transmitted to Anna, deciding in each case what could be mentioned to Thompson and what not.

Business taken care of, Berthold said, "By the way, I've changed hotels. Did you know the Reichsbahn has a longstanding business relationship with the Excelsior, as well as a direct tunnel from the train station and our offices to the hotel. I'm on the same floor as you."

***

It soon became clear to Berthold that many of the Nazi leaders were truly fed up with Hitler's refusal to become part of the government, thus denying them the jobs and other benefits to which they thought they were entitled. They all knew that Gregor Strasser was pushing for Nazi participation in a coalition government, even if Hitler did not become Chancellor, and many of them were starting to think Strasser had a better idea. Berthold could see the panic in Goebbels' eyes as he gave him these reports.

Anna wrote an article describing the chaos within the Nazi organization and sent a telegram to Pilsudski urging him to enjoy what they had agreed to call his "French baguette" as soon as possible.

Chapter 62

Anna and Dorothy Thompson continued to get on famously, despite the fifteen year difference in their ages. Thompson was fascinated with the story of Anna's emergence from a remote *shtetl* in Poland to international recognition, and of course Anna was thrilled to learn more about Thompson's legendary career, including her famous interview with Hitler in Munich the previous year.

Thompson leaned forward and whispered, "I haven't published this yet, but here's my description of Hitler: he is formless, almost faceless, a man whose countenance is a caricature, a man whose framework seems cartilaginous. He is inconsequent and voluble, ill poised and insecure. He is the very prototype of the little man."

"What does cartilaginous mean?" Anna asked.

"It means having a skeleton of cartilage instead of bone, in other words not fully formed, underdeveloped, childlike." She thought for moment. "Maybe I should leave that out."

They laughed together, loud enough to draw attention.

"Does 'little man' refer to the book just published by Hans Fallada?"

"So you're well-read in addition to well-connected," Thompson said. "Yes it does."

Thompson ordered a plum brandy called Slivovitz to top off the meal.

"This is a favorite in Poland," Anna said.

"I ordered it in your honor."

Thompson sipped her drink and got serious again.

"Now for real business. Do you know that Schleicher is still trying to convince Gregor Strasser to join his cabinet?"

"There's been talk in Nazi circles for weeks," Anna said. "Has a meeting actually been set?"

Thompson looked at her watch.

"It should be happening just about now."

***

"I will never get tired of seeing you like this," Berthold said as they rolled out of bed and began to gather their clothes.

Anna blushed and stared lustfully at Berthold, who was also naked, until he blushed as well. They came together and caressed each other for several delicious minutes, then reluctantly dressed and went to the dining room.

"What is Schleicher trying to do?" Anna asked Berthold after they had ordered dinner.

"It seems he's trying to split off the Strasser faction and bring the Strasser-oriented Nazi Reichstag delegates into the government. The rumor is he'll offer Strasser the Vice-Chancellorship, thus excluding Hitler from the government and perhaps destroying the Nazi Party."

"Is that possible?"

"I wish," Berthold said, "but it's not likely. Schleicher and Strasser are both naïve. When it comes down to a decision, I doubt there will be a Strasser faction. Gauleiters and District Leaders may be complaining, but would they actually oppose Hitler? His response would be immediate and brutal, and they know it. Strasser is a brilliant organizer and manager, but he's not a fighter. I think Hitler will crush him. But that doesn't mean either Hitler or the Nazis will survive. It could still fall apart, and soon."

"Can I write that?"

"Please do. Just don't quote me."

***

"It's another disaster," Putzi exclaimed.

"Strasser?" Berthold asked.

"No, Hitler will deal with him. I'm talking about Thuringia. There was a local election there yesterday and the results were awful. On top of everything else, this could kill us."

"But Thuringia is just a small state," Berthold said. "How could it be so important?"

"It's important because Hitler predicted a huge victory and we lost almost forty percent from our vote total in July."

***

The attack unleashed by Hitler against Gregor Strasser was vicious, quick, and effective. As Berthold had predicted, Strasser never had a chance. Berthold and Anna met with Putzi to discuss what had happened.

"Hitler," Putzi said, "spoke with every District Leader, Gauleiter and stormtrooper captain. There must have been twenty meetings in two days. He began each meeting by stammering with a sob that he had been shocked by Strasser's treachery. He finished each meeting by extracting from each man a solemn oath of loyalty, not to the Party, certainly not to Germany, but to him personally."

"What happened then," Anna asked.

"Hitler called Strasser to the Kaiserhof and openly accused him of being a traitor, stating that his only recourse was to shoot himself."

"Will he?" Anna asked.

"No," Putzi said, "but he did resign all of his Nazi Party posts and took the train to Munich."

"And his seat in the Reichstag?" Anna asked.

"Very perceptive, Fraulein Gorska" Putzi said. "So far he's kept his seat, and his vote."

So the game, Berthold thought, was still not quite over.

"Who will run the district organizations now?" he asked, fearful that Goebbels would look to him for expanded duties.

"That will be a huge problem," Putzi said. "Between them, as I'm sure you know, Hitler and Goebbels couldn't begin to do what Strasser was doing. If we gain power soon, it won't matter. If not, everything will fly apart and it'll all be over."

Putzi shook his head and smiled without a hint of joy. "Hitler has always been given to the throw of the dice, taking the all-or-nothing risk. I believe this will be the final throw. Chancellor or suicide are now Hitler's options, and it will happen quickly."

"Can I write that?"

"As long as you don't attribute it to me," Putzi said.

Chapter 63

December 31, 1932 - Berlin

By the time Hitler made his appearance the New Years' Eve party at the Kaiserhof was in full swing but the mood changed for the worse with his arrival. The *Führer* was in a foul mood which he made no effort to hide. He sat in a corner sipping a beer, a scowl on his face, and nobody dared to approach him.

Hitler finished his one beer and left, never having said a word. Goebbels, who was only there because Hitler was, also left, and without those two in the room, conversations began again. Berthold picked up snatches as he wandered from group to group.

One of the Nazi District Leaders from northern Germany was the most outspoken. "It's fine that the *Führer* cast out Strasser," the District Leader said. "We've all sworn loyalty to Hitler, and we are loyal. But many are still wondering why their leader refuses to join the government and obtain for us the jobs and other spoils that such participation would bring."

Berthold also heard more than one of the stormtrooper commanders say it was time for more direct methods. "We have 400,000 men under arms," one said. "It's time we use them."

Just at that moment, as if to emphasize the stormtroopers' frustration, a bloody man dressed in a tuxedo arrived to report a huge and still ongoing confrontation between communists and Nazis, not two blocks from the Kaiserhof, with dozens wounded and many under arrest. Several rushed out to see the battle, and Berthold and Putzi found themselves alone in one corner of a now almost empty room.

"You know Hitler is suicidal again," Putzi said. "Has been for weeks. I think he feels his moment has finally passed and will not return."

Putzi downed his champagne, poured another, and downed that too.

"Adolf is saying quite openly that if he's convinced nothing will come of his dreams, he'll end his life with a bullet."

"Would he actually do that?" Berthold asked.

"Whether his threat is real or not," Putzi continued, "his assessment of the situation is not exaggerated and he is truly panicked for the first time since I've known him."

Putzi stumbled and caught himself on a chair, but kept right on talking.

"Oh how the tide ebbs! In July we had a huge victory, but it wasn't enough to gain control. Now, we're on the verge of extinction."

***

A very different party was taking place at the Adlon Hotel where many of the international correspondents had gathered. Dorothy Thompson introduced Anna to her colleagues, most of whom knew her name and had seen the photograph of her with Hitler. Franklin Roosevelt's victory and Hitler's recent troubles were the main topics of discussion. Several correspondents stated their opinion that Hitler was done, except perhaps as part of a coalition in which he would be an insignificant partner.

"It seems likely," Anna said, "that Hitler will never gain a majority of voters or seats in the Reichstag, but it seems equally true he will never agree to become part of a coalition where he does not have the ultimate power."

"Hitler may make progress with the right-wing parties," someone said, "but the German bishops despise him and most Catholics voted against him."

"The Vatican seems to feel differently," Anna said.

A slew of surprised faces instantly turned to her. Apparently this was not common knowledge among the reporters.

"Herman Göring," Anna said, "has been negotiating with Cardinal Pacelli in Rome for months."

"What does Hitler have that the Vatican wants?"

"For one thing," Anna said, "he's seen in Rome as the best hedge against a Communist Party takeover in Germany."

Anna paused, uncertain whether to mention the desire of Rome for a Reich Concordat, but she was saved from making that decision when a new drunken voice entered the conversation. Thompson whispered to Anna that the speaker was the head of the New York Times' European news service.

"When will these people learn?" the Times man asked. "Schleicher, Papen, Schacht, the Vatican - it's always the same dream. They think they can use the Nazi movement for their own purposes, and they are very, very wrong. The Nazi movement belongs to Adolf Hitler and cannot be used by anyone else."

Several people asked Anna about Marshal Pilsudski and rumors of a Polish invasion of Germany. Anna said she knew nothing about such rumors.

The conversations went on, everyone sang *Auld Lang Syne* at midnight, and when the serious drinking began, Anna walked back to the Excelsior a few blocks away. Berthold was already there.

"Is it really possible?" Anna asked. "Do we dare hope that we will soon see the end of Adolf Hitler?"

Chapter 64

January 1933 - Berlin

"It's incredible," Putzi said. "Just when it seemed everything was lost, Papen has asked Hitler to meet."

So, Berthold thought, as former Chancellor Papen had told Anna, the game was definitely not over. Without realistic hope and perhaps on the verge of suicide, was it possible that Adolf Hitler's hope of ruling Germany would be rescued by another man's ambition?

"The meeting is supposed to be secret," Putzi said, "but I've already notified a photographer."

"Are you sure photos are a good idea?" Berthold asked. "Suppose the meeting doesn't go well?"

"Doesn't matter," Putzi said. "Just the fact that Hitler and Papen are meeting will be enough to revitalize the *Fuhrer's* image."

Before it was Adolf and now it was the *Fuhrer*. Berthold wondered if this was the result of Hitler's vicious treatment of Strasser.

"What does Papen want?"

"He wants his job back," Putzi said, "but even more, he wants revenge against Schleicher for convincing Hindenburg to dump him."

Just then Goebbels burst in.

"The *Führer* has returned," he said. "Papen wants to form an alliance to replace Schleicher. Did your photographer get pictures?"

Putzi raised his phone, spoke briefly, and broke into a big smile. "There are pictures of each of them entering the house. The presses have been stopped and the story is being inserted at the top of page one."

Goebbels raced out to tell Hitler the news. Berthold hurried to the Excelsior to tell Anna.

The next day, Putzi reported that Papen had spoken with President Hindenburg and come back with the news that the President would support a Papen cabinet including Hitler but not a cabinet led by Hitler. This was of course unacceptable to the *Führer* and it seemed that every possible route to a Hitler Chancellorship was now again blocked, with time running out.

Hitler, however, did not commit suicide, and instead went frenetically from one bizarre meeting to another, with nobody understanding what was happening or where it would end.

***

"Do you know anything about *Osthilfe?*" Dorothy Thompson asked.

"Never heard the term," Anna said. "What does it mean?"

"*Osthilfe* was a program instituted by the German government three years ago to give financial support to bankrupt estates in East Prussia. It was implemented, in spite of the generally dire economic situation and paucity of funds, because the government was seeking to retain the political support of the influential owners of these estates."

"I smell a scandal," Anna said.

"Well," Thompson said, "it turns out that some of these favored landowners spent the money on things like new cars and vacations on the French Riviera."

"For a scandal to be of interest, there must be some significant names involved."

"The name Hindenburg has been mentioned," Thompson said, pausing to see the effect. "Significant enough?"

***

Hitler led a march of twenty thousand stormtroopers to the St. Nicholas Cemetery where another memorial to Horst Wessel was unveiled. That evening he addressed a large crowd of stormtroopers at the Sportpalast. While attention was focused elsewhere, Hitler quietly left the stage, entered a waiting limousine, and drove with Hermann Göring and former Chancellor Papen to the villa of Joachim von Ribbentrop, where they were joined by Oskar von Hindenburg, the President's son, along with several members of Hindenburg's staff.

Instead of the meeting that had been planned, Hitler demanded to speak privately with Oskar and they went to a side room, where they stayed for over an hour. After they emerged, a visibly shaken Oskar was heard to say, "I still oppose Hitler, but I now see no way to turn down the deal he is proposing."

"It seems," Putzi told Berthold later, "that President Hindenburg was deeply involved in the *Osthilfe* scandal, to the extent that the family estate might be forfeit if all the facts came out. At the least, the President would be disgraced and his reputation forever tarnished."

"Hitler blackmailed Oskar?" Berthold asked.

"Nobody knows exactly what was said in that room, but the *Fuhrer* is very good in negotiations where grave threats are involved. Believe me, if he ever has something on you, you will have every reason to be terrified."

Putzi raised his eyebrows and Berthold felt a chill.

Chapter 65

1990 - Jerusalem

"January 1933 was a horrible month for us," Anna said. "We were together in Berlin, but the tension was so great there was no time for joy. We felt helpless and terrified, two insignificant people standing against a raging flood."

"And yet Hindenburg continued to hold out," Marissa said.

"That was our only hope," Anna said. "There were some days when it seemed Hindenburg would, even in the face of all the pressure he was feeling, still reject Hitler. We were also hoping Marshal Pilsudski would make a deal with the French, but of course that never happened. Then, adding to Hitler's case, there was a rumor the Vatican approached Hindenburg and told him that Rome would not oppose the appointment of Hitler as Chancellor. On the other side, Chancellor Schleicher continued to try to recruit Strasser to split from the Nazi Party, the stormtroopers were at the edge of revolt, and the party still had huge debts. It kept going back and forth."

"The tension must have been unbearable," Marissa said. "Most Germans had no idea what was going on, but you and Berthold had a ringside seat."

"It was a question," Anna said, "of who would crumble first, Hindenburg or Hitler. Marshal Pilsudski had predicted that Hitler would eventually out-maneuver and outlast the old man and in the end the Marshal was right. Hindenburg was old, exhausted, and so beaten down by everybody pulling at him that he just wanted to be done with the whole business. Hitler stood firm and became, as was always his objective, the last man standing. At the end of the month, Hindenburg asked for Schleicher's resignation and appointed Hitler as Chancellor of Germany."

Chapter 66

January 30, 1933 - Berlin

Berthold and Anna watched from the garden outside Hindenburg's office as former Chancellor Papen led Hitler and the others who would be part of the new Cabinet to meet with the President. The entire affair took less than ten minutes and not a single photograph was taken; Hindenburg didn't want any and Hitler had forgotten to bring his photographer. Hitler was sworn in as Chancellor, thus becoming the tenth Chancellor in the fourteen years of the Weimar Republic, the fourth within the last year. Papen became Vice-Chancellor.

Later that day, Anna interviewed Papen, who seemed to think he had accomplished a master stroke. As he described it, his brilliantly conceived plan had put Hitler in a position which required him to act responsibly. The ministries which controlled foreign policy, finance, economics, labor and agriculture were all headed by experienced professionals, none of them Nazis, and control of the army remained with President Hindenburg.

When Anna suggested that Papen was ignoring the significance of Göring becoming the Prussian Interior Minister, which gave the Nazis control over the police in the most important part of the Reich's territory, Papen said with apparent sincerity, "No, you're mistaken. There's no danger at all. We've simply hired Hitler for our act."

***

At least one formerly powerful person disagreed.

Later that day, President Hindenburg received a hand-written letter from General Erich Ludendorff, co-commander of the German Army in World War I and Hitler's co-conspirator during the 1923 *Putsch*. Ludendorff, who had long before split with Hitler, wrote:

You have delivered up our holy German Fatherland to one of the worst demagogues of all time. I solemnly prophesy that this accursed man will cast our Reich into the abyss and bring our nation to inconceivable misery. Future generations will damn you in your grave for what you have done.

There is no record that Hindenburg ever responded.

***

When darkness fell, the parade began. Goebbels later claimed there were hundreds of thousands; the police estimated thirty thousand. To the ear-splitting blare of martial music, the stormtroopers formed up in the Tiergarten, lit their torches, passed under the Brandenburg Gate and marched along the Wilhelmstrasse.

Hitler stood at a window in the Chancellery, which was now his home, smiling broadly and saluting the crowd. Hindenburg, at a window of the Presidential Palace, showed no outward emotion but was seemingly as overwhelmed as any ordinary German at the sheer scale of the pageantry Goebbels had arranged on very short notice.

Berthold and Anna, standing on the street and shivering from the cold and also from fear, watched the Nazis celebrate, understanding as most others either did not know or would not admit, that this was not the culmination of the Hitler revolution, but rather its commencement. They huddled together, silent amidst the uproar, lit by the flickering torches, each thinking about how this momentous day would impact their lives and finding no cause for optimism.

***

In bed that night, Berthold and Anna felt compelled to tell each other things they already knew, as if in repeating the story it might somehow end differently. Finally, pressing her head into the pillow, Anna cried out, "Words! Useless words! Nobody was willing to act, and now ..."

Berthold filled the gap. "... now that Hitler has power, he'll never give it up. He has a private army and he controls the police. His government will use violence and terror in a way most people still refuse to allow themselves to imagine."

"Could we have done more?" Anna asked. "Can we still do more, or ..."

"... or what?" Berthold asked. "Give up? Should we give up? Leave? Go to America with Richard?"

"I don't know," Anna said in a whisper that filled the darkness.

Berthold had never heard her sound so helpless and defeated.

* * *

Hours later, after Berthold had tossed and turned and not slept, and Anna had held his hand in the terrible silence, he finally revealed his deepest secret.

"I killed Albert Mueller," he said, the words spilling out into the darkness as if with a mind of their own.

"What? You did what? You said it was an accident."

"No. It was murder," Berthold sobbed. "I could never find the courage to tell you. I pushed Albert off the train. I was afraid of what he would tell Goebbels."

Anna said nothing.

"Now I'll lose you too," Berthold said. "You'll hate me. You should hate me. I hate myself."

When Anna finally reacted, it was not with words. She put her arms around him and held him tightly. Many minutes later, she disentangled herself and spoke.

"It is a terrible thing to take another human life, but I don't judge you, Berthold Becker. I judge God. God put Hitler's evil in this world and we, weak as we are, can either go along or fight. You and I have chosen to fight, as best we can."

There was just enough moonlight in the room for Berthold to see the look of firm resolution come onto Anna's face.

"I choose," Anna said, "to continue to fight, with you at my side whenever possible and always in my heart."

***

Still later, unable to sleep, Anna slipped out of bed and wrote in her diary.

> *I sounded so brave when I spoke to Berthold but what I felt most was guilt.*
>
> *The risk has always been unequal. He takes far greater risks than I do, and he takes them because of me, because he won't leave me.*
>
> *If I'm honest, I must admit that I share responsibility for the murder he committed.*

Chapter 67

April 1933

Dearest Anna:

The Nazis have taken over everything. Within days, Hitler easily brushed aside Papen and the other non-Nazis in the cabinet. Then the Catholic Center delegates kept Cardinal Pacelli's deal and provided the votes to pass the Enabling Act which made Hitler an absolute dictator.

There is virtually no government at any level, no professional organization, no university or anything else, that isn't now run by Nazis. They called it *Gleichschaltung*. In Northeim, Ernst Krueger walked into the City Hall and proclaimed himself mayor. No one dared object.

Those who do protest are arrested and sent to special prisons the Nazis are calling concentration camps. There's one in Dachau, just outside of Munich. Communists, socialists, Jews, homosexuals, and anybody else the Nazis define as an enemy of the State are confined. It's called protective custody; no charges are filed and there is no day in court. People are just taken away.

The Goldmanns have gone to America. Richard sold the store to Mother and me, so it is no longer in Jewish hands. Mother is in charge and she's doing a good job of it and it keeps her busy. So now we are wealthy. It was awful when the Goldmann sign came down.

I don't know how much longer it will be safe to communicate using the two stores. There are new Nazi organizations designed to spy on Germans, including other Nazis. Reinhard Heydrich is becoming the most feared man in Germany and I'm afraid I'm very much on his to-be-watched list.

My job at the Reichsbahn is going well. The signals project is a great success and I will soon begin a new assignment, one which I proposed, to evaluate all internal investment options and rank them in terms of which improvements will produce the best return on investment. Goebbels now has a whole government full of people and doesn't need me, so I'm left alone to do my Reichsbahn work.

How will we see each other again? I'm so sorry there are no pictures of the two of us together and now maybe there never will be. I'm enclosing a photograph of me at my Reichsbahn desk. Would you send me one of you at your desk?

I cannot find words to express how much I love you. Perhaps the right words will fly from the kiss with which I now seal this letter.

***

Berthold my love:

I cried over your letter. Surely I love you as much as any woman can love any man. It is with that love foremost in my heart that I have concluded we must no longer communicate on any matters which put you at risk. We can write about other matters, personal matters, but that is all.

***

Dearest Anna:

I do not accept your decision. The flood of evil Hitler has unleashed is just beginning and there may yet be opportunities to slow down or derail Hitler's progress. If we are to behave as you suggested, then we should have gone to America, and even now we should go. Not too long ago you said you chose to continue to fight, with me at your side and in your heart. We must continue this struggle and I cannot do so without knowing, even if we are physically apart, that you are with me. Please do not leave me alone on this path.

***

Dearest Berthold:

You mentioned a concentration camp in Dachau, which is apparently near Munich. There are many frightening rumors about that camp. Can you arrange for me to see it?

Chapter 68

May 1933 - Munich

"Are reporters permitted to visit the concentration camp at Dachau?"

Putzi's face blanched in a way Berthold had never before seen. In the three months since President Hindenburg had appointed Hitler Chancellor, Putzi had several times mentioned to Berthold his increasingly inability to mollify foreign correspondents who were asking questions about the brutality of the Nazi takeover, especially the so-called "protective detention" of political enemies. Putzi was being blamed for the bad stories.

"Does Anna want to see Dachau?" Putzi asked.

"Yes."

"That's a really bad idea."

"For her or for me?" Berthold asked.

"For both of you." Putzi seemed to agonize before he added, "and for me. Heydrich is involved. You don't want to have anything to do with him."

"Would he know if she went there?"

"That's a stupid question. Of course he would know."

"Who is the next reporter scheduled to visit Dachau?"

"A New York Times reporter, next week."

"Suppose he had an assistant."

"I will have nothing to do with making any such arrangements," Putzi said. "We never had this conversation."

***

Berthold called Anna, and she in turn had called Dorothy Thompson in New York to make the arrangements. Anna met the New York Times reporter in Munich and they drove together in a taxi paid for by the newspaper. The trip from Munich to Dachau took about twenty minutes, mostly over a

317

bucolic roadway lined with trees and open fields. The town itself was pleasant enough with cobblestone streets and charming country homes.

Commandant Hilmar Wäckerle received the American reporters at noon, resplendent in his black SS uniform and highly polished riding boots, holding a muzzled attack dog on a leash. They were given numbered white arm bands identifying them as visitors, and Wäckerle and the dog led them into the walled compound that had until recently been the remains of a dilapidated Royal Powder and Munitions Factory.

"You had a problem here last week?" the reporter asked.

"Yes," the Commandant answered. "Some communists tried to escape and were killed in the attempt."

He pointed.

"There's the wall where it happened. They were shot from those guard towers. Foolish men, to try to escape."

***

When they reached her hotel near the Munich train station, and Anna was leaving the car, the reporter said, "Please tell Dorothy Thompson she owes me one."

Berthold was in the lobby when Anna arrived but he barely recognized the blond, overweight, distinctly American woman in sunglasses who walked past him without so much as a nod and continued to the desk, where she retrieved her key and headed for the elevator.

Five minutes later, Berthold followed.

"What happened," he asked when Anna opened the door.

"Later," she said. "It's been way too long. Help me out of these clothes."

Anna had already removed the outer layer, but that was just the beginning. With Berthold's enthusiastic assistance, more clothes fell away until Anna stood lean and luscious and naked.

"Now you," Anna said, pulling at Berthold's clothes while he kissed her eyes, her lips, her breasts, her stomach and hips, and between her legs.

***

"I believe I recognize this woman," Berthold said as they lay damp and exhausted on the bed, "but perhaps a little more exploring, just to be certain, before Monsignor Johannes gets here."

"A priest is coming here!" Anna screamed, moving her hands to cover herself.

"We're to meet in the restaurant down the street."

***

Berthold went to the restaurant while Anna got dressed and arranged her hair. The place was filled with noisy storm troopers and loud women. Johannes was sitting alone at a small table in the back. Berthold joined him and they each had a beer while they waited.

Anna came into the restaurant dressed in her Warsaw clothes and of course without her wig. She waved to Berthold and the Monsignor and walked to their table. Berthold did the introductions and Anna ordered a glass of wine.

"The Cardinal told me to extend his gratitude," Johannes said. "He wants you to know how much he appreciates what you did."

"Tried to do," Anna said. "We failed. The Pope never read the Brüning papers and the Catholic Center Reichstag delegates all voted for the Enabling Act. So now we'll see what Hitler does when he has unlimited authority."

"There are many who think his time as Chancellor will be short," Johannes said. "Hindenburg still has the power to remove him."

Berthold and Anna didn't argue with the Monsignor, but both raised their eyebrows in disbelief.

"I don't think we got the full story today," Anna said. "Commandant Wäckerle was quite polite, and we got a very complete tour, but ..."

"I've been to Dachau several times," Johannes said. "I conducted Easter Mass there and I've met many of the prisoners. The place is inexpressibly horrible."

"Do you know about the communist escapees who were killed?" Anna asked.

"There were no communist escapees," Johannes said. "They were Jews. They were selected, taken into the yard, and murdered."

"Do you have proof?"

"The prosecutor does, and he will soon bring the perpetrators to trial."

"Can I meet him?"

"He's agreed to meet if you promise not to publish anything until his case becomes public."

***

"I am meeting with you," Deputy Prosecutor Josef Hartinger said to Anna, "because Cardinal Faulhaber said you can be trusted." He smiled. "I always listen to my Cardinal."

"I understand," Anna said, "that while you're still accumulating evidence, you've already concluded the official version of events is not true."

"A total fabrication," Hartinger huffed. "This was a clear case of murder, from the selection of the four Jews to be killed, to the method of killing, to the clumsy attempts to cover up what had been done."

"Do you have proof?"

"The autopsy reports," the prosecutor said, "show that each of the four men died from a bullet to the back of the head fired from just a few feet away.

"One of the victims lived long enough to give a statement to the attending physicians. That statement, which is appended to the medical records, describes how the four men were called out, taken to the yard, and shot from close range. Unfortunately, the witness died before I could interview him."

Chapter 69

Anna prepared a draft of her story, including a carbon copy for Berthold. The next morning, she and Berthold went to the re-named Becker Department Store to visit with Elisabeth and were pleasantly surprised to find that Henri Bousquet had arrived from Paris.

"Henri is helping me re-organize the fashion departments," Elisabeth said. "We will soon have the most elegant store in Munich."

Elisabeth tried to smile but could not pull it off. The underlying devastation which had been her constant companion her since the Goldmanns left for America quickly surfaced.

"If it wasn't for the strength I get from my son and Henri," Elisabeth said, "I would long ago have collapsed."

They talked for awhile about store business and the impact of the Nazi takeover in Bavaria, which had been rapid and brutal, until it was time for Berthold and Anna to leave.

"I'm going to Berlin with Anna," Berthold said, "but I'll be back in a few days." To Henri he added, "Thank you so much for everything you're doing for Mother."

Before they left, Henri took a photograph of Berthold and Anna together, promising to send prints to both of them.

***

Berthold had arranged first class tickets for himself and Anna, anticipating a quiet ride, snuggled together, lulled by the sound of the train and the scenery. They were joined in their comfortable compartment by an older couple, and were still saying hello and getting settled when a commotion erupted outside the train.

Through the window they could see several black-uniformed SS officers shouting and giving orders. Two SS officers burst into their compartment and brusquely demanded that the older couple leave but that Berthold and Anna remain.

A few seconds later, Reinhard Heydrich came into the compartment and sprawled across the now empty seat. The train pulled out and Berthold and Anna were trapped, alone with Heydrich for the next six hours.

***

"How fortunate to have run into you like this," Heydrich said to Berthold. "This must be your friend Anna Gorska about whom Goebbels has told me so much."

He raised his eyes in what could be interpreted as a leer.

"Please introduce us."

Heydrich rose, clicked his booted heels and reached to kiss Anna's hand, which she reluctantly offered to him. He resumed his seat and smiled, but it did not seem like a friendly smile.

"How was your visit to ... Munich?"

Heydrich had paused in asking the question; both Anna and Berthold thought he was going to say Dachau. Did he know?

"My own trip was quite brief," Heydrich continued, after Anna had quietly said that her visit to Munich had been just fine. "I came to Munich to deal with a recent incident at Dachau. Perhaps you heard about it."

Heydrich stared at Anna. Berthold watched with pride as Anna held Heydrich's penetrating look without faltering.

Heydrich continued, "Some communists tried to escape and were killed. The local prosecutor had become confused and thought there might be something more to it. I set him straight. His misguided investigation has been terminated."

It took every effort Berthold could summon not to touch the pocket in which he had placed his copy of Anna's draft, which clearly stated that it was SS guards, under Heydrich's control, who had murdered the Jewish prisoners.

The conductor came by to take their tickets, giving Berthold, for the first time since Heydrich had joined them, an

323

opportunity to look at Anna. There was a mixture of panic and determination in her eyes, and despite the courage she had already shown, he was far from sure which would prevail in the hours ahead, for her or for him.

"How is your mother doing with the store?" Heydrich asked. "What is the arrangement with Richard Goldmann? Does German money go to the Jew in New York?"

Heydrich didn't wait for any answers and gave no indication he wanted any. It seemed certain he already knew all the answers and that this was not an interrogation - not yet.

"How is your friend Leonard doing at Bloomingdales?"

Some time elapsed in ominous silence and then Heydrich talked about the Nazi takeover of the Bavarian government, including the new roles for himself and his boss Heinrich Himmler.

"I've moved my main office to Berlin, but I still have a presence in Munich."

He laughed, a cruel laugh.

"My office here is too close to that Hanfstaengl character. What a strange man. I don't understand what the *Fuhrer* sees in him, but I understand you're all quite friendly."

And so it went, all the way to Berlin. Heydrich talked about his plans for the development of a far-ranging SS intelligence service, for using Dachau as a model for the additional concentration camps that would be needed, and many other topics.

Berthold talked, when he couldn't avoid it, mostly about his new project for the Reischbahn, a subject in which Heydrich was clearly not interested. Anna nodded occasionally and never volunteered anything.

Eventually, their interminable ride ended, Heydrich politely said he would like to invite them to dinner but had other obligations. Berthold and Anna went as quickly as they could to their room at the Excelsior Hotel.

***

Their hug was a mixture of intense affection and even more intense desperation, fingers digging into each other's back. Finally they let go, but both continued to breath in huge gulps.

"He's a terrifying man," Anna said.

"It will get worse," Berthold said. "From what he said he already knows a lot about us."

"Far too much," Anna said quietly. "Why did he tell us? Was he bragging?"

"He's sending us a message," Berthold said. "I'm sure he wants something from me, or maybe even from you. He understands boxing; this was just the first round."

"He's far worse than Goebbels," Anna said.

They looked at each other with despair at what lay ahead.

"He's trying to frighten us," Berthold said.

"Well, he succeeded."

"You can't publish your article. It would be a death sentence for that prosecutor."

"Of course," Anna said. "Will you let Herr Hartinger know that what he told me will never be published."

"I'll find a way to do that," Berthold said. "But what they did at Dachau must be known. The Nazi government selected Jews and murdered them, and then covered it up. This is no longer just Hitler's private army of stormtroopers, bad as they are. This is the German government, the state, committing official murder. The world needs to know what these people are doing. This surely won't be the last time something like this happens."

Anna thought for a moment. "Do you think Monsignor Johannes could get the facts about the Dachau murders to someone who would care. Maybe the American Ambassador?"

"I'll ask him," Berthold said.

***

They had dinner in their room, and then they made love, this time slowly and sadly, holding together as long as they could, after which they lay together, fully awake, legs and arms intertwined, until dawn.

Berthold took Anna to the train station. Rain poured down on them as they stood hugging and crying on the platform.

***

When he got back to Munich, Berthold approached Monsignor Johannes, who said he would discuss the Dachau incident with the Cardinal, but nothing ever came it.

The truth about those first murders at Dachau in the spring of 1933 was not made known until six million more Jews had perished.

Chapter 70

1990 - Munich

Abraham and Marissa knocked on Berthold's door but there was no answer. When the concierge let them in, they found Berthold lying unconscious on the floor. At the hospital, they were told Herr Becker had suffered a mild heart attack.

"Before we sedated him," a nurse said, "he was briefly awake; he kept saying 'call Anna.' Do you know someone named Anna?"

***

Marissa had called Anna and offered to fly to Jerusalem and join her for the return flight, but Anna insisted she could make the trip by herself. Now here she was in Munich, striding firmly from the baggage area, carrying one small suitcase.

"He's regained consciousness," Marissa said.

"I know," Anna said. "I spoke with him as soon as I landed."

***

Anna, Abraham and Marissa sat in a waiting area near Berthold's hospital room. "This is not the first attack he's had," Anna said, "and the doctors believe he will once again survive. He's always been a very tough man."

Marissa and Abraham looked at each other, sensing there was more to be revealed.

Anna spoke softly. "As you may have guessed, this is not my first trip to Munich. I've been here many times since Berthold was released from prison. Had you looked in his closets you would have seen my clothes. Actually, I also visited him several times at Spandau."

Anna saw the look of surprise on Marissa's face.

"So you haven't yet checked the visitor logs," Anna said with a smile.

"I'll bet there's a lot we haven't learned yet," Marissa said. "For instance, Anna, you're a reporter, a good one with an impressive roster of international publications. Why didn't you write this story yourself?"

"We tried," Anna said, "but we found it unbearably painful. Berthold was convinced his life was a failure and his story not worth telling. He was embarrassed, humiliated really, by his participation in the Nazi horror, whatever his motivations. Every attempt to write it down ended badly."

Anna shifted slightly, gathering herself.

"We were afraid that if we continued we would hurt each other so much we would lose the little bit of happiness we've managed to have together. With so few years left, that's a risk we were not willing to take."

A nurse walked down the hall and they looked up expectantly, but it wasn't Berthold's nurse.

"We had all but given up," Anna continued. She smiled. "Then you came along, a professional historian with special access to Berthold's Nuremberg prosecutor and the perspective to tell our stories better than we could do it ourselves."

"And just how was it that I came along?" Marissa asked.

"I think," Anna resumed, ignoring Marissa's question, "you understand what a huge price we've paid, dedicating so much of our lives to a series of endeavors which essentially came to nothing. And yet, if Berthold's story is told fully and correctly, maybe in the end there will be some lasting value to our efforts."

Marissa felt, even more than she had before, a huge responsibility to ask the right questions, to hear the nuances, to get it down properly. Then she saw the look in Anna's eyes just a second before Abraham did. They looked at each other, puzzled.

"The visitor logs at Nuremberg," Anna said, "were not the only thing you missed. Have you spoken recently with Professor Polonsky?"

Marissa's mouth dropped. She had never mentioned her Brandeis mentor to Anna.

"Do you think it was an accident your professor suggested this project for you?"

"What ...? I suggested it to him."

"Not really," Anna said. "Berthold and I had been organizing our notes for years, and I was looking for a way to tell our story without destroying our relationship. I had of course read Dr. Polonsky's work, and also yours. I had corresponded with him several times, so it seemed natural for me to visit him at Brandeis. I presented my plan and he agreed, including that you were not to know where the idea originated unless I decided to tell you."

Anna swallowed and pursed her lips. "Are you angry?" she asked.

"Actually," Marissa said, "I've never been so pleased to be manipulated. You two are masters at deception, but then we know that by now. I feel honored to have been trusted with your stories."

***

Berthold recovered and returned to his apartment. When Marissa and Abraham came to visit, they were moved to see, for the first time, Berthold and Anna together, sitting quietly, holding hands, smiling at each other frequently.

On the table next to the pictures of Berthold's parents and brother was a third frame containing a photograph of Berthold and Anna. This had not been displayed on any of Marissa or Abraham's prior visits.

"Is that ..." Marissa started to ask.

"Yes," Berthold answered. "Henri Bousquet took that picture. Anna lost her copy when the Nazis took her, but mine has never left this apartment. It was the first thing I looked for when I got out of Spandau."

The visit passed quietly and then Marissa and Abraham left, having made arrangements to resume their interviews in a few days. They walked to the Ludwigsbrücke, crossed the Isar, and headed on toward their hotel.

Marissa broke the silence.

"They've been through so much over so many years and here they are, still very much alive and still enthralled with each other. What a love story. I can picture the two of them on the train to Paris, almost sixty years ago, when they first held hands."

"I don't believe Berthold," Abraham said.

"About what?" Marissa asked, startled.

"He keeps saying he feels only humiliation and regret about what he did when he was a Nazi. I'm sure he does feel that way, but not exclusively. I believe he must also feel, along with Anna, a fierce sense of accomplishment. If nothing else, they tried when so many others looked away."

NOTE: A sequel, covering Berthold and Anna's lives in the years 1934 to 1946, is currently being researched and written.

GLOSSARY

Beitar ... a Revisionist Zionist youth movement founded in 1923 in Riga, Latvia, by Vladimir Jabotinsky.

Blood Banner ... the Nazi flag used in the failed Beer Hall Putsch in Munich, Germany on 9 November 1923, stored in Munich at the Brown House.

Brown House ... The Brown House was the national headquarters of the Nazi Party. A large stone structure, it was located at 45 Briennerstrasse in Munich. It was named for the color of the party uniforms. It was acquired in 1930 and renovated with funds provided by industrialist Fritz Thyssen. The Brown House was damaged in October 1943 and largely destroyed in an allied bombing raid late in World War II. The rubble was cleared away in 1947, leaving an empty lot.

Concordat ... an agreement or treaty between the Holy See of the Catholic Church and a sovereign state that deals with the recognition and privileges of the Catholic Church in a particular country and with secular matters that impact on church interests. In this book, the primary reference is to the Concordat entered into between the Vatican and Hitler's Third Reich in 1933.

Der Angriff ... in English "The Attack," a German language newspaper founded in 1927 by Josef Goebbels.

Droshky ... a light, low, four-wheeled, open vehicle used mainly in Russia, in which the passengers sit astride or sideways on a long, narrow bench.

Enabling Act ... an amendment to the Weimar Constitution that gave the German Cabinet, in effect Adolf Hitler, the power to enact laws without the involvement of the Reichstag. It was passed by the Reichstag on March 24, 1933, and signed by President Paul Hindenburg later that day. The act required two thirds vote of the Reichstag and would not have passed without the votes of the Catholic Center delegates.

Gauleiter ... the party leader of a regional branch of the Nazi Party, to whom Local District Leaders reported.

Kiddish cup ... a decorated wine vessel, usually silver, through which comes blessing and sanctification. Kiddish also refers to the prayer said over the wine at the beginning of a meal: Blessed are You Our God, King of the Universe, Creator of the fruit of the vine.

Lag b'Omer ... The Torah commands that Jews count forty-nine days beginning from the day on which the Omer, a sacrifice containing an omer-measure of barley, was offered in the Temple in Jerusalem, up until the day before an offering of wheat was brought to the Temple on Shavuot. Lag b'Omer is celebrated on the 33rd day of the Counting of the Omer. This day marks the anniversary of the death of Rabbi Shimon bar Yochai, and also the day on which he revealed the deepest secrets of kabbalah in the form of the Zohar, a landmark text of Jewish mysticism.

Protocols of the Elders of Zion ... a fabricated text purporting to describe a Jewish plan for global domination, first published in Russia in 1903, translated into multiple languages, and disseminated internationally in the early part of the 20th century. According to the claims made by some of its publishers, the Protocols are the minutes of a late 19th-century meeting where Jewish leaders discussed their goal of global Jewish hegemony. Henry Ford funded a printing of 500,000 copies distributed throughout the US in the 1920s. Adolf Hitler was a major proponent. It was studied, as if factual, in German classrooms after the Nazis came to power in 1933 despite having been exposed as fraudulent by *The Times* of London in 1921.

Putsch ... German word for coup d'état, a violent forcible change of the government. In this book, the Putsch organized by Adolf Hitler in Munich in November 1923, which was an utter failure.

Reich ... the former German state, most often used to refer to the Third Reich, the Nazi regime from 1933 to 1945. The First Reich was considered to be the

Holy Roman Empire, 962–1806, and the Second Reich the German Empire, 1871–1918.

Reichsbahn ... The Deutsche Reichsbahn (DRG), was the name of the German national railway created from the railways of the individual German states of following the end of World War I.

Reichstag ... the German Parliament ... also refers to the building in Berlin in which the Parliament met.

SA/Stormtroopers/Brownshirts ... an unofficial paramilitary organization of thugs used by Adolf Hitler to cause trouble and punish political opponents, both before and after Hitler came to power in 1923.

SD/Sicherheitsdienst ... the intelligence agency of the SS and the Nazi Party in Nazi Germany ... first formed in 1931 ... headed by Heinrich Himmler and Reinhard Heydrich.

SS/Schutzstaffel ... founded in 1925, personal bodyguards for Hitler ... had grown to 50,000 men by 1933 when Hitler took office.

Unter den Linden ... a boulevard near the Brandenburg Gate in Berlin, named for the linden trees that line the grassed pedestrian mall between two carriageways.

Versailles ... a suburb of Paris, the site of the magnificent palace of the French kings, at which was held the meetings which resulted in the 1919 Treaty of Versailles marking the end of the First World War.

BIBLIOGRAPHY

Abel, Theodore ... *Why Hitler Came into Power*

Allen, William Sheridan ... *Nazi Seizure of Power: The Experience of a Single German Town 1922-1945*

Baird, Jay ... *To Die for Germany: Heroes in the Nazi Pantheon*

Bennett, Edward W ... *German Rearmament and the West, 1932-1933*

Bitter, Alexander ... *Kurt Von Schleicher- The Soldier and Politics in the Run up to National Socialism*

Blobaum, Robert ... *Antisemitism And Its Opponents In Modern Poland*

Broszat, Martin ... *Hitler and the Collapse of Weimar Germany*

Burleigh, Michael ... *The Third Reich: A New History*

Conradi, Peter ... *Hitler's Piano Player: The Rise and Fall of Ernst Hanfstaengl, Confidante of Hitler, Ally of FDR*

Coppa, Frank J. ... *The Papacy, the Jews, and the Holocaust*

Cornwell, John ... *Hitler's Pope: The Secret History of Pius XII*

Davies, Norman ... *Heart of Europe: The Past in Poland's Present*

Dederichs, Mario R. ... *Heydrich: The Face of Evil*

Domarus, Max ... *The Complete Hitler - Speeches and Proclamations*

Dornberg, John ... *Munich 1923*

Dorpalen, Andreas ... *Hindenburg and the Weimar Republic*

Eliach , Yaffa ... *There Once Was a World: A 900-Year Chronicle of the Shtetl of Eishyshok*

Evans, Richard ... *The Coming of the Third Reich*

Ferguson, Adam ... *When Money Dies: The Nightmare of Deficit Spending, Devaluation, and Hyperinflation in Weimar Germany*

Fest, Joachim ... *Hitler*

Fest, Joachim ... *The Face Of The Third Reich: Portraits Of The Nazi Leadership*

Fischer, Klaus ... *The History of an Obsession: German Judeophobia and the Holocaust*

Godman, Peter ... *Hitler and the Vatican: Inside the Secret Archives That Reveal the New Story of the Nazis and the Church*

Goebbels, Josef ... *My Part in Germany's Fight*

Gold, Ben-Zion ... *The Life of Jews in Poland before the Holocaust: A Memoir*

Gordon, Harold J. ... *Hitler and the Beer Hall Putsch*

Gutman, Yisrael ... *The Jews of Poland Between Two World Wars*

Haffner, Sebastian ... *Defying Hitler: A Memoir*

Hanfstaengl, Ernst ... *Hitler: The Memoir of the Nazi Insider Who Turned Against the Fuhrer*

Hanser, Richard ... *Putsch!*

Harsch, Donna ... *German Social Democracy and the Rise of Nazism*

Hastings, Derek ... *Catholicism and the Roots of Nazism: Religious Identity and National Socialism*

Heller, Celia Stopnicka ... *On the Edge of Destruction: Jews of Poland Between the Two World Wars*

Herzl, Theodor ... *The Jewish State*

Heschel, Abraham Joshua ... *The Earth Is the Lord's: The Inner World of the Jew in Eastern Europe*

Hetherington, Peter ... *Unvanquished: Joseph Pilsudski, Resurrected Poland and the Struggle for Eastern Europe*

Hitler, Adolf ... *Mein Kampf*

Hoffman, Eva ... *Shtetl: The History of a Small Town and an Extinguished World*

Jedrzejewicz, Waclaw ... *Pilsudski: A Life for Poland*

Junger, Ernst ... *Storm of Steel*

Kershaw, Ian ... *Hitler: 1889-1936 Hubris*

Krieg, Robert ... *The Vatican Concordat With Hitler's Reich*

Lewy, Guenter ... *The Catholic Church And Nazi Germany*

Manvell, Roger ... *Doctor Goebbels: His Life and Death*

Mendelsohn, Ezra ... *The Jews of East Central Europe between the World Wars*

Mendelsohn, Ezra ... *Zionism in Poland: The Formative years, 1915-1926*

Michlic, Joanna Beata ... *Poland's Threatening Other: The Image of the Jew from 1880 to the Present*

Mierzejewski, Alfred C. ... *The Most Valuable Asset of the Reich: A History of the German National Railway Volume 2*

Modras, Ronald E. ... *The Catholic Church and Antisemitism in Poland*

Mommsen, Hans ... *The Rise and Fall of Weimar Democracy*

Morris, Douglas G. ... *Justice Imperiled: The Anti-Nazi Lawyer Max Hirschberg in Weimar Germany*

Mosse, George L. ... *Germans and Jews: The Right, the Left, and the Search for a Third Force in Pre-Nazi Germany*

Nagorski, Andrew ... *Hitlerland: American Eyewitnesses to the Nazi Rise to Power*

Niewyk, Donald L. ... *Socialist, Anti-Semite, and Jew: German Social Democracy Confronts the Problem of Anti-Semitism, 1918-1933*

Nowicki, Ron ... *Warsaw: The Cabaret Years*

Patch, William L. ... *Heinrich Brüning and the Dissolution of the Weimar Republic*

Pease, Neal ... *Rome's Most Faithful Daughter: The Catholic Church and Independent Poland, 1914-1939*

Peterson, Edward Norman ... *Hjalmar Schacht: for and against Hitler; a political-economic study of Germany, 1923-1945*

Plach, Eva ... *The Clash of Moral Nations: Cultural Politics in Pilsudski's Poland, 1926-1935*

Polonsky, Antony .... *From Shtetl To Socialism: Studies From Polin*

Polonsky, Antony ... *Polin: Studies in Polish Jewry, Volume 8: Jews in Independent Poland, 1918-1939*

Remarque, Erich Maria ... *All Quiet on the Western Front*

Remarque, Erich Maria ... *The Road Back*

Reuth, Ralf ... *Goebbels*

Richarz, Monika ... *Jewish Life in Germany: Memoirs from Three Centuries*

Roth, Joseph ... *The Wandering Jews*

Ryback, Timothy W. ... Hitler's First Victims: The Quest for Justice (Dachau)

Schacht, Hjalmar ... *My first seventy-six years*

Schatz, Jaff ... *The Generation: The Rise and Fall of the Jewish Communists of Poland*

Scholder, Klaus ... *The Churches and the Third Reich: Preliminary History and the Time of Illusions 1918-1934*

Sciolino, Anthony J. ... *The Holocaust, the Church, and the Law of Unintended Consequences: How Christian Anti-Judaism Spawned Nazi Anti-Semitism*

Segel, Binjamin & Richard Levy ... *A Lie and a Libel: The History of the Protocols of the Elders of Zion*

Sinclair, Upton ... *Dragon's Teeth*

Singer, Isaac Bashevis ... *The Manor*

Smaldone, William ... *Rudolf Hilferding: The Tragedy of a German Social Democrat*

Stachura, Peter D ... *Gregor Strasser and the Rise of Nazism*

Stachura, Peter D ... *Poland Between the Wars, 1918-1939*

Stehlin, Stewart A. ... *Weimar and the Vatican, 1919-1933*

Time Life ... *Fists of Steel*

Toland, John ... *Adolf Hitler: The Definitive Biography*

Turner, Henry ... *Hitler's Thirty Days To Power*

Ventresca, Robert ... *Soldier of Christ: The Life of Pope Pius XII*

Wasserstein, Bernard ... *On the Eve: The Jews of Europe Before the Second World War*

Watt, Richard M. ... *Bitter Glory: Poland and Its Fate, 1918-1939*

Weitz, Eric D. ... *Weimar Germany: Promise and Tragedy*

Whaley, Barton ... Covert German Rearmament, 1919-1939: Deception and Misperception

Wolf, Hubert ... Pope and Devil: The Vatican's Archives and the Third Reich

Yasni, A. Wolf.... Memorial Book of the Ciechanow Jewish Community

Zamoyski, Adam ... The Polish Way: A Thousand-Year History of the Poles and Their Culture

Zbrowski, Mark ... Life is With People : The Culture of the Shtetl

ACKNOWLEDGMENTS

First and foremost is my wife Pat Lenny, my best reader and most aggressive critic, whose mantra "don't tell me everything you know" ultimately reduced this novel by almost 200 pages from its original draft.

Also John Banville (aka Benjamin Black) who, at a recent Key West Literary Seminar, articulated his belief that it is a writer's obligation to make every single word as good as it can be. That thought has been my constant writing companion ever since.

Renni Browne and Dave King wrote a wonderful book, "Self-Editing for Fiction Writers," to which I have turned many times in my quest to apply Banville's commandment, deleting adverbs and unnecessary repetitions at every editing pass.

Finally, I have been aided by many "early readers" who have given generously of their time and perspectives. Many of their suggestions have found their way into my story. Thank you to ... Judie Amsel, Donald Baraf, Randy Becker, Michael Brunet, Barbara Capuana, Brewster Chamberlin, George Collins, Ed Demore, Linda DiBiasio, Cindy Emmet, Jeremy Emmet, Amy Ferguson, Steve Freiberger, Joly Girard, Grazyna Gulczynska, Hank Hanahan, Lisa Hawkins, Dr. Andreas Heusler, Lilo Huhle-Poelzl, Julia Hürter, Cheryl Kennedy, Norma Klein, David Lee, Pat Lenny, Pat Mastrobuono, Charles McClelland, Rose Moorse, Susan Otradovec, Susie Savitch, Joanna Schmida, Ashwini Sharma, Sandy Sheehy, Andrew Short, Nancy Stairs, Douglas Stone, Terry Swartzberg, Anne Trieber, Jon Weinstein, and Bill Workman

Thanks for reading my novel.

I'd love to hear what you think of it.

You can email me at ...

authorlewweinstein@gmail.com

You can learn more about my research
and writing, including my progress on
Book Two of A FLOOD OF EVIL,
at my author blog ...

http://lewweinsteinauthorblog.com/

Made in the USA
Charleston, SC
09 February 2017